Almost a Clean Getaway

Doreen Diller Humorous Mystery Trilogy, Volume 2

Margaret Lashley

Published by Zazzy Ideas, Inc., 2022.

Copyright

Copyright 2022 Margaret Lashley
MargaretLashley.com

All rights reserved. No part of this book may be used or reproduced by any means, graphic, electronic, or mechanical, including photocopying, recording, taping or by any information storage retrieval system without the written permission of the author except in the case of brief quotations embodied in critical articles and reviews.

The scanning, uploading, and distribution of this book via the Internet or via any other means without the permission of the publisher is illegal and punishable by law. Please purchase only authorized electronic editions, and do not participate in or encourage electronic piracy of copyrighted materials. Your support of the author's rights is appreciated.

For more information, write to: Zazzy Ideas, Inc. P.O. Box 1113, St. Petersburg, FL 33731

This book is a work of fiction. While actual places throughout Florida have been used in this book, any resemblance to persons living or dead are purely coincidental. Unless otherwise noted, the author and the publisher make no explicit guarantees as to the accuracy of the information contained in this book and in some cases, the names of places have been altered.

What Readers are Saying About Doreen Diller

"*A great plot, exceptional storytelling and a whole new cast of fun characters make this one a must-read.*"

"*What a delightful start to a new cozy mystery series by one of my favorite contemporary Southern authors!*"

"*Doreen Diller is pretty sure she didn't kill her boss. But, could the last few stressful days have turned her into a psycho-eyed homicidal maniac? Read it and find out!*"

"*I love books that grab me from the start, make me laugh and cry, and keep me glued to the end. This book is all that and more.*"

"*Ms. Lashley takes loads of quirky characters, a twisty mystery, a pinch of romance, and a heaping helping of humor to create this masterpiece!*"

"*This book is hilarious. I couldn't believe how funny Doreen is. The craziness in this story was such fun to read. Doreen is my new favorite character.*"

More Mysteries by Margaret Lashley

Available on Amazon in Your Choice of Ebook, Paperback, Hardback & Audiobook:
Doreen Diller Mystery Trilogy (Three-Book Series)
https://www.amazon.com/gp/product/B0B2X3G3G7
Val Fremden Midlife Mysteries (Nine-Book Series)
https://www.amazon.com/gp/product/B07FK88WQ3
Absolute Zero (The Val Fremden Prequel)
https://www.amazon.com/dp/B06ZXYK776
Freaky Florida Investigations (Eight-Book Series)
https://www.amazon.com/gp/product/B07RL4G8GZ
Mind's Eye Investigators (Two-Book Series)
https://www.amazon.com/gp/product/B07ZR6NW2N

Prologue

I'd fantasized about accomplishing a lot of things before I turned forty. Escaping a murder rap wasn't one of them. Neither was discovering that I had a secret family in Florida with ties to the mob. Did I mention that one of them was a serial killer?

Sammy the Psycho.

And he was on the lam.

Fun times.

If that weren't enough to curl a girl's hair, in less than a week, I, Doreen Diller, would turn the big four-oh. That meant I only had *five days left* to become a movie star, marry Keanu Reeves, and cure cancer.

Yeah. Like any of that was gonna happen.

Anyway, if life really *did* begin at forty, I was going to need a do-over like the Titanic needed more life rafts. Because, as I was about to find out, despite all the crazy crap that went down with my new family last week, I'd barely seen the *tip* of the lunatic iceberg bobbing around in their gene pool ....

Chapter One

"Cheese curds?" I asked, then sank back into the hideous brown recliner my Aunt Edna referred to as "the good chair."

The old Barcalounger had come off the assembly line well before I was born—and, as I mentioned, I was no spring chicken. Aunt Edna might've been an immaculate housekeeper, but she hadn't redecorated her living room since Disco Duck gasped out his last *quack*.

"Yeah, cheese curds," my aunt said, her gaze fixated on a clear plastic bag full of gooey white globs.

The nasty things reminded me of somebody's cerebellum.

Yuck!

The bag of curds was dangling from the geriatric hand of Jackie Cooperelli, my aunt's squirrely sidekick. The thin, pewter-haired woman was smiling and holding the gross-looking blobs up as if they were goldfish she'd just won at the county fair.

From what I'd observed in my brief time with these ladies, Jackie possessed the slightly dim-witted, yet annoyingly cheerful disposition of Edith Bunker in *All in the Family*. And, like Edith to Archie, Jackie's perpetual good mood rankled Aunt Edna to no end.

A sturdy, no-nonsense woman, my aunt had shown herself to be one incredibly tough cookie. But at the moment, the bag of cheese curds appeared about to push her to the verge of crumbling. She wiped her palms on her apron and took a step toward me. Wobbling unsteadily, she grabbed ahold of the back of the avocado-green couch for support.

"You okay?" I asked.

"Huh? Yeah," she muttered absently, her voice husky and strained. She turned to her companion. "Hey, Jackie. Anything else come with those curds?"

"Lemme check." Jackie peeked inside the small Styrofoam cooler.

The lumps of white cheese had arrived mere minutes ago. Someone had dropped the box on the front doorstep, rapped hard with the knocker, then taken off before we could catch a glimpse of them.

"Yeah, there's a note," Jackie said. She plucked a damp piece of paper from the cooler with her long, bony fingers. "Now ain't that nice!"

"Gimme that!" Aunt Edna leaned forward and snatched the note from Jackie's hand. As she read it, her face took on the kind of hopeless, slack-jawed expression generally seen in doomsday films, right before the asteroid struck.

"What's it say?" Jackie asked, beating me to it.

Aunt Edna's hand fell limply to her side. "It says, '*Atta girl.*'"

Jackie cocked her narrow head sideways like a curious hound. "Who's Atta?"

Aunt Edna didn't answer. But based on the scowl tightening her jawline, I figured she was contemplating sending Jackie back to the pound. Or maybe to a kill shelter ...

"Uh ... is that some kind of congratulatory note?" I asked, trying to break the tension between the long-suffering pair.

Aunt Edna pursed her lips. "That's *one* way to look at it, I suppose."

My upper lip snarled. "What's the *other* way?"

Aunt Edna grimaced. "Sammy *knows.*"

My eyes opened wide. "Sammy? As in that psycho dude Sammy?"

"That's the one," Jackie said merrily.

"What do you mean *he knows*?" I scooted to the edge of the recliner. "Knows *what*?"

My aunt's lips were a thin, white line. "I dunno. Maybe nothing. Maybe everything." She turned to me and sighed. "Dorey, there's a lot you don't know about this family."

"No kidding. I only found out ten days ago that you guys even *existed.*"

"Not our fault," Jackie said, wagging a finger at me.

She was right. The blame for that fell squarely on the shoulders of my mother, Maureen Diller. Until a week and a half ago, I'd been under the assumption my mother was an orphan. It wasn't until I'd told her I was in St. Petersburg, Florida filming a TV show that she'd ever mentioned a single word about having relatives here.

Ma had given me Aunt Edna's number. To be honest, I hadn't exactly been in a hurry to make the call. I'd figured that if Ma hadn't kept in touch with her sister, why should I? But before I could pack my bags and skip town back to L.A., fate had intervened—in the form of a murder rap.

Yeah. A murder rap.

The night Sunshine City Studios wrapped up filming of their hokey slasher serial set on St. Pete Beach, life had imitated art. Someone had stabbed to death Tad Longmire—my boss and star of the show. Since I was the only one in town who knew Tad, the local cops had pinned me as the prime suspect. They'd also advised me to stick around while they conducted the homicide investigation.

Unfortunately, their suggestion hadn't come with an offer to pay for my room and board. Being a hot tourist town, St. Petersburg's hotel prices could blaze a hole through a wallet faster than the new girlfriend of an A-list celebrity.

Seeing as how I was both freshly unemployed and not-so-freshly broke, I was so desperate at the time that staying at a relative's house had sounded like a good idea. So, I'd rung up Aunt Edna.

When she'd politely invited me for tea, I'd been relieved. Excited, even. On the way to her house, I'd envisioned having a gentile chat with Maggie Smith from *Downton Abbey*. What I got instead was bushwhacked by Anne Ramsey from *Throw Momma from the Train*.

Before I knew what hit me, Aunt Edna and Jackie had drugged my tea, tied me to a bedpost, and interrogated me with a rolling pin and a can of Raid. The pair had thought I was a hit-woman sent to "rub them out."

After finally convincing them that I was Maureen Diller's daughter, I found out why Ma had never talked about her family. According to Aunt Edna, it had been against "Family" rules. Which Family? A little-known southern branch of the mafia referred to as the Cornbread Cosa Nostra.

Once the two had removed the zip-ties from my wrists, my aunt had explained the whole situation to me. Back in the 1970s and '80s, their entire limb of the mafia had been cut down by the long arm of the law. Nearly every single one of the Cornbread mob men had either been killed or were busy finishing out life sentences in Sing Sing.

But the mob *women* were still very much alive and kicking—and they wanted to stay that way. (At least, that's the reason they gave me for our not-so-cute meet-cute. Though I suppose, to be fair, it hadn't helped that I'd arrived at their doorstep in the trunk of a Chevy Caprice. But that's another story.)

Given how it had ended for their men, the women left standing after the Cornbread Cosa Nostra crumbled had sought to shield themselves from unwanted attention. As part of their cover, they'd moved into Palm Court Cottages, a small apartment complex in an older neighborhood near downtown St. Petersburg, Florida. They'd also renamed themselves the Collard Green Cosa Nostra, or the CGCN for short.

Jackie Cooperelli and Aunt Edna were two such women. And although both of them were pushing seventy, they still carried a healthy fear of mobsters.

One in particular.

Sammy the Psycho.

And, unfortunately, he just happened to love cheese curds.

Chapter Two

I sat up in the old recliner and studied my aunt. She was staring blankly at the bag of gooey cheese globs still dangling from Jackie's hand. Her face had taken on the same sickly shade of green as the sculptured carpeting beneath her feet.

"Do you really think Sammy the Psycho sent those things?" I asked.

"Maybe." Aunt Edna gnawed her bottom lip. For the first time since meeting her, my aunt appeared to have lost the pep that fueled her typical steamroller personality.

"I thought Sammy was dead," Jackie said, gawking at the plastic bag full of white, lumpy goo. She hoisted it up to eye level again for our viewing pleasure.

"Maybe he *is*, maybe he *ain't*." Aunt Edna collapsed onto the velvet couch and shook her head slowly. "The last news I got on Sammy was over two years ago."

"Oh, yeah?" Jackie crinkled her long, thin nose. "What news was that?"

Aunt Edna sighed. "I heard a rumor he's in a vegetative state."

Jackie gasped. "Sammy's in *Idaho*?"

Aunt Edna glared up at Jackie. A pained look flashed across her face. She spoke in a weary, half-whisper. "Seriously, Jackie. I've got a bad feeling about this."

I leaned closer to my aunt. "Isn't there someone you can call to find out?"

She shook her head. "Sammy's not somebody you can just casually bring up in a conversation."

"Why not?" I asked.

Jackie twirled a finger next to her temple. "They don't call him Sammy the Psycho for nuthin', you know."

I squirmed in my seat. "So why exactly *do* they call him that?"

"Molasses," Aunt Edna said.

Molasses was the code word my Aunt Edna used for secrets. Or, more accurately, how secrets should be revealed.

Slowly. Drip by drip.

According to my aunt, it was better to give people time to gently soak in bittersweet information by giving them just a little sample. That way, they could acquire a taste for it without losing their appetites completely. She'd tried her method on me. But after already having swallowed a bellyful of family secrets, I was craving something more akin to a shot of Kentucky Bourbon.

"Come on," I said. "Just give it to me straight."

Jackie folded her arms across her chest. "Edna, if you don't tell her, I will."

Aunt Edna blew out a breath that could fill a hot-air balloon. "Okay, okay. All right, already." She locked eyes with me. "Dorey. Get comfy. This could take a while."

• • • •

AS I SAT ON THE COUCH and munched homemade snickerdoodles, Aunt Edna settled herself into the good chair and proceeded to lay out a tale that would've been hard to swallow even *with* a bourbon chaser.

According to her, Sammy the Psycho had been an on-again, off-again hitman for the Cornbread Cosa Nostra. And she'd meant that quite literally.

If Aunt Edna was to be believed, Sammy had performed his "services" in an altered state of consciousness, like some Southern-fried *Manchurian Candidate*. She'd explained that during their childhood years, Sammy's fellow teen-mobsters-in-training had discovered they could turn his murderous talents on and off like a switch.

"On the surface, Sammy was your average Joe Mafioso," Aunt Edna said. "But the guys found out that when he got boiling mad—and then drunk as a skunk—Sammy turned into a murderous, *Hulk*-like monster capable of just about anything."

"But here's the *real* kicker," Jackie chimed in. "Afterward, Sammy couldn't remember a thing."

My nose crinkled in disbelief. "Seriously?"

"You're darn tootin'," Jackie said. "The mob guys used Sammy like a Polaroid camera. Just pointed him and said, 'Shoot.'" She winked and shot me with a bony finger gun.

"I know it sounds crazy," Aunt Edna said, wiping an errant strand of gray hair from her face. "But it's true. As you can imagine, Sammy's blackout brain came in pretty handy during police investigations. Not being able to remember nothin', he could sail through interrogations and polygraphs like a pigeon through a wind tunnel."

I gulped. "So, what happened to him?"

"Nothing," Aunt Edna said. "Despite a boatload of suspicions, the cops could never pin so much as a jaywalking charge on Sammy."

"Wow," I said. "Sounds like he was one lucky guy."

Jackie shrugged. "Not really. Sammy avoided the slammer, but then the Family started avoiding *him*."

My right eyebrow shot up. "Why?"

"Because," Aunt Edna said. "If *our* men could use him to get rid of their enemies, what was to stop someone else from flicking Sammy's switch to get rid of *us*?"

"Sammy was a ticking time bomb," Jackie said. "And nobody wanted to get caught holding the magic eight-ball."

My brow furrowed. "I don't get it. It seems to me that all you guys had to do was keep Sammy away from the booze and he'd be fine."

"Yeah," Aunt Edna said. "And all you gotta do is drain the ocean and you got anchovies." She shook her head. "Look, Dorey. Maybe what you said could've worked. But nobody was willing to put their life on the line to find out. Besides, there was more to Sammy than your typical, rage-filled booze hound."

My nose crinkled. "What do you mean?"

Aunt Edna tapped a finger to her graying temple. "Maybe the booze wiped out his memory. *Or* maybe, just maybe, *Sammy was faking it all along.*"

"Faking it?" I frowned. "How could he? I mean, beating all those polygraphs and stuff?"

"I can think of *one* way," Aunt Edna said.

"Oh!" Jackie piped up. "Was it because he wore a disguise?"

Aunt Edna ground her teeth. "No." She turned to me. "Maybe Sammy played us all because he knew in his rotten little mind that he could beat the system. Maybe he really *is* a bona fide psychopath."

My mouth fell open. "Are you saying you think Sammy *knew* what he was doing when he killed people?"

"How could he *not*?" Aunt Edna scowled. "But enough about him. Talking about Sammy is bad luck." She pursed her lips and crossed herself.

"Bad luck?" I asked. "How could it be bad—"

"Edna's right," Jackie blurted. "It's bad luck because *Sammy* was bad luck. Talk about him and his bad luck finds you. You know, like the Dim Reaper."

Aunt Edna shot me a tired look. "I rest my case."

I frowned. "Come on. That doesn't make any sense."

"Sure it does," Jackie said. "Everybody knows Sammy was a natural-born killer. The poor guy was doomed from birth. You know. On account of the 'Curse of the Psycho Eye.'"

Jackie beamed at me, then shrunk back and grimaced. "Oh. No offense, Dorey."

My shoulders slumped. "None taken."

The "Curse of the Psycho Eye" Jackie had referred to was the fact that Sammy had been born with one brown eye and one pale-blue one.

Just like *I* had.

Heterochromia iridum (mismatched irises) ran in the Family. I'd inherited a nearly identical pair as Sammy's. Whether I'd *also* inherited the drunken-rage-serial-killer trait was still up for debate. But I had no plans to hang around to find out.

Just a little over an hour ago, Sergeant McNulty of the St. Petersburg Police Department had cleared me of all suspicion in the death of my old boss, Tad Longmire. Given the insanity I'd just been through with the cops and my wacko new mob family, all I wanted now was to make a hasty exit back to my pathetic, but comparatively quiet life as a would-be actress back in L.A.

"Anyway, Dorey," Aunt Edna said. "Now that the news about your eye is out, we need to keep an eye out for Sammy."

What the?

I was going to ask her why, but decided not to. Instead, I stood up and said, "Well, ladies, it's been fun. As much as I'd love to help you find Sammy, I better get back to—"

Bam! Bam!

A loud knock sounded at the door.

The three of us froze.

"It's Sammy!" Jackie squealed. "He found us!"

"Hush!" Aunt Edna whispered. "I *told* you it was bad luck to say his name!"

"What are we gonna do?" Jackie whispered.

"Pull yourself together!" Aunt Edna barked, rocking herself to standing. "Run to the kitchen and get the bug spray—and bring me back my rolling pin!"

"What about me?" I asked.

"Go put Jackie's sunglasses on. If it ain't him, we don't want to be scaring any Girl Scouts to death."

Chapter Three

The knock sounded again at the door—louder and more insistent this time. Apparently, Sammy the Psycho not only had no conscience, but no patience to boot.

I glanced at my aunt and Jackie and nearly groaned out loud. Armed with nothing but household gadgets, the three of us stood poised to do battle with a psychotic killer.

We were doomed.

All six of our knobby knees shook as Aunt Edna crossed herself, then gave the "go" signal to her reluctant sidekick. Jackie gulped and nodded.

Slowly, one of her bony hands raised, then hovered over the doorknob like a hairless, liver-spotted tarantula. Her other hand had a white-knuckle grip on an industrial-sized can of Raid.

"Who's there?" Jackie squealed into the gap in the front door.

A trickle of sweat ran down my back. The three of us held our breath, waiting for a reply.

"Me," a man's voice answered.

Jackie gasped and turned to us. Horror sagged her usually sunny expression. "Edna! That sounds just like Sammy!"

"Crap!" I said. "What are we gonna do?" My hand was shaking so badly I nearly dropped the weapon they'd given me—a toilet brush.

"Hush! Lemme think!" Aunt Edna hissed. "Jackie, whatever you do, don't open the door."

Jackie grimaced. "Are you sure?"

"Yes!" Aunt Edna and I said simultaneously.

"Okay, here goes," Jackie said.

She grabbed the knob and flung open the door.

"Ack! Noooo!" I screeched. I slammed my eyelids shut and braced for the oncoming hail of bullets from a Tommy gun.

"Gee. Am I *that* repulsive?" a man's voice asked.

My eyes sprung open. Instead of a mad serial killer in a double-breasted suit, a cop in a blue uniform stood just outside the doorframe. A very handsome cop. One who'd helped save my bacon when it was about to fry for the murder of Tad Longmire.

"Brady!" I yelled. "What are *you* doing here?"

"I could ask you the same thing," he said. "I thought you were on your way back to L.A."

"Oh. I was," I fumbled, suddenly flustered. "I mean, I *am*. This evening."

"Unless we can convince her to stay," Aunt Edna said, no hint of fear left in her voice. "You got any ideas?"

"Well, you could start by not making her clean the johns," Brady quipped.

"What?" I followed his gaze up my raised arm, where the toilet brush hovered like a club in my hand. "Oh." I let out a nervous laugh and lowered the brush.

Jackie laughed. "Dorey was getting ready to clean your clock, Brady."

"Remind me not to hire her as a maid, then," he quipped.

Aunt Edna and Jackie laughed. But I was dumbstruck—and impressed.

"Geez, Brady," I said. "You didn't even *flinch* at the sight of three armed women. That's pretty impressive."

Brady grinned. "You forget. This isn't my first ride on the Palm Court Express."

I smirked. I hadn't forgotten.

As a friend of the family, Officer Brady made a habit of dropping by once or twice a week to check up on, and sometimes share a meal with, the elderly women living at Palm Court Cottages. From what I could tell, it was a mutually beneficial arrangement. Aunt Edna provided the main course in the form of delectable Italian cuisine. In return, Brady provided dessert—in the form of mouth-watering eye candy.

Blessed with a full head of mink-brown hair, a muscle-man's physique, and a boyish, friendly face, Officer Brady was quite the dish, all right.

"Well?" Aunt Edna asked, nudging Brady with her rolling pin. "You gonna get Dorey to stay, or what?"

"I can't exactly cuff her to the bedposts," he said. "But I might be able to think of something to persuade her."

Brady shot me a grin that made me wonder if the whole cuffing thing might not be such a bad idea after all.

My cheeks grew hot. If Brady noticed, he didn't show it. Instead, he turned to Jackie and said, "That is, if you ladies don't *exterminate* me first."

"Oh," Jackie giggled at the can of Raid still locked in her bony grip. "Sorry. We thought you was somebody else."

"Who?" Brady asked. "The abominable Orkin man?"

"Close," I said. "Sammy the Psycho."

"Can it!" Aunt Edna hissed, jabbing an elbow into my ribs.

"You sayin' I should spray Brady?" Jackie asked.

"No!" My aunt shook her head. "That's it, Jackie. Tomorrow we're getting you fitted for a Miracle Ear."

"Wait a minute," Brady said, his grin evaporating. "Are you serious? You thought I might be some kind of psycho?"

"No!" Aunt Edna protested too loudly.

Brady's eyes made a quick study of us all. "Then what's going on here?"

Aunt Edna softened her tone. "It's just that, you know, somebody sent us some cheese curds. That's all."

"Ah. The case of the killer curds," Brady said. "Why didn't you say so in the first place?"

"It's no joke," I said. "They think they came from Sammy the Psycho."

Aunt Edna shot me a dirty look. Brady noticed. His friendly voice switched to no-nonsense policeman mode. "Where are they?"

Jackie grimaced. "They? There's just *one* Sammy, right Edna?"

"The curds are in that cooler over there," Aunt Edna said, pointing to the Styrofoam box on the floor beside the door. "They just got here ten minutes ago."

Brady knelt by the cooler and opened the lid. "No return address?"

"Nope," Jackie said. "Kinda rude, eh?"

Brady carefully picked up the baggie of curds and studied them. "Hmm. They appear to be direct from Wisconsin."

Jackie stared at Aunt Edna. "I thought you said *you-know-who* was in *Idaho*."

The tendons in Aunt Edna's neck grew taught. She closed her eyes and turned away from Jackie. "Brady, how do you know those things came from Wisconsin?"

"Well, it's a little known fact," he said. "But I happen to have majored in cheese-curd forensics."

"Really? Wow!" Jackie said, the whites of her eyes doubling.

Brady laughed. "Well, *that* and there's this nifty little label on the bag. It says, *Waylan's Famous Wisconsin Cheese Curds*. Also, based on the dry ice in the cooler, these curds have traveled a long *whey*. Get it?"

Jackie laughed. Aunt Edna and I groaned.

"So they weren't sent locally?" I asked.

"It doesn't appear likely," Brady said. "Otherwise, they'd have used regular ice. Tell me, ladies, did this psycho of yours send any kind of message along with these weapons of mass arterial destruction?"

"Yeah," I said. "A note—"

"Saying to enjoy them in good health, that's all," Aunt Edna said, her voice drowning out my own. "But it wasn't signed."

"Hmm." Brady eyed the lumps of cheese. "Well, if you ask me, these curds either got delivered to the wrong address, or they were likely meant as a gift for one of you. Anybody have a special occasion coming up?"

Jackie perked up. "Hey, maybe—"

"Nope. Nobody," Aunt Edna said, slipping the rolling pin back into her apron. She dusted off her hands and shot me and Jackie her distinctive *shut your trap* glare. "So, I guess that's that. It was just an innocent little mix-up at the post office."

"Uh, yeah," Jackie said. "That's it."

"Okay," Brady said, but the look on his face said he wasn't buying it.

"Oh well, their loss is our gain," Aunt Edna said, trading her angry glare for a brilliant smile. She beamed up at Brady and said, "So, who's up for some nice cheese curds and tea?"

Chapter Four

"You always wear sunglasses?" Brady asked me.

"Doreen's a big star in Hollywood," Aunt Edna said, shoving us out the front door and into the courtyard. "Doesn't want to get recognized by the paparazzi."

He smirked. "I see."

"I bet you do," Aunt Edna said, then ushered Brady and me to the wrought-iron picnic table that stood at the center of Palm Court Cottages' tropical courtyard. The small, jungle-like oasis was surrounded on all sides by quaint, single-story wooden cottages, each nestled amidst a riot of colorful foliage on the verge of going rogue.

"Sit right here," my aunt said, and motioned to two chairs right next to each other. She set a platter of Ritz crackers and gooey cheese curds down on the table. "Now, you two make yourselves comfortable and enjoy your snacks."

As we settled into our cushioned seats, Jackie came strolling down the paved path toward us, humming *Strangers in the Night*. In her hands was a tray laden with two plates, two sets of silverware, and a pair of tall glasses filled with iced tea.

"Here you go," she said, setting the tray down in front of Brady and me.

"Well, doesn't that look delicious?" Aunt Edna said, winking at Brady. "Oh, dearie me. I forgot something on the stove."

"You did?" Jackie asked. "That ain't like you, Edna."

Aunt Edna rolled her eyes. "Geez, Jackie. Too bad they don't make a Miracle *Brain*." She hooked Jackie's arm in hers and tugged her, begrudgingly, back toward their cottages.

Brady and I watched as they disappeared into the fading light of dusk. A few seconds later, a string of festive party lights blinked on over our heads.

Brady laughed. "So much for subtlety."

I smirked. "I don't think my aunt knows the meaning of the word. Still, I'm glad to catch a moment alone with you."

Brady's dark brown eyes brightened. "You are?"

"Yes. I'm surprised at you. Making light of Sammy the Psycho. Aunt Edna and Jackie seem genuinely worried about him. Is their safety all a joke to you?"

Brady blanched. "Not at all. It's just that ...." Brady chewed his bottom lip for a second. When he spoke again, his tone was more serious. "Let me put it this way, Doreen. I've known these ladies a lot longer than you have. I've learned to humor them, okay?"

My back bristled. "*Humor* them?"

"Yes." Brady picked up a fork, stabbed a cheese curd, and doled it onto my plate. "Let's just say the women in your family appear to be blessed with *exceptional imaginations*."

My right eyebrow angled sharply. "Am I supposed to take that as a compliment or an insult?"

Brady grinned. "Use your imagination."

My jaw tightened. "I'm serious! Those two are acting as if their lives are at stake."

"I understand," Brady said. "But what you don't know is, their lives are *always* at stake."

I nearly choked on a sip of iced tea. "*What?*"

"There's always *something* going on with them. Last month, Jackie was sure the neighbor's dog was wearing a wire. The month before that, your aunt was convinced someone had sent her a death threat on a potato chip."

The indignation went out of my righteousness sails. "Oh." I grimaced. "And?"

Brady smiled softly. "In Jackie's case, the poor pooch had gotten tangled in an old telephone cord."

"And the potato chip?"

"Edna told me the chip had the perfect outline of a coffin burned onto it."

My upper lip snarled. "Did it?"

He shrugged. "I don't know. Jackie ate it before I had a chance to see it."

"Geez." I slumped into my chair. "So, you think Sammy the Psycho is just something they made up?"

"More likely a figment of their paranoia," Brady said. "Actually, this is the first time I've ever heard of him."

I locked eyes with Brady. "Do you think he could actually exist?"

"Theoretically, sure." Brady put a cheese curd on his plate. "As a cop, I've learned virtually anything, no matter how improbable, can be possible. On the other hand, after you've heard as many tales as I have, they all tend to sound suspiciously familiar."

"What do you mean?" I frowned and watched a moth flittering around the party lights above our heads.

Brady stabbed another curd with his fork. "Okay. Let me guess. Sammy murdered a bunch of people, right?"

My shoulders stiffened. "Yes."

"And he's on the lam?"

I blushed. "Uh ... yes." I poked a fork at the nasty lump of cheese on my plate. "But there's more to it than that."

Brady put a cracker on my plate. "Like what?"

I frowned. "Well, according to Aunt Edna, Sammy can be programmed to kill."

One of Brady's thick eyebrows ticked up slightly. "Programmed? How?"

"By getting him all fired up with alcohol and rage."

"I see." Brady put his fork down. "Well, I hate to break it to you, Doreen, but there's nothing unusual about that. Especially here in Florida."

"Maybe not," I argued. "But Sammy's different."

"How?"

"He ... well, Aunt Edna says that after Sammy kills someone, he says he can't remember a thing."

"Wow," Brady said, tapping a finger on his chin. "A criminal who can't recall his crimes. I've never heard *that* one before."

I groaned.

Brady grinned at me. "Sorry, Diller. You've got to do better than that."

"Okay, fine! He's got the Curse of the Psycho Eye, okay?"

Brady blanched. "Excuse me?"

I whipped off my sunglasses and scowled at Brady. "Sammy's got a wonky eye. Just like mine. Jackie says that means he's a natural-born killer."

Brady's face lit up with horror. "Oh my God!"

His eyes darted maniacally around in the fading light, causing my heart to quicken. He grabbed my hand and whispered, "Anything else you can tell me about this hideous, murdering, Frankenstein mobster?"

"Argh!" I jerked my hand away. "Yes. He loves cheese curds!"

Brady burst out laughing. "Well, that proves it."

I eyed him with suspicion. "Proves *what*?"

"That you're not like Sammy, if that's what you're so worried about."

I nearly gasped. How did he know my secret fear?

I winced. "So my eye doesn't gross you out?"

Brady shook his head. "I'm a cop, remember? I've seen it all. If it makes you feel any better, I can show you the hairy mole on my back."

I gave him half a smile. "Thanks, but I'll pass." I locked eyes with him. "But tell me, how can cheese curds prove I'm not like Sammy?"

"Because you obviously *hate* them," Brady said. "At least, that's what I gather from the look on your face." Brady nodded at my plate. "Go on. Prove me wrong."

I glanced down at my plate. My nose crinkled at the thought of the slimy, white goo touching my lips. But I wasn't going to wimp out in front of Brady.

"Fine." I steeled myself and stabbed a cheese curd with my fork. I lifted it to my nose and took a whiff. It smelled like sour milk.

Eeew!

"Go on," Brady coaxed. "Be brave. Take a bite."

Battling my pride *and* my gag reflex, I took a nibble. To my surprise, the disgusting glob *squeaked* against my teeth. I nearly heaved.

"Gross!" I blurted, spitting out the rubbery white morsel.

Brady laughed. "And there's your proof. You hate cheese curds. It's official. Doreen Diller is no Sammy the Psycho."

I smiled. But inside, my gut was summersaulting.

To my utter horror, that disgusting-looking cheese curd had tasted even better than Aunt Edna's clam linguine.

Chapter Five

Last night, I'd had every intention of asking Brady take me to the airport after our less-than-subtle set-up by Aunt Edna. But while the cheese curds she'd served us had been flown in from Wisconsin, my aunt had neglected to inform either of us that the *iced teas* had come directly from Long Island.

"Great," I grumbled.

I held my thumping skull together with my hands and slowly crawled out from under the covers. Careful not to lean over far enough for my brain to slosh out of the top of my cranium, I grabbed ahold of the handle on my ratty suitcase and hoisted it up onto the bed.

I yanked open the zipper. The case was empty.

WTH?

"You up in there?" Aunt Edna's voice boomed through the bedroom door.

"Uh ... yes!" I yelled back, causing my head to pulse along to the beat of my heart.

I blinked my bloodshot eyes at the baby-pink walls and yellowing French provincial furniture that had been my home base for the last week and a half. As dated as the room was, it still beat the one I shared in a rundown flat in a crappy area of South Park, California.

"Then you'd better get a move on," Aunt Edna bellowed. "You wouldn't want to miss your flight back to L.A. now, would you?"

"My flight last night!" I gasped. "I missed it!"

"Don't worry," she said through the door. "I helped you rebook it for 9:45 this morning. You know you giggle a lot when you're drunk?"

"So I've heard."

I glanced at the clock radio on the nightstand. It was 9:38 a.m. I nearly choked on my own spit. Even with a *Star Trek* transporter,

I couldn't make it on time. Thank goodness my ticket was exchangeable.

I flopped back onto the bed. The sudden jerking motion jarred my brain, causing it to thump like an angry orangutan against my skull. I couldn't believe it. Once again, my aunt had rendered me unconscious. Only this time, her drug of choice had been alcohol.

Geez! Is everyone in Florida bonkers?

I lay back on the bed pillows and sighed. The people I worked with back in L.A. were odd. But actors and producers were *predictably* weird. It didn't take a lot of work to peg them as phonies, narcissists, or egomaniacs. But here in St Petersburg, my powers of perception had turned as vague as what's covered by an insurance policy.

Florida seemed to possess its own unique brand of weirdos. From what I'd been able to ascertain so far, Jackie Cooperelli was a harmless one. Granted, she was a lamebrain who thought dogs were capable of both espionage *and* sniffing out deadbeats, but harmless nonetheless.

Aunt Edna, on the other hand, was proving trickier to diagnose. Though she seemed relatively normal on the surface, I suspected her culinary mastermind could be peppered with more than a mere pinch of delusional paranoia. And I had to hand it to her. She sure knew how to incapacitate a gal.

Then there was the annoyingly attractive Officer Gregory Brady. Where he fit into this goofball crew was still a total mystery to me.

Brady was handsome, smart, and cared about my aunt and Jackie. That was obvious. But what secret cards was he holding close to his vest? And what was up with that warped sense of humor of his? Was it an unavoidable side effect of being named after a TV character?

I pictured Brady's face amongst the tic-tac-toe vignettes on the opening jingle to *The Brady Bunch* and laughed out loud.

What a bunch of nut balls. Geez. If Sammy the Psycho really does exist, he might turn out to be the sanest one of us all.

• • • •

"WHY DIDN'T YOU WAKE me up?" I asked, stumbling into the kitchen in my pajamas.

"Do I look like your personal valet?" Aunt Edna asked, barely glancing up from the newspaper crossword puzzle. "You're a grown woman, Dorey."

Unable to argue her point so soon after regaining partial consciousness, I settled for the consolation of a cup of coffee and a bowl of Lucky Charms. As I sipped and munched across the table from my aunt, I got busy thumbing through my phone for flights back to L.A.

"What's a seven-letter word for a guest who don't pay?" Aunt Edna asked.

I glanced up at her. "Is that part of your puzzle, or are you trying to make a point?"

Aunt Edna laughed. "You know—"

A sharp creaking sound interrupted her. Someone had just opened the front door.

"Who's that?" I asked, lurching back in my seat. The sudden movement made me wish some of those marshmallow thingies in my cereal were aspirins.

"Anybody home?" Jackie's voice rang out, answering my question.

"We're in here," Aunt Edna said. She smirked at me and quipped, "My, you're jumpy this morning. Guilty conscience?"

Before I could answer, Jackie came bouncing into the dining room. She was wearing white shorts and a golf shirt so orange it forced me to shut my eyes.

"Morning!" she said. "Any coffee left?"

"In the pot," Aunt Edna said. "Like it always is."

"Fantastic!" Jackie grinned with such cheer that both Aunt Edna and I winced.

"Hey, did you see the news?" Jackie asked, holding up a rolled newspaper as if she were about to use it to swat a fly. "Another old-timer bit the dust at Shady Respite."

I shrugged. "What's so unusual about that? Isn't Florida God's waiting room?"

"If you ask me, somebody's getting tired of waiting," Jackie said, arching a drawn-on eyebrow. "This is the third one in less than a month."

"You're kidding," Aunt Edna said, looking up from her crossword.

"Nope." Jackie tapped a bony finger on the folded paper. "Says so right here in this article."

"Lemme see that." Aunt Edna snatched the paper from Jackie's hand. As she unrolled it, I recognized the title running across the top of the page. It was a local tabloid called the *Beach Gazette*.

I watched silently as Aunt Edna chewed a mouthful of bagel and read the article circled by Jackie with a red marker. Suddenly, her eyes grew wide. She dropped the paper and sprang to her feet.

"This is worse than I thought," she said. "We need to talk to Sophia. *Now!*"

I stuck my spoon into my magically delicious cereal. "Who's Sophia?"

My question seemed to startle Aunt Edna, as if she'd forgotten I was there. She shook her head. "Molasses."

"No molasses," Jackie said sternly. "It's time Doreen got to know the Family."

Aunt Edna let out a groan and closed her eyes. "Fine. Sophia's the head of the CGCN. The Queenpin, so to speak."

My right eyebrow arched. "So, she's like ... Cosa Nostra *royalty*?"

An image of Michelle Pfeiffer in *Scarface* popped into my mind—an elegant woman in a sleek, sequined ball gown, lying atop a piano smoking a cigarette with one of those long, tapered holder-thingies.

"Sorta," Jackie said.

I perked up at the opportunity to meet a real, live mob queen in action. I figured I could gather a few useful tips for future auditions back in L.A.

"Okay, I'm in," I said. "As long as you can get me back to the airport in time, that is. I just rebooked my flight for this evening at seven."

Aunt Edna shrugged. "Sure. It shouldn't take too long."

I smiled. "Cool. So, where does Queen Sophia live?"

"In apartment three, across the courtyard," Jackie said, returning from the kitchen with a cup of coffee. "But at the moment, she's ... um ...." Jackie's voice trailed off. Her eyes darted left, then right. She cupped a hand to her mouth, leaned over and whispered in my ear, "She's in a *facility*."

I blanched.

Geez. This seals it. This whole family is 100% nuts!

"Drug rehab or mental breakdown?" I asked, imagining a crazed, big-eyed Bette Davis holed up in the attic in *Hush, Hush, Sweet Charlotte*.

"Neither," Aunt Edna said. "Convalescent center. Busted hip. Sophia's about to turn a hundred years old."

"Oh." My image of the CGCN Queenpin degenerated from 'dapper diva' to 'dowager in Depends.'

Jackie smiled coyly and winked at me. "Rumor has it Sophia came over from Sicily in a wooden ship."

I frowned, my former curiosity replaced with suspicion. "Rumors seem to run rampant around here."

Jackie smirked and clapped a hand on my shoulder. "Dorey, you got no idea."

I grimaced. "That's what I'm afraid of. You know what? You guys go ahead without me. I think I'll just stay here and re-pack for my trip back to L.A. Speaking of which, who unpack—"

"Come on," Jackie pleaded. "One little Family visit won't hurt nothing. Then we'll come straight back here and get you to the airport on time. I promise."

I chewed my lip. "Well ..."

"Oh, crap!" Aunt Edna bellowed. "Would you look at the clock? It's almost lunchtime and I got nothing in the oven!"

I glanced at the gaudy cherub clock casting aspersions at us from the wall above our heads. The dial in its pudgy, golden arms registered quarter past ten.

In Aunt Edna's world, lunch was served promptly at eleven, followed by dinner at four o'clock. I didn't know if the early-bird arrangement was her own personal preference or a CGCN regulation. Either way, I'd learned not to ask if I could help out with the preparations. Setting foot in the kitchen when Aunt Edna was cooking was a risky proposition. The woman had a cleaver and she knew how to use it.

Aunt Edna wrung her hands. "Geez, Louise. Good thing I already got most of it together. I'll pop the cacciatore in the oven and we should still be able to make it in time."

"In time for what?" I asked.

"Saturday lunch with Sophia," Aunt Edna said, sprinting toward the kitchen. "It'll sweeten the pot."

My brow furrowed. "*What* pot?"

Aunt Edna shrugged. "Sophia can be cranky when it comes to surprises."

"What's the surprise?" I asked.

"You," my aunt said.

"Oh." I glanced over at Jackie. She was already licking her lips in anticipation. I couldn't blame her. Aunt Edna might've been rigid when it came to rules, but her cooking could steal the "Bam!" right out of Emeril's envious, drooling mouth.

Looking at Jackie made me think of my own mother. She was a total disaster in the kitchen. The best recipe she'd ever come up with was a tin of tuna dumped into a can of cream-of-something soup, poured over a box of macaroni and cheese and microwaved until the plastic bowl half-melted. To be honest, until I'd met my aunt, my idea of a gourmet meal had been a Denny's Grand Slam. I wasn't even sure there was a functioning stove in my apartment back in L.A.

I drained my coffee mug and chewed my lip. While I tried to decide whether Aunt Edna's cacciatore was worth missing my flight over, Jackie reached across the table and patted my hand.

"Come with us and meet Sophia," she said. "It'll be fun."

"I dunno," I said. "I don't even know her."

Jackie made googly eyes at me. "Hello? Earth to Doreen. *Meeting* Sophia is how you *get* to know her."

I hesitated. The delectable aroma of Aunt Edna's cacciatore was busily eroding my resolve.

"Do it for your Aunt Edna," Jackie said. "Do it for your *Family*."

My eyebrows shot up. "The same family that drugged me, hog-tied me to a bed, and nearly scratched my eye out?"

Jackie shrugged. "Hey. We didn't know you was Family then. Besides, ain't that exactly what *you* did to that soap-opera hunk boss of yours?"

I frowned. "I never *drugged* Tad."

Jackie smirked. "No. You just threatened to cut off his body parts."

I winced, caught in my own trap. "Just his *bangs*. And cuticle scissors never killed anybody!"

Jackie smirked. "Honey, a good hitman can turn a *broken toothpick* into a deadly weapon."
I grimaced.
Geez. I wonder how she knows that?

Chapter Six

That *'70s Show* had nothing on Aunt Edna's living room. I parked my butt in her brown Barcalounger and stared blankly at the urine-colored lamps flanking either side of the green velveteen couch. While I waited for the two women to get ready for our trip to visit Godmother Sophia, I found myself caught in an internal debate—one I couldn't win despite the fact that I was arguing both sides.

My brain kept telling me to leave this whole Collard Green Cosa Nostra craziness behind while I had the chance. Just call a cab and get my butt to the airport. But the smell of Aunt Edna's chicken cacciatore baking in the oven had my traitorous stomach shredding through my sensible escape plan like a tornado in a trailer park.

Admittedly, I *was* more than a smidgen curious about meeting the CGCN's leading lady. And I couldn't deny a niggling sense of duty to Ma's family, no matter how nutso they were.

I chewed my lip, then let out a sigh.

What would be the harm in staying a few more hours? Face it, Doreen. The only cook waiting for you back in LA is Chef Boyardee.

"So, you coming or not?" Jackie asked.

I nodded, letting the deciding point go to the cacciatore. The aroma alone made me feel as if I'd died and gone to Sicily. "Okay," I said. "I'm coming."

"All right!" Jackie hooted. "Edna, she's going with us!"

Aunt Edna stepped out of the kitchen and beamed at me. "Good girl! Now, let's get a move on, you two. Jackie, you carry the casserole dish. Dorey, you grab the keys. You're driving."

"I am?" I asked.

"Yes." She looked down at my bare feet. "Put on those new flip-flops we gave you."

I didn't argue. What was the point?

• • • •

AS I SCOOTED INTO THE driver's seat of Jackie's ancient, olive-drab Kia, my mind flashed back to my suitcase. I'd left it lying open at the foot of the bed like a gutted fish. I needed time to repack before my flight back to L.A. this evening. Would we make it back in time?

I glanced over at Aunt Edna climbing into the passenger seat beside me. An unfamiliar emptiness shot through me. I told myself it was a hunger pang, but it felt more substantial than that. She and Jackie had been kind enough to feed and house me for well over a week, asking nothing in return. I'd never known such selflessness. Nobody in L.A. did *anything* without an ulterior motive. The least I could do was drive them over to have lunch with this Queenpin lady.

I turned the key in the ignition. In a minor miracle, the car coughed to life without having to be beaten about the solenoid with a socket wrench. But as I shifted into reverse, something felt off to me.

Neither of the other two women appeared overly excited about the trip.

Aunt Edna was staring blankly out the window, chewing her thumbnail to the quick. In the backseat, Jackie anxiously drummed her fingers on the side of the harvest-gold casserole dish nestled on a dishtowel in her lap.

"You two look nervous," I said, reversing out of the parking space. "Anything wrong?"

"Not a thing," Aunt Edna said. "I just hope Sophia likes her lunch, that's all."

"Don't worry," Jackie said. "Chicken cacciatore is Sophia's favorite. She'll love it. Unless she went and lost her dentures again. Then all bets are off."

Aunt Edna sighed. "If it weren't for us, I swear that poor woman would starve to death in that place."

"Why?" I asked, steering the Kia onto the street. "Is the food that bad in there?"

Aunt Edna shrugged. "I dunno. I've never tried it."

"Sophia won't touch it either," Jackie said. "She thinks somebody's trying to poison her."

I nearly drove the Kia into the curb. "*Poison* her? Why would she think *that*?"

Aunt Edna shot me a cockeyed glance. "When you're the Queenpin of the CGCN, your head's always on the chopping block."

I grimaced. "It *is*?"

"Hello?" Aunt Edna said. "Welcome to the mafia, Dorey. Sophia's rivals have been trying to do her in since before you were born."

I shot a paranoid glance in the rearview mirror at Jackie. "If that's so, how does Sophia know you haven't put cyanide in that chicken cacciatore of yours?"

"Because we've been taking care of Sophia for over thirty years," Aunt Edna said wearily. "If I wanted to poison her, I'd have done it by now."

"Sophia's not just our *boss*," Jackie said. "She's our cash cow, too. She knows she can trust us 'cause if *she* dies, the money dies with her."

I blinked hard at Aunt Edna. "Is that true?"

My aunt shot Jackie a dirty look in the rearview mirror, then turned to me. "Yeah, pretty much. Unfortunately, we mob women were better at *hiding* dough than *making* it."

"Then where does Sophia get *her* money?" I asked.

Aunt Edna frowned and stared at the road ahead. "The Family Fund. And to be honest, I think they're getting tired of shelling out the greenbacks for her."

Jackie snorted. "I'm pretty sure they hadn't counted on Sophia living to be a bazillion."

Aunt Edna smirked sourly. "As they say, nothing ensures longevity like a monthly stipend."

"Huh." I turned right onto Fourth Street. "So, who's in charge of the Family Fund?"

"I think it's—" Jackie blurted.

"Can it, Jackie!" Aunt Edna yelled. "Look, Dorey. All you need to know right now is that keeping Sophia alive keeps *us* alive. Now, no more questions. Capeesh?"

I grimaced. "Capeesh."

Geez. This pair have more secrets than a call girl's condom box.

I shut my mouth and stared at the road ahead. As I drove, I mentally repacked my suitcase to beat a hasty retreat back to L.A. before I became a Cosa Nostra casualty myself. The two women in the car may have looked harmless, but I knew better. I didn't want to stick around and feel the wrath of Jackie's Raid ...

My head still hummed from my "iced tea" hangover. And my ghostly left eye still ached from when Jackie had accidently scratched my cornea during our "get acquainted" interrogation. It was still too irritated to conceal with a contact lens like I normally did. As a makeshift alternative, I'd been forced to don Jackie's huge, wrap-around glaucoma sunglasses instead.

I glanced at myself in the rearview mirror and blanched.

Geez. I'd better get out of here fast. All I need is a blue-tinted wash-n-set, and I'll be one of them!

Chapter Seven

At the reception window at the convalescent center, we showed our IDs to a bored, middle-aged medical tech clad in dingy gray scrubs. Ms. Rodriquez eyed us up and down and said, "None of you are afraid of dogs, are you?"

"No," Aunt Edna said. "Why?"

"We got a lady making the rounds with a therapy dog," she explained, pushing her mountain of frizzy black hair away from her face. "It's good for the patients' mental health. Unless, of course, they're terrified of dogs." She stared at us with dull, disinterested eyes. "It happens more than you'd think. That's why I have to ask. It's a matter of liability."

"Liability?" I asked.

"Yeah." Rodriquez sighed. "I thought it was stupid, too. But I looked it up. Dogs kill like 25,000 people a year."

"Geez," Jackie said. "I better be nicer to Benny."

"I'm okay with dogs," I said. "What about you two?"

"Sure," Aunt Edna said.

"Me, too," Jackie said.

Rodriquez nodded. "Okay, then. Go on through. Ms. Lorenzo is in room 113."

Jackie, Aunt Edna, and I made our way down the dreary beige corridor. The hallway hummed with the insect-like buzz of dying fluorescent lightbulbs hanging from the drop ceiling. Pine-scented disinfectant assaulted our noses.

Even the flapping noise generated by our pink flip-flops seemed to add a foreboding eeriness to the dank passageway. Our rubber sandals were the official leisure footwear of the CGCN. Aunt Edna had insisted we wear them as a sign of respect to the Queenpin.

According to Aunt Edna, the only thing Sophia hated more than being disrespected was being surprised. And while she had the hearing of a bat, the Queenpin couldn't see squat without her bifocals. Thus the flapping of our sandals would provide Sophia with fair warning of our approach.

I'd shrugged at the news. Given the crap I'd had to put up with as a Girl Friday back in L.A., it seemed a more than reasonable enough request.

"Here we go," Aunt Edna said as we reached room number 113. She cautiously rapped her knuckles on the door in a kind of SOS-like code.

Tap. Tapity-tap. Tapity-tap. Tap. Tap.

"Enter," a quavering voice said from the other side.

Suddenly I felt silly, as if I were auditioning for a bit part in a comical mobster movie. I giggled—a nervous habit—then took a step toward door number 113. Aunt Edna put a hand on my shoulder and held me back.

"Listen, Dorey," she said. "No stupid questions, okay? And no sudden moves. Smile and be humble. You think you can handle that?"

Smile and be humble?

I nearly laughed out loud.

My old job at the L.A. production studio had entailed catering to stars' outlandish whims at all hours of the day and night. As a "human gopher," I'd once been summoned at 2 a.m. by a D-List celebrity who'd insisted I smell his armpits and "describe the aroma in the voice of an android sent from the future." Like all my assignments, I'd done it with a smile—albeit a fake one.

I nodded at my aunt. "Yeah. I think I can handle it."

She looked me up and down. Worry lines etched her face. "Okay. But keep Jackie's sunglasses on, for crying out loud. We don't want to give Sophia a heart attack with that wonky eyeball of yours. Capeesh?"

"Capeesh." I pushed Jackie's huge glaucoma glasses up higher up on the bridge of my nose. "Ready when you are."

Aunt Edna nodded solemnly. "Okay. We're going in."

Like all L.A.-trained actors, I instinctively took a deep breath to center myself. Then I straightened my posture, set my attitude to *Can do!* and followed the two women into the nursing-home lair of the reigning Queen of the Collard Green Cosa Nostra.

Doña Sophia Maria Lorenzo.

Chapter Eight

The heavy metal door creaked open to Doña Sophia Maria Lorenzo's room at the convalescent center. Aunt Edna licked her lips nervously, cleared her throat, and pushed the door open a bit wider.

"Doña Sophia?" she said softly, aiming her voice at the backside of a wheelchair. It had been turned to face a small window in the stark, hospital-like space. "I'd like you to meet my niece, Doreen Diller."

A mechanical buzz sounded, as if in reply. It reverberated oddly off the blank, white walls as the wheelchair swiveled slowly around to face us. As it turned, it revealed its occupant—a shriveled, milky-white old woman shrouded in a black crocheted shawl.

If there'd been an audition for the part of Vito Corleone's grandmother in *The Godfather*, Doña Sophia would've been a shoe-in for the role.

A shiny silver turban sat atop the ancient woman's ghostly head like a bulbous, comical crown. But there was nothing funny about the dour, narrow face staring at us from beneath the Jiffy-Pop headdress. I recognized Doña Sophia's countenance well. "Regal disgust," was a popular attitude among celebrities.

The wheelchair buzzed to a stop. Doña Sophia jutted her sharp chin upward and studied the three of us silently with a pair of green, cat-like eyes.

Her intelligent, humorless visage reminded me of Celia Lovsky, the woman who played the Vulcan leader T'Pau in the *Star Trek* episode *Amok Time*. (The one where Spock fought Kirk to the death, driven mad by a desire to get laid. *Et tu*, Spock?)

For a moment, my eyes scanned the room, wondering if a hormone-crazed Vulcan might be hiding behind the bathroom door, preparing to lunge at me with a double-sided axe.

The mechanical buzz of Sophia's chair sounded again, drawing my wandering attention back to her. One of her gnarled fingers was pressing a button on the arm of her customized wheelchair. Slowly, the seat rose up, enabling Doña Sophia to look down her nose at us through a set of bejeweled bifocals.

"So you're Maureen's daughter, Doreen," she said slowly, apprising me with her almond-shaped eyes.

"Yes, your majesty." I curtseyed awkwardly, unsure of how to address the queen of the CGCN. "It's a pleasure to meet you."

"She came here all the way from L.A.," Aunt Edna said.

"Hmm." Sophia's eyes dulled, apparently unimpressed by my curtseying skills or my place of residence. Her attention shifted over to Jackie. "What's in the casserole dish?"

"Chicken cacciatore," Jackie answered. "You hungry?"

"Yes. Prepare me a plate."

"Yes, your Queenship," Jackie said reverently.

While Jackie carefully arranged a plate for Sophia, the old woman leaned her thin frame toward the small table beside her hospital bed. A spidery arm jutted from under her shawl and mashed a call button on an old landline phone.

"Freddy?" she said into the intercom. "Come over. *Now.*"

Before I could even ask who Freddy was, an old guy in a hospital gown tapped twice on the door, then stuck his pasty, half-bald head inside.

"Come in," Sophia said, offering him the first smile I'd seen grace her thin lips.

"Yes, ma'am," Freddy said, bowing as he entered. The old man was small and wiry. Not much bigger than Sophia herself.

"Here you go, my dear," Sophia said. "Have a plate of homemade cacciatore. Compliments of my Family."

The old man's eyes lit up. He grabbed the plate from Jackie. "Thanks, Soph. You're the best!"

"Yes. I know," she said dully. "Now run along and eat it before it gets cold." She shooed him out of the room with a flick of a blue-veined wrist.

Confused, I turned to Jackie and whispered, "What's going on?"

"Shh!" Aunt Edna hissed.

"Freddy is my food tester," Sophia said, eyeing me intently as she smoothed the lap of her black dress with a ghostly, liver-spotted hand.

I nearly blanched. "Food tester?"

Aunt Edna walked over and wedged herself between me and Jackie. "Yeah, in case someone tries to poison her," Jackie said, earning her an elbow in the ribs from Aunt Edna.

My mouth fell open. "Are you serious? People are willing to risk their lives like that for *money*?"

Doña Sophia tutted as if I'd amused her. "Don't be ridiculous, Doreen. Freddy's not getting *paid*. Except, of course, with some of Edna's excellent Italian cuisine."

My nose crinkled. "But …. I mean, how did you get him to put his life on the line like that for you?"

"Easy," Sophia said, the right corner of her mouth angling upward. "He doesn't know."

"Wha—" I managed to utter before Aunt Edna's elbow knocked the wind from my lungs.

Sophia's smirk broadened into a thin-lipped smile. "Take it from me, young Doreen. A woman can never be too careful, or a man too dumb to be useful."

"But surely you must know by now that Aunt Edna's food is safe," I said.

"Of course." Sophia sighed as if my protestations bored her. "I can't kill every man with every morsel I offer. Word would get around."

"*Every* man?" I asked, my throat suddenly dry. "You've done this *before?*"

Sophia sighed. "Freddy's the third tester I've had this month. The other two didn't, shall we say, *pass the test.*"

I gasped. "You *killed* them?"

Suddenly, the room went wonky. I tilted on my heels. Aunt Edna reached out and grabbed my upper arm.

"Thanks," I said, assuming my aunt had taken hold of my arm to keep me from falling over. But then I felt a sharp pinch. She was squeezing my upper-arm flab!

"Ouch!" I whined, pulling my arm away. "What'd you do *that* for?"

Aunt Edna hissed through her fake smile. "Cool it with the twenty questions already."

"*I* didn't kill those two men," Sophia said indignantly. "Whoever was trying to kill *me* is to blame. Besides, they could've died of natural causes. In a place like this, you can never be too sure."

"But ... why would someone want to kill *you?*" I asked.

Aunt Edna grabbed my arm flab again. "Like I said, lay off with the inquisition, okay?"

"Heavy is the head that wears the crown," Sophia said. She sighed dramatically and shook her head. "Didn't these two tell you?"

I glanced at Aunt Edna, then Jackie. "Tell me what?"

"Whoever kills me gets to take over the Family." Sophia reached up and adjusted her silver turban. "Believe me, Doreen. You don't last as long as I have by being careless. You might not believe this young lady, but I'm about to turn a hundred on Tuesday."

Actually, that was the easiest thing to believe that I'd heard since arriving in St. Petersburg.

"Tuesday?" I said. "Wait. That's June twenty-first, right?"

"Yes."

I smiled. "Huh. What do you know? Looks like you and I have the same birthday. Only, *I'll* be forty, of course."

"Humph," Sophia snorted. "I've got corsets from Sicily older than you. Take off those sunglasses, child. Let me see your face."

I glanced over at Aunt Edna for her consent. She grimaced, then gave me a tiny nod.

Slowly, I pulled off the wraparound glaucoma glasses, revealing my ghostly left eye. To my surprise, Sophia didn't even so much as a blink. Instead, the ancient Queenpin sat up straighter in her wheelchair and said, "Come closer."

I blanched. "What?"

Aunt Edna pushed me forward. I took a single, cautious step toward the mysterious, possibly murderous queen of the CGCN.

"Closer," Sophia said, beckoning me with a curl of her gnarled index finger.

I swallowed a dry knot in my throat. Hesitantly, I inched forward another half-step. Fear pricked my spine.

What does this old lady want from me? Is she going to stab me with a silver dagger hidden under her shawl? Or—God forbid—hand me a specimen bottle to take to the nurse's office?

"Closer!" Sophia demanded.

"I ... uh ... I'm right here, Doña Sophia," I stuttered, taking another infinitesimal step. It landed me about foot and a half from her wheelchair. Not daring to come any closer, I asked, "Can I do something for you?"

"Yes, Doreen. You can." The old woman reached a dry, withered hand from under her shawl and grabbed ahold of my forearm.

"What do you want?" I nearly squealed.

"I'm hungry," she said, then flashed a set of ivory dentures at me.

I gasped.

Dear lord! Is she about to taste-test me?

I stared, frozen in horror as Sophia's other arm emerged from beneath her inky shawl. Her ancient, knobby hand reached out and softly patted my own.

"Now then," she said. "Be a dear and go see if Freddy's dead or not."

Chapter Nine

After escaping my own brush with death with the spooky Queenpin—whether imagined or not—I was relieved to find Freddy was also still alive and well. The old man was in the convalescent center's cafeteria, scarfing back a plateful of fish sticks and tater tots. Apparently, the wiry little guy could really pack away the grub.

"Looks like Freddy survived the chicken cacciatore," I announced as I returned, albeit somewhat reluctantly, to Sophia's room.

I studied the three women's expressions, looking for a glimmer of mirth that would tell me I'd just been sent on a wild goose chase—that this had been some silly CGCN prank of theirs. If that was the case, nobody was letting me in on it. At least, not yet.

"Good to hear," Aunt Edna said, waving me over. "Now, let's eat!"

The trio were hovered over a small table in the corner of Sophia's room, admiring the cacciatore as if it were a newborn baby. As I walked over to them, Aunt Edna grabbed a large spoon and began portioning the casserole onto plates. After serving Sophia, Jackie, and herself, she picked up my dish.

"That's okay," I said. "Have a rest. I'll serve myself."

Aunt Edna surrendered the spoon, but not her watchful gaze. "Take another scoopful," she said after I'd already heaped my plate with enough chicken and pasta to choke a goat.

"Yeah," Jackie said. "You don't eat enough to keep a Dodo bird alive." She winked at me. "That's why they went extinct, you know."

Feeling a little more at ease, I smirked. "The only thing extinct about *me* is my size-six thighs. I'll never see *those* babies again."

"Ha!" Aunt Edna said. "You can say that again."

Balancing a mountain of steaming cacciatore on my plate, I took a seat beside Aunt Edna at the cheap, laminate-topped card table. After a quick round of crossing themselves, the three women dug in like rabid wolves.

"Well, here go my size *eight* thighs," I said, and joined in the feast.

• • • •

SOPHIA'S ROOM AT THE convalescent center might've been dreary, but the conversation was anything *but*.

Between mouthfuls of delectably cheesy chicken and pasta, Doña Sophia loosened the reins on her dour, regal persona and regaled us with recollections of what she referred to as the "Golden Age"—the time when the Cornbread Cosa Nostra ruled most of Florida.

"We were as untamed as the swamp gators back then," the Queenpin said, her green eyes sparkling with a faraway glow. "It was the Wild West all over again—only instead of rattlesnakes and cactus, we had mosquitos and palm trees."

Seeing the softer side of the Queenpin caused my worry about being on the old woman's hit list to dissipate considerably. I grinned at her. "Florida must've been something to see back then, Doña Sophia."

"Oh, it was. Believe me." Sophia sighed and shook her head sadly. "If only I could wave a magic wand and go back to the days before RICO, when the booze was flowing and the bolita balls were still rolling."

"Bolita balls?" I asked, a forkful of cacciatore poised halfway to my mouth.

"Yeah," Aunt Edna said. "It was a gambling game. Kind of like the state lottery. But back then it was run by the Family."

My eyebrows rose half an inch. "Seriously? I've never heard of bolita."

Sophia tutted softly. "Nowadays, nobody has. Bolita's gone the way of the Dodo bird and your skinny thighs, young lady. But back in the day, let me tell you. Bolita was *huge.*"

"She ain't lying," Jackie said. "You could buy a bolita ticket at every street corner, grocery store, and backroom bookie in the state."

"Backroom bookie?" I asked. "So bolita was a scam?"

"No!" Sophia slammed a gnarled hand on the table. Her sharp eyes narrowed in on me. "No more than that stupid state-run lottery is today!"

"I'm sorry," I backpedaled. "I didn't mean to upset you."

Sophia crumpled into her wheelchair. The four of us sat in silence for a few minutes, as if paying respects to a dearly departed friend. When Sophia finally spoke again, her voice was still fiery, but it had lost a significant bit of its spark.

"Bolita was better than the lottery," she said. "Way better. Back then, it didn't cost an arm or leg to play. You could place a bet for as little as a penny."

"That seems like a good deal," I said, mainly to appease her. "So, how did bolita work exactly?"

"Simple." Aunt Edna set down her fork. Italian to the core, she used her hands to demonstrate as she spoke. "Every week, people would bet on a number from one to a hundred, hoping their number would be picked. On Saturdays, the heads of the bolita games would draw from a bag with a hundred numbered balls in it. The lucky winners got paid. The bolita runners kept the rest."

Sophia sighed. "Rain or shine, the Family always won the biggest pot."

"With penny bets?" I smirked. "I bet those 'pots' were *humongous.*"

Sophia jabbed a fork into her cacciatore. "I'll have you know, young lady, those pennies added up."

"To *what*?" I snickered, imagining some kids in old-timey clothes sorting through a wheelbarrow full of dirty pennies.

"A *lot*," Sophia grumbled.

"Okay," I said. "So, how big was the take on an average week?"

Aunt Edna shrugged. "Well, you've gotta remember this was back in the fifties and sixties, so everything is relative. But back then, I'd say it was around half a million a week."

My shoulders straightened. "Pennies?"

"*Dollars*," Sophia said, trumping my smirk with a bigger one of her own.

My gut fell into my shoes. "Holy crap!"

Sophia grinned like a fox with a bellyful of hen-house chickens. "Crime might not pay, Doreen Diller. But *organized* crime sure does." She sighed. "Or, at least, it *did*."

I shook my head. "Geez. You can say that again."

"Organized crime used to pay," Jackie said brightly, earning her another dirty look from Aunt Edna.

Sophia frowned and picked at her cacciatore with her fork. "Like all good things in life, bolita didn't last." She glanced up at me. "I was a mere slip of a girl like you when it all started to go belly-up. In fact, I remember the exact day the grits hit the fan, so to speak."

"You do?" I asked.

"Of course I do." Sophia's face grew dark again. "It was the summer of 1961. I was in the kitchen helping my mother make pasta e fagioli. My father came home and announced that Congress had formed that blasted BATFE. Ma dropped the pot of soup right on the floor." She shook her head. "Two complete disasters in one day."

"BATFE?" I whispered to Aunt Edna while Sophia stared at her plate and ruminated. I didn't want to ask another stupid question and tick off the old Queenpin even more. After all, if Jackie knew how to kill someone with a broken toothpick, what could Sophia do with that fork in her hand?

"The Bureau of Alcohol, Tobacco, Firearms and Explosives," Aunt Edna whispered back. "It was really bad news for bookies."

Sophia muttered into her cacciatore, oblivious to the other passengers on board as her trip down memory lane derailed. She shook her head. "Then they passed that damned RICO act and went after the Family with a vengeance!"

Aunt Edna must've read my face. She leaned over and whispered, "Racketeer Influenced and Corrupt Organizations Act. That's what really did the Cornbread Cosa Nostra in."

"That's right!" Sophia said. She banged her bony fist on the table. "When that blasted Bureau got going, there was no stopping them! Before we knew it there was a Fed on every corner and a G-Man in every pot!"

The old woman sighed and stared out the window. "In less than twenty years there was nobody left standing but us women folk. Us and the handful of man-rats who beat the rap by selling the others down the river."

"Wow," I said softly. "I get why you'd be so angry. Was Sammy the Psycho one of those rats?"

A loud, shattering *crash* sounded right beside me.

I whirled my head to the left to see Jackie frozen in place, her face aghast. Her half-eaten plate of cacciatore lay in a tomato-covered heap on the floor like the victim of a drive-by pasta shooting.

"Sammy wasn't never no rat!" Sophia bellowed.

I blanched with confusion. "But ...," I stuttered. "I ... I didn't mean anything by it. I just thought he might be. You know, since he's trying to kill you, and everything."

"What?" Sophia hissed.

"She don't know what she's talking about," Aunt Edna said, her elbow rocketed sideways into my ribcage. "Stuff a sock in it, Doreen!" She turned to Jackie. "Go get a mop! Now!"

Jackie bolted for the door. Aunt Edna sopped up the sauce on the table with her napkin.

I turned to Sophia. "I'm sorry. It's just that, well, if *Sammy's* not trying to poison you, who *is*?"

Sophia leaned forward until her face was mere inches from mine. "*Humpty Bogart*, that's who."

"What?" My mind whirred with confusion. Either I hadn't heard her right, or Sophia was totally off her rocker. I glanced over at Aunt Edna for a clue. Her stern, angry face offered no conclusive evidence one way or the other.

"Humph," Sophia growled. "Why on earth would you think *Sammy* would want to poison *me*?"

I chewed my lip, unsure of how to proceed. No matter what I said, I figured it would earn me either a hard elbow to the ribs or a fork in the eye.

I am SOOO going back to L.A.

I clamped my mouth shut. Then a thought hit me.

If I'm leaving tonight anyway, why not go for it? What have I got to lose?

"Well," I said, "it's just that Aunt Edna looked pretty upset when we got those cheese curds last night."

Sophia choked on a sip of water. "What did you say?"

"Someone sent us cheese curds," I repeated. "They came with a note that said, 'Atta girl.' What do you think that means?"

Aunt Edna stopped cleaning, closed her eyes, and groaned.

Sophia set her fork down and slowly straightened to perfect posture. Her glowering gaze shifted to Aunt Edna. "What's she talking about?"

Aunt Edna squeezed on a painful-looking smile. "I was going to mention it after we ate."

"Then your timing's perfect," Sophia said, her face puckered with anger. "I've suddenly lost my appetite."

• • • •

"ERR ... THE CURDS ARRIVED in a cooler yesterday evening," Aunt Edna explained, her tone soft and apologetic. "Along with the note, just like Dorey said. But it was already way past visiting hours here at the facility, see? So we waited until this morning. I wanted to tell you in person. We headed over as soon as I got the cacciatore ready. A good cacciatore takes time, as you well know, Doña."

Sophia glanced down at her plate. Her angry countenance barely softened. "That's true. But still, you should've called me as soon as you knew."

"Knew what?" I asked.

"Molasses," Aunt Edna growled at me.

"No molasses," Jackie said, sweeping up the broken plate of cacciatore at her feet.

"What's with this *molasses* business?" Sophia demanded. "This some kind of new code, Edna? Something *else* you haven't bothered to tell me about?"

"No. It's nothing. I swear," Aunt Edna said. "But with all due respect, I have to ask, Doña Sophia. Do you think Sammy might've sent the curds? We're not sure of his ... um ... current *state of health*."

Sophia studied the three of us as if trying to decide which to kill first. Finally, she said, "It could've been *anybody*."

"Does that mean Sammy's still alive?" I asked.

Jackie let out a squeak, then nearly dropped her dustpan full of mangled cacciatore on the floor again.

"Maybe," Sophia growled. "Or maybe somebody just wants you to *think* he's still alive."

I frowned. "What about—"

"Anybody got a roll of duct tape?" Sophia growled, glaring at me. "If I hear another question out of this one's mouth, I'm gonna stuff a sock in it!"

Aunt Edna grabbed me by the arm and yanked me toward the door. "Sorry about all the bother, Sophia. We'll be going now. You need your rest. I'll be back tomorrow with a nice linguine Alfredo."

The old woman frowned and waved a dismissive hand at us. "If I live that long."

"Take care, Queenie," Jackie said, bowing and scraping as she backed herself out the door. She waved the broom handle like a magic wand. "May you remain forever in good health."

What the?

As Jackie cleared the doorframe, Aunt Edna jerked me by the elbow into the hallway.

"Ouch!" I said, wincing. "What did *I* do?"

"I told you not to ask dumb questions! Nobody's allowed to ask Sophia about Sammy."

My nose crinkled. "Why not?"

"There you go with your dumb questions, again," Aunt Edna said. "Sophia's touchy when it comes to Sammy."

"But why?" I asked.

Aunt Edna frowned. "Molasses!"

"But—" Jackie protested.

This time Aunt Edna held her ground.

"I *said* molasses!"

Chapter Ten

"I've never seen Sophia so pissed off," Aunt Edna said, gingerly tiptoeing away from the door to the Queenpin's room at the convalescent center. "We need to get outta this joint and let her cool down." She shot me a *this is all your fault* glare that sent a twinge of panic racing along my spine. "You got a big mouth, Dorey."

I cringed. "Sorry!"

Great going, Doreen. Now you've gone and ticked off the head of the southern mafia! What happens now? Is Sophia already dialing H for hitman on that ancient landline of hers? Am I about to be fitted for a pair of cement shoes?

I gotta get back to L.A.— A.S.A.P.!

"Don't just stand there like a couple of knuckleheads," Aunt Edna barked. "Come on." She turned on her pink heels and headed down the hallway.

"We're coming!" Jackie said, ditching the dustpan in the corridor. She grabbed me by the arm and yanked me along. "Come on, Dorey. Let's go!"

I scrambled to keep up with the women's quick pace. As we rounded a corner in the hallway, I spotted a ray of sunlight glaring through the set of glass exit doors. Feeling bad about blowing it big time with Sophia and my aunt, I was eager to make amends before I ended up on the wrong side of a poisoned gelato.

I sprinted past the two women, intent on opening the door for them to show my respect. But just as my fingers touched the push-handle on the exit door, an old woman sitting on a bench nearby sprang to her feet. She raised a huge, purple umbrella over her head, then sent it crashing down on my unsuspecting noggin.

"Argh!" I cried out, shocked by her unexpected attack. "What'd you do that for?"

"Because you're a murderer!" she yelled.

I flinched. "What?"

She jabbed at me with the umbrella. "You killed my boyfriend!"

My mouth fell open. "Uh ... I'm sorry, but I didn't—"

I glanced around for a dementia nurse. No such luck.

"I *saw* you do it," she grumbled. "On TV!"

"Ma'am, I assure you ..." I said. Then something clicked inside my brain. My voice trailed off.

Today is Saturday.

Yesterday afternoon, the last episode of *Beer & Loathing*, the TV show I'd come to St. Pete to film with Tad Longmire, had aired on Channel 22. In it, I'd played a mysterious, unidentified, crazy-eyed psycho killer.

But in the final episode that aired yesterday, the rubber mask I'd worn to conceal my identity had been ripped away. The face of my murderous character, Doreen Killigan, had finally been revealed to the world—just as I'd fake-stabbed Tad Longmire to death.

Killigan's face was also *my* face. Wonky eye and all.

I groaned.

Somehow, the old woman had the mental wherewithal to recognize me, but not enough to tell the difference between reality and TV.

Given the current state of the world, I kind of got that. But what I *couldn't* understand was how the old woman had pegged me as Killigan. My wonky eye and half my face were hidden behind Jackie's giant glaucoma glasses.

Or were they?

I nearly slapped myself on the forehead. After giving Sophia a look at my face, I'd forgotten to put the stupid sunglasses back on.

"You killed Tad Longmire!" the old woman yelled, confirming my theory. She reared back and swung her umbrella at me again. This time, I was able to deflect it with my forearm.

"Sheesh, lady! I'm no killer," I said, rifling through my purse for Jackie's glasses. I slapped the big, black frames onto my face. "That was just a role I played on TV."

A deep scowl creased the suspicion already lining the elderly woman's face. "Yeah. That's what they *all* say." Then, for good measure I suppose, she raised her umbrella and beaned me with it again.

"What's going on here?" Aunt Edna yelled as she and Jackie came flip-flopping up to us.

"Help me nab her, ladies," the old woman yelled. "She's a killer!"

Jackie and Aunt Edna both stopped in their tracks and stared at me.

"Ha! I knew it!" Jackie said.

I gasped. "I'm not! I didn't! Geez. It's just ... uh ... This is just a funny *misunderstanding*."

"If you say so," Aunt Edna said. She shot Jackie a dubious glance, then the pair took off out the exit door like buckshot from a double-barreled rifle.

"Hey! Wait!" I yelled after them.

Hot on their heels, I chased them through the parking lot as they made a mad dash toward the battered old Kia. "Why are you running?"

"Like Queenie says, a girl can ever be too careful," Aunt Edna said as she reached the Kia. She leaned on it, huffing and puffing.

"You really think I'm a killer?" I asked.

"Unlike you, I don't ask questions I don't want to know the answer to," Aunt Edna said. "Now unlock the fakakta car and let's get the H-E double toothpicks out of here before some wiseguy gets a bead on us!"

I gulped, not sure if she was serious or not. Unwilling to wait around to find out, I scrambled into the driver's seat.

The old Kia creaked and bobbed like a rickety old boat as the three of us piled in. I slammed the door, locked it, and scanned the parking lot for snipers.

"What are you waiting for?" Aunt Edna said. "*Hit it*, Dorey."

I shot her a worried look. "You really think someone's after us?"

Thwack! Thwack! Thwack! Thwack!

"What the?" I screeched, as a hail of bullets riddled the windshield.

Chapter Eleven

"Oh my gawd!" I squealed and ducked for cover between the seat and the dashboard. "Somebody's shooting at us!"

"Those ain't bullets," Jackie said, craning her long neck for a better look from the backseat. "Just acorns. That nutso umbrella lady's throwing them at us."

"Really?" I asked, staring up at Aunt Edna.

She smirked down at me. "Yes, really. "I remember when I had reflexes like that."

I felt my face heat up. I scooched myself up from the floorboard and back in the driver's seat. The "shell casings" littering the hood of the Kia were green and brown—and wore cute little caps with stems at their centers.

Jackie snorted with laughter. "Thank goodness that old geezer ain't packin' an Uzi. She's got deadly aim."

I scanned the parking lot. In the shade beneath a huge oak tree, I spotted the old lady with the purple umbrella—or, more accurately, I spotted her backside. She was bent over gathering another handful of ammunition.

"Start the car already, Dorey," Aunt Edna said.

"Oh. Right." I turned the key in the ignition. All three of us let out a collective sigh of relief when the hunk of junk started on the first try.

Aunt Edna crossed herself. "Thank you, Saint Frances of Rome."

"Saint Frances of Rome?" I asked, backing out as another hail of acorn artillery blasted the side of the car.

"Yeah." Aunt Edna shrugged. "She's the patron saint of car drivers. Closest I could come up with on short notice."

"I'll take it," I said, shifting into drive. "Right about now, I could use a little help from above."

"Couldn't we all," my aunt said. "Now step on it. That dingbat old woman's almost done reloading again."

I reversed out of the parking spot and hit the gas so hard it plastered Aunt Edna flat against the passenger seat. I glanced in the rearview mirror at Jackie. She was grinning from ear to ear.

"Woohoo!" she giggled. "That was one for the bucket list! I ain't never been attacked by a rabid squirrel in a muumuu before."

My nose crinkled.

Who ever had?

Aunt Edna snorted despite herself. "Jackie's right. Dorey, you sure know how to bring out the *animal* in people."

"Ha ha," I sneered. "You two laugh all you want. But it's not funny. Sophia hates me. And now some crazy old woman recognized me from TV. She thought *I killed Tad*!"

"You *did*," Aunt Edna said.

I frowned. "I mean *for real*."

"You *did* for real," Jackie said. "With those tiny little cuticle sciss—"

"Okay, Okay!" I said, drowning out Jackie. "Enough with the jokes on me, already! Can we change the subject?"

"Fine with me," Aunt Edna said, stifling a smirk.

"And you're wrong about one thing," Jackie said. "Sophia don't hate you."

"She doesn't?" I asked.

"Naw," Aunt Edna said. "I mean, no more than she generally hates everybody."

"Good to know," I said. "Mind if I ask a question?"

Aunt Edna shot me a look. "*Now* you're gonna ask my permission?"

I winced. "Sorry about asking about Sammy," I said. "I was just trying to look out for you. You know, because of the curds. You two looked so worried when they came."

"Thanks, kid," Aunt Edna said. "But we can look out for ourselves. So, what do you want to know?"

I cleared my throat and tried to sound casual. "When we were leaving Sophia, I heard Jackie call Sophia *Queenie*. I thought she was the *Queenpin*."

"I didn't say Queenie," Jackie said. "I said Queen '*E*'. You know, like Queen Elizabeth."

My brow furrowed. "I don't get it."

"Sophia's like Queen Elizabeth," Aunt Edna said, staring out the windshield. "And we're like a bunch of Prince Charles's."

My eyebrows rose an inch. "Prince Charles's?"

"Yeah." Aunt Edna sighed. "We've been waiting around so long for Sophia to die that in the meantime, we've all turned into old coots ourselves."

"Oh." My brow furrowed. "But why is everybody waiting around? I thought whoever killed Sophia got to be the new leader."

"Not everybody's ready to murder to get their own way," Jackie said, then shot me another wink.

I scowled. "Gimme a break." I pulled up to the exit for the parking lot. "For the millionth time, I didn't kill—"

Suddenly, my voice died in my throat. I'd been struck dumb by the sign for the convalescent center we were leaving.

It was Shady Respite.

Chapter Twelve

Shady Respite! That's the name of the place where those three people died. Good gawd! Could this whole poisoning nonsense be real after all?

I stared, wide-eyed, at the sign for the convalescent center.

"What are you waiting for?" Aunt Edna asked. "The lane's clear."

"Oh. Right," I muttered, and steered the battered old Kia onto the highway. I punched the gas pedal to the floorboard. But as we made a hasty getaway from the potential scene of three poisoning deaths, I suddenly felt more in danger than ever.

"Wait a second," I said to Jackie and Aunt Edna. "You guys never told me Sophia was staying where those other people died. Is that the *real* reason we came here? Not for lunch, but to make sure nobody had poisoned her?"

Aunt Edna cocked her head. "Well, we sure as heck didn't come here to check out the vacation rentals. Right Jackie?"

Jackie grinned at me. "Look at you, Miss Detective. You figured it out all on your own!"

I shook my head. "Why didn't you just tell me that in the first place?"

"Because Edna still ain't a hundred percent sure about you," Jackie said. "You might still be a hitman. Only you're after Sophia instead of us."

I turned and stared at my aunt. "Is that true?"

She shrugged. "Naw. Well, maybe it *was*. But not anymore." She patted me on the shoulder. "Nobody who knows nothing about the Family would've talked to Sophia that way."

"You had her on the ropes," Jackie said. "Sophia will either love you or hate you for that."

"How will I know which one?" I said sourly.

Aunt Edna laughed. "Good question. At least we know now you're not after Sophia." She grinned at me. "Turns out *you're* the one with a price on your head. Or is that *an acorn?*"

Jackie snorted.

I gritted my teeth and turned back to the road ahead. "I'm so glad you two find my death threat so amusing."

"Sorry," Jackie said, drying tears of laughter from her eyes. "But you gotta remember, we're used to 'em. Somebody's always trying to bump us off. Now more than ever."

Like that stray dog wearing a wire? Yeah, right.

"Anything *else* pertinent I should know?" I asked.

"Yeah," Aunt Edna said. "You found us at a pivotal moment in CGCN history, Dorey. As you might've noticed, Sophia can be a real pain in the bunions. But if she manages to live to her hundredth birthday, Family rules say she can step down peacefully and name her own heir."

"So?" I said. "What's so pivotal about that?"

"Like I said, *timing*," Aunt Edna said. "If some wiseguy wants to be head of the CGCN, they've only got until Tuesday to bump off Sophia and claim the crown. It's now-or-never time. After Tuesday, she can live in peace, without a target on her head."

Jackie reached forward and put a hand on my shoulder. "That's why we was so suspicious when you showed up last week in the trunk of that Chevy Caprice. See?"

"Okay," I said. "I kind of get that."

Jackie winced. "Sorry again about your eye."

"Thanks." I turned to Aunt Edna. "So, who's your number one suspect for poisoning Sophia? Sammy?"

She shrugged. "No. He's already waited this long. Why would he want to kill his mother *now*, with just a few days to go?"

I nearly wrecked the Kia. "Wait. Sammy is Sophia's *son?*"

"Yeah," Aunt Edna said.

I shook my head. "Another tiny fact that would've been good to know. So that means we can probably rule him out."

"Why do you say that?" Jackie asked.

"Seriously?" I asked. "She's his *mother*!"

Aunt Edna shot me a sideways glance. "You never thought about killing your own ma, Maureen?"

I cringed. "Look. Surely, if Sammy's alive, Sophia will name him to take over, right? So there's no need for him to kill her."

"You'd think so," Aunt Edna said. "But in case you weren't listening, Sammy's loyalties aren't exactly what you'd call 'predictable.' He could go nutso and take any of us out at any time. Why do you think the Family's been hiding from him all these years?"

My heart skipped a beat. "And now you think he's found you? Because of the cheese curds?"

"That's his calling card," Jackie said. "Like E.T., he just phoned home."

I grimaced. It made sense now why they were so worried. "So, how do you think Sammy figured out where you are?"

Jackie shrugged. "Maybe he got the Google on us."

"Or it could be that Sophia summoned him home for her big birthday party," Aunt Edna said.

I chewed my lip. "That would make sense, I guess, if she's going to name him as the new Kingpin."

"Sammy the Psycho our Kingpin?" Aunt Edna hissed. She crossed herself. "God forbid!"

"Nobody wants him in charge," Jackie said. "Not even Sophia!"

"Then why in the world would she tell him where you are?" I asked.

"I didn't say she *did*," Aunt Edna said. "It's just a theory."

"A theory that doesn't hold water," I said.

"Sure it does," Aunt Edna said. "Look at it this way. Say Sophia *is* gonna name somebody besides Sammy as the new leader of the

CGCN. She could be leading him on, telling him she's gonna name him Kingpin. Then pow! She names somebody else during the party. Dropping news like that, she's gonna need protection."

My nose crinkled. "Protection?"

Aunt Edna tapped a finger to her temple. "Think about it, Dorey. If Sammy finds out the news with an audience around, it'll be harder for him to kill Sophia on the spot."

Geez. And I thought my *mother was a cold fish.*

"But it's just a theory," Jackie said. "I got one, too. Wanna hear it?"

Before either of us could object, Jackie told us anyway.

"What if Sammy caught old-timer's disease, and wants a chance to be Kingpin before he forgets how to bowl?"

Aunt Edna and I groaned simultaneously.

"I've got a question," I said.

"What a surprise," Aunt Edna said. "You ask more questions than a kid in a candy store."

I shot her some side eye. "What if Sophia dies of natural causes before she turns a hundred? What are the Family rules then?"

Aunt Edna sat up straight. "Sammy would take over automatically. Why do you think we work so hard to keep her alive?"

"Poor Sophia," Jackie said. "For her, Sammy's always been a double-edged swordfish."

I shot a glance at Aunt Edna. "What does she mean?"

Aunt Edna shifted in her seat. "On the one hand, Sammy's Sophia's good-luck charm. Nobody dares bump her off for fear of Sammy taking over and exacting his revenge."

"And the other hand?" I asked.

"Sammy's a nut case. Sophia's had to hide out from him just like the rest of us. That's why she won't tell nobody whether he's still alive or not. If people knew for sure he was dead, it'd be open season for her."

I frowned. "But Sophia told me people are *always* trying to get her."

Aunt Edna's lips twitched to one side. "About that. We kind of ... feed her *stories*."

My eyebrows rose an inch. "Stories?"

Aunt Edna shrugged. "That's how we keep her in check. Otherwise, she'd be wandering the streets, accusing the neighbors of working for the FBI. We'd be found out in a heartbeat."

Jackie giggled. "Sophia thinks everybody's after her lucky charms—just like that little gnome on your cereal box."

"Leprechaun," I said.

"Lepers, cons, whoever," Jackie said. "Sophia thinks *everybody's* out to get her."

I sighed.

I guess that *runs in the Family, too.*

Chapter Thirteen

On the drive back to Palm Court Cottages, I mulled over the bizarre events of the last few hours.

I'd met a mafia Queenpin in a turban who was convinced she was being poisoned by Humpty Bogart. I'd spied on a hapless food taster to see if the old man had survived Aunt Edna's cacciatore. I'd found out Sammy the Psycho is real—and that he's Sophia's son. And I'd been attacked with an umbrella and acorns by an old lady in a muumuu.

If I'd have written this as a screenplay, Hollywood producers would've laughed me off the set. It was all just too absurd to be plausible. As I pulled up to a red light, it finally dawned on me.

That's it! The only way this makes sense is if it's all an elaborate joke on me.

"Okay, I need you to be honest with me," I said, turning to Aunt Edna in the passenger seat. "I'm not mad. But did someone put you up to this?"

She turned and studied me. "Up to what?"

I threw my hands up. "This whole thing! Ever since those curds arrived last night, I've felt like the only one not in on the joke. Are you pranking me? Did my roommate Sonya back in L.A. put you up to this?"

"I don't know what you're talking about," Aunt Edna said. "I swear, Dorey, none of this is a joke. I wish it was."

"She ain't lying," Jackie said from the backseat. "Believe me, the CGCN ain't got that good a sense of humor."

I frowned. If the joke wasn't on me, maybe it was on someone else. "Aunt Edna, you said you tell Sophia stories to keep her in line. This whole poisoning thing. Is it one of those?"

My aunt shot me a hard look, then her face softened a notch. "To tell you the truth, Dorey, I don't know anymore. When Sophia first brought it up, I thought it was just another one of her paranoid delusions. That is, I did until this morning, when Jackie showed me that article in the *Beach Gazette*."

"What did the paper say, exactly?" I asked, then hit the gas.

"Nothing specific," she said. "Just that there'd been a rash of deaths. Three in less than two weeks. That's unusual, even for a place like Shady Respite."

"And don't forget, Edna," Jackie chimed in. "Sophia said the old geezers who died were all her taste testers."

I shot my aunt a look. "Yet *another* fact that would've been good to know."

"Excuse me," Aunt Edna said, "but your ears work better than mine. You were there when Sophia said that. Whether it's actually true or not, who knows? The newspaper didn't name names."

I grimaced, then nodded. "Okay, fair enough."

"Humph," Aunt Edna grunted. "All I know for sure is that we need to keep Sophia alive until she turns a hundred."

"I second that emotion," Jackie said.

I gripped the steering wheel tighter. "Okay, ladies. Let's get hypothetical here for a minute."

"What do you mean?" Jackie asked.

I chewed my lip. "Let's say Sammy *is* in town. And that he wants to do in Sophia. He'd need to kill her before Tuesday, right? Because after she turns a hundred, Sophia sure isn't going to name him Kingpin herself. Correct?"

"Yeah, I guess so," Aunt Edna said. "What's your point?"

"My point is, I don't see how poisoning Sophia would be Sammy's method of choice."

"Why not?" Jackie asked.

"Too risky." I tightened my grip on the steering wheel. "What if the poison only made her sick? Sophia could still live long enough to name somebody else as heir to the throne."

"Hmm," Aunt Edna said. "Yeah, I suppose that could be a problem."

"I know, right?" I said. "Sammy would want to make sure she was a hundred percent dead before Tuesday. And from what you've told me, Sammy was more of a gun guy anyway."

"Another good point," Aunt Edna admitted.

"Wait a minute," Jackie said, piping up from the backseat. "If Sammy's not trying to poison Sophia, who is?"

"That's what we need to find out," Aunt Edna said. She looked my way. "Got any more ideas, Miss Detective?"

I nodded. "One. But it's kind of weird. Sophia told me she suspects some guy named Humpty Bogart is the one trying to do her in. No disrespect, but could Sophia be as psycho as her son?"

Aunt Edna's eyes narrowed. "Why would you say that?"

"Uh ... didn't you hear me? Sophia told me she thought *Humpty Bogart* was trying to kill her."

Aunt Edna locked eyes with me. "Like I said, lots of folks wish they could bump off Sophia."

"Right. But *Humpty Bogart*?" I shook my head. "You've got to admit, that name is well ... *ridiculous*. I think Sophia could be suffering from the same thing as that old lady with the umbrella."

"Old timers?" Jackie asked.

"No," I said. "Well, maybe a little bit. I'm referring to her confusion over what's real and what's something she watched on TV."

Aunt Edna shot Jackie a look in the rearview mirror. "Eh," she grunted. "You could be right, Dorey. Take the next right onto Fourth Street."

I did as instructed and steered the Kia south in the direction of Palm Court Cottages. As I drove, a boatload of questions swirled in my mind, but I decided to keep my mouth shut. After all, what did it matter? I'd be back in L.A. tonight.

Yep. In a few short hours, this would be their *circus.*

Their *psycho monkeys.*

Even so, I just couldn't resist finding out what else might be lurking under the CGCN Big Top.

"Besides Sammy, who else would want to kill Sophia?" I pondered aloud. "She seems nice enough. You know, besides using Freddy as a human guinea pig and all."

Neither Aunt Edna nor Jackie said a word.

"Sophia's just a little old lady," I tried again. "How hard could it be to bump her off?"

"Like we told you," Aunt Edna said. "Everybody's afraid of what Sammy would do. Paybacks are hell when a psycho's holding the purse strings."

"That's why everybody's dying to find out whether Sammy's still alive or not," Jackie said. "If he really *is* out of the picture, Sophia's throne is up for grabs *right now*—for *any* of us—with nobody standing in the way."

"Except Sophia," I said.

"Well, yeah," Aunt Edna said. "That goes without saying."

I shook my head. "I still don't get it. If Sophia's such a pain in the butt, why hasn't someone at least taken a pot-shot at her by now?"

"And if they missed?" Aunt Edna said. "They'd be found out and fall from Sophia's good graces forever. Even if they survived Sammy's revenge, they'd lose any chance of being picked to take over the reins."

"Then it makes no sense for someone to be trying to *poison* her," I said.

"Sure it does," Aunt Edna said.

I crinkled my nose. "How do you figure that?"

"Because poisoning is *anonymous*. If it fails, well, nobody's the wiser. But if it *works*, and Sammy doesn't show up and chop the culprit's head off, the killer can step up, take the credit, and grab their prize."

My left eyebrow ticked up a notch.

Geez. What's wrong with my world that that kind of makes sense?

Aunt Edna turned her gaze to the windshield. "Let me tell you something, Miss Detective. Sophia may be old, but she's one tough broad. Take my word for it, the woman is harder to kill than Rasputin."

My right eyebrow shot up to meet the left. "You've *tried*?"

Aunt Edna scowled, then muttered something under her breath. I'd have sworn it was the word, "Molasses."

Chapter Fourteen

As I steered the Kia past the shops and strip centers along Fourth Street, my mind boiled with burning questions about Sammy the Psycho.

I'd have already chalked the whole crazy business up to the demented suspicions of a couple of old ladies except for two things. First, the cheese curds were definitely real. I'd seen them with my own eyes. But even if they were Sammy's calling card, anybody could've sent them. Second, Aunt Edna and Jackie seemed genuinely worried about Sammy.

Is he still alive? Is he the one who sent the cheese curds? Is he really psycho? Is he here to kill his mother and take the title of Kingpin? Or is he just a figment of what Brady had referred to as my relatives' "exceptional imaginations?"

I turned to my aunt. "If Sammy—"

"Enough talk about him already," Aunt Edna barked. "Everybody put a sock in it before his bad mojo finds us again."

"Fine." I turned my attention back to the road.

What do I care? I'll just to keep my trap shut and wave goodbye to this whole mess from the plane back to L.A.

"Take a right here," Aunt Edna said. "Let's stop by Morty's bakery."

I blanched. "What? I thought we were going straight home."

"We are. Right after this. It won't take a minute. I wanna see how the *torta alla panna* is coming along for Sophia's birthday party."

"The tortellini *what?*"

"Torta alla panna," Aunt Edna repeated. "Traditional Italian birthday cake. Didn't Maureen teach you anything?"

The corner of my mouth curled downward.

Nope. Not even about Betty Crockeroni.

Aunt Edna blew out a breath and shook her head. "If it were *my* party, I'd personally rather have a nice peach cobbler. But Sophia's a stickler for the old ways."

"What's this torta thing made of?" I asked.

"Finally, a question I don't mind answering," Aunt Edna said. "Okay. First, you start with a *pan di Spagna*—uh, sponge cake. Then you fill it with vanilla pudding and cover it in homemade whipped cream. If you want, you can top it with seasonal fruits."

That's handy, considering how there's no shortage of seasonal "fruits" hanging around.

"What's your favorite fruit, Doreen?" Jackie asked from the backseat.

"Uh ... strawberries, I guess. Why? I won't be there for Sophia's party."

"You won't?" Jackie asked.

"No. That reminds me. Who keeps unpacking my suit—"

"You can't leave now!" Jackie blurted. "And miss Sophia's big centennial bash?"

"She's right," Aunt Edna said. "Now that you've met her, the Doña would consider it extremely rude of you to skip out on her big celebration. And believe me. You don't want to see Sophia when she's ticked off."

My eyebrows shot up. "I thought I already had. She threatened to duct tape my mouth shut, remember?"

Jackie giggled. "That's nothing. When she mentions a chainsaw? *Then* you start worrying."

I gulped. "Chainsaw?"

"Jackie's just pulling your leg," Aunt Edna said. "Anyway, what will it hurt to stay a few extra days? You can meet the Family at the party. Then we can have a little celebration right after, just for *your* birthday."

I chewed my lip. "I dunno."

"Maybe Miss Bigshot's got bigger plans waiting for her back in Hollywood," Jackie said.

Aunt Edna turned and studied me. "*Do* you?"

I thought back to my thirty-ninth birthday and cringed. I'd been working in Hollywood on the set of a low-budget western. As the two lowest grunts on the totem pole, my roommate Sonya and I'd been assigned to "trailer-trash crewing." In other words, we were doomed to satisfying the weird whims of the celebrities cooped up in trailers in the back lot.

Given our luck, we'd been assigned the worst shift—6 p.m. to 6 a.m. As we'd started work that night, Sonya had surprised me with a chocolate cupcake with a candle sprouting from the center of its gooey frosting. Desperate to catch a few badly needed winks, I'd blown out the flame and wished for no middle-of-the-night celebrity meltdowns.

My birthday wish had not been granted.

Around 3 a.m., my cellphone had buzzed. For a brief second, I'd thought it was Sonya pulling a birthday prank.

No such luck.

Instead, I'd been summoned to the trailer of octogenarian Arthur Dreacher. As usual, the dirty old man had answered his trailer door wearing nothing but a pair of saggy cotton underpants. After beckoning me inside, between slugs of Old Milwaukee he'd laid out to me his urgent, life-or-death emergency.

The creep had wanted me to clip his thick, fungus-yellow toenails.

The job had required bolt cutters.

"Ugh," I grimaced aloud, still scarred by the disgusting memory.

"Is staying with us so bad?" Aunt Edna asked.

"What? No." I winced. "I was just—"

Jackie tapped my shoulder from the backseat. "The light's green, hun."

"Oh, right." I hit the gas. "Uh ... regarding my birthday, I think my friend Sonya might have something planned for me, that's all."

"Call her and find out," Aunt Edna said. "We need a headcount for Morty."

Jackie laughed. "So you're turning the big four-oh, eh? You know, by the time I was your age, I'd been divorced twice already. Figuring out how to kill dirtbag losers and get away with it was pretty much all I ever thought about back then. I couldn't get enough of *Forensic Files*. But look at you. You're way ahead of me. You've already gone and done it."

My shoulders stiffened. I glanced at Jackie in the rearview mirror. "You know I didn't *actually stab* Tad Longmire. Right?"

"Right." She shot me an exaggerated wink. "You only tied him up and threatened to cut off his body parts if he didn't do what you said."

I groaned. "For the millionth time, they were *cuticle* scissors. And I only threatened to cut off his—"

"Slow down!" Aunt Edna grunted. She pointed to her right. "Turn in here."

I glanced over at a generic strip center. Painted on the glass display window of one of the shops were the words, *Morty's Bakery*. I pulled into the narrow lot.

"You guys go on inside," I said, shifting into park. "I'm gonna call Sonya."

"You do that," Aunt Edna said. "Then come and join us inside."

I nodded. "Will do."

I waited until the Kia coughed itself out and the two women had ambled into the bakery.

Then I made a call.

But it wasn't to Sonya.

Chapter Fifteen

After spending a crazy morning with my new mob Family, I needed a reality check that wasn't going to bounce.

I needed to talk to Officer Brady.

Last night, during our sketchy date over a plate of cheese curds and Ritz crackers, I'd had so many things I'd wanted to ask Brady about my aunt and Jackie. But I'd been sidetracked by two rather unexpected developments.

First, I'd lost my nerve after the cheese curds had turned out to be freaking delicious. And second, I'd lost my train of thought after chugging down my tea as I pretended to wash the "horrible" taste from my mouth. Little had I known that Aunt Edna had replaced Lipton with her special Long Island blend.

I still wasn't sure how I'd made it to bed last night. And I wasn't sure I wanted to find out. But now, in the sober light of day, as I sat in Jackie's old Kia in front of Morty's Bakery, I figured it was time for a dose of reality. And Brady was the only one I knew of who could possibly deliver.

I raised my index finger to punch in his number, then hesitated. What was I going to say to him?

It was barely three o'clock and I'd already lived through a quadruple dose of the *Twilight Zone*. Sophia the Queenpin. Sammy the Psycho. Freddy the food taster. And an unnamed acorn assassin.

Geez. The guy's gonna think I'm nuts.

I shoved the phone back into my purse and crossed my arms.

But hell. I'm leaving anyway. What does it matter?

I dug my phone back out of my purse and called Brady's number before I lost my nerve. When it went directly to voice mail, I felt both disappointed and relieved.

Just as well. I mean, what could I say to him that would make any sense, anyway?

"Brady here. Leave your message at the tone," his recorded voice said.

Beep!

"What?" I gasped. "Oh! Uh ... Hi. It's just me, checking to see if I'm insane or not, hee hee. But seriously ..."

Oh, God! Hang up, Doreen! Hang up now!

I clicked off the phone and groaned. My face was the temperature of the sun. Panic shot through me. I closed my eyes and took a deep breath.

It's okay. With any luck, he won't know it was me.

But even *I* wasn't buying it.

Who do you think you're talking to, Doreen? With any luck? Since when have you had any luck?

"Crap!" I muttered, then tossed my phone into my purse.

I gulped in another lungful of oxygen to calm myself. Then I grabbed the phone again and quickly punched in another number before I had time to analyze what just happened with Brady and go throw myself under a bus.

The phone rang. This time, it didn't go to voicemail. Accustomed to dealing with non-stop emergencies, Sonya answered on the first ring. "Hello?"

"Sonya, it's me, Doreen. How's it going?"

"Uh ... okay. I heard you beat the murder rap. Good for you."

"Well, if by 'beat the rap' you mean that I didn't kill Tad, then yes. I beat it. Uh ... listen. I'm thinking of coming back home today."

"Today? Uh ... about that. Well ...."

"Well what?"

"Okay, I'll just say it. I sublet your part of the apartment."

I blanched. "You *what*? Why?"

"You lost your job. You missed the rent. I thought you were going to jail. Sorry."

I slumped into the seat. "Sorry for renting my space? Or for not believing in me?"

"Uh ... both? But hey, if you need to, you can bunk with me. Still better than the studio cots, right?"

I pursed my lips in frustration. Sonya could be such an airhead. But at least she'd always remembered my birthday.

"So ... anything *special* going on next week?" I asked, trying to drop a hint.

"Not that I know of," Sonya said. "Oh, wait. There is *one* thing."

I grinned. "What?"

"I hear Arthur Dreacher might drop in at the studio. He always asks about you, you know."

My stomach turned. That was one encore performance I never cared to see again. "Gee, thanks. Hey Sonya? Could you do me a favor?"

"Sure. What?"

"Could you box up all my stuff?"

"Already done. Just tell me where to send it."

I nearly dropped my phone. "Seriously? I just meant so the new person doesn't mess with my junk."

"That's why I did it," she said unconvincingly. "So, you coming back or not?"

I frowned. "I'll have to get back to you on that. But don't lease out the other half of your bed just yet, okay?"

"I'll try. But if I run into Johnny Depp, all promises are null and void."

"Got it. Thanks."

I clicked off the phone and sighed. L.A. was a fickle place. Hollywood was even crueler. If you made it big, you were only as good as your last acting role. If you *didn't* make it big, you were only as good as your last rent check.

I glanced through the windshield at the dismal-looking strip center in front of me.

Would it just be more of the same here in St. Pete?

I blew out a breath and stared at the luscious desserts in the bakery's display window.

Geez. Maybe my best bet for a real birthday cake is in Morty's hands after all.

Chapter Sixteen

As I walked up to the glass storefront to Morty's Bakery, I could see Aunt Edna and Jackie inside. They were chatting up a plump, sweaty guy wearing a crisp, white apron tied around his belly. He bore the crooked mug of an ex-prize fighter. I immediately thought of Vic Tayback, the guy who played Mel, the diner cook on that 1980s sitcom, *Alice*.

I pushed open the door, causing a bell affixed to the top to clang. Jackie, my aunt, and the aproned guy looked my way and clammed up. A millisecond later, they unfroze and shot me a trio of smiles that seemed way too enthusiastic for the occasion.

Even over the heavenly scent of vanilla and cinnamon, I smelled a rat. Were they secretly plotting together to rub Sophia out? Or were they merely haggling over the price of baguettes? Or, worse yet, was I turning into a paranoid schizophrenic like the rest of them?

"Hey. What's going on?" I asked, trying to sound breezy.

"Nothing," Aunt Edna said. "Morty, this here's my niece Doreen from L.A. Doreen, this here's Morty."

"From Brooklyn," he said, then offered me a hand as big as a baseball glove.

I smiled sheepishly and shook it. "Hi."

"You should try Morty's famous cannoli," Jackie said.

"Yes, she most definitely should." Morty grinned at me. "Hold on a second."

He snatched a small sheet of wax paper from a dispenser on the counter, then reached into the display case and plucked out a golden-brown, tubular pastry. He held it out for me. "A cannolo for the beautiful young lady."

"Cannolo?" I asked. "I thought Jackie called it a cannoli."

"*One* cannolo, *two* cannoli," Morty said, his smile never wavering. "Little known fact. Go on. Take a bite."

I sunk my teeth into the crispy pastry. An unusual flavor tickled my taste buds. "That's delicious," I said. "But what's the cream—"

"They're filled with banana pudding!" Jackie blurted.

My eyebrow shot up. "Whoa. That's unusual. I've never heard of that before."

Morty beamed. "That's because *I* invented it. I like to take the best of Italian and Southern cooking and combine them into something fresh and new."

"Well, this is a match made in heaven," I said. "Who knew the two could blend so well?"

"*I* did." Morty stuck out his chest and hooked his thumbs into the armpits of his apron. "Actually, when it comes to food, you'd be surprised how close the two countries are. Take grits for example."

"Grits?" I took another bite of cannolo and studied Morty. I'd been right. Up close, he was the spitting image of Mel, the rough-and-tumble hash slinger.

"Yeah," he said. "Think about it. Grits are just polenta you eat for breakfast."

"Huh." I smiled. "I never thought about that."

"Hey, Dorey," Aunt Edna said. "You know what the *real* difference between polenta and grits is?"

"What?" I asked.

She smirked. "About ten dollars a bag."

"Ha!" Jackie cackled. "Good one, Edna!"

The bell on the front door clanged again. We all turned to look.

The door flew open. A balding, sixty-something man with a round belly walked into the shop. He could've been Morty's twin, except that he was about a foot shorter than the baker, and as bald as a boiled egg.

"Morty!" the man called out chummily. "I'm here for my ... *usual*."

"Got it all ready for you," Morty said, his smile growing less generous. He reached for something behind the display counter.

"So, what are you three old hens clucking about?" the man asked.

"Grits," I said.

Morty handed the guy a white paper bag. "That's right. I was just saying how you should put basil in your grits. You know, the good, sweet basil from Italy."

The man took the bag. "Really? I'll have to give it a try."

"You be sure and do that, and let me know what you think." Morty scrambled past us to the door and held it for the man. He ushered his customer out, then closed the door behind him.

"Basil in grits?" I asked Morty. "I'd have never thought about doing that. Is it good?"

"Did I *say* it was good?" Morty shook his head. The ingratiating smile he'd worn for the man was gone. "Actually, it's disgusting. But then again, so is *that* douchebag."

My eyebrows rose an inch. I turned and stared through the display window, watching the roly-poly figure of a man climb into a Lincoln Continental.

"Who is he?" I asked.

Morty shook his head and spat, "That piece of work there? You're looking at none other than the dirtbag we call Humpty Bogart."

Chapter Seventeen

"You mean Humpty Bogart *isn't* a figment of Sophia's imagination?" I asked, dumbfounded as I slid the keys into the Kia's ignition.

"Why would you think that?" Jackie asked from the backseat.

Uh ... why wouldn't *I?*

I shrugged. "I just thought Sophia was trying to get me off the topic of Sammy the—"

"Shhh!" Aunt Edna hissed. "Enough with him, already! We don't need any more bad luck! You want to know about the jerk who came into the bakery? Fine. His real name is Humphry Bogaratelli."

After saying his name, Aunt Edna turned her head and pretended to spit.

"Geez," I said. "What's so bad about the guy?"

"Didn't you hear him call us a bunch of old hens?" Jackie groused. "I'd like to turn him into Al *Capon*!"

I smirked. "Wow. That's pretty foul, Jackie."

"Humpty ain't no joking matter," Aunt Edna said. "The guy's a total shyster. When the Feds were busy busting the Family apart in the '70s and '80's, Humphry told us he was working on putting the pieces of the Family fortune back together. But what did he *really* do? He bogarted most of the money for himself."

"That's why we call him Humpty Bogart," Jackie said. "Get it?"

"Got it." I turned the key in the ignition. The Kia made a clicking sound, but didn't start.

"Fantastic," Aunt Edna grumbled. "Here we go again."

"Sit tight." I leaned over and grabbed the socket wrench from the floorboard beside her feet. "I'll be right back."

I climbed out of the Kia and lifted the hood. Leaning over the engine, I gave the solenoid a solid whack with the wrench. As I raised my hand to deliver a second blow, I called out to Aunt Edna. "Hey. What do think was in the bag Humpty picked up from Morty?"

"Lemon bars." The man's voice sounded so close behind me that I jerked upward and banged my head on the hood.

"Geez!" I yelped, turning to see Morty standing less than two feet away. "Where'd you come from?"

"The bakery. Where else?" He pointed a meaty thumb back toward the storefront. "I practically live there. So, solenoid, eh?"

"Yeah."

Morty leaned sideways so he could see past the Kia's open hood and into the passenger compartment. "I told you two to get a decent vehicle already. This fakakta thing is a piece of kaka!"

"Hey, you wanna pay for us a new car, we'll be glad to have it," Aunt Edna shot back.

Morty took the wrench from my hand and tapped the solenoid on the side. "Go give her a try now."

I hopped into the driver's seat. The Kia cranked to life. I leaned my head out the window. "Thanks!"

Morty closed the hood and handed me back the wrench. "Some things just need a man's touch." He waggled his grey eyebrows at me.

"Careful Morty," Aunt Edna said. "Dorey's got a wrench and she knows how to use it. And in case you haven't noticed, she's half your age."

"I'm not *eighty*," Morty said. "Geez, Edna. Gimme a break."

"I'd love to," she quipped. "We talking femur or kneecap?"

Morty smirked, causing his large nose to dent in at the tip. "You still got the fire, Edna. But you and me don't got the spark no more."

Aunt Edna scowled. "Maybe not. But we all know my niece here is a real fireball. She's already shown us some pretty slick moves. So watch your step around her, Morty. And no more funny business. Capeesh?"

I smiled sheepishly. "Uh ... nice to meet you, Morty. Thanks for the cannolo."

He smiled and winked. "Plenty more where that came from if you play your cards right."

Unsure whether to smile back or slap his face, I rolled up the window. Then, as quickly as I could, I reversed the Kia out of the parking lot.

Morty watched us intently as we pulled away. He certainly appeared to be longing for something, all right. But what? Me? Aunt Edna? Or something else entirely?

"Schmuck," Aunt Edna muttered.

"What's the deal with you and Morty?" I asked as I steered the Kia down the street. "Did you two used to date or something?"

"Or something," Aunt Edna said. "Now, no more questions about Morty."

"What about Sam—"

"Or him, either."

I frowned. "I thought you wanted me to get to know the Family."

"I do," she said. "I just need some time to think about *what* I want you to know."

Chapter Eighteen

Aunt Edna wasn't the only one who needed time to think things over. When we got back to her cottage apartment at half past three, it was crunch time.

I needed to decide whether to risk hanging around a few days for my birthday, or repack my suitcase and catch the red-eye back to L.A. before I ended up dating Morty the ex-con faced baker—or I got whacked to death by a random old lady who couldn't tell the difference between reality and a lousy TV show.

Geez. I'm not sure which would be worse...

I needed advice. *Sane* advice. With Brady unavailable and Sonya dumping me like a hot-to-trot potato, I was left with only one real choice.

Dear old Ma.

Like I said before, my mother Maureen was what you might call a "cold fish." Distant. Secretive. And hard to catch—especially in a good mood.

To be honest, ever since seventh-grade biology class, I'd been fairly certain Ma was the spawn of one of those weird, sharp-toothed, big-eyed creatures that lived in the darkest depths of the ocean. She was beautiful to look at, I'd give her that. But anyone who tried to get too close fell prey to her painfully sharp barbs.

On the other hand, what Ma lacked in warmth she more than made up for in cold rationality. And a sane voice in the wilderness was exactly what I desperately needed right now. My life back in L.A. was disintegrating by the second. If I stayed here with Ma's family, my life might not last another minute.

Ain't life grand?

I plopped down on the chenille bedspread and fished my cellphone from my purse. I wanted to get Ma's take on whether her sister and her friends were really dangerous, or merely delusional.

While I was at it, I also wanted to ask Ma why she'd never told me that her family were mobsters. And, more importantly, *why on earth* she hadn't used her mafia connections to get me a decent acting gig in Hollywood? I mean, what was the good of being a mob moll if you couldn't throw your weight around a little?

I pushed her speed-dial button and held my phone to my ear. While I could never depend on Ma for cuddles, I could always rely on her to answer her phone. I listened to her line ring five times, then go to voicemail. I didn't leave a message.

Great. Now what?

I grabbed my purse and rifled through it for my *Hollywood Survival Guide*. A gag gift from Sonya, the little book had actually helped me out a few times since I'd gotten to St. Pete. Maybe there was some bit of sage advice inside that would set me on the right path now, as well. At this point, what the heck did I have to lose?

I flipped through the little volume with a cover the color of a yellow caution light. Tip #53 seemed appropriate, but vaguely unhelpful:

> *When you come to a fork in the road, pick it up and eat cake with it.*

I crinkled my nose.

What the heck is that *supposed to mean?*

My phone rang, startling me. I snatched it up. "Ma?"

"Not exactly," a man's voice said. "But I *am* calling to check up on you."

My face ignited into flames. "Brady! What do *you* want?"

"Just to see if you survived the Long Island iced tea massacre. When you called earlier, you sounded ... well, a bit flustered?"

I cringed, too mortified to speak.

"Sorry," Brady said. "Is this a bad time?"

"Huh? No. It's just that ...."

My voice trailed off. After the scatterbrained voicemail I'd left him earlier, maybe the less I said now, the better.

"You still there?" Brady asked.

"Yes."

"Something you want to talk about?"

Only a gazillion things. All of which would prove to Brady once and for all that I was a complete nut job. No thanks. I was definitely going back to L.A. The sooner, the better.

"No, nothing," I said. "Listen, I've got to go. I still have to pack for my flight."

"So you're leaving?"

"Yes."

"I see. Well, have a good flight. "It was nice meeting you."

"Thanks. You, too."

• • • •

FRUSTRATED AND BUMMED out, I padded into Aunt Edna's living room. The green sculptured carpet was truly hideous, but it felt good on my bare tootsies. Aunt Edna was parked in the old Barcalounger, sipping a glass of iced tea. She appeared lost in thought.

"Aunt Edna? Sorry to bother you, but I can't get ahold of my mother. I haven't talked to her in over a week."

"Geez, Louise," Aunt Edna said, setting her glass of tea into the plastic cup holder hooked to the armrest of the vinyl recliner. "I forgot to tell you. Maureen called this morning. She's in Anchorage."

"Alaska?"

"Yeah. She went on one of those summer solstice cruise deals. Said the phone reception there is terrible. I could barely make out what she was saying. Anyway, she said to wish you happy birthday."

"Oh. Okay."

She shot me a weak smile. "How's about a nice iced tea?"

"Uh, sure. Thanks."

I followed Aunt Edna into her kitchen domain, feeling like a lost child.

"Don't worry. Maureen always *was* her own girl," Aunt Edna said, pouring me a glass of strong, brown brew. "So, you staying a while?"

"I don't know yet," I said, not wanting to hurt her feelings.

"Well, just so you know, me and Jackie would like it if you did."

"Really? I ... I just need a little time to think."

"Take all the time you want." My aunte winked at me. "Your plane doesn't leave for another three hours."

"Oh. Right."

She patted me on the shoulder. "Well, I better get busy with dinner. Let me know if I should set a place for you or not."

"I will. And thank you for your hospitality. I really appreciate it."

"You're family, Dorey. Hospitality is for strangers. And there's no need to thank me. It's been my pleasure getting to see how Maureen's daughter turned out."

I hugged my aunt, but when she opened a kitchen cabinet and reached inside, I sniffed my tea for alcohol. Aunt Edna might be sentimental, but if I'd learned anything about her and Jackie, it was that the pair were craftier than they looked.

And I didn't particularly feel like waking up tied to the bedposts again.

• • • •

I TOTED MY GLASS OF tea outside into the tropical courtyard at the center of the cottage apartments. I pulled out a chair and sat down at the wrought iron table to think things through. Even though it was sweltering outside, under the shade of the massive, yellow umbrella overhead it felt at least ten degrees cooler.

As I glanced around at the cute cottages and colorful foliage, I suddenly felt as hollowed-out as a Halloween pumpkin. Palm Court

Cottages wasn't posh by any means. But compared to the ramshackle apartment I shared with four—make that *five*—other would-be actresses back in L.A., this place looked like the Ritz.

And *here* I had my own bed. And I didn't have to live out of boxes. Just a suitcase.

A magical, self-unpacking suitcase.

I took a sip of tea and wiped a trickle of sweat from my forehead.

How can it be that I'm about to turn forty and I have absolutely nothing to show for it?

I shook my head slowly. Hitching my wagon to Tad Longmire had been a colossal mistake. When his acting career went off the rails, it had taken mine down with it.

Who are you kidding, Doreen?

My career hadn't exactly been going gangbusters *before* I met Tad. Actually, after fifteen years in the cutthroat world of Hollywood, I hadn't been able to land a real *friend*, much less a real movie role.

I chewed my bottom lip and pondered my options.

One, I could go back to Snohomish and live with my mother until I figured things out. Two, I could go back to Hollywood and beg sleazebag Jared Thomas to give me back my crappy job at the production studio as a human grub. Three, I could stay here with Aunt Edna for a few more days and see how it goes. Or four, I could go back to L.A. and throw myself into the La Brea Tar Pits.

I took another sip of tea and looked up at the palm leaves waving softly in the late afternoon sky. As I stared into space, a weird, déjàvu feeling overcame me. It felt as if I'd been here and done this all before. I shook my head.

Geez. I wonder how many lives I've led as a total loser.

Aunt Edna and Jackie had made a life here in St. Pete. It was a weird life, sure. But a bona fide life, nonetheless. Not like my fake-it-till-you-make-it life back in L.A. I'd faked it and faked it and faked it. When did the "make it" part kick in?

Would it ever?

I blew out another long, hot breath.

Should I stay? Should I go? Should I throw myself under a bus?

I closed my eyes and said a silent prayer to whoever might be listening.

Please. If anybody's up there, I need a sign.

Suddenly, my cellphone buzzed. I bolted upright in my chair and stared at the display.

The caller ID read: *Unknown.*

Chapter Nineteen

I couldn't take my eyes off my cellphone. It was ringing on the picnic table next to my frozen hand.

Panic shot through me. Had my prayer been answered? If so, was God going to tell me to go back to my mother in Snohomish?

Please, no! Anything but Snohomish!

I quickly promised God that I'd never swear again or stick my chewing gum under another bus seat if *only* I didn't have to go to Snohomish. The pact sealed, I swallowed hard and clicked the answer button on my cellphone.

"Hello?"

"Doreen? Hi! It's me!"

I nearly melted with relief. The voice on the other end of the line wasn't God. It was Kerri Middleton.

Kerri was the manager of Sunshine City Studios. She was also the reason I'd come to St. Pete in the first place. She'd hired Tad Longmire to star in *Beer & Loathing*. As his personal assistant, I'd been obligated to come along to keep the gorgeous lout both on his mark and off the booze.

Kerri was also who I had to thank for my first real acting gig. (Unless you counted playing a decapitated hooker in a dumpster, but that's another story.) When the original killer in the *B&L* script—an inflatable shark—had burst before its maiden performance, quick-thinking Kerri had cast me as its replacement. That's how I'd ended up playing a serial slasher on TV.

Come to think of it, that's *also* how I'd become the unwitting victim of an old lady's purple umbrella. I guess fame really did have its plusses and minuses.

"Doreen? Are you there?" Kerri asked, interrupting my trip-and-fall down memory lane.

"Oh. Yes. Sorry," I said. "How are things at the studio?"

"Not bad. Actually, I'm calling to see if you're still in town."

"Yes. But I'm getting ready to—"

"Excellent! I've got another job offer for you!"

"What?" I nearly choked on my own tongue. "A new season of *B&L*? Did Channel 22 pick it up after all?"

"It's related," Kerri said. "More like a spinoff. Can you come in on Monday and talk about it?"

"Uh ..."

"Great. See you at ten thirty?"

"Err ... okay."

She clicked off the phone before I could ask any more questions.

Typical Kerri. Cut and run while she was ahead.

I frowned.

Huh. Maybe I should do the same.

But as I glanced up at the palms gently swaying in the afternoon sky, it dawned on me that I'd already made my decision. I'd stay. At least for a few more days, anyway.

I looked up at the clouds. The universe had given me my answer after all. I smiled and mouthed the words, "Thank you."

"How's the tea," Aunt Edna asked. She'd walked up the courtyard path while my gaze had been skyward.

I looked at her smirked. "Not as strong as *last night's*."

She laughed and pulled out a chair. "Southerners love a ton of sugar in their tea. I guess that's where the Italian in me draws the line."

"I like it unsweetened, too," I said, raising my glass to her. "Besides, I don't need the extra calories. I'll save those for Sophia's birthday cake."

Aunt Edna's face brightened. "So, you're staying?"

I nodded. "At least through Tuesday. Actually, I might have another film gig here. I'll know more on Monday."

"That's excellent news," Aunt Edna said. "Now, how about a nice piece of veal scaloppini?"

I grinned. "I thought you'd never ask."

••••

AFTER DINNER, AUNT Edna and I sat out in the courtyard and watched the sky turn pink. It was Jackie's turn to do the dishes, and we both were grateful for a little silent star gazing.

As the streetlights came on, Aunt Edna turned to me. "So, a job at the studio, eh?"

"Yes," I said brightly.

"Doing what?"

"I'm not sure yet. But it's an acting role, not grunt work."

Aunt Edna beamed. "I'm glad for you Dorey. You know, we could really use—"

"Really?" I squealed, surprised at my own enthusiasm. I sat up straight. "You know, I was thinking that if things work out with this offer, maybe I could move into Sophia's apartment. While she's not using it?"

Aunt Edna's smile evaporated. She glanced around the courtyard, then leaned over and whispered, "No way. If I let you into her place, Sophia would kill us both."

Brrrzz!

The cellphone in Aunt Edna's apron pocket blared like a time's-up buzzer, startling us both. She pulled her phone out and glanced at the display. Her face turned to stone. "It's Sophia."

I flinched. "Geez! Has she got this place bugged or something?"

"I dunno." Aunt Edna cleared her throat and answered her phone. I could hear Sophia's voice on the other line.

"Sophia. Everything okay?"

"Edna! Thank goodness you picked up. I've got bad news."

"What?"

"Freddy's dead."

Aunt Edna's jaw dropped. "I swear it wasn't the cacciatore!"

"I know that," Sophia said. "Freddy keeled over ten minutes after I gave him a cookie. It came from the Neil Mansion."

"The funeral home on Central?" Aunt Edna asked.

"Yeah," Sophia said. "Either those grave diggers put a hit out on me or they've come up with one hell of a new marketing strategy."

Aunt Edna grimaced. "What kind of cookies were they?"

"Sneaky bastards," Sophia hissed. "They sent my favorite. Lemon bars."

Chapter Twenty

Aunt Edna clicked off the phone and slammed her fist on the picnic table, causing my iced tea to nearly topple off onto the ground.

"Lemon bars!" she hissed. "Who *does* that?"

I gulped and grabbed my glass just before it fell.

Oh, no! That's what Morty told me he'd given Humpty Dumpty at the bakery!

Aunt Edna and Morty definitely had some past chemistry. I needed to tread carefully. "Um ... you don't think Morty and Humpty are working together to bump off Sophia, do you?"

Aunt Edna eyed me, incredulous. "No way. Morty and Humpty *hate* each other."

Jackie stepped out of the shadows like a gray-haired ghost. She pursed her lips and said. "Maybe they do, or maybe they don't."

"What do you mean?" I asked.

Jackie sat down in the chair next to me. "You know the old saying, 'The enemy of my enemy is my fiend?'"

"*Friend*," I said. "It's Sanskrit."

Jackie's nose crinkled. "You got a friend named Sand Grits? Is he related to Joey the Sandman?"

My nose crinkled. "Uh ... I don't think so."

Aunt Edna groaned and shook her head. "Listen. If you two are done with the Abbott and Costello routine, we need to get serious here. Apparently, somebody really *is* trying to poison Sophia."

"Holy cow," Jackie said. "So, what's the plan?"

Aunt Edna glanced around the courtyard, then leaned in and whispered, "We need to bust Sophia out of Shady Respite. She's not safe in there anymore."

"You got it," Jackie said, springing up out of her chair. "Let's go!"

"We can't right now," Aunt Edna said. "Visiting hours are over for the night. That place will be locked up like Fort Knox."

"Oh," Jackie said. "Then we ride at dawn. Or as soon as breakfast is over. Whichever comes first."

Aunt Edna nodded, then locked eyes with me. "You in, Dorey?"

"Uh ... *sure*."

Like I had a choice.

• • • •

WE DIDN'T ACTUALLY ride at dawn. It was more like 8:45. Visiting hours at Shady Respite didn't start until nine o'clock.

Even though this was supposed to be a covert operation, Aunt Edna had insisted we wear the neon-pink flip-flops that branded us as members of the CGCN. Her rationale was that she didn't want to confuse Sophia so early in the morning, in case her meds hadn't had a chance to kick in yet.

We arrived at the convalescent center armed not to the teeth, but more like to the ankles. Aunt Edna had her trusty rolling pin tucked into her pocketbook. Jackie had her can of Raid hidden under a lime-green vest. As for me, I carried a very bad feeling in the pit of my stomach ...

As I shifted the Kia into park, my nerves began to unravel like a cheap sweater.

If I help kidnap Sophia from Shady Respite, is that considered a felony in Florida?

I chewed my lip.

I just beat a murder rap a couple of days ago. If Sergeant McNulty finds out, he'll throw the book at me!

"You coming?" Aunt Edna asked as she climbed out of the car.

I hesitated in the driver's seat, my fingers gripping the steering wheel like a life ring in a Nor'easter. "Uh ... I don't know about this."

If all I do is drive the getaway car, will my jail sentence be shorter?

"Dorey," Aunt Edna said softly. "We could really use your help. Freddy's dead. Sophia could be next."

I swallowed hard and unclenched my fists.

"Okay. I'm coming."

• • • •

"WHERE'S THE LEMON BARS?" Aunt Edna shouted as she burst into Sophia's room, her rolling pin at the ready.

"Oh, it's you," Sophia said, sitting up in bed. "Thank God. I thought it was that stupid woman with that therapy mutt again. It's getting to where a person can't die in peace anymore."

"You're not dying. Not yet, anyway," Aunt Edna said. "And you won't be on my watch. We're here to get you out of this place."

"It's about time." She threw the covers off her torso and scooted to the edge of her bed. She was fully clothed—all the way to her sensible shoes.

"I see you were expecting us," Aunt Edna said dryly. "So, where are these deadly lemon bars?"

"Under the bed," Sophia said, brushing a wrinkle from the skirt of her black dress.

Aunt Edna turned to me. "Dorey, get down there and grab them."

I cringed. "Why *me*? Because I'm the most expendable?"

"No. Because you're the one most likely to be able to get back up off your knees." Aunt Edna reached into her pocketbook. "Here, wear these rubber gloves, just in case the poison leaked through the sack." She whipped out a pair of latex dishwashing gloves as pink as our CGCN flip-flops.

I dutifully slipped them on, got on my hands and knees, and looked under the bed. I half expected to see some kind of homemade bomb-like contraption oozing icky green poison. Instead, lying amongst an impressive collection of dust bunnies, was a decidedly *unimpressive*, crumpled white paper bag.

It was the same kind I'd seen Morty hand over to Humpty Bogart.

"Uh, I think I see them," I said.

"Congratulations," Aunt Edna said. "Now be a dear and actually get them out from under there."

I grimaced and inched my arm and shoulder under the bed until I could reach the bag. I snatched it with my gloved hand and dragged it out from under the box springs.

"Here you go," I said, holding it out to Aunt Edna.

"Not so fast," my aunt said. "Open it first. To be sure."

Sure of what? That it's not going to explode?

I gulped, then cautiously opened the paper sack. To my great relief, it didn't detonate.

"Uh … they look like ordinary lemon bars," I said.

"Right." Aunt Edna turned to Sophia. "How do you know these things came from the Neil Mansion? Did one of your moles tell you?"

"No." Sophia sat down in her wheelchair and wrapped her shawl tighter around her thin shoulders. "The delivery man said so himself."

Aunt Edna's face grew red. "They let a delivery guy into your room?"

Sophia scowled. "That's what I just said, didn't I?"

"You sure did, Queen E," Jackie said, grinning and nodding like a bobble-head toy. "Hey, Edna. Maybe we should *both* go get Miracle Ears!"

Aunt Edna's jaw flexed. "The security here is ridiculous," she growled to Sophia. "Why didn't you call us earlier? During visiting hours? We could've come for you yesterday."

"I called you right after he left," Sophia said. "Someone let the delivery man in last night, after visiting hours were over."

"What?" Aunt Edna bellowed. Tendons protruded from her neck. She glanced around the room. "They probably have your room bugged, too."

"Those dirty cockroaches," Jackie said. "Where are they? I'll spray them in the face with Raid!"

"That's *it*," Aunt Edna growled. "We're not waiting around for someone to take another potshot at you. We're busting you out of here. *Right now.*"

Sophia shrugged. "Well, okay. If you insist."

Chapter Twenty-One

H ere's a tip that should've been in my *Hollywood Survival Guide*:

If you ever need to make a clean getaway, don't wear flip-flops.

After wheeling Sophia out of her room, the four of us burned rubber as we raced down the dreary corridor of Shady Respite convalescent center. The ruckus our flip-flops made was enough to wake the dead—which was ironic, considering we were trying to sneak Sophia out of there before she bit the dust herself.

I'd been assigned to "Queenpin detail," which involved pushing the cantankerous old lady down the hall in her fancy throne wheelchair as fast as my legs could take us. Aunt Edna and Jackie had taken up positions on either side of us. Their job was to guard our flanks using their signature weapons of choice, a rolling pin and a can of Raid.

If I'd been asked to star in this movie, I'd have turned it down.

Our mission, though outwardly ridiculous, wasn't without tactical thought. Aunt Edna had chosen to strike at precisely 9:45 a.m., twenty minutes after the convalescent center served breakfast. According to my aunt, that was when the hallway would be at its most quiet.

I'd asked her how she knew that, then had instantly regretted it.

According to Aunt Edna, a quarter to ten was peak hour for patients to be occupied with what she called their "post-coffee constitutionals."

My aunt had a strategy for the staff, as well. They'd been lured away to the breakroom by the plate of Snickerdoodles she'd drop off at the reception desk.

As I pushed Sophia's chair with all my might, I could scarcely believe my aunt's crazy plan had actually worked. We'd made it all the way down the hallway without being noticed by a single soul.

But our luck didn't last. Fifteen feet from the exit doors, a silver-haired fly buzzed into our ointment.

The sour-faced head of an old woman poked out of a doorway as we flapped noisily by. She looked me up and down and snarled. My gut dropped. It was the same muumuu-clad lady who'd beaned me with her umbrella yesterday.

"You!" she screeched. Then she hobbled out into the hallway and yelled, "Look out, everybody! Killigan's back to kill again!"

My back bristled. I stumbled to a stop. "Look, ma'am. We're just here to—"

"Help!" the old lady hollered as I turned toward her. Her high-pitched voice reverberated down the empty corridor. "Help! Killigan's kidnapping an old lady! She's gonna murder her, too!"

I'd had enough of her crap. I frowned. "Ma'am, if you would just let me—"

But the old lady didn't stick around to hear my argument. Having completed her public service announcement about a killer in the hallway, she ducked back inside her room and disappeared behind the metal door like a geriatric cuckoo clock.

"That's just fantastic," Sophia said. "Now we've got about three seconds before Gloria hits the emergency button in her room."

"Gloria?" I asked.

Sophia elbowed the back of her wheelchair, poking me in the gut. "Don't just stand here, girl! Get going before she rounds up her walker posse!"

I grimaced. "Her *what*?"

"Step on it!" Aunt Edna yelled.

I did as I was commanded and kicked into high gear. The four of us raced out the exit while Jackie held the doors open wide. We'd just made it out the door when an alarm bell sounded.

"Shizzle!" Sophia grumbled.

I winced. "What should we do now?"

"Keep going," Sophia ordered. "Hopefully they'll think Gloria is nuts and ignore her."

"What are the chances of that?" I asked, pushing her down the sidewalk toward the parking lot.

"Pretty high," Sophia said. "Because she *is*."

"Save the conversation for tea and crumpets," Aunt Edna yelled. "Get a move on!"

• • • •

MANEUVERING THE WHEELCHAIR through the parking lot was relatively easy. But once we got to the Kia, I suddenly felt at a loss as to what to do next. How was I supposed to get frail-looking Sophia the Queenpin inside the car without breaking her?

"Don't just stand there," Aunt Edna said. "Lift her up and put her in the passenger seat. Jackie and I'll fastened her wheelchair to the tow hitch in the back."

I glanced over at the entrance to the convalescent center. A mob of gray-headed avengers was forming. "Uh ... I'm not sure we have time for all that."

"Oh, geez," Sophia said, hopping out of her wheelchair. "Stop complaining already. Help those two stuff this thing into the trunk. I'll get in the car on my own steam."

"You're getting' in the steamer trunk?" Jackie asked.

Sophia shook her head. "Mother Mary. Maybe I'm better off here at this crappy old folks' home."

"Let me help you," I said, reaching for Sophia's arm.

"Mitts off," she said, then hit a button on the wheelchair's armrest. To my surprise, the chair folded down to a rectangle the size of a large suitcase.

"There they are!" someone hollered from across the parking lot.

I looked over and spotted the top of a purple umbrella bobbing toward us from between the parked cars.

Not again!

"Everybody in! Now!" I yelled. "I'll get the chair."

While the others scrambled into the Kia, I heaved the wheelchair into the trunk. I managed to wedge it inside, then I scrambled for the driver's seat. Once behind the wheel, I crossed my fingers and said, "Okay, everybody. Hold your breath."

I turned the key in the ignition. The car fired right up.

"Halleluiah," Aunt Edna yelled from the backseat. "Now get us the H-E double toothpicks out of here, Dorey. That nutcase is almost on top of us!"

She wasn't kidding. Umbrella-toting Gloria was only about ten feet away. She raised a fist and flung it our way. Acorns blitzed the side of the car.

Jackie rolled down the back window. "Come any closer and you'll get a faceful of Raid!"

"Oh, yeah?" Gloria yelled back. "Bring it, Killigan! I ain't afraid of you!"

I did, in fact, *not* bring it. Instead, I peeled out of the lot before Jackie could get off a killer shot of bug spray.

"Sheesh. That was a close one," Aunt Edna said as we sped away. "Good driving, Dorey."

"That Gloria Martinelli is a real piece of work," Sophia said. She glanced over at me from the passenger seat. "Who's Killigan?"

"That's the name of a character I played on TV."

Sophia's green eyes narrowed. "Wait a minute. You mean the serial killer who took out Tad Longmire?"

My face went slack. "You saw that?"

"Of course." Sophia took a parting glance back at the convalescent center. "In that place, you only have two choices to pass the time. TV or Tiddlywinks. And let me tell you, young lady. Most of the folks in there haven't got the brains for Tiddlywinks."

"Come on, Dorey," Aunt Edna said, putting a hand on my shoulder. "Step on it."

"Okay, okay!" I shook my head to clear it. "Where to?"

"Home," Aunt Edna said. "We'll get Sophia settled, then we'll go check out this Neil Mansion funeral home that sent these fakakta lemon bars."

"There's no need to curse," Sophia said. "I've got another idea. I've been cooped up in that smelly old nursing home for weeks. I need some fresh air. I'm coming with you."

I glanced in the rearview mirror. Aunt Edna was scowling, but she gave a quick nod. I don't think she had much choice in the matter. I was beginning to know exactly how she felt.

"Yes, ma'am, your Queenpin," I said.

"Now *that's* what I like to hear." Sophia reached over and placed a gnarled hand on my thigh and squeezed it.

"Punch it, Killigan Girl," she said. "Let's see what this baby can do."

Chapter Twenty-Two

According to Jackie, the Neil Mansion funeral home was run by the same family that owned the discount baby goods chain known as Babies or Bust.

"These Neil folks got the perfect racket going," she said from the backseat of the Kia.

The four of us were speeding down the road, having just busted Sophia out of Shady Respite convalescent center. I felt like I was starring in a low-budget remake of *Thelma and Louise*—and, as much as I hated to admit it, I kind of liked it.

"What do you mean by the 'perfect racket'?" I asked, locking eyes with Jackie in the rearview mirror.

"They get your first dollar coming into this world, and the last one leaving it," she said. "It's a real 'cradle to gravy' operation, as they say."

My eyes shifted in the mirror to Aunt Edna. She rolled her eyes and turned away from her backseat companion. Apparently, my aunt wasn't in the mood to fight over semantics. Neither was Sophia. She simply sighed and shook her head.

"You probably don't know this, Doreen," Sophia said. "But the Neil Mansion really *is* an old mansion."

"It's true," Aunt Edna said. "It used to be a fancy estate. Sat on some nice acreage, too. But then the government took the land around it by eminent domain."

"Why?" I asked.

"So they could build that fakakta interstate," Aunt Edna said. "Now the poor old house butts up to an exit ramp." She shook her head. "A lousy, postage-stamp lot. That's all the government left the poor owners."

"It was a real tapestry of justice," Jackie said. "But one man's disaster is another man's treasure. The Neils bought the place for cheap and turned the dance parlor into a casket showroom. Now if that ain't using your noodle, what is?"

"In your case, we may never know," Sophia said. "But I agree. Neil Mansion is still the best place in town to hold your send-off. When my time comes, I want the works."

My jaw nearly dropped. "What? Even though they just tried to poison you with those lemon bars?"

"We don't know that for sure, Dorey," Aunt Edna said. "That's what we're going there to find out. And we need to do it without ticking them off."

"Why?" I asked. "What does it matter?"

"It matters because Sophia's final send-off is all arranged and paid for with them, that's why." Aunt Edna reached over from the backseat and laid a hand on Sophia's shoulder. "When your time comes, you don't have to worry about a thing."

"Except the dying part," Sophia muttered.

"Here it is, coming up on the right," Jackie said.

Just left of the 1-275 overpass, I spotted a stately, three-story, Victorian-style mansion. It was painted the purplish-black color of a semi-ripe eggplant. The ornate trim was mint green. Against all odds, the combination just ... well, *worked*.

"Okay, we're here," I said, pulling into the parking lot. "What's the plan? Hold a pastry gun to their heads until they confess?"

"I wish," Sophia said. "Back in the day, when this whole place was nothing but dirt roads and pine trees, you could get away with stuff like that."

Aunt Edna's hand moved from Sophia's shoulder to mine. "Dorey, the plan is for you to go in. *Alone.*"

I blanched. "Me? Alone? Why?"

"Because they don't know *you*," she said, squeezing my shoulder. "You can go in without raising suspicion. So hop out and snoop around while we wait in the Kia."

My eyebrows met my hairline. "Snoop around? What am I? A Basset Hound?"

"Of course not." Aunt Edna lifted her hand from my shoulder.

"If Benny was here, she'd sniff out the backstabbing deadbeat from a hundred yards," Jackie said, referring to her ancient pug.

"You're absolutely right," I said. "I'm definitely no deadbeat-smelling dog. And I'm no Sherlock Holmes, either. Look, ladies. I have *no clue* how to 'snoop around.' I've never investigated a murder before."

"Sure you have," Jackie said. "The one you just got away with."

I turned and stared at the pewter-haired woman in the backseat. "I've told you a ... *argh*! Forget it. Look, what am I supposed to say to these funeral people? 'Read any good books lately about how to poison lemon bars?'"

Sophia snickered.

"No," Aunt Edna said. "You never want to confront a suspect outright like that."

"Not unless you're packing heat," Jackie said.

My brow furrowed. "Why not?"

"Amateur move." Aunt Edna tutted and shook her head. "Rule number one, Dorey. Never let a suspect know you're onto them. You gotta keep your cool and use it to your advantage."

Somebody shoot me now.

I closed my eyes and let out a breath. "And how do I do that?"

"Easy." Aunt Edna shrugged. "Just keep it casual. Strike up a nice little conversation. You know, about funeral arrangements and stuff. And then see what happens."

"*See what happens*?" I balked. "That hardly seems like—"

"Look," Aunt Edna said. "I didn't want to say this in front of the head of the CGCN, but you need *training*, Dorey. If you're gonna make the cut, you've gotta develop an eye for detail. No pun intended."

"Make the cut for *what*?" I argued. "And excuse me, but I believe I already *have* an eye for detail. No pun intended."

Aunt Edna smirked. "Okay, then. If you're so smart with the details, answer me one simple question and you're off the hook."

"Fine." I folded my arms across my chest. "Go ahead."

Aunt Edna waggled her eyebrows. "What's my last name?"

I grimaced. "Uh ... *Diller*?"

Aunt Edna snorted. "Heh. That's what I thought. Now, get going, Killigan Girl."

Chapter Twenty-Three

"So, this is your basic midrange model?" I asked, knocking my knuckles on the smooth, polished oak of a casket labelled *Settler's Rest*.

"Yes," Neil Neil answered. "It's our most popular choice."

I'd almost done a double-take when the man had introduced himself as Neil Neil. I'd thought maybe he had a stutter. But then I'd spotted the name placard on his desk and realized his only impediment was being born to a set of parents with either no imagination or a twisted sense of humor.

I was certain Neil Neil himself couldn't have possibly inherited those unappealing attributes—or any flaws at all, for that matter. From outward appearances, the man running the Neil Mansion funeral home was absolutely *perfect*.

Neil Neil's shiny blond hair and clean-shaven face were impeccably groomed. Dressed in an immaculate blue suit with fashionably coordinating tie, he appeared ready to step into a *GQ* magazine photoshoot.

Tall and slim, he was head and shoulders above most of the schleps I'd auditioned with back in Hollywood. If he had any flaw at all, it was that he reminded me of how irritatingly gorgeous Tad Longmire had been.

In other words, Neil Neil was just my type. But the wedding picture of him and his husband displayed on his desk informed me that I was definitely not *his*.

"How much?" I asked, slapping a palm on the shiny hull of the Settler's Rest.

"For the casket or the whole service?" Neil asked, raising his chin as if he found my question distasteful.

I crinkled my nose.

What is it with doctors and undertakers? Are we not supposed to ask how much it costs to live or die?

"The whole shebang," I said. "How much?"

The prospect of a big sale made the pinched look on Neil's handsome face disappear. The corners of his perfect mouth curled upward slightly.

"Let me check." He sat down at his desk and began punching a calculator as if his life depended on it. After a minute or so of banging away, he stopped.

"Okay, here we go," he said. "The casket, plot, ceremony, and premium burial service come to $15,355."

I nearly swallowed my tonsils. "Holy smokes!"

"No," he said dryly. "Cremation is $595 extra."

I laughed. Neil smiled.

"Good one," I said. "I guess … well, I'm sorry. I just had no idea funerals were so expensive."

"I agree it can be a real *eye* opener," he said, dropping a hint for me to remove Jackie's giant glaucoma shades that were hiding my mismatched eyes.

Not happening.

"Indeed," I said.

Neil cleared his throat. "That's why we recommend the prepaid plan. With all your arrangements preset, your relatives can't blow your burial budget on things like tattoos and marijuana edibles."

My left eyebrow shot up.

Neil closed his eyes and nodded. "Happens a lot more than you'd think."

"Hmm. That's something I never considered. But I can see how prepayment makes sense."

Neil stared up at me patiently from his desk, his perfect smile brightening the otherwise slightly morbid space. He and I both knew it was my turn to make a move. But I wasn't sure what to do. I had to get busy grilling him for information about the lemon bars. Otherwise, he might charm me into becoming the next owner of my own shiny, satin-lined Settler's Rest.

A tinge of panic swept through me as we faced off within the pregnant void. I wracked my brain to think of a way to steer our conversation toward the true goal of my mission.

I couldn't exactly ask Neil Neil outright why the Neil Mansion had delivered poisoned lemon bars to Sophia at the nursing home. Besides the fact that Aunt Edna had warned me not to give away that I knew anything about it, if he was the murdering type, Neil Neil could easily stuff me into the Settler's Rest never to be seen again. Then again, the coffin was probably more comfortable than the cot waiting for me back in L.A. But still, it wasn't exactly how I'd pictured my grand finale panning out ...

"So, are you ready to put together a plan?" Neil asked brightly. "We offer layaway."

My upper lip twitched. "*Layaway*? That seems rather—"

"Not for *bodies*," Neil said. "I was referring to monthly payments toward future funeral services."

"Oh. Uh ... do you guys ever have any promotions?"

"You mean *sales*?" Neil appeared a bit horrified. "Sometimes, I suppose. On outdated models."

My nose crinkled. "Just exactly how does a casket get outdated?"

Neil's brow furrowed. "I beg your pardon?"

"Sorry." I shot him a tentative smile. "I guess this whole death business makes me a little nervous. What I *meant* was, how do you get your customers? Do you, I dunno, maybe hand out business cards at churches? Or at *old folk's homes*, perhaps?"

Neil's chin raised a full inch. "We're undertakers, not ambulance chasers. But occasionally, we do extend tokens of community goodwill."

"Really?" I perked up. "Like what?"

Neil exhaled sharply. "We sponsor races. Donate to school sports programs. Things like that. Why?"

"I was just wondering if you ever use local caterers. Or maybe supply food to senior centers?"

Neil stiffened. "Are you here seeking a donation?"

I seized on the lead he'd handed me. "Well, now that you mention it, I *am* thinking about putting together food baskets for elderly shut-ins. And those poor old folks in nursing homes and convalescent centers."

"I see. Well, we generally avoid programs where food is involved."

My eyebrow shot up. "Really? Why's that?"

"In a word? *Liability*. Food is wrought with dangers, Ms. ... I'm sorry. What was your name?"

"Diller," I said, then kicked myself for not coming up with an alias. "Dangers? What kind of dangers?"

"All kinds." Neil pulled a sheet of laminated paper from his desk drawer. It was an article he'd clipped from a magazine.

"See here?" he said, pointing to the plasticized sheet. "In any given year, over forty-eight million Americans get food poisoning. Five-thousand die from choking on food alone!"

He slapped the article down on his desk and looked up at me. "Don't even get me *started* on deaths related to obesity and diabetes."

"Geez," I said. "You sure know a lot about how people die."

"I should. It's my business."

You don't say ...

"Oh. Of course," I said. "So, what if you became aware of an upcoming death? You know, someone on their last legs. How much notice do you need to get a funeral together?"

"Well, we can't exactly *plan* these things, now can we?"

The tone of Neil's voice told me his patience was growing thin. I could barely blame him. I studied him as he blew out a breath and glanced out the window beside him. All of a sudden, his handsome jaw went slack.

I followed his gaze out the window and nearly choked on my own spit.

In the parking lot, ten yards away, stood the beat-up old Kia. From the open passenger window, Sophia glared at us like an angry cadaver sporting a Jiffy-Pop wig.

Holy crap!

Neil turned a hardened face toward me and glared. "We don't take *early delivery*, either, Ms. Dither, if that's what you're after. We serve the *dearly* departed here. We're not a boarding kennel for the *nearly* departed."

"Uh ... of course you aren't," I backpedaled. "That's not what I meant ...."

"So, exactly what *can* I do for you today?" he asked, his lips a tight, white line. "Or are we through here?"

"Uh ... just your business card will do for now." I plucked one from the stand on his desk. "Thank you for your time. I'll be in touch."

• • • •

"NEIL TOLD YOU HIS COMPANY doesn't mess around with food?" Aunt Edna asked as I drove us back to Palm Court Cottages. "That's all the goods you got on that crew?"

"Like I told you," I said. "I'm no murder investigator."

"Maybe it's that crappy nursing home that's behind all this," Sophia said. "So many old geezers die in there they've got a conveyor belt from the lunchroom to the morgue."

"I knew it!" Jackie said.

"Knew what?" I asked.

"*Shady Respite*," she said. "Never trust a company with *shady* in their name. Am I right?"

"Well, at least we've got the lemon bars for evidence," Aunt Edna said, holding up the bag.

"That's right," Sophia said. "We can use Kitty to test them for poison."

I blanched. "Now you're going to poison a *cat*?"

"No," Jackie said. "Kitty lives in apartment four. She's our resident gardener and potioneer."

My nose crinkled. "Potioneer?"

"She cooks up stuff," Jackie said. "Like the knock-out drugs we used on you." She shot me a grin. "Pretty effective, eh?"

Sophia nodded her determined-looking face. "Kitty will be able to tell us what's in the lemon bars that shouldn't ought to be there. Let's get her going on that as soon as we get home."

Aunt Edna cleared her throat. "Um ... Doña Sophia? I've been meaning to tell you. Kitty took a short vacation while you've been away. She should be back any day now."

Sophia frowned and crossed her thin arms across her bony chest. "What *else* are you not telling me, Edna?"

"Nothing," Aunt Edna said. "I swear."

"Humph," Sophia grunted. "Today's Sunday. We talking today or tomorrow? You know how much I hate to wait."

"Yes, I know," Aunt Edna said. "But—"

Aunt Edna's phone buzzed. She glanced at the display. "Crap. It's Shady Respite. They must've figured out Sophia's flown the coop."

"Don't answer it!" Sophia barked.

"I've got to," Aunt Edna said. "You don't want the cops poking around your place, do you? I'll just tell them we checked you out early."

"Humph," Sophia grunted.

Aunt Edna clicked on the phone. "Hello? Uh-huh. Oh, no. She's fine. Yeah, sure." She put her hand over the speaker and said, "Sophia? Someone wants to talk to you."

"Who?" the grumpy Queenpin asked.

Aunt Edna glared at her. "He says his name is Freddy."

Chapter Twenty-Four

"All right," Sophia admitted with a shrug. "So I may have exaggerated a smidgen about the current state of Freddy's health. But I did give him some lemon bars this morning, so I couldn't exactly be sure."

"I thought you said you gave them to him last night," I said. I glanced in the rearview mirror at Aunt Edna. Her face was so red I feared it might explode like a rotten tomato.

"Does it matter?" Sophia said, raising her skinny arms in a *what's the big deal* gesture. "Look. I needed to get out of that crap hole to save my own skin. When that punk with those lemon bars showed up last night, I figured the clock was ticking on me biting the big one in there."

I grimaced. "So you really think someone's trying to poison you?"

"Absolutely." Sophia folded her arms across her bony chest. "Either that, or kill me by pure mental torture. I'm telling you, if I had to hear Gloria Martinelli talk about her gallbladder one more time, *I'd* be the one up on murder charges. Besides, all the nurses in that place do is walk around and check who's asleep—so they can wake us up and jab us with needles. God only knows what they've got in those syringes of theirs."

My shoulders stiffened. My fingers curled into a death grip on the steering wheel. "Hold on a minute. Are you saying I just humiliated myself at the Neil Mansion *for nothing*?"

"Nobody told you to humiliate yourself," Sophia said. "That's on *you*."

My jaw dropped. If I'd been searching for a sympathetic ear, I'd definitely paddled up the wrong auditory canal. I glanced back at Aunt Edna. She leaned forward and whispered, "Welcome to *my* world, Dorey."

• • • •

BY THE TIME I PULLED the Kia up to Palm Court Cottages, I found myself once again seriously debating whether to skip town while I had the chance.

On the one hand, on Monday I had a potentially career-making acting job waiting for me here with Kerri Middleton at Sunshine City Studios. On the other hand, I was currently bunking with a posse of sketchy mob molls and it was three days to the showdown at the Sophie Corral.

I parked the Kia and turned off the ignition. Before I could say a word, Aunt Edna began barking orders from the backseat like a drill sergeant.

"Doreen! You get Sophia's wheelchair ... I mean *throne* ... out of the trunk. Jackie! You get Sophia settled into her cottage while I make lunch."

"No!" Sophia protested. "I want *Doreen* to help me."

I glanced back in the rearview mirror. Jackie appeared just as shocked as I was. Her mouth was opening and closing like a fish out of water. As for Aunt Edna, the fact that Sophia had taken a shine to me had seriously dulled the usual glint in her eyes.

"Fine," Aunt Edna said, her face puckering. "Jackie, *you* get the throne out of the trunk. And Dorey, *you* get Sophia back to her cottage. It's number three, in case you forgot."

• • • •

AS I'D PUSHED SOPHIA and her wheelchair down the path past the courtyard picnic table, I'd pictured the inside of her apartment as a dusty, gray hovel laden with crocheted doilies and cobwebs. Possibly even a skeleton lying in a corner. But to my surprise, the hard-nosed Doña's apartment turned out to be quite the opposite of my dreary machinations.

If Aunt Edna's place was stuck in the 1970s, Sophia's cottage was a portal back to the 1950s.

The living room sported a brilliant teal sofa flanked by two lemon-yellow armchairs. The kitchen was furnished with vintage pink appliances and a matching dinette set. I hadn't seen that much chrome since Henry Winkler played The Fonz on *Happy Days*.

"Set my purse on the table," Sophia ordered.

"Yes, ma'am. I hear you came over on a boat from Sicily," I said in a nervous attempt to make conversation.

"You did, did you?"

I cringed. "Uh ... that must've been quite an adventure."

Sophia chortled, but said nothing as I helped her to the low-slung, peg-legged couch.

I glanced around the place as she settled herself into the cushions. Uncertain whether I was supposed to stay and keep her company or leave and let her be, I suddenly realized just exactly how much I knew about Cosa Nostra etiquette.

Exactly diddly squat.

"I guess I'll be going," I said, and took a step toward the door.

"Stay."

I looked over at Sophia. She was staring at me with those cat eyes of hers as if she expected something.

"Uh ..." I fumbled.

"Uh, what?" Sophia said. "Speak up, Doreen Diller. I don't care for mealy-mouths."

I found another inch of backbone. "Okay. I was wondering. Why did you ask *me* to help you instead of Jackie?"

Sophia shrugged. "I need to get a feel for you. Don't get me wrong, but the rest of my crew is a bunch of goomahs."

I nearly blanched. "*Goomahs?*"

She smiled at me like I was a bug and she was an entomologist. "You like them, don't you?"

"I guess."

"Mealy-mouth."

I straightened my shoulders. "Yes, ma'am. I think they're nice ladies."

"Nice ladies," she repeated as if it amused her. "Now, don't get your hackles up, Doreen. Goomah is just what we call mob wives and mistresses. Jackie and Edna are good women. They both bring their own skills to the table. But neither of them has ever been *made*."

She studied me for a moment. "I'm not sure any of the goomahs left in the Family have the gumption I'm looking for to take over the Collard Green Cosa Nostra. You catch my drift?"

Uh ... not really.

The first time I'd met them, Jackie and Aunt Edna had drugged me, tied me up, and interrogated me before I'd known what hit me. Sure, it'd been an ambush. And their weapons of choice had been garbage-bag zip-ties, a rolling pin, and a can of Raid. Nevertheless, they'd definitely held the upper hand on me. If that wasn't gumption, what was?

"Well ..." I managed to utter before Sophia cut me off.

"You see, Doreen, the mafia is like a bunch of hermit crabs."

I blanched. "*Hermit crabs?*"

"Yeah." Sophia picked a piece of lint from the lap of her black dress. "When one crab finds a bigger shell, the whole lot get in line. You know, to trade up." She locked her green cat eyes with mine. "But you can't have the bigger shell unless you fit. And to fit, you have to prove yourself."

I winced out a fake smile. "So, how do you prove yourself?"

The ancient Queenpin cocked her turbaned head. "By making your bones. Don't you know *anything*?"

I grimaced. Apparently not.

"Making *my bones*?" I asked.

"Bumping somebody off." Sophia smiled coyly. "From what I hear, you already *did* that."

• • • •

AFTER FETCHING SOPHIA some water, an aspirin, and her pocketbook, I left her resting on the couch in her cottage and returned to Aunt Edna's. As usual, my aunt was busy in the kitchen. And *I*, as usual, began obsessing about what I should do next.

I was short on cash, but long on apprehension. From what I could tell, the whole CGCN mob was convinced I'd actually whacked Tad Longmire and gotten away with it scot free. And they also thought I had "big shoes to fill."

A thought hit me between the eyes like a stray bullet.

O.M.G! Do they expect me to be their new hitman? Am I supposed to take over for Sammy the Psycho?

I jumped up off the couch and took a flying step toward the bedroom. If that was the case, I needed to pack my suitcase and get my butt out of Dodge! As I made my way to my bedroom, another thought froze me in place.

But what if that acting role Kerri Middleton has for me is my big break? If I leave now, I'll be throwing fifteen years of acting lessons, humiliation, and grunt work down the drain!

I nearly groaned out loud.

What am I gonna do?

As I agonized in my petrified state, a third thought wormed its way into my seesawing mind.

Kerri let me stay at her place once before. Now that she knows I'm not a murderer, she might let me again. I can throw my crap in my suitcase and be out of here in ten seconds flat!

I glanced around to make sure the coast was clear. Then I pulled out my cellphone, dialed Kerri's number, and scurried into the spare bedroom where I'd been staying. As I closed the door behind me, the call went straight to voicemail.

Crap!

I glanced around for secret listening devices, then I cupped my hand to my mouth and whispered an urgent message for Kerri to call me back, A.S.A.P.

Then I opened my suitcase and started flinging my junk into it like my life depended on it.

Chapter Twenty-Five

"Lunch is ready!" Aunt Edna called out down the hallway. Startled, I slammed my crammed suitcase shut and stuffed it under the bed as if I were hiding a murder victim. My mind reeled with trepidation. Would going to Kerri's place hurt Aunt Edna's feelings? Would it turn the whole CGCN against me?

If it meant escaping a future as the new Sammy the Psycho, it was a chance I had to take—right after I finished off a plate of my aunt's ridiculously good food.

"Coming!" I yelled.

Geez. Why am I such a sucker for Aunt Edna's cooking? Is her secret recipe cocaine or something?

I cautiously stuck my head into the kitchen, expecting to find my sketchy aunt sprinkling mysterious white powder onto plates of linguine. Instead, I found her humming away, dutifully rolling paper napkins around sets of silverware.

She looked as wholesome as June Cleaver.

My nose crinkled. Guilt washed over me. Had I read these ladies wrong? I mean, June Cleaver would never hire a hitman, would she?

The only way to be sure was to stay for lunch and pump these ladies for more information. It was only right to give them a fair shake, right? Plus, whatever was cooking in that huge pot on the stove smelled absolutely divine.

"Smells great in here," I said, taking a cautious step into the carefully guarded domain of my aunt's kitchen.

She smirked. "It's my new perfume. Eau de garlic and onions."

I smiled. "Heavenly. Hey, can I ask you something?"

"Sure. As long as you lend a hand while I answer."

"Of course."

Aunt Edna handed me a napkin and set of silverware to roll. "So, shoot."

"Well, first off, I'm curious. Why do you call Sophia the Queenpin? I thought that, you know, *technically*, she's the Godmother."

Aunt Edna sighed tiredly. "She is. But when you're the Godmother, people call you what you *tell* them to call you. If Sophia wants to be Queenpin, you call the lady Queenpin. Or Doña. She likes that, too."

"Good to know." I laid the rolled silverware on the counter and picked up another set. "So, how does this whole CGCN thing work?"

"What part?" Aunt Edna asked, her tone sharpened a notch. She plucked four bowls off the shelf of a fake woodgrain cupboard, then eyed me carefully as she handed them to me.

"Well ... the *hierarchy* part, I guess," I said, taking the bowls.

"You doing some kind of research on us, Dorey? You a monkey eager to climb up the Family tree?"

"No!" I blurted. "I ... I was just wondering, you know, how you all ended up here together. Taking care of Sophia. I mean the *Queenpin*. She told me that to get bona fide, you have to crush somebody's bones."

Aunt Edna snorted. "You mean you have to make your bones."

"Yeah, that's it." I looked her square in the eye. "Have *you*?"

"If you're asking me if I've ever whacked somebody, the answer is no." Aunt Edna stacked four laminated placemats atop the bowls in my hands. "But there are other ways to prove your worth, Dorey. How else do you think I got to be the Capo?"

"The Capo?"

Aunt Edna shook her head. "Geez. I forget how green you are to all this. The *Capo* is the one who leads the crew when the Godmother's not around. I'm second fiddle to Sophia, so to speak."

"Oh. What about—"

"No more questions. We gotta get lunch on the table before the Queenpin has a meltdown. She gets crabby when she's hungry." She winked at me. "And she's *always* hungry."

"I've noticed."

Aunt Edna chuckled and shoved the rolls of silverware into my free hand. "Go set the table in the courtyard. It's good weather. We'll eat outside today. And while you're out there, do me a favor and go see what nonsense Jackie's up to. She should be rounding up Sophia."

I smirked. "I'm on it, Capo."

Aunt Edna laughed and swatted me on the butt with the kitchen towel. "That's right. And don't you forget it!"

• • • •

OUT IN THE COURTYARD, I found Jackie on her hands and knees under the picnic table, spraying the ground with Raid.

"Hey, Jackie," I called out, then coughed. I waved a hand in front of my face to whisk away the fumes. "Aunt Edna says lunch is ready."

"Good. I'm starving. I'll go get the Queenpin."

As I watched Jackie sprint down the pathway, I thought twice about setting the dining ware down in a cloud of toxic bug spray. I toted them back into Aunt Edna's cottage.

"What's going on?" she asked, glancing down at the bowls and placemats still in my hands.

"Uh ... technical difficulties," I said. "Does Jackie always blast the courtyard with Raid?"

"Ugh!" she groaned. "I told her not to."

"Is it to keep away the mosquitoes?"

Aunt Edna closed her eyes and let out a long, slow breath. "That woman. Who needs mosquitoes when Jackie's already sucking the life out of me?" She opened her eyes and shook her head. "I swear. Raid is that woman's answer to everything. One of these days she's gonna do us all in with that stupid bug spray of hers."

I cocked my head. "Then why do you put up with her? After all, you're the Capo."

Aunt Edna shot me a sly look. "Think about it, Dorey. Then take a guess."

I shrugged. "Out of loyalty and friendship?"

Aunt Edna sighed. "Eh. Partly. But think harder. A successful mob leader always has a good reason for everything she does."

My eyes widened. "Don't tell me you keep Jackie around for the jokes!"

Aunt Edna laughed. "I said *good* reason." She grinned. "I'll admit, that's part of Jackie's 'charm'—and I used that term loosely. But no. Think *strategically*, Dorey. Like a wiseguy. This is the *Family* we're talking about here."

I grimaced. "Because she's your *sister*?"

Aunt Edna crossed herself. "Heavens no! We're no relation, thank God."

Suddenly the front door flew open. A second later, Jackie burst into the kitchen. "What's taking so long?" she asked. "Sophia's out there chomping at the bit like a pierogi-fish in the Amazon."

I shot Aunt Edna a pursed-lip smirk. "Sorry, Jackie. It's my fault. I've been holding up Aunt Edna with questions about the CGCN."

"Oh, *have* you now." Jackie's shoulders broadened. "Well, I say it's high *crime* you learned all about the Family." She snickered. "High *time*—high *crime*. Get it?"

"We got it," Aunt Edna said. "Jackie, you take the place settings out to the table. Tell Sophia that Doreen and I are coming right behind you with the food."

"You got it." Jackie grabbed the bowls, placemats, and rolls of silverware from my hands, then winked at me. "Looks like you'll have to save your questions for the dinner table, Doreen. The Doña's getting restless."

Aunt Edna watched Jackie go, then handed me a pot full of soup. "Okay. So you want to know the main reason I keep Jackie around?"

I nodded eagerly. "Yes. I really do."

"It's simple." She tapped a finger to her temple. "Pretend you're Sophia. Between me and Jackie, which one would *you* choose to be the Capo?"

My right eyebrow shot up.

Well played, Aunt Edna. Well played.

Chapter Twenty-Six

"Where's the linguini already?" Sophia grumbled as Aunt Edna brought out a gorgeous, magazine-worthy platter of ripe, red tomato slices. A slab of milky mozzarella was sandwiched between each juicy slice, accompanied by a healthy sprinkling of bright-green, aromatic basil leaves.

"The linguini's for *dinner*," Aunt Edna said. "For lunch we're having a nice caprese salad and a bowl of my homemade minestrone. They're good for your constitution."

Sophia frowned. "My mouth was all set for linguini."

I frowned. So was mine.

"But I guess I can make do," Sophia said.

"Much appreciated," Aunt Edna deadpanned. "Now let's eat."

I doled out the soup with a ladle, then sat down and dug in with the rest of them. One mouthful of Aunt Edna's minestrone and I forgot all about my packed suitcase stuffed underneath my bed like a stiff.

"Geez, this is fabulous," I said to Aunt Edna. "What's your secret?"

"She'd tell you, but then she'd have to kill you," Jackie quipped.

I laughed and glanced over at Aunt Edna. Her Mona Lisa smile sent mixed signals as to the seriousness of Jackie's statement. I supposed thirty years of Jackie's bad jokes and Sophia's bad temper had taught my aunt how to cloak her true feelings better than a Klingon bird of prey.

"Ah," Sophia said after guzzling her soup like a starving hobo. "It's good to feel the sunshine on my face again. And smell the fresh air at last."

I smirked. "Wow. The way you talk, people would think you just did a stint in San Quentin instead of Shady Respite."

"What's the difference?" she grumbled. "I barely got a wink of sleep in that old-folks warehouse." She sniffed the air. "Hey. What's that flowery bouquet I smell?"

"Beats me," Jackie said. "If Kitty was here, she'd know."

I sniffed the air.

I believe it's called a Raid blossom.

"Enjoy the outdoors while you can, Queenpin," Aunt Edna said. "After lunch, you're on lockdown. We need to keep you under wraps until your birthday celebration at the Coliseum."

I blanched. "The *Coliseum*? In *Rome*?"

"Naw," Jackie said. "The one over on Fourth Avenue."

"Wait till you see it, Dorey," Aunt Edna said. "It's grand."

"It is?" I asked.

My aunt nodded. "Yeah. It's a classy dance hall built back in the roaring '20s. Wood floors. Crystal chandeliers. Domed ceiling. It's really something to see."

"I met my husband there at a USO dance," Sophia said, her eyes fixed on some faraway point in time and space.

"Really?" My eyes lit up. "Was he in the military?"

"No," Sophia growled. "Harvey was in the waste management business. I thought you knew that."

My nose crinkled. "The garbage business?"

Aunt Edna leaned over and whispered, "That's a euphemism for organized crime."

"Oh." I smiled at Sophia. "Was it love at first sight?"

An infinitesimal smile cracked Sophia's pale lips. "You could say that. Let me tell you, Harvey Lorenzo was quite the Dapper Dan."

"He sure was," Aunt Edna said.

"This one's gonna be a party for the history books, Doreen," Jackie said. "We're pulling out all the stops! Everybody in the business is gonna be there vying for the Queenpin's favor. Ain't that right, Edna?"

"That's right," my aunt agreed. "Everybody who's anybody will be there."

Aunt Edna smiled and raised her glass of tea to Sophia. "Think of it. At the stroke of midnight, our very own Sophia Maria Lorenzo, Doña of the Collard Green Cosa Nostra for the past forty years, will turn one hundred years young."

Sophia stuck her chin up proudly. "And then, young Miss Doreen, all bets are off. At the stroke of midnight, I'll no longer be a moving target for every two-bit goodfella trying to make his bones and take my throne."

"Here, here," Aunt Edna said as we all chinked our glasses together.

Sophia grinned smugly. "I'll be *untouchable*. And I can name my own heir." She laughed. "After that, instead of every goombah in town trying to *kill* me, they'll be falling all over themselves to pay tribute and win my favor."

As my glass clinked with Jackie's, my face froze into a grimace. I wasn't sure whether to be glad for Sophia or afraid for her. My mind's eye envisioned an old-fashioned ballroom filled with a conga line of hermit crabs—each toting machineguns in their claws and scrambling for a shot at the biggest conch shell before the clock struck midnight.

I'd once had a hermit crab as a pet. When it died, it had stunk to high heaven. Was this party going to end the same way?

Sophia cackled. "It's going to be like Oscar night. And I'm a shoe-in for best director."

I gulped.

Or it's gonna be like Apocalypse Now *at an all-you-can whack crab-leg buffet.*

• • • •

WHILE JACKIE TUCKED Sophia securely away in cottage number three, I helped Aunt Edna by washing up the lunch dishes. She was busy rummaging through the cupboards for the ingredients for the linguini Alfredo she'd promised Sophia for tonight's supper.

The thought of missing out on her pasta sent a ting of disappointment through me. So did the fact that once I heard from Kerri I'd be skipping out on her and the CGCN crew. But after hearing about the time bomb ticking down to the Queenpin's party, I was more convinced than ever that the prudent thing to do was to, as my aunt would say, "Get the H-E double toothpicks outta here."

I'd checked my cellphone after lunch. Kerri still hadn't returned my call.

"I'm curious," I said, dawdling over a dirty soup bowl in the sink.

"That you certainly *are*," Aunt Edna said, then chuckled.

"I'm serious," I said. "Are you really so worried about somebody trying to bump off Sophia that she has to go on lockdown until the party on Tuesday?"

Aunt Edna pursed her lips. "It could happen. There's still over two days to go."

"Come on. Do you really think someone poisoned those lemon bars, or is she just paranoid?"

My aunt set a package of flour on the counter. "Nobody's tried to pop Sophia in years. I think most of her competitors got too old to give a damn anymore. To be honest, half the people she wanted me to invite are already dead."

"Oh."

She eyed me up and down. "Now that I think about it, it's been pretty quiet until *you* showed up. You got plans you're not sharing with us, Dorey?"

"What? Me? No!"

Aunt Edna laughed. "Okay. If you say so."

I dawdled with the dishtowel. "If Sophia is in danger, why'd you let her stay at Shady Respite in the first place?"

Aunt Edna shrugged. "She fractured her hip. I'm too old to lift her. What else could I do? Besides, I thought Shady Respite was safer for her than this place. That is, I did until that guy with the lemon bars showed up in her room last night."

"How do you think he was able to get in after hours?"

"I don't know. Either somebody let him in, or he actually came before visiting hours were up. As you've seen for yourself with Freddy, with Sophia the truth is like a bra strap. Adjustable to suit her needs."

"Are you saying she's a *liar*?"

"I'm only saying that the whole lemon bar story could be just part of her scam to make us get her out of that place."

"And the food testers, too?"

"Bazinga."

"But she actually *had* the lemon bars," I said.

Aunt Edna yanked a dozen eggs from the refrigerator. "She could've ordered them over the phone."

"True." I hadn't thought about that. "But according to the *Beach Gazette*, three people really *did* die in Shady Respite during the time Sophia's been in there."

"Yeah, but *which* people? The article didn't say. And one of them *wasn't* Freddy, obviously."

"Fair enough."

Aunt Edna's phone rang. She pulled it from her apron pocket. "It's Shady Respite. I better get this."

While I dried glasses and put them away in the cupboard, I eavesdropped on her conversation, but only caught dribs and drabs.

"Uh-huh, I see," Aunt Edna said. "Yes, we'll take care of it. Thank you for letting us know. Goodbye."

"What did they want?" I asked.

"The usual." She slipped the phone back into her apron pocket.

"The usual?"

"They want us to pay the final bill and go pick up Sophia's stuff."

"Oh."

Aunt Edna put her hands on her hips and scowled at the sack of pasta flour on the counter. "Sheesh. I can't believe it."

"What's wrong?" I asked.

"Sophia."

She plucked her rolling pin from her pocket and slammed it onto the counter. "I gotta hand it to her. That woman always keeps me on my toes."

My nose crinkled. "What did she do now?"

"Nothing. Or maybe everything."

I grimaced. "What do you mean?"

Aunt Edna shook her head and stared at the kitchen counter. "According to the lady at Shady Respite, Freddy's dead. For *real* this time."

Chapter Twenty-Seven

I nearly dropped the glass I was drying. I set it down and grabbed Aunt Edna by the arm. "Sophia *wasn't* lying? The lemon bars really *are* poisoned?"

"Either that or something *else* got Freddy."

She turned and stared blankly into the open cupboard. Worry lines creased her brow. "I didn't take Sophia seriously when she told me she was using the old guys at the nursing home as taste testers." She hung her head. "I guess I should've."

"How could you have known?" I put my hand on my aunt's shoulder. "Besides, the deaths might be totally unrelated. Like you said about Freddy. It wasn't necessarily *poison* that killed them. They could've died of *anything*."

Aunt Edna pursed her lips. "Two might be a coincidence, Dorey. But *three*? That's a much harder pill to swallow." She sighed tiredly. "Anyway, now with Freddy dead too, I'm beginning to think Sophia was right. Somebody really *was* slipping something into her food at Shady Respite."

I cringed. "It seems so ... *implausible*."

Aunt Edna locked eyes with me. "Get this straight, Dorey. Sophia may stretch the truth sometimes, but she's no fool."

I bit my bottom lip. "Okay, suppose she's right about someone trying to poison her. Who would do such a thing? I'm pretty sure Neil Mansion had nothing to do with it."

"With the clock ticking down on Sophia's hundredth birthday, my money's on somebody in the Family. Anybody who's got their heart set on being the new boss is running out of time to seal the deal."

"I thought we agreed that poisoning wouldn't be the method of choice for someone wanting to make sure she died before Tuesday."

Aunt Edna scowled. "Ever hear the term, 'Desperate times call for desperate measures'?"

Yeah. Pretty much every day of my life.

I frowned. "Sophia thinks Humpty Dumpty is behind it. And, I didn't want to say anything, but Morty gave him a sack of lemon bars. He told me so himself."

"My Morty?" Aunt Edna eyed me funny. "When?"

"When we stopped at his bakery yesterday."

"Impossible," Aunt Edna said.

"Look, I know you and he had a thing—"

"Ancient history. And that ain't why it's impossible."

"Then why not?"

"Morty don't make lemon bars."

My shoulders straightened. "Yes, he does."

"No, he don't."

"But he told me so himself," I argued. "I asked Morty what he gave Humpty in that paper sack. He said it was lemon bars."

Aunt Edna's furrowed brow went slack. She laughed. "That's a euphemism for *cash*, Dorey. Little golden bars. Why do you think it's Sophia's favorite cookie?"

"Oh." I frowned sourly. "If they're Sophia's favorite, why doesn't Morty make them?"

"He used to. But they were never good enough for the Queenpin. Morty's no masochist."

Crap. There goes my theory about Morty the Masher.

"If Humpty didn't get the lemon bars from Morty, he still could've gotten them from somewhere else."

"Eh." Aunt Edna plucked a can of roasted roma tomatoes from the cupboard. "I'm not saying it couldn't be Humpty. But there are plenty more suspects where he came from."

My eyebrows shot up. "Like who?"

"Well ... Vinny Zamboni, for one."

"Who's he?"

"A bagman. Like Humpty."

"Bag man? Those guys are *homeless*?"

Aunt Edna's lips puckered. "Hardly. A bagman is what we call a money runner. Sort of like a banker who makes house calls, if you catch my drift."

"Huh?"

"Humpty and Vinny pick up and drop off loot for the Family. That's all I'm saying. Capeesh?"

"Capeesh. Why do you think Vinny would want Sophia dead?"

"Who knows? She's not exactly Mother Teresa now, is she?" Aunt Edna set a large pot on the stove. "Maybe the Family's tired of paying Sophia's widow's pension and gave Vinny a little 'extra homework' assignment."

"Or maybe he wants to be Kingpin himself?"

"Vinny?" Aunt Edna shook her head. "I don't see it. He ain't what I'd call *management material*. When it comes to work, he's more like a fireman."

My brow furrowed. "A fireman?"

"Yeah. He likes to drop and roll. No time for chit-chat."

"Just like Humpty. He got his sack of so-called 'lemon bars' from Morty and took off with barely a word."

"Exactly. In their line of work, the less said, the better." Aunt Edna plucked a wooden spoon from a canister on the kitchen counter.

"You know what? Maybe the lemon bars weren't poisoned. Maybe Freddy just died of natural causes. Then there'd be *nobody* to blame, would there? All of this could just be a figment of Sophia's imagination."

Aunt Edna blew out a big sigh. "Sure. That could be true. But unless we can figure out what actually killed those old geezers at Shady Respite, we're just a bunch of cuckoos on a wild goose chase."

"Well, the first thing to do is find out their names," I said.

"Yeah, I guess you're right." Aunt Edna pursed her lips. "Geez. I wish Kitty was back already. She could test the lemon bars and we'd have our answer to—"

The creaking sound of the front door opening caused Aunt Edna to stop mid-sentence. She pushed me behind her protectively and snatched up her rolling pin.

"Who's there?" my aunt called out.

"It's me," a voice said from just beyond the kitchen door.

The hair on the back of my neck pricked up.

Oh, no. Here we go again!

Chapter Twenty-Eight

I had a death grip on Aunt Edna's apron strings I peeked over her shoulder as the sturdy old woman stood her ground, rolling pin at the ready. Slowly, a head peeked into the kitchen door frame.

If it was Sammy the Psycho, he'd arrived in drag.

"Kitty!" Aunt Edna exclaimed. "You and your silly tricks. It's about time you got back."

Kitty laughed. "I came as soon as I got your message. What's 'gone all fakakta' on you?"

Aunt Edna reached around and pulled me from my hiding place behind her. "Dorey, meet Kitty Corleone, our resident prankster and chemical engineer."

"Chemical engineer?" I stared at the woman. The job title seemed so ... *unlikely*.

Judging from the lines on her face, Kitty Corleone was in her late sixties. Petite and busty, she was dressed from head to toe in pink—from her blousy shirt and leggings all the way to her sunglasses, purse, and coordinating pink rinse in her silver hair. Oh, and, of course, her obligatory pink flip-flops.

So much for better living through chemistry.

"Nice to meet you," I said, woozy with relief that I was shaking her hand and not dying in a blaze of Sammy's gunfire.

The lady in pink grinned. "Likewise. I hear you're settling in well here. Welcome to the Family."

"Uh ... thanks." I shot her a sheepish smile. "So, what's 'chemical engineer' a Family euphemism for?"

Aunt Edna and Kitty exchanged knowing glances.

"Nothing," Kitty said, peering at me through the top of her heart-shaped sunglasses. "It's just Edna's fancy title for what I do. Which is mostly tend the posies and make magic potions. So, what's your job around here? Or haven't they told you yet?"

"She's our new associate in training," Aunt Edna blurted.

I blanched.

I am?

"And *she's still got a lot to learn*," Aunt Edna added in a tone that implied Kitty should be careful what she said around me.

"I see." Kitty lowered her sunglasses and studied my face. "Spooky pair of peepers you've got there, Doreen."

I frowned. "Thanks for noticing."

She laughed. "So you want to become a garbage woman, huh? Well, let me be the first to welcome you to waste management 1-0-1, collard-green style. How do you like it so far?"

"It's been an experience," I said.

"I bet it has." Kitty's mischievous eyes darted back and forth between me and Aunt Edna. "So, what were you two busy gossiping about? From the looks on your faces, I don't think it was the recipe for linguini Alfredo."

"No," Aunt Edna said. "Lemon bars."

• • • •

WHILE AUNT EDNA BREWED the tea, she brought Kitty up to speed about our theory on who might be trying to poison Sophia. Exactly four minutes later, my aunt poured the steeping tea into dainty cups. We each took one and moved to the living room so Kitty could fill us in on what *she'd* been up to.

"I don't know anything about Freddy," Kitty said. "But neither of the other two taste-tester guys Sophia used keeled over while I was on watch."

"While you were on watch?" I asked.

Kitty glanced at Aunt Edna, then said, "Yeah. The three of us took turns watching over Sophia while she was at Shady Respite. One week on, two weeks off for vacation. Didn't Edna tell you?"

"No, she did not." I looked over at Aunt Edna. "Are you saying you guys put Sophia in Shady Respite so you could have *a vacation*?"

My aunt crossed her arms. "You've met Sophia. Can you blame us?"

I frowned. "What about the fractured hip?"

"Eh, cover story," my aunt said.

My brow furrowed. "But—"

"I used to date a guy in the X-ray department," Kitty said. "You've seen one busted hip, you've seen them all. Dr. Mancini didn't even notice."

Aunt Edna shrugged. "As they say, no harm, no foul."

"But what if somebody had actually managed to bump off Sophia while she was in there?" I asked.

"They couldn't have," Kitty said. "Believe me, we took turns keeping a close eye on everything going on in the place. Especially the food."

"But four people have died at Shady Respite in the past two and a half weeks," I said. "And at least one of them was Sophia's taste-tester."

"Two of them were," Kitty said.

I gasped. "What?"

"Take it easy, kid," Kitty said. "Two of Sophia's testers died on my watch. But they didn't die of poisoning. Charlie choked on an apple fritter. And poor Ernie strangled to death on a cheese Danish."

"How is that possible?" I asked.

"Hazard of the trade." Kitty shrugged. "Look, Doreen. You can't choose a picky eater as a taste-tester. You need somebody with what you call a 'healthy appetite.' Charlie and Ernie were the kind of guys that if you give 'em a free pastry, you gotta count your fingers afterward. You know what I meant?"

"Not really."

Kitty ran her fingers through her pink hair. "You'd think they never ate in their lives. Believe me. For them, choking to death was just a matter of time."

Aunt Edna scowled at Kitty. "Why didn't you tell me about them dying?"

"I didn't want to worry you unnecessarily," Kitty said, setting her teacup down on the coffee table. She leaned toward us. "I figured the whole poisoning thing was just another one of Sophia's paranoid imaginings."

"Ha! Me, too," I said.

Aunt Edna's back stiffened. "That's not why—"

"Wait. I'm not finished," Kitty said. "Edna, I'm no sloppy Sally. I did my due diligence. When those two gluttonous guys died, I chatted up Dr. Mancini. He's the attending physician at the joint. He told me both of them died of old age, exacerbated by insufficient oxygen."

"Oh," Aunt Edna said.

Kitty turned to me and wagged her silver eyebrows like Groucho Marx. "Choking on food will do that to a person."

"Is that what their autopsies said?" I asked.

Kitty shook her head. "As far as I know, none were ordered. Dr. Mancini said there was no point, seeing as both were well into their eighties. He chalked them up to age-related disease."

"*Life* is an age-related disease," Aunt Edna said, shaking her head. "That diagnosis could mean anything."

"Sure." Kitty shrugged. "But the bottom line is this. No foul play equals no autopsy. Same with the old lady that died. Eunice, I think. But she had a heart attack."

I glanced over at Aunt Edna. Kitty noticed. "Wait a minute," she said. "Why the sudden interest in these two old dead guys?"

"Because another one died today," Aunt Edna said. "A guy named Freddy Sanderling. And he just happened to be—"

"Don't tell me," Kitty said. "Sophia's latest 'taste-tester.'"

"Bazinga," Aunt Edna said.

Kitty's perfectly arched eyebrows knitted together. "As they say, when it comes to coincidences, three's a crowd."

Aunt Edna nodded. "My sentiments exactly. Something's up. It's gotta be."

"So, what do we do now?" I asked.

"First things first," Kitty said, picking up her teacup. "I'll drop by Shady Respite tomorrow and talk to Dr. Mancini. Maybe with Freddy being number four, he'll be doing an autopsy."

"Good." Aunt Edna set down her cup. "And while you're there, I need you to pick up Sophia's stuff and pay the bill. Let me tell you, it's pretty hefty."

Kitty smirked. "But worth every penny, right?"

Aunt Edna nodded. "Best two weeks of my life."

"What'd you do with *your* free time?" Kitty asked.

Aunt Edna grinned. "Read books and ate Thai take-out every night. I'm telling you, there were cobwebs in the kitchen."

Kitty laughed. "Good for you." She turned to me. "I went to Miami. Took a class in botany."

"To each his own," Aunt Edna said. "But now it's time to pay the piper."

Kitty pursed her lips. "We're gonna need to get the money from Sophia. I'll see if I can squeeze it out of the old cash cow at dinner."

"Dinner!" Aunt Edna yelped. "I forgot all about it! I gotta get the sauce going for the linguini!" She gripped the sides of the old recliner and began rocking herself up and out of it.

Kitty shot me a smirk. "In case you don't know it yet, kid, we need to stay the hell out of Edna's kitchen."

"By threat of death," I said. "It's the first thing she taught me."

"Hey, don't talk about death to *me*," Aunt Edna said, pulling herself to standing. "If anybody knows how to kill somebody, it's Kitty.

Why do you think I don't want her in my kitchen while my back is turned?"

"You could poison somebody a lot easier than me," Kitty said. "You're the cook."

"True," Aunt Edna said. "And my food is so good it'd be worth dying for. Right, Doreen?"

I blanched.

Kitty laughed. "From the look on the kid's face, Edna, I'd say she's pleading the Fifth."

Chapter Twenty-Nine

A few short hours ago, I'd made up my mind to stay in St. Pete, albeit with Kerri Middleton if she'd have me. But as I stood there listening to Aunt Edna and Kitty Corleone casually volley back and forth about which one of them was better at poisoning people, I kind of felt like it'd be better to put some distance between myself and them.

Like, 2,549 miles to be exact, according to Google.

I chewed my lip nervously and wondered if I could still catch a flight back to L.A. tonight. I might not become a star, but at least I'd still live to audition another day.

"Uh, I'm not feeling so well," I said as Aunt Edna headed for the kitchen. "I need to go to the restroom."

"Edna's food can do that to a person," Kitty quipped.

"I heard that!" Edna bantered back.

I smiled wanly. "Excuse me."

I sprinted down the hall to the bathroom and shut the door. Once out of their sight, I crossed my fingers and checked my phone, hoping Kerri had called. I was out of luck.

I chewed my lip and wondered, was the woman in pink merely an eccentric old lady, or a deadly hit-woman in disguise? What about Aunt Edna? She'd just called me an "associate in training." Did that mean they were planning on teaching *me* how to kill so they could retire to Florida?

Wait. They already *were* in Florida ...

Crap!

What do I actually know about any of these CGCN women? Do I really want to be around for Sophia's party? What if her birthday bash turns into a midnight massacre?

No. I needed to get out of Palm Court Cottages before the CGCN thought I knew too much. Once I'd crossed that line, I had a feeling there would be no turning back.

But without Kerri Middleton to run to, where could I go? Thank goodness I'd already packed. All I had to do was sneak out to the street and grab a taxi to the airport. Heck, I could sleep in the ladies' room if I had to!

Like a ninja, I sprinted out of the bathroom, across the hall, and into the spare bedroom. Carefully and silently, I closed and locked the door behind me.

After kicking off the pink flip-flops Aunt Edna had given me, I yanked my suitcase out from under the bed. It was so light it flew across the room and banged into the wall.

What the?

I pulled the old suitcase to me and unzipped it. It was empty. Someone had unpacked my luggage. *Again.*

I glanced around the room. From my toothbrush to my underwear, everything I'd crammed into my suitcase a few hours ago was now neatly tucked back inside the closet, drawers, and atop the bureau.

Suddenly, I knew how Bill Murray felt in *Groundhog Day*. The only difference was, I knew who was pulling the strings. Now, how did I get them to stop?

"Doreen?" Kitty's voice sounded at my bedroom door, startling me. "You in there, hun?"

"Um ... yes."

"I've got something I want to show you."

"I'm kind of busy," I said.

"Well, get un-busy. Edna says it can't wait."

My knees went weak. I flopped onto the edge of the bed.

Crap! Did I already know too much?

Chapter Thirty

Kitty rapped harder on my door. "You okay in there? What's taking you so long?"

I sat on my bed and chewed my thumbnail to the quick.

Just a major panic attack, that's all.

When I'd arrived at my aunt's doorstep last week, she and Jackie had suspected me of being an assassin sent there to kill them and Sophia. Now I was worried the crafty old ladies had turned the tables on me. Had they hired Kitty Corleone to bump *me* off?

No. That's crazy.

Are you sure about that? Aunt Edna did claim to see a coffin in a potato chip...

I glanced around wildly for a weapon. Thanks to the mystery suitcase unpacker, everything I'd brought with me was within easy reach. I grabbed my cuticle scissors from atop the bureau. They'd come in handy once before. Besides, it was either them or my hairbrush. I'd watched every horror movie ever made. Not once had I ever seen anyone bite the dust from a hairbrush.

I palmed the tiny scissors, then cautiously opened the door. "Yes?"

Before I knew what hit me, Kitty grabbed my free hand and tugged me out of the room. I couldn't help but notice she had a dark leather bag in her hand. Was her hit-man gear inside?

"Come on, Doreen," Kitty said, yanking me into the hallway. "I don't have much time."

Does that mean I don't, either?

"Where are you taking me?" I squealed.

"While we're waiting for Edna to get dinner ready, she says I should give you the nickel tour of my place."

A trickle of relief worked its way into my stunted lungs. "Oh. Okay."

Kitty grinned. "That's a good girl! By the way, did you know you can kill somebody with a nickel?"

• • • •

THE FIRST THING I SAW when I entered Kitty's spare bedroom was a whole roll of red biohazard bags. They were hanging casually on a spool—as if we'd just entered the homicide section of the local grocery store.

I gasped and glanced around. On every wall, clear jars of what appeared to be dried herbs and pickled roots were lined up neatly on open, wooden shelves. Next to a stainless steel sink big enough to conduct an autopsy in, stood a Bunsen burner and an impressive collection of brown and blue glass bottles.

I hadn't seen so many test tubes since I'd flunked high school chemistry.

"What is this place?" I asked.

"My lab," Kitty said. "What did you think?"

You don't want to know.

Kitty plunked her leather bag onto the smooth, concrete countertop and grinned at me. "I guess it's time to get to work."

"Work?" I asked.

Kitty unclicked the latch on the bag. My body stiffened. I doubled down on my death grip on the cuticle scissors hidden in my hand. "What do you mean by 'work'?"

"The lemon bars," Kitty said. "It's time we got to testing them for poison. You can be my assistant."

"Oh," My tight gut let go a tiny bit. "Uh...sure."

Kitty pulled on a pair of rubber gloves. "Any time we suspect poisoning, that's when *I* kick into gear."

My nose crinkled. "Why don't you just send the lemon bars to a professional lab?"

Kitty pulled a white paper sack from the leather bag. "Poison, by its very nature, is a covert business, Doreen. Its success lies in its *anonymity*. You don't exactly send nudie pictures to get developed at Kodak, now do you?"

"No."

At least, not for the last twenty years, anyway.

Kitty cocked her head. "The authorities tend to get suspicious if you keep sending in samples, if you catch my drift."

I nodded. "I get it."

"Good." Kitty grabbed a pair of tongs from a drawer, wiped them with a cotton swab dunked in alcohol, then opened the paper sack. "Besides, those so-called professional lab tests only cover your run-of-the-mill poisons."

"Run-of-the-mill poisons?" I asked.

"Yeah. Your everyday cyanides, arsenics, heavy metals, stuff like that." She scoffed. "Amateurs."

My nose crinkled. "What other kinds of poison *are* there?"

Kitty laughed. "Tons of things."

"Like what?"

Kitty playfully snapped the tongs at my nose like a lobster claw, then used them to pluck a lemon bar from the paper sack. She carefully placed it in a sterile petri dish.

"Doreen, poison is all around you," she said carving off a small sample of lemon bar and dropping it into a test tube. "All you've gotta do is know where to look."

A knock sounded on Kitty's front door. A second later, Jackie appeared in the doorframe.

"Playing doctor again?" Jackie quipped. "F.Y.I., Edna says to let you know dinner will be ready in exactly five minutes."

"Got it," Kitty said, but Jackie was already gone.

"Okay, we better hurry, Doreen. Take a sample from each bar and put it in a separate test tube. I'll mix up the reagent."

"Does this make me a partner in crime?" I asked, only half joking.

"No." Kitty reached for one of the brown bottles. "That is, not unless you plan on stabbing me with those cuticle scissors you've got hidden in your hand."

Chapter Thirty-One

"You did good for a first-timer," Kitty said, pulling off her rubber gloves. "We should have the results from the lemon bars after dinner."

I smiled. "Thanks. Sorry about the cuticle scissors. I just—"

"No worries. I'm used to not being trusted."

"Sorry," I said again. "So, how did you get into this ... uh ... profession?"

"Natural curiosity." Kitty ushered me out of her lab and shut the door behind her. She snapped closed the padlock. "Doreen, poisons don't just come from some diabolical chemist's lab, you know."

"They don't?" I asked, following her down the hall and out into the tropical courtyard.

Kitty stood on her front porch and put her hands on her hips. "Look around you. From where I stand I can see maybe a dozen things I could poison you with."

I blanched. "Are you serious?"

"Serious as a heart attack," Jackie said, appearing out of nowhere. "Kitty here has a degree in botulism."

"*Botany*," Kitty said tiredly. "Speaking of which, you'd better go get Sophia before we end up on Botany Bay."

"I'm on it," Jackie said, and disappeared.

"Are you referring to that *Star Trek* episode where they wake up Khan and his crew and they try to hijack their ship?" I asked.

Kitty laughed. "Yes. That's the one. *Space Seed*. You a Trekkie?"

"Kind of."

"Me, too." Kitty held her hand up, then spread her fingers into the shape of a V. "Here's to living long and prospering, Doreen."

"Thanks. It'd be really nice to do both."

"You worried you won't?"

I eyed her with suspicion. "*Should* I be?"

Kitty laughed again. "Good answer. But let me tell you, kid. No matter where you go or what you do, life doesn't come with any guarantees."

I frowned. "I know that."

"Do you? Then follow me and I'll prove it."

My gut flopped again. I trailed a few steps behind Kitty as she walked down the paved path toward the center of the courtyard, where, if I survived the trip, dinner awaited us.

Suddenly, Kitty stopped. "Look, Doreen. See this cute little palm with the small, feathery-looking leaves?"

"Yeah."

"It's called a Coontie."

I smiled. "That's a cute name."

"Deceptive, isn't it? The little devil should be called *Killer* Coontie."

"Why?"

"Eat a seed pod and drop dead."

I grimaced. "Geez. I had no idea an innocent-looking plant could be so lethal."

Kitty shrugged. "Few people do. But toxic plants are everywhere. Especially here in Florida. See that tree over there with the yellow flowers hanging down like bells?"

I spotted a slim, fleshy-trunked tree about eight feet tall. A mass of yellow flowers hung face-down from its limbs like frilly-edged blow-horns. "Yeah. So?"

"That's an angel trumpet tree. Mash up the flowers to make a tea, and you can hear God calling you home." Kitty smirked. "Maybe you survive the hallucinations. Maybe you don't."

"Wow." I glanced around, wondering what else might be waiting to kill me in the courtyard. "What about this vine?"

Kitty laughed. "That's poison oak. Despite the name, it won't kill you. But touch it and you'll itch until you wish you were dead. As far as a potential homicide weapon, it's not a good candidate. But you could sure get even with somebody by rubbing it on their undershorts."

I studied Kitty's face. "Are you speaking theoretically or from experience?"

Kitty chuckled. "Like I said before, poisoning is a *covert* business." She knelt down next to a row of colorful plants lining the pathway. "See these fun little guys here?"

"Yes." I smiled at the heart-shaped leaves speckled with splotches of pink and white, as if they'd just been sprinkled with confetti. "Caladiums, right?"

Kitty's eyebrow shot up. "Very good, Doreen. But did you know they're also called Heart of Jesus?"

"No. Why?"

Kitty winked. "Nibble on a bulb and the only way you'll live through it is to be born again."

"Geez, Louise!" I shook my head. "I had no idea I was walking around in a tropical courtyard of death."

"Hmm," Kitty said, rising to her feet. "'Tropical courtyard of death.' I like that. Sounds like a euphemism for life itself."

I frowned. "What do you mean?"

Kitty locked her blue eyes with mine. "Like I said. Life doesn't come with guarantees. Never forget, kid. Everything survives by killing something else."

I grimaced. "How do you figure that?"

An insect landed on Kitty's arm. "Think about it. We're all just like this little ladybug here." Kitty's face lit up like a child's as she played with the ladybug, allowing it to crawl along the top of her index finger.

"How so?"

"Everybody's got to eat to live," she said. "And whatever you eat—animal or vegetable—has to give up its life energy for your survival."

I let out a breath. "I can't decide if that's poetic or bleak."

"It's neither," Kitty said. "It's just nature's way."

She blew on the ladybug. It flew away. "Doreen, we only exist in the tiny moment of time allotted to us by our parents. And by that, I mean Mother Nature and Father Time. While we're here, we need to make the most of it."

"By growing poisonous plants?"

Kitty stroked a bush that had long, blade-like leaves dotted with yellow. "If that's what it means to follow your heart? Then, yes. By growing poisonous plants."

"To each their own, I guess," I said. "Have you got any more felonious foliage to show me?"

Kitty laughed. "I sure do. A whole greenhouse full behind my cottage. Want to see?"

"Uh ..."

"Dinner's ready!" Aunt Edna hollered into the courtyard.

Kitty turned and winked at me. "How about right after we eat?"

I smiled weakly. "Uh ... sure thing."

Chapter Thirty-Two

Instead of eating dinner outside in the courtyard, Aunt Edna insisted that it be served promptly at four o'clock inside the confines of her drab dining room.

We took our places around her old, oak dining set. A beige vinyl tablecloth covered the table, while five dung-brown placemats marked the place settings. Atop each ugly laminated rectangle sat the most hideous melamine dinner plates I'd ever seen. Dull beige, they were rimmed in a brownish-gold hue that perfectly matched the twin wheat-stalk motif stamped onto their centers.

I'd seen L.A. homeless shelters with more ambiance.

Was everybody back in the '70s tripping on acid or something?

While I poured the tea, Aunt Edna dished out the pasta. On the wall above us, a picture of Mother Mary watched over us, her hands clasped in prayer. Beside her, wrapped in swaddling clothes, baby Jesus stared down at the linguini with envy.

"My compliments to the chef," Sophia said, eagerly swirling a forkful of pasta around the bottom of a spoon. "Edna, I do believe this is your best Alfredo yet."

"Eh," Aunt Edna shrugged nonchalantly, but the pride on her face was unmistakable.

"Absolutely delectable," Kitty said, wiping her mouth with a napkin. "I lost four pounds while I was gone. I think I'm gonna find them all again right here on this plate."

"Four pounds? Ha! That's nothing," Sophia said, a forkful of pasta poised inches from her mouth. "I think I dropped twenty in that stupid nursing home. I've got to make up for lost time."

Kitty nodded. "Speaking of nursing-home food, I heard you lost a third food taster today, Sophia. A guy named Freddy, right?"

"Men." Sophia shook her head. "You were there for the first two, Kitty. First Charlie chokes on that apple fritter, then Ernie bites it on a cheese Danish. Such weaklings. While you were gone, the goons tried to get to me with my favorite."

"Freddy was your favorite?" I asked.

Sophia eyed me as if I'd just fallen off the collard green truck. "No. *Lemon bars.*"

"So you never took a bite of the other desserts?" Jackie asked.

"Nothing doing." Sophia's shoulders broadened. "I did like Kitty told me. After giving the guys a sample, I waited to see what happened. Good thing, too. Or right now I'd be six feet under along with the rest of them."

"What did the guys say when you gave them the desserts?" Jackie asked.

"What do you think?" Sophia grumbled. "Thank you."

Kitty cleared her throat. "I think what Jackie means is, did any of them mention any symptoms or problems after eating them?"

Sophia frowned and shook her head. "Nothing that I can recall." She twirled more pasta on her fork. "Except for Freddy." She smiled. "For a small guy, he sure could pack away some food."

"What do you mean, 'Except for Freddy.'?" I asked.

Sophia shrugged. "After I gave Freddy a lemon bar, he was back in a flash for more. He went on and on about how delicious they were. He was such a pest I gave him two more just to shut him up. And then, just like that—bam!"

I gasped. "He died on the spot? But I thought—"

"No!" Sophia grumbled. "Before I could stop him, Freddy laid one on me. Right on the kisser!" She shook her head in disgust. "God knows what he would've tried if you guys didn't come get me out of there. Anyway, the next thing I hear, that jerk's dead, too."

"Gee. I'm sorry for your loss," I deadpanned.

"Loss, schmoss," Sophia said. "I think that horny toad gave me herpes!" She pulled down her lower lip to reveal a blister on her gums.

Aunt Edna let out a deep, soulful sigh. She leaned over and whispered in my ear, "Probably from her caustic tongue."

"What was that?" Sophia demanded, her green cat eyes narrowing to slits.

"I said it was probably caused by some ... uh ... caustic agent," Aunt Edna said. "Did you switch from Crest to Pepsodent again?"

"No!" Sophia scowled. "You think I'm crazy or something?" She turned to Kitty. "Pussycat, what did you find out about the toenail clippings?"

I nearly spewed my mouthful of linguine. "Toenail clippings?"

Sophia eyed me funny. "Kitty took samples from all my tasters. To test for poison. Ain't that right, Kitty?"

"Yes," she answered softly.

My nose crinkled. "Gross! Why not just get hair samples?"

Kitty sighed. "Both Charlie and Ernest were bald as billiard balls."

"Well?" Sophia demanded. "What did the lab results say while you were out having a big time on vacation?"

"I was gone *four whole days*," Kitty said.

"Excuse me?" Sophia said.

Kitty wilted. "Sorry, Queenpin. The results haven't come back yet. But if Charlie and Ernie died within hours of ingesting poison, the toxin wouldn't show up in their hair or nails anyway. For that, we'd need blood or urine for analysis."

"Don't look at me," Sophia said. "The only adult diapers *I'm* touching are my own."

Aunt Edna groaned. "Could we can it with the—"

"Anyway, it's a moot point now with those two," Kitty said. "No autopsy was conducted on either man. And Charlie and Ernie were both cremated."

"How do you know that?" I asked.

"Obits, honey," Kitty said. "There's no way to get samples from them now. But Freddy's still fresh. There's a chance we could still nab some swabs from him."

"Good thinking," Aunt Edna said. "You can do it while you're there paying the bill in the morning. Take a sneak peek in the morgue for Freddy. And while you're at it, ask around about who was working the late shift. Somebody might've let that creep with the lemon bars in after visiting hours."

"You got it, Capo," Kitty said.

Aunt Edna chewed her bottom lip. "Look, guys. We've only got a couple of days to figure this out. If somebody's trying to poison Sophia, they need to have their invitation to the party revoked."

My back stiffened.

Was that a mob euphemism for murder?

• • • •

AFTER DINNER, I CHECKED my cellphone. Still no word from Kerri. What was up with that?

While we cleared the dinner dishes and set the table for dessert, Jackie helped Sophia to the bathroom. With the Queenpin out of earshot, I had a few delicate questions I wanted to ask. I set a clean dessert plate on the table and took my shot.

"Excuse me, Kitty," I said. "I'm curious. Freddy either ate the lemon bars last night or this morning. But he didn't die until this afternoon. Is there a poison that takes hours to kill someone?"

"Sure." Kitty laid a fork beside my plate. "Poisoning someone isn't like in the movies where somebody up and dies in seconds. Most poisons take time. Only strychnine and cyanide can kill you in a flash. Well, them and the bite of a Fer de Lance."

"Fair de what?" I asked.

"A snake that lives in Central America. But that's not important right now."

"Oh."

Aunt Edna came in carrying a key lime pie. "Feast your eyes on this beauty," she said. "Homemade with love."

"Just so long as that love isn't the lethal kind," Kitty quipped. She tapped a pink fingernail on the table. "You know, Edna, the tartness of those key limes would make an excellent cover for a bitter toxin. So would that linguine sauce, come to think of it."

Aunt Edna laughed. "You got some imagination, Kitty."

She grinned. "It runs in the family."

My aunt's face turned somber. "Listen, you two. I didn't want to say this in front of Sophia, but I'm worried somebody's gonna take a shot at her before Tuesday. That's why we're eating inside tonight. I didn't want to take the risk."

Kitty nodded solemnly. "I think you're right to play it safe, Edna. This close to her centennial party, Sophia's like a sitting duck in the posies. Does this mean we're going back to overnights?"

"Yeah."

"Overnights?" I asked.

"We're all gonna have to do guard duty at Sophia's cottage overnight," my aunt explained. "To keep the wolves at bay."

"So we'll split the time into four shifts?" Kitty asked.

"No. *Three*." Aunt Edna put a hand on Kitty's shoulder. "You can't do a shift. You'll be busy analyzing those lemon bars. Dorey will take up the slack."

Kitty nodded. "You got it, Capo. Thanks, Dorey."

I grimaced. I guess my fate was sealed for the night. I couldn't exactly ditch them in their time of need, could I? Besides, what had I been thinking? All I had to do was get through tonight, then I could ask Kerri about staying with her when I saw her tomorrow for the interview at ten thirty.

That settled in my mind, I turned to Kitty. "I'm curious. Did you test the apple fritter and the Danish?"

"Nope."

My eyebrows shot up. "Why not?"

"Nothing left to test. Sophia only got one of each. She gave them both to the guys."

My jaw dropped. "If Sophia only got one apple fritter and one Danish, why didn't she just throw them away, instead of making those guys eat them?"

"Sophia never lets down her guard," Kitty said. "That's why she's managed to live for so long."

"That's an important lesson for you, Dorey," Aunt Edna said.

I frowned. "What lesson?"

Aunt Edna's eyebrow crooked. "Monkey business usually starts way before the circus tents show up."

Kitty nodded. "She's right. And if you ask me, the clowns are circling the wagons as we speak."

Chapter Thirty-Three

After dessert, Kitty left with Sophia to get her settled for the evening in her apartment. Meanwhile, Jackie and I got busy cleaning up the dinner dishes under the watchful eye of Aunt Edna. She was also sorting out the shifts for overnight guard patrol of the Queenpin's cottage.

"So, Dorey, you familiar with the undertaker's friend?" my aunt asked.

My nose crinkled. "Neil Neil? Not really. I just met him this morning."

Jackie snorted.

Aunt Edna shook her head. "Undertaker's friend is mob-speak for a *gun*, Dorey. You ever shoot one?"

I grimaced. "Uh ... no."

Aunt Edna smirked. "Oh yeah. I forgot. You prefer *knives*."

Jackie hooted. "Ha! Good one, Edna!"

I blew out a breath and shook my head. "Whatever."

"You're gonna take the amateur shift, Dorey. You're on from 3 a.m to 6 a.m. So you better get some shuteye soon."

I eyed her with suspicion. "*Amateur* shift? Is that mob-speak for the *worst* one?"

Aunt Edna grinned. "No. Not *this* time, anyway. Statistically, it's actually the *easiest* shift. Three to six in the morning are the hours when it's least likely for a violent crime to go down."

I frowned. "How do you know that?"

"When you're in the garbage business, you learn the schedule," Aunt Edna said.

"That's right," Jackie said. "And we're smack dab in the deadliest month of the year."

"June is the deadliest month?" I asked.

"Yep." Jackie grinned. "And the time you're most likely to get murderized is from midnight to three in the morning. I thought everybody knew that."

I stared at Jackie as if I'd just spotted a horn growing out of her forehead.

"She's not kidding," Aunt Edna said. "Summer is high season for homicide. The only deadlier time is December." She shot Jackie a sideways glance. "Probably because of all the relatives visiting."

I sighed. "I heard *that*."

"Anyway," Aunt Edna said, "even in the heat of summer, things cool down after three in the morning. They pick up again after sunrise. So there you go, Dorey. Three to six. The amateur shift."

I shook my head. "The things you two think are common knowledge blow my mind. I guess the next thing you're going to tell me is that Sunday's the deadliest *day*, too?"

"Ha! It sure is, kid!" Jackie said with glee.

"Unfortunately, Jackie's right." Aunt Edna's face pinched with concern. "Another reason we need to keep a tight watch over Sophia."

Jackie studied her wrist. "How can I, Edna? I haven't worn one since 1999."

I crinkled my nose. "Worn what?"

"A watch," Jackie said. "I threw mine in a dumpster on New Year's Eve. How was I supposed to know Lionel Ritchie was just kidding about 2000 being the end of time?"

Aunt Edna groaned. "Don't listen to her, Dorey. At any rate, your shift doesn't technically start until tomorrow. And Monday's the least deadly day of the week."

"Huh," I said. "I'd have thought the existential dread of having to go to work would've bumped it up at least higher than say, *Tuesday*."

"Yeah, you'd think so," Jackie said. "Poor working stiffs." She laughed at her own joke. "Stiffs. I guess all that killing on Sunday wears a homicidal maniac out. They need their rest on Monday."

Aunt Edna rolled her eyes. "Enough claptrap already. Jackie, go start your shift." She reached into a gap between the wall and the refrigerator. "Here, take Kate with you." She handed Jackie a shotgun.

"You got it, Capo." Jackie grabbed the gun and headed for the door.

"The gun's name is Kate?" I asked, slack-jawed as Jackie disappeared out the door.

"Yeah. Any more questions? Or can I go take a load off now before I have to start *my* shift?"

"Uh, sure. But could I ask just one more little question? Who keeps unpacking my suitcase?"

Aunt Edna laughed. "That would be Jackie. She's our resident ninja. You might not believe this, Dorey, but that woman can move like the wind. She's also got a photographic memory."

I shook my head. "You're right. I don't believe it. That woman is a walking malapropism."

"Excuse me?" Aunt Edna growled defensively. "You calling Jackie maladjusted?"

"No! Not at all! A malapropism is when you switch a word with one that sounds similar, but isn't right. You know. Like when she said mobsmacked instead of gobsmacked."

Aunt Edna's stern face softened. "Oh. Well, yeah. Jackie ain't too great on remembering words. But she's like one a them idiot savant people. Jackie can take one look at something and remember every single little detail."

"Like where every item in a suitcase goes?" I said sourly.

She smirked. "Exactly."

"And yet she can't seem to remember that I'm going back to L.A." I shook my head. "From the looks of it, Jackie doesn't want me going anywhere."

Aunt Edna took my hand in hers. "None of us do, Dorey. Don't you know that by now?"

An odd twinge pricked my heart. "Really?"

"Yeah, really. It'd be nice to have you around, kid."

I swallowed a lump in my throat. "Thanks."

"You're welcome. Now get your ass in bed." She swatted me on the butt with a dishtowel. "You're gonna need your sleep. Three o'clock will be here before you know it."

"Okay." I turned to go.

"Hold up a minute, you two," Kitty said, poking her head in the door. "I took a look at the lemon bar results."

"And?" Aunt Edna asked.

"There's something in them, all right. But I gotta say, this one's got me stumped. I'm gonna have to run some more tests."

Aunt Edna pursed her lips. "So Sophia wasn't making this up."

"It would appear not," Kitty said.

My aunt's broad shoulders slumped. "Be sure and tell Jackie we've got a live one, eh?"

"I will." Kitty turned to me. "Oh, here, Dorey, take this for a bedtime story." She handed me a beautiful, leather-bound journal.

"What's this?" I asked.

"My life's work. I didn't have time to give you a tour of the greenhouse tonight, so I thought I'd bring the greenhouse to you."

"Oh." I opened a page of the journal. Inside was a beautiful, hand-painted watercolor illustration of a plant. "Wow. You did this?"

"Yeah. It's a curated collection of my favorite deadly plants. It'll make good reading while you're on shift."

I flipped to another page and shook my head. "Geez. Who knew there were so many ways to die?"

Kitty grinned. "*I* did."

• • • •

I NEVER HEARD THE ALARM go off at quarter to three. Instead, I was awakened by a gentle nudge on the shoulder and the smell of fresh-brewed coffee. I opened my eyes to find Jackie standing over me, holding a white coffee cup. It seemed to glow like a lantern in the darkness.

"Rise and shine," she said softly.

I sat up with a start. "Did something happen to Sophia?"

"Nope. All's quiet on the Southern front. But if you're one second late for your shift, it won't be. Edna can get pretty vocal when she's grumpy."

"You don't have to tell *me* that." I smiled and took the coffee. "Thank goodness it's a short commute."

Jackie laughed softly. "Take my advice. Wear your pink flip-flops over to Sophia's. As a safety precaution. They're in your closet, right next to your black pumps."

"Okay," I said sleepily.

"Those things practically glow in the dark, you know. You can best bet Edna's got her eyes peeled on the walkway, and it's still pretty dark out there."

"Okay, will do. Thanks for the coffee."

"You got it, kid. Glad to have you on board."

Jackie slipped out the door and closed it behind her. I sighed, thankful for a brief moment of privacy. I took a sip from my cup. Suddenly, my eyes bulged in their sockets. The coffee was so strong and bitter it sent a jolt racing through my body.

Either that, or I'd just been done in by the CGCN.

I bolted to sitting and swung my legs over the bed. My dangling feet hit something roundish and hard on the floor beneath my feet. My mind went haywire.

Oh, lord! Is that a severed head beside my bed? Or—worse yet—the head of an assassin waiting to do me in?

My heart thumped in my chest like a kettle drum. I leapt out of bed and over the severed head. In the dim light, I raced to the light switch and flipped it on.

Then I wanted to kick myself in the ass.

The object on the floor wasn't a head—detached or otherwise. It was the round corner of my suitcase peeking out from under the bed. I'd put it there myself after scrounging my toothbrush and pajamas from it. The rest I'd left packed, waiting on Kerri's call.

As I walked over to haul my suitcase onto the bed and grab some yoga pants, I spied my favorite sweatshirt hanging on the back of the door.

What the?

I glanced over at the bureau. My hairbrush and toiletries lay on top of it, all neatly organized. My clothes were stowed away in the closet—including the pink flip-flops.

Right next to my black pumps. Just like Jackie'd said.

I shook my head.

How does she do that?

• • • •

"KEEP YOUR EYES PEELED like boiled eggs," Aunt Edna said, handing me the shotgun at the front door of Sophia's cottage at three in the morning. "I'll send Jackie over to relieve you at six. Keep your phone handy, just in case."

"Okay." I took hold of the shotgun as if it were a venomous snake. "Where's Sophia?"

"In her bedroom sawing logs. She could sleep through a hurricane. With any luck, she might just snooze right through to the end of your shift."

A sudden wave of apprehension swept through me. I'd never spent more than a few minutes alone with the Queenpin.

"What do I do if she wakes up?" I asked.

"Whatever she tells you to do. Capeesh?"

I nodded. "Capeesh."

I stared out the front window and watched Aunt Edna slowly amble along the courtyard path in the dark. I kept my eye on her until I saw the glow of her front door opening, then closing behind her. A weird mixture of relief and pride and something else I couldn't name caused my heart to feel oddly warmer in my chest.

I glanced up at the sky. Beneath a nearly full moon, huge, feathery palm leaves swayed in the amethyst sky. The moon was so bright it glinted off the glass candleholders on the picnic table in the center of the courtyard. In the warmth of the night, the tropical foliage surrounded the tiny apartment homes like a leafy hug—albeit a potentially lethal one.

I let out a long, slow breath.

Maybe Kitty was right. Life doesn't come with any guarantees. You just have to make the most of the hand you're given.

And, unlike me, these women had found a way to do just that.

Chapter Thirty-Four

Despite my fear that crazed mobsters would descend in hordes upon Sophia's cottage during my watch, except for a wayward possum that tripped a motion-activated light on the courtyard path, all remained quiet on my "amateur shift."

Until a few minutes before six, that was.

I'd been sitting by the front window, trying to stay awake by skimming through Kitty's poison journal. It was full of impressive illustrations of deadly plants, and even more impressive lethal recipes that could be made from them. All in all, the tome was what I imagined Charles Darwin would have written if he'd been a serial killer.

Annihilation of the Species.

Suddenly, I heard a strange rustling coming from behind Sophia's bedroom door. Immediately, my thoughts flashed back to Tad Longmire. I'd heard noises in his bedroom too—right before I'd found him stabbed to death!

I sprinted toward Sophia's bedroom, my heart racing faster than my feet. As I skidded to a barefoot stop in front of her door, I realized I didn't know the proper etiquette for addressing the Queenpin in such a situation.

Should I bang on her door? What if I startle the poor old woman and give her a heart attack! If she died, would I have to take over the CGCN? Holy Crap!

I put my ear to the door's cool, wooden panel. I heard the faint rustling again.

"Sophia?" I called out in a voice just a notch above a whisper. "Are you okay in there?"

The rustling sound ceased. In the silent void, I could hear my heart thumping in my ears.

"Sophia?" I said a little louder. "It's me, Doreen. Are you okay?"

No answer.

Holy crap! Someone's in there trying to murder her!

I grabbed the doorknob and tried to turn it. It was locked.

What were you going to do if it opened? Scream for them to go away? Go get Kate, you dolt!

I scrambled back to the living room and grabbed the shotgun leaning against the wall. I skittered back to the bedroom and rapped my knuckles hard on the door this time.

"Sophia? Are you awake?"

"I am *now*," I heard her grumble from behind the door. My shoulders drooped.

Oops.

"I want coffee," she said, her voice gravely from sleep. "Get me some."

"I ... I can't," I said, reeling with relief. "I can't leave you alone in the cottage."

"You ever heard of a coffee pot? I got a kitchen, you know."

I winced. "Yes, ma'am. I'm on it."

• • • •

AFTER PERKING A POT of coffee, I went back to find Sophia's bedroom door cracked open a few inches. I tapped lightly on it, then slipped inside with a cupful. Sophia was sitting up in bed.

"Good morning," I said brightly, setting the coffee on her nightstand. "Need help getting up?" I reached toward her.

"Don't touch me!" she hissed. "I can get up on my own. I'm not an invalid!"

"I know that. It's just—"

"Plump my pillows," she demanded, sitting up on her elbows. "And then hand me my coffee."

I did as she commanded. "Anything else?" I asked, leaving off an unspoken "*your majesty.*"

Sophia settled into her warm nest of cushions. "Yeah. Pull up a chair. I got something I want to say to you."

Oh, no! Did she detect my hint of sarcasm? Am I about to face the wrath of Khan?

"Uh, sure. I'll be right back."

I scurried into the living room and grabbed my cup of coffee and gulped down a mouthful. Fortified with caffeine, I dawdled slowly back to Sophia's room, feeling like a child who was about to get her butt spanked.

As I enter her bedroom, Sophia nodded, wordlessly, toward a wicker chair in the corner. I picked up the chair and strategically placed it arms-length away from the side of her bed. I wasn't going to give the crotchety old woman a chance to grab me again.

I took a moment to survey her lair. Sophia's bedroom was surprisingly small. To accommodate her full-sized bed, the other side of it had been positioned mere inches from the wall. In the middle of that wall, just above the chenille of her bedspread, was a window covered in lace curtains.

"Ahem," Sophia said, clearing her throat. She eyed me up and down.

"Yes, your Queenpin." I braced myself for a lecture about the atrocities of waking her up too soon. Or, possibly, of some other offense of which I had yet to be made aware.

"Doreen, I don't know what the others have told you about me, but I'm no liar."

Realizing this wasn't about me, I perked up like a kid being released from detention. "I know tha—"

"Don't interrupt me," she barked. "I'm not crazy, either. Charlie and Ernie were poisoned. Freddy, too. You know how I know?"

I stared into her green cat-like eyes. Uncertain whether to answer with a reply, or follow her orders to not interrupt, I settled for a small shake of my head.

"Because the same guy who brought me the apple fritter and cheese Danish also dropped off the lemon bars."

"Oh." Shocked, I asked, "Do the others know this?"

"Not yet. I want you to tell them."

"Why me?"

"Because I got my pride," she said. "I know they just stuck me in that old folks' home so they could have a break from me."

I winced. "You don't miss much, do you?"

"Ha!" Sophia said, sitting up straight in her bed. "So I'm right!"

Crap. I've just been outwitted by a lady in a Jiffy Pop turban. Some detective I am.

• • • •

"SO THAT'S WHY I DIDN'T try a lemon bar, even though they're my favorite," Sophia said and drained her coffee cup. "I knew it was the same guy."

She shook her head and sighed. "Back in the good old days, the bad guys wore normal hats. Take my advice, kid. Never trust a guy in a hoodie. You can't get a good look at him. What's he trying to hide?"

"Do you think you could make out the delivery guy in a lineup?"

Sophia scoffed. "Who are you? Joe Friday? I just told you I couldn't see his face."

I flinched, recalling Aunt Edna's warning right before I met Sophia for the first time at Shady Respite. *Don't ask stupid questions.*

Too late. But then again, maybe Aunt Edna didn't ask *enough* questions. I dared another.

"There's got to be some other way to identify the guy. Did he walk funny? Have any kind of nervous ticks or something?"

Sophia frowned. "No. But he *did* act all haughty-like."

Haughty like? In a hoodie?

"What do you mean?" I asked.

"You know. All fancy-schmancy. Like he was too good for the likes of me."

"Anything else?"

Sophia's brow furrowed. "Now that I think about it, I could see his chin poking out of the hoodie. It had a cleft. And like I said, the jerk sounded all hoity-toity when he spoke."

I blanched. "He *spoke*? What did he say?"

Sophia's nose crinkled as if she'd just smelled a skunk. "The creep stuck his nose in the air and said, 'I hope you enjoy these sweet treats M' Lady, compliments of the Mansion Neil.'"

"You mean Neil Mansion?" I asked.

"That's what I said," she grumbled.

My mind flashed back to Neil Neil at the funeral home. Of all the people I'd met to date, he was by far the most pretentious of the lot. But his handsome chin definitely didn't have a cleft. I tried to recall details of the picture of him with his husband. Had his partner's chin been cleft?

"Hmm," I said. "What about—"

All of a sudden, the bushes outside the window above Sophia's bed began to quiver. I leapt out of the chair. In the moonlight, I caught a glimpse of a ghostly hand reaching toward the glass.

"Duck, Sophia!" I yelled.

"What?"

Instinctively, I grabbed the shotgun and leapt into bed on top of the old Queenpin.

"What the hell!" she yelled, squirming underneath me.

"Hush!" I leaned across Sophia and took a tentative peek between the lace curtains.

I was right. Somebody *was* out there.

And whoever it was had a knife.

Chapter Thirty-Five

So much for this being the "amateur shift."

Just before my watch guarding the Queenpin was about to be over, I spotted someone in the bushes right outside her bedroom window. And they had a blade in their hand.

I was so freaked out I'd jumped in the bed with Sophia.

"Quick! Get under the bed!" I whispered.

"With you on top of me?" Sophia grumbled. "How am I supposed to do that, genius?"

I rolled off of her. "This is no time for jokes. I'm serious. There's an assassin out there with a knife!"

"Look again," Sophia said, reaching for her turban on the nightstand. "Is this 'assassin' of yours wearing pink?"

"What?"

I pulled back the lace curtain a crack and took a cautious peek, hoping not to get stabbed between the eyes. The hitman was indeed wearing pink.

The tension in my gut went limp. "How'd you know?"

"Because that's Kitty. She's on morgue patrol."

I blanched. "Morgue patrol?"

I flung the curtains open wide. Sure enough, there stood Kitty, a huge pair of garden shears in her hand. I felt like a complete fool.

"Who died?" I asked, rolling over and practically spooning Sophia.

"Nobody. *Yet*." Sophia pushed me away. "Unless this is purgatory and nobody told me."

Geez. Stuck with Sophia through eternity? I'd rather go back to Ma in Snohomish. I think ...

"So, what's morgue patrol?" I asked.

Sophia shrugged. "Every morning I don't wake up dead, I open the curtains a little to let the crew know I'm still alive. Kitty likes to peek in and wave." Sophia shook her head. "She's one of those annoying morning people."

I glanced back out the window. As if on cue, Kitty waved. Like an idiot, I waved back. Kitty turned away and started clipping the leaves on a bush.

"What's she doing out there messing around in the dark?" I asked.

"Checking on her plants. They're the same as people to her. Now do me a favor, kid."

"Sure. What?"

"Get out of my bed!"

"Oh. Yes, ma'am."

I scooted down the side of the bed against the wall, using the shotgun like an oar. As I reached the foot of the bed, I heard the front door to the cottage open. I sprung up off the mattress and scrambled to cock the shotgun.

"Shift's over!" Aunt Edna hollered, her voice echoing down the hallway. "It's quarter to six. Breakfast will be on the table in fifteen minutes!"

I nearly melted from relief. I relaxed my finger on the trigger and stood there, heart racing, feeling like a fool for the third time in under two minutes.

Behind me, I heard the mattress creak. I turned to see Sophia crawling out of bed in her turban and a flannel nightgown I'd swear I once saw on an episode of *Gunsmoke*. After planting both feet on the floor, she grinned up at me. I braced myself, expecting her to bust my chops again.

"Well aren't you a little miss Quick-Draw McGraw," she said, patting me on the shoulder as she passed by. "Good thing I was already done with my coffee."

As she took a few steps down the hallway, I heard her say, "Thanks, kid."

I nearly dropped the shotgun in my hands.
Had I actually done something *right* for a change?

Chapter Thirty-Six

Thanks to Aunt Edna, in less than two weeks I'd become as food-motivated as a lab rat. Like Pavlov's dogs, just the sound of my aunt's voice yelling, "Food's ready!" caused my mouth to salivate.

After hearing breakfast would be ready in fifteen minutes, I'd rushed back over to Aunt Edna's and taken a quick shower, trying not to drool from the aroma of cinnamon buns baking in the oven. I pulled on a sundress, put my hair in a ponytail, and headed for the kitchen.

"Can I do anything to help?" I called through the door.

"Go get Sophia," Aunt Edna called back. "We're eating in the courtyard."

"I'm on it!" I dashed out the door.

After my little talk with Sophia, I was no longer filled with trepidation. That is, I wasn't until I spotted someone leaving Sophia's apartment and running out the back gate.

He was wearing a hoodie.

I nearly swallowed my own tonsils.

Oh my God! The poisoner is back!

I ran toward the frail old Queenpin's cottage and onto the porch. I flung open the door, expecting to find Sophia lying dead on the floor, some kind of pastry shoved halfway down her throat. What I found instead surprised me even more.

The old lady was humming to herself as she poured a takeout Starbucks coffee into a ceramic mug.

"Ack!" she hissed as I barged in. "Close the door!"

"What?" I gasped. "Why?"

The queen of the CGCN glared up at me. "One word of this to Edna and you're a dead woman. Got it?"

I cringed. "But ... I don't—"

"Ah!" Sophia said after taking a sip from the steaming cup. "Now *that's* a real cup of joe."

"Don't drink that!" I yelped. "It could be poisoned!"

Sophia chuckled, then looked me up and down. "Hardly. What can I say? When I was at Shady Respite, I got hooked on Starbucks."

My mouth fell open. "What?"

Sophia took another sip. "Don't get me wrong, kid. When it comes to pasta, your aunt is Michelangelo with a spoon. But her coffee is the pure devil's handiwork. Even worse than yours. Now, promise on your mother's grave you won't say a word about this."

"But my mother's not dead. She's in Alaska."

The Queenpin stared at me for a second. Then the old woman burst out laughing so hard she sloshed her Starbucks coffee onto the floor.

••••

IF ANYTHING COULD HELP calm my nerves after two false murder attempts, it was cinnamon rolls, bacon, and scrambled eggs. This perfect trifecta of breakfast foods was what awaited us in the courtyard. Starving after a morning full of adrenaline rushes, not even the ugly wheat-patterned melamine dishes could dull my appetite.

"Good morning. *Again*," I said to Kitty as I led Sophia to her seat at the head of the table.

"Good morning," she said, setting a centerpiece bouquet on the table.

The blooms were simple, five-petal flowers of canary yellow with pink centers. Even over the aroma of Aunt Edna's breakfast feast, I could smell their heavenly fragrance—as sweet and buttery as raw sugar-cookie dough.

"What are those?" I asked.

"Plumeria Apocynaceae," Kitty said. "Also known as Frangipani, or Hawaiian lei flower."

"Kitty knows everything about plants," Jackie said, pulling up a chair.

Kitty smiled, then glanced to her right and waved. I followed her gaze and spotted an old woman waving back from a second-story window across the back alley.

"Don't encourage her, Kitty," Aunt Edna grumbled. "That busybody is worse than Mrs. Kravitz on steroids. Sit down, already. So we can eat. Any luck with the lemon bars?"

"A little," Kitty said, shifting the seat cushion on her chair. "I found something unusual in a couple of the samples. But we can definitely rule out arsenic or cyanide."

"How?" I asked.

Kitty shot me a grin. "Either one of those two and Freddy would've dropped dead practically where he was standing."

"Well, we know *that* didn't happen," Aunt Edna said, her eyes darting to Sophia as she jabbed a fork into her scrambled eggs.

"Kitty, what happened to your hand?" I asked, noticing a Band-Aid on her right index finger. "Cut it with the pruning shears?"

"No." Kitty stared at it absently. "I must've brushed it up against my Bunsen burner."

"Oh." I thought back to dissecting frogs in high school science class, then wished I hadn't. "That reminds me, I'd still like to see your greenhouse."

"That's gonna have to wait," Aunt Edna said, unrolling a chunk of cinnamon bun. "After breakfast, I need you two to go to Shady Respite and pay up before they send the bill collectors out on us."

"Yeah," Jackie said, shooting us a wink. "We don't want them coming out and repossessing Sophia, now do we?"

Aunt Edna pursed her lips and muttered, "If only."

"No problem," Kitty said. "Well, *one* problem. How are we going to pay the bill?"

"This ought to cover it," Sophia said. She reached into the bosom of her thin, cotton dress and pulled out a roll of bills big enough to choke an elephant.

I gasped. "Holy Moses! Where'd that come—"

But I didn't get to finish. The dire looks on the faces of the other ladies caused my voice to dry up in my throat.

As usual, there was a lot more going on around me than I had any clue about. In fact, these ladies were virtually swimming in their own secrets.

The only thing I knew for sure was, wherever that money had come from, it sure wasn't Sophia's change back from buying Starbucks.

Chapter Thirty-Seven

On the way to Shady Respite to collect Sophia's things and pay the bill, Kitty filled me in on yet another thing I had no clue about—the Queenpin's subtle reign of terror over the other residents while she'd been at the convalescent center.

Kitty shook her head and laughed. "I'm sure everyone in there was glad to see her go."

"I can only imagine," I said, steering the old Kia down Fourth Street.

"Sophia had a whole harem of men doing her bidding in there." Kitty cracked her gum. "I don't know how she does it, but Sophia can make a man eat shredded cardboard if she wants."

"Or poisoned lemon bars," I deadpanned.

"Exactly." Kitty studied her pink fingernails. "Don't let her fool you. Sophia can't see squat without her bifocals, but her tongue is still as sharp as Occam's razor. It has to be some kind of miracle for her to have made it this long, right?"

"That and Aunt Edna's food."

"Oh, yeah." Kitty patted her stomach. "There's nothing like it. I'm gonna miss it when I die and have to eat whatever crap they serve in Heaven."

I laughed, then caught myself. "I feel sorry for those poor guys who died being her food tasters."

"Charlie and Ernest? Don't feel too bad about them. At their age, good food was one of the last pleasures left in life."

My brow furrowed. "What do you mean?"

"Listen. If all you had to look forward to was a steady diet of lumpy porridge and mushy green peas, I bet you'd be ready to cash it all in for a good cheese Danish, too."

Geez. In a way, I kind of already am. Is that what happens when you turn forty and have nothing left to live for?"

"I guess," I said. "But that hardly seems charitable."

"Don't judge. You weren't there." Kitty frowned. "Charlie was always hungry. Poor guy wandered the halls looking for scraps."

I blanched. "He did not!"

"Wanna bet? When Sophia told Charlie about the apple fritter, he was at her door before she hung up the phone." Kitty shook her head. "Anyway, the plan was to only give him one bite. But before I knew it, he'd wolfed the whole thing down while I clipped his toenails."

"Gross!"

"You're telling me! Gluttony is one of the seven deadly sins, you know."

"I mean about the toenails." I cringed, fighting back the urge to retch. "You said at dinner last night they wouldn't show evidence of poisoning. So why did you ... ugh ... *clip* them?"

Kitty blew out a breath. "Sophia's orders. Believe me, it wasn't my idea."

"Sophia's orders?"

"Yeah. Sometimes you have to take one for the team, kid." She looked out the window. "Sophia had this great idea for me give her 'boy-toy tasters' pedicures while they ate. It was a ruse she thought up so I could watch for symptoms. I have to say, her idea was both diabolically clever and absolutely disgusting at the same time."

"You aren't kidding." I swallowed the bile rising in my throat. "I suffer psychological trauma every time I even *think* about ADT."

Kitty's head cocked to one side. "You got issues with home security systems?"

"No. ADT is my code for Arthur Dreacher's Toenails."

"Huh?"

I shivered with disgust. "Long story. Just suffice it to say that 'toenails' has become a trigger word for me."

"Ah." Kitty laughed. "Well, take it from me. Trigger words are a hell of a lot better than having a *real* trigger pointed at you, that's for sure."

• • • •

AS WE APPROACHED THE front desk at Shady Respite, I began to wonder how Kitty had ended up with the CGCN. Dressed in soft pink from head to toe, she seemed more intellectual and introverted than the others. Mild-mannered and meek didn't seem like attributes that would be highly sought after by the mafia. But then again, what did I know?

I followed behind Kitty as she walked up to the receptionist's window. She smiled like a pink cherub at the haggard woman sifting through papers at her desk.

"Good morning!" Kitty cooed. "I'd like to speak with Dr. Mancini, please."

The receptionist peered up at her through her bifocals. "You have an appointment?"

"No, honey. I'm afraid I don't."

The woman at the desk turned her attention back to the stack of papers on her desk. "Sorry, but the doctor is only available by appointment."

"Oh, dear," Kitty said sweetly. "It's kind of urgent."

The receptionist blew out a tired breath. "It always is. Which patient is this regarding?"

"Mr. Freddy Sanderling."

The woman's tired face grew pinched. "Are you a relative?"

"Why, no, ma'am," Kitty said softly. "My, what a lovely necklace you have on!"

"Look lady. You want to speak with Dr. Mancini, you're going to need an appointment."

"No. *You* look, sweetheart," Kitty said, still smiling sweetly. "I'm here to see the doctor. Then I'm going to pay the bill for Sophia Lorenzo's stay. In that order. *And in that order only.* Got it?"

The woman's brow furrowed in anger. She stuck her nose up. "Like I said—"

"Listen, honey," Kitty said sweetly. "You work hard for a living. Don't make the job even harder on yourself."

"What are you talking about?" the woman asked.

"This." Kitty pulled Sophia's wad of cash from her purse and laid it gently on the counter in front of the hole in the Plexiglas window. "Do you really want to have to explain to your boss why you turned away a customer and their twenty grand in cash?"

The woman gulped. She shook her head.

"Oh, you don't want it?" Kitty asked, snatching up the money. "Okay, have it your way, Miss. Good luck with the unemployment paperwork."

Kitty turned on her heels to face me and shot me a devious wink. "Come on, Doreen. We did our best to avoid the impending catastrophe. It's in God's hands now."

"Wait!" the woman cried out, leaping up from her desk. "Let me make a quick call."

"Oh, that'd be swell," Kitty said, beaming from ear to ear. "You're an angel!"

I watched in awe as the receptionist jabbed digits on her landline phone. If she really had been an angel, she sure as heck didn't play the harp. Her true talent appeared to be grinding glass to dust with her teeth.

I exchanged glances with Kitty. Not only was this odd woman in pink a botanist and potioneer. She was also the smoothest talker I'd come across since my date with Lenny Hobovitz back in 1999.

The receptionist hung up the phone. "Dr. Mancini is on his way," she said. "Now, hand over the cash. I mean, pay your bill."

"Not so fast," Kitty said. "Doctor first. Cash second."
I smiled, amused with my new friend's style and poise. *Whoa! Miss Kitty's got claws.*

Chapter Thirty-Eight

After dodging two assaults from umbrellas and acorns, hijacking a mob Godmother in a getaway wheelchair, and now participating in soft-core extortion with a mob moll in pink, I really didn't think Shady Respite could possibly hold any more surprises for me.

Boy, was I wrong.

While Kitty and I stood waiting at the reception area for Dr. Mancini to arrive, a tall, thin woman in jeans and a t-shirt walked up to the window. Something about her made me do a double take.

Lying across her shoulders beneath her short, bleach-blonde hair was a huge, gray-green lizard. The languid reptile sat there motionless, draped around her neck like the world's most hideous neck shawl.

"Hi, Melanie," the receptionist said. "And who have you got for us today?"

"My old pal Iggy," she said, petting the lizard's head. "Where do you want us?"

"They're all waiting for you in the rec center."

"Okay, then." Melanie turned her head and spoke to the lizard. "We better get to it, hon."

"Uh, excuse me," I said, rolling my tongue back into my mouth. "What's up with the lizard?"

"Iggy's not a lizard," Melanie said. "He's an iguana. From Guatemala. Wanna pet him?"

"Ick. I mean ... no thanks. Why is he ... you know, *here*?"

Melanie laughed. "He's a therapy animal."

Kitty's nose crinkled. "I thought therapy animals were supposed to be cute and fuzzy."

"That's pet discrimination," Melanie said. "A social issue I'm trying to change. Here, have one of my flyers." She reached into her purse and handed me a yellow slip of paper. Across the top was a headline that read, *Dander Danger*.

"Dander danger?" I asked.

"Yeah. It's a real thing. A lot of folks are allergic to dander. Makes them choke and wheeze. Iggy is furless, so he doesn't cause a reaction."

"Right," I said.

Unless you're allergic to freaking ugly giant lizards.

"Can you believe people actually eat these poor little things?" Melanie asked, stroking the horny fringes on the iguana's head.

"No." I watched Iggy's pink tongue flick in and out of his mouth. "I absolutely can't believe it."

"Oh. Here comes Dr. Mancini," Kitty said, grabbing my arm.

"I gotta go," Melanie said. "Come to the rec room if you want to see Iggy in action."

I smiled weakly. "Sure thing."

What's he gonna do? Barf up a beetle?

• • • •

"I APPRECIATE YOUR CONCERN, Ms. Corleone," Dr. Mancini said in a tone that implied the exact opposite.

The skinny, fastidious physician had whisked us into his office after spotting the hoagie-roll-sized wad of cash poking out of Kitty's purse. Having just seen my colleague work her magic with the receptionist, I decided to hang back and let Kitty do the talking.

"Why thank you, doctor," Kitty said sweetly. "You see, I'm worried about what happened to Freddy Sanderling. He was a good friend of my mother's."

"Uh-huh." The doctor studied her from behind his thick glasses. "Well, I believe your concerns are totally unfounded. Unfortunately, elderly gentlemen choking to death is a rather common occurrence. Mr. Sanderling is just the latest statistic."

Kitty shot him a look of doe-eyed concern. "What did his autopsy say?"

"That's none of your .... Ahem, that's *confidential*. Besides, I saw no need to conduct one. I've already ruled Frederick Sanderling's death as due to natural causes."

One of Kitty's claws came out. "What *kind* of natural causes?"

"Mr. Sanderling was eighty-four," Dr. Mancini said dismissively. "He was underweight and frail. It's my belief his heart stopped due to complications exacerbated by aspiration."

"Huh. That wouldn't be the first time aspiration killed somebody, would it?" Kitty said, wagging her eyebrows.

"Good one," Dr. Mancini said without a trace of amusement. "Mr. Sanderling swallowed improperly chewed food that then lodged in his throat and blocked his airway."

"What was the food?"

"Nothing we served here at Shady Respite, of that you can be assured," Dr. Mancini said indignantly. "We don't allow our patients to eat sugar-laden foods. Mr. Sanderling choked on contraband goods. Macerated lemon bars, I believe."

"Oh," Kitty said as innocently as *Betty Boop*. "Why do you believe it was lemon bars?"

"Because Mr. Sanderling told me so himself." Dr. Mancini's face drew pinched. "He even offered me one, but I refused." He patted his flat stomach. "What kind of example would that have set?"

My eyebrow arched.

I dunno. A human *one?*

"So you had the chance to save him from eating contraband food, but you didn't," Kitty said.

Meeoow!

"I ..." Dr. Mancini fumbled.

"Don't worry about it," Kitty said, smiling up at him. "So, did Freddy complain about the taste of the lemon bars?"

Sweat began to trickle down Dr. Mancini's right temple. "No. Not that I recall. Wait." He stuck his chin in the air. "I remember Mr. Sanderling saying they were delicious. The best he'd ever had."

"And that's when he choked to death on your watch?" Kitty asked sweetly.

How many claws did that make now? I've lost count.

"No!" Dr. Mancini gulped. "Mr. Sanderling returned to his room to take a nap. Unfortunately, he never woke up."

"How tragic." Kitty tutted and shook her head. "What a comfort it will be for my mother to know this. Thank you, Dr. Mancini."

He eyed her dubiously. "Uh … you're welcome."

"So," Kitty said. "Where is dear Freddy now?"

Dr. Mancini appeared confused. "Um…heaven or hell, I suppose. I'm a doctor, not a judge."

"I meant his *body*." Kitty shot him a brilliant smile.

Dr. Mancini's eyebrow rose an inch. "I assume it's still in the morgue downstairs. He's slated for pickup and cremation today. Thankfully, Mr. Sanderling had made his pre-arrangements with the Neil Mansion."

"You don't say," I said to Kitty.

"Well, thank you so very much for your precious time," Kitty said, shaking Dr. Mancini's hand. She thrust the wad of cash into his palms. "We'll be going now." She patted his hand. "Just mail us a receipt, hon. I trust you."

Kitty spun on her heels. I tagged along after her, leaving Dr. Mancini standing in the corridor with his mouth hanging open.

"Where are we going?" I asked, trotting up to her side.

"Where do you think?" she whispered out of the side of her mouth. "To the morgue."

"What? Without the doctor?"

"That old tomcat has a new toy to keep him occupied. So now the mice can play."

"But why not just ask—"

"The good doctor?" Kitty scoffed. "You saw that pretentious jerk. He'd never let me in there to see Freddy. So why bother asking and arousing suspicion?"

I grimaced. "But ... how will we get in?"

"Don't you worry about that." She patted her purse. "I've got the key right here."

Chapter Thirty-Nine

As it turned out, the key to the morgue wasn't made of metal, but paper.

"You've got five minutes," the orderly said, counting out the bills in his hands. "Follow me."

"A couple a Ben Franklins can open a lot of doors," Kitty said, shooting me a wink.

The orderly led us into a room so cold it made Jackie's glaucoma sunglasses fog up instantly. I didn't dare take them off and give the guy a look at my wonky eye. He'd probably think I was a zombie. So I stood back and watched through the hazy lenses as the morgue attendant wheeled out a long, narrow table covered in a white sheet.

He pulled back a cloth. "This the one?"

Kitty glanced over at me. "Well?"

"I'm not sure," I said. "It's hard to see."

"Then get over here and take a closer look," Kitty said.

I stepped up to the corpse and stared at the lifeless body of Freddy Sanderling. "Yes. That's him."

"Okay," the orderly said. "I'm going on smoke break. When I get back, you two are gone. Correct?"

"Absolutely," Kitty said.

"Geez. Now what?" I asked, watching the orderly slip out of the room.

"I check for poisoning symptoms and *you* clip his toenails."

"What!" I nearly screeched.

Kitty laughed. "Just kidding. You really *do* have toenail PTSD."

I cringed. "Please stop saying *toenails* and I'll do whatever you want."

Kitty grinned and tutted. "How easy the young ones cave."

She picked up Freddy's arm and let it drop. "Good. No rigor mortis. That makes it easier."

I grimaced. "Easier to *what*?"

"Steal his wallet." Kitty shook her head at me. "What do you think? Get the samples!"

"Oh. Right."

"Okay, now. Doreen, you hold his mouth open while I put a penlight down his throat."

I suddenly felt woozy. "Uh ... can I retract my last statement and clip his toenails instead?"

"Quit grumbling or you'll do *both*." Kitty whipped out two pairs of rubber gloves from her purse. "Here. Put these on first."

"Thank you," I said, truly meaning it. I quickly donned the gloves, swallowed a retch, winced until my eyes were almost shut, then pried open Freddy's mouth. The unexpected smoothness made my eyes open a notch.

"Geez!" I said, startled. "All his teeth are gone!"

Kitty shrugged. "Eh. They usually recycle the spare parts off a cremee. Take my advice. Don't buy your dentures at a thrift store."

The hair on the back of my neck stood up. "Are you serious?"

"Yeah, but that's not important right now."

"Huh?"

Kitty leaned over Freddy's body and aimed the small flashlight in her gloved hands at his head. "Hold his mouth open as wide as you can. I'm going in."

A shiver went down my spine as Kitty shoved the penlight down Freddy's throat and leaned in for a look. Any closer and her right eyeball would've been inside his mouth.

"Huh. Would you look at that," she said.

"What is it?" I asked, not wanting to know.

"See those blisters on his tonsils?"

"Err...no."

"Get closer."

I winced. "Do I have to?"

"Grow up, Doreen. You want to be in the Family, you gotta learn the biz."

"I never said I wanted—"

"Look, hun," Kitty said, shooting me a look. "The clock's ticking. I don't have time for a philosophical discussion about your life right now. Just be a good do-bee and stick your face in there and get a good look, okay?"

I held my breath, sucked up some courage, and did as I was told. In retrospect, I probably shouldn't have closed my eyes as well. As I leaned over his body, I accidently bumped noses with Freddy's corpse.

"Arrgh!" I squealed, and lurched back in revulsion.

"Did you see the blisters?" Kitty asked.

"Uh ... yeah," I lied. "I absolutely, most certainly did."

Kitty nodded and chewed her lip. "I figure they had to be caused by some kind of caustic agent."

My nose crinkled. "You mean like battery acid?"

Kitty laughed. "You watch too many mafia movies, Doreen. Life ain't like the movies. I'd say it was more likely Draino. Or a rodenticide."

"A *what*?"

"Rat poison."

"Oh." I slapped my sunglasses back on. "But wouldn't Freddy have tasted it? The doctor said he told him the lemon bars tasted good."

Kitty shrugged. "Like I said before, lemon is a strong flavor. Good for masking unpleasant tastes." Kitty took another look down Freddy's throat and grunted.

"What now?" I asked.

"There's nothing blocking his windpipe. Freddy couldn't have aspirated."

"Maybe they cleared his throat up during the examination."

Kitty pursed her lips. "Maybe. But only if they shoved a garden hose down his throat."

I cringed at the imagery. "Are we done here?"

"Almost. Open wide one more time, Freddy." Kitty shot me a look. "By that, I mean *you*, Doreen."

"Oh."

I grimaced and pulled Freddy's jaws apart again. Kitty pulled out a pack of cotton swabs on foot-long stems.

"Okie dokie, now," she said. "Just gonna get some nice little samples of his throat skin, and some of that juice inside those blisters."

Bile boiled up in my throat. "Fine. But could you do it *without the commentary*, please? And hurry!"

"Sure thing." Kitty laughed. "I forgot this is your first time."

Despite trying not to watch, my eyes kept returning to Kitty and her grisly task. I saw her place six different cotton swabs into six separate plastic tubes.

"I think we're done here," she said, peeling off her rubber gloves. "That's two of our three chores completed. Now all we've got to do is ask around about who worked the late shift for the last two nights."

"Thank God," I said, tossing my gloves into the hazardous waste bin. "Let's get out of here before that creepy orderly comes back."

"Aww, he wasn't that bad. You should see the guys working down at the city morgue. Talk about *Invasion of the Body Snatchers*."

My eyebrows met my hairline.

What the?

• • • •

AFTER LEAVING THE MORGUE, Kitty and I crossed the hall and rode the elevator up to the second floor. The doors opened right across from the entrance to the cafeteria.

I blanched.

Geez. Maybe Sophia's right. Maybe this place really does *have a conveyor belt directly from the cafeteria to the morgue. Or at least a dumb waiter ...*

"Why are we going to the lunch room?" I asked Kitty. "I, for one, have absolutely *no* appetite right now."

Kitty laughed. "You're a riot, Doreen. I just want to check on what they served in the cafeteria the last couple of days. See if those blisters might be from food allergies."

"Oh." I glanced around the cafeteria at the old folks busily gumming their plates of ground hamburger steak, instant mashed potatoes, and broccoli cooked to a slimy green mush.

"I think we can rule out a reaction to seafood," I said. "They probably only serve shrimp and lobster on Tuesdays."

"Heh, heh," Kitty giggled. But then her lip snarled as an old man walked by with his tray. She leaned over and whispered in my ear, "You're right, Doreen. From the looks of the food they're serving, allergic reaction is a long shot. I bet they don't let a peanut within fifty miles of this place."

Suddenly, a loud shriek rang out from across the cafeteria. "Murderer!" a woman yelled.

My eyes darted to across the room and landed on the sour face of Gloria Martinelli. The old woman jumped to her feet and begin waving a purple umbrella at me menacingly.

"Oh, crap," I said. "Not *her* again."

"I'm gonna get you, Killigan!" Gloria screamed, causing the old man next to her to spit out a chunk of watermelon.

"Whoa," Kitty said. "What'd you do to Gloria Martinelli?"

"You *know* her?"

"You catch on quick," Kitty quipped. "So, what happened between you two?"

I shook my head and took a step toward the door. "Long story. Now, can we just get the hell out of here? Please?"

Kitty grinned. "You got it, killer."

Chapter Forty

"And that's why that crazy old lady thinks I'm a murderer," I said as I steered the Kia down Fourth Street.

Kitty laughed. "Because Gloria saw you stab a guy on a TV show? Ha! What a hoot!" She shook her head. "What's this world coming to, when people can't tell fact from fiction anymore?"

"I blame reality TV."

"Yeah, I can see where that crap could blur the lines. Especially if you're already skating on thin ice. Mentally, that is."

"What a misnomer. Reality TV is about as far from reality as it gets." I grimaced. "At least, I *hope* it is."

Kitty shot me a knowing look. "You and me *both*, kid."

I pulled up to a traffic light and turned to Kitty. "So how do you know Gloria Martinelli, anyway?"

Kitty shrugged. "She and Sophia used to be good friends when they were young. Not many people who remember are still alive, but as a teenager, Gloria had her heart set on marrying Harvey Lorenzo."

"Sophia's husband?"

"Not at the time, but yeah. But, too bad for Gloria. Harvey met Sophia and ditched her like a cold cannelloni."

"That explains a lot." I hit the gas. "But that was like—a gazillion years ago. You'd think the two would've kissed and made up by now."

Kitty laughed. "You really *don't* know anything about the mafia, do you?"

"Not much," I admitted. "But I feel like I've been taking a crash course the past few weeks."

"I bet."

"Hey. I've got another question for you. How could it be that Dr. Mancini never noticed the blisters in Freddy's throat?"

Kitty stared out the windshield. "Could be any number of reasons. Laziness. Oversight. Or maybe he saw them, but didn't think they were relevant."

"Are you saying you think he's incompetent?"

Kitty shrugged. "Not exactly. But I wouldn't rule it out. They guy's up to his knees in sick, ornery old people every day of his life. Maybe to him, Freddy was just a frail old man whose time was up. Aspirating on food was as good a cause of death as any. I bet ruling it natural causes saved him a lot of paperwork."

My eyebrows inched together. "That's diabolical!"

"Don't throw the doctor in the slammer just yet," Kitty said.

"Why not?"

"Just going out on a limb here, Dorey. But maybe he's actually right and Freddy really did just choke to death on a plain old lemon bar."

My brow furrowed. "I don't buy it."

Kitty sighed. "Me neither. Just trying to be objective."

"Come on. You said yourself you detected something strange in the bars when you tested them last night. That has to mean foul play, right?"

"Not until we know for sure what it is. Right before breakfast, I set up some secondary tests in my lab. I'm hoping they'll tell us more when we get back."

"Good."

Kitty drummed her pink fingernails on the door panel just below the window. "In the meantime, let's do a quick review of the facts. The doc said Freddy ate the lemon bars and told him they tasted good. Then Freddy went to his room, laid down, went to sleep, and died sometime during the night."

"That sounds about right."

"Yeah. Too bad it's wrong."

"What do you mean?"

Kitty blew out a breath. "That story doesn't pan out with the evidence."

"Why not?"

Kitty pulled up a picture on her phone and shoved it in my face. "With all those blisters?"

"Gross!" I yelped, and pushed the phone away.

"No way. Freddy's throat would've felt like it was on fire. Who could sleep through that?"

"Maybe he had help nodding off," I said.

"Like somebody suffocated him?"

"Uh ... I was thinking more along the lines of Freddy complaining and a nurse giving him a sleeping pill."

"Oh." Kitty chewed her bottom lip and nodded. "That could work. Good thinking, Dorey."

"Thanks." I pulled up to another traffic light. "So, where to now?"

"A drugstore." Kitty held up a half-gallon baggie containing the tubes of sampling swabs. "I'm fresh out of drug-testing kits."

I glanced at her quizzically. "But you have your own testing lab."

"That's right. But for *poisons*, not drugs. Why bother with all that hocus-pocus when, for fifty bucks, I can buy a drug-screening panel that tests for over a dozen legal and illicit drugs in one fell swoop?"

"So you think some kind of *drug* caused those blisters in Freddy's throat?"

"Maybe. Maybe not. What you said earlier got me thinking. You may be onto something, kid."

"On to what?"

Kitty wagged her eyebrows. "Maybe somebody not only helped Freddy die—they also made his death a little easier to swallow."

• • • •

I WAITED IN THE CAR while Kitty went in the drugstore. I needed time to think, and to check my phone. Somehow, it had gotten switched off. I turned it back on, and was excited to see a text message from Kerri Middleton. After reading it, however, I wasn't so excited.

Where are you? It's nearly 10:30.

"What?" I said aloud.

Suddenly, I felt the color drain from me. In all the confusion over the past few days, I'd forgotten today was Monday. And, according to my phone, it was now 10:45.

"Oh, crap!" I yelled.

I scrambled to dial Kerri's number, my fingers trembling on the keypad. It rang once. Twice. Three times.

Come on, pick up!

After the fourth ring, it went to voicemail. I groaned.

I can't believe my own stupidity! There goes my best chance at an acting career.

Desperate, I sent Kerri a text.

> *I'm so sorry! I had a few family matters come up. Set up another meeting anytime, anywhere, and I'll be there. I promise! And I'll take the part, whatever it is.*

I pressed *Send*, then drummed my nails on the steering wheel and stared at my phone display. Nothing.

As I obsessed about whether I'd ever hear back from Kerri, a movement outside the Kia made me look up. Kitty had come waltzing out of the drugstore swinging a plastic bag and grinning, like a kid who'd just scored a bag full of candy. For her, life looked as rosy as the outfit she had on.

As for me? Not so much.

Chapter Forty-One

"There you two are," Jackie said as Kitty and I pulled up in front of Palm Court Cottages. "I was about to send out a search party. I thought you might've gotten jacked, carrying around all that loot, you know."

"No," Kitty said. "Everything was smooth sailing. We just had to stop at two different drug stores before I found one with the test kits I needed. Who knew drug testing was getting so popular?"

Smooth sailing? Popular? I wish I could say the same about my *life. At this point, I'd settle simply for not going down the drain.*

I shook my head.

Geez. I just met a damned lizard *with a better job in the entertainment industry than I have. What's wrong with me?*

"Well, I better get to my lab," Kitty said, waving her drugstore bag.

"Uh, can I go with you?" I asked. "I kind of want to see how it all works."

Plus, I suddenly find myself in need of a new career.

Kitty beamed. "Sure, kid. Maybe I can teach you a thing or two."

"Lunch is ready!" Aunt Edna bellowed from the courtyard.

"It's eleven already?" Kitty shot me a wink. "How about right after we eat?"

I sighed. "Sure thing."

As I followed Kitty and Jackie toward the courtyard, my phone buzzed. It was text from Kerri.

Tomorrow. 10 a.m. sharp. No excuses!

My knees nearly buckled as relief washed through me. Maybe I wouldn't be outdone by a lizard after all.

• • • •

IN THE COURTYARD. AUNT Edna was busy putting lunch on the table. At her feet, Benny, Jackie's ancient pug, was begging for scraps.

"So, everything all settled at Shady Respite?" Aunt Edna asked as she doled out heaping helpings of fragrant mushroom risotto, along with a side of steaming collard greens.

I was salivating before the food even hit my plate. So was Benny. Either that, or she always had drool hanging out of the corners of her mouth. The threadbare little pooch hobbled along with every step my aunt took, an eternally hopeful glimmer shining in her big, bulging eyes.

"All done," Kitty said. "I paid Sophia's bill in full. They're sending a receipt."

"Good. We'll need it for taxes," Aunt Edna said, then chuckled and almost tripped over Benny. "And the Freddy business?"

"Done, too," I said, not wanting Kitty to get started with any gory details and ruin my appetite. "We're running tests right after lunch."

"What about my *things*?" Sophia asked. "Where are my cherished belongings you were supposed to pick up?"

I glanced over at Kitty and winced. "Crap. We'll have to go back."

Sophia shook her head. "I swear, Kitty. You'd forget your head if it wasn't attached."

"Hey, remember that time she did?" Jackie said.

"Geez, not with the pumpkin head again," Kitty said. She turned to me. "My colleagues at the lab I used to work for gave me a retirement-slash-Halloween party. I went as Ichabod Crane, but I forgot to bring the pumpkin head. I come home later and find these three had murderized it and stuck it under my bedsheets for a joke." She looked at the other women. "Ha ha."

A round of laughter emanated from Jackie, Sophia, and Aunt Edna. After a moment, Kitty shrugged and joined in. "Hey. Nobody's perfect. At least *I* had a *real* career."

"What's that supposed to mean?" Jackie asked.

Kitty smirked and wagged her eyebrows at me. "Oh. Excuse me. Ms. Jackie Cooperelli over there majored in 'cocktail waitress' at a Biloxi casino," she said, air-quoting the term with her fingers.

"*Head* cocktail waitress," Jackie corrected.

Aunt Edna laughed. "Hey, Dorey. You know how you can tell who the head waitress is?"

I shook my head. "Uh ... no."

Aunt Edna snorted. "She's the one with the dirty knees."

Raucous laughter filled the courtyard. Jackie laughed along with us. "Hey, a girl does what she can to make a living. No shame in earning money the hard way."

"Just exactly how *hard* was it?" Kitty quipped.

Sophia chuckled, then took a bite of her risotto. "Hey. Speaking of too hot to handle. Edna, you were a little heavy with the pepper today."

Aunt Edna took a bite of risotto and frowned. I tried it as well. Sophia was right. It was a bit spicy, but still delectable in my book.

"My apologies," Aunt Edna said unapologetically.

Sophia raised a hand to her throat and dramatically downed half a glass of iced tea. I braced myself for more deprecating banter, but Sophia set her glass down and chewed the corner of her mouth as if in deep thought.

"What's wrong?" Aunt Edna asked. "You need a Tums or something?"

"No." Sophia frowned. "I just remembered something about when I gave Freddy those lemon bars. He came back for more, saying they went down sweet, and that he liked the peppery aftertaste."

"The lemon bars that came from the Neil Mansion?" Jackie asked.

"No," Sophia said. "The ones that came from the moon. Isn't that where people who wear hoodies come from? The moon? And speak in British accents?"

Jackie shrugged. "How should I know? I ain't never been there."

"Wait a minute," I said. "The guy in the hoodie spoke with a British accent?"

"Yeah," Sophia said. "I thought I told you that."

"No. You said the guy spoke all hoity-toity."

Sophia shrugged. "What's the difference?"

I opened my mouth to answer, but thought better of it. "You know, when I talked to Neil Neil at the funeral home, he sounded kind of haughty. Do you think it could've been him?"

"Maybe," Sophia said. "What's Neil's voice sound like?"

"Medium, I guess. Kind of nasally pitch."

Sophia shook her head. "This guy's voice was deep. Gravelly, even. He sounded like that snooty butler on *Downton Abbey*."

"What do you mean?" Kitty asked.

"Like when he said m'lady," Sophia said. "And instead of saying the lemon bars were compliments of the Neil Mansion, he said it like the Brits—*the Mansion Neil*."

Kitty choked on her iced tea. "The Mansion Neil? Are you sure that's what he said?"

"I may be old, but I've still got my marbles," Sophia grumbled.

Kitty shook her head. "This makes total sense now."

"What are you talking about?" Aunt Edna asked.

"The lemon bars were poisoned, all right." Kitty said, "And they didn't come from the Neil Mansion or the Mansion Neil. I'd bet dollars to donuts that whoever sent them laced the bars with poison from the *Manchineel* tree!"

I nearly dropped the forkful of risotto poised at my lips. "What are you talking about?"

Kitty gasped. "Nobody take another bite! The risotto could be poisoned!"

"No way," Aunt Edna said. "Not on my watch!" She hung her head. "Okay, already. So I might've accidently dropped the pepper container into the—"

"Thank the lord!" Kitty said, holding a hand to her heart.

Aunt Edna scowled. "You don't gotta be so dramatic about a little extra pepper, Kitty."

"You don't understand." Kitty rose to her feet. "The Manchineel has a peppery taste. It's one of the deadliest plants in the world. If you ingest too much of it, you're a goner. Even standing under one in the rain can cause your skin to blister."

"Geez!" I pushed my plate away.

"What makes you think this Manchineel plant is to blame?" Aunt Edna asked.

"Because of the symptoms," Kitty said. "Upon first eating the fruit, it tastes sweet. Kind of like a plum. Then the toxic juice turns peppery in your mouth. A few minutes later, it burns like drain cleaner down your throat."

My mouth fell open. "That sounds like what happened to Freddy!"

"Exactly," Kitty said. "I'll run some tests in my lab, but I'm quite certain that's what killed him."

"Hold up," Sophia said. "So you're saying this blister on my lip isn't from Freddy giving me herpes?"

Kitty's eyes made half a roll. "Probably not."

"But how would somebody get ahold of a Manchineel plant?" I asked.

"Actually, they're native to Florida," Kitty said.

Aunt Edna shook her head. "I've lived here my whole life. How come I never heard of it before?"

"Probably because they're really rare. And they're not of much commercial value," Kitty explained.

"Commercial value?" I asked.

Kitty shrugged. "They're homely to look at, and they're really hard to grow. The Manchineel needs tropical conditions to thrive. Nowadays, they're only found in a handful of places down south, where their natural habitat hasn't been destroyed."

"I dunno," Aunt Edna said. "This whole thing seems like a longshot to me. You said this plant is nothing to look at. And you gotta go traipsing through the jungle to find it. It doesn't add up. Why bother? Besides, who would even know about it besides a plant nut like you?"

"Yeah," Jackie said. "How would some average Joe lay his hands on a machine eel around here?"

Kitty winced. "Uh ... I have one in my greenhouse."

"Geez Louise!" I gasped. "Should we call the cops and tell them about it?"

"No need," a man's voice sounded behind us.

I turned to see a familiar face staring at us from behind the mirrored lenses of a pair of aviator sunglasses.

I closed my eyes in disbelief.

Oh, dear God. Not again.

Chapter Forty-Two

"McNutsack," Aunt Edna muttered under her breath.

"What are *you* doing here?" I asked.

Sergeant McNulty, the man who'd accused me of stabbing my old boss Tad Longmire to death, eyed me with a familiar suspicion. It'd been less than a week since I'd been cleared of charges in that case. As he stood there in the courtyard staring at us, I could almost hear him opening another file on me in the computer of his mind.

"I'm responding to an anonymous tip," McNulty said. He folded his arms across his chest and scowled. I sensed his dark brown eyes noting every detail, even from behind the mirrored lenses of his sunglasses.

"Anonymous tip?" I asked.

"Yes." He unfolded his arms. "Someone reported that seniors were being murdered at Shady Respite, and that the person behind the killings was hiding out at this address."

"That's preposterous," Aunt Edna scoffed.

"Is it?" McNulty's eyes scanned each of us seated at the table. "From what I just overheard, the potential murderer and murder weapon are still on the premises."

"What are you talking about?" Aunt Edna growled.

McNulty turned his attention to Kitty. "What's your name?"

"Uh ... Kitty Corleone."

"Well, Ms. Corleone, I think it's time I had a look inside that greenhouse full of poisonous plants I heard you talking about."

• • • •

"OFFICER MCNULTY, I'M a trained botanist," Kitty explained as she led him toward the greenhouse behind her cottage. Aunt Edna and I followed closely behind, leaving Jackie in the courtyard to watch over Sophia.

"Is that so?" McNulty said. "I'll be sure and make a note of it."

"What I mean is, I'm a *responsible scientist*," Kitty said. "I keep all my specimens under lock and key."

As if to prove her point, Kitty stopped in front of the greenhouse and pointed to an impressive looking padlock still hanging on the entry door. "See?"

"Unlock it," McNulty said.

Kitty reached for the padlock. It fell apart in her hands. "Oh my word!" she exclaimed.

McNulty stepped forward and examined the metal pieces that had fallen onto the concrete paver path. The heavy duty lock had been cut clean through.

"I ... I secured the greenhouse before I left for my trip," Kitty stuttered. "I swear I did."

"Well, from the looks of it, someone *un*secured it," McNulty said.

He pushed on the door. As it slowly creaked open, a steamy blast of ultra-humid air walloped us like an ocean wave.

"I don't see any footprints inside," he said, turning to Kitty. "Shall we go in?"

"Yes, sir."

We all took a step toward the greenhouse. "Not you two," McNulty said to me and Aunt Edna. "Stay outside. But don't go anywhere." He turned back to Kitty. "Okay, Ms. Scientist. Which one is the machine eel?"

"Manchineel," Kitty said. "If you have a hard time pronouncing it, you can call it by its common name. Beach apple."

"Do you take me for some kind of simpleton?" McNulty asked.

"No sir!" Kitty said.

He shot her a sour look. "So which one is it?"

"That one." Kitty pointed to a small tree over in the back right corner.

I peered inside the eight-by-twelve greenhouse, craning for a look. Beyond the tables crammed with pots of herbs and orchids stood a small, scraggly looking tree with oval, yellowish-green leaves. If Charlie Brown was to ever have a tree named after him, this one would be it.

"That pathetic-looking thing is a deadly Manchineel?" McNulty asked.

"Yes." Kitty winced. "It may not look like much, but the *Hippomane mancinella* is considered to be the most toxic tree on Earth. If you don't believe me, check the *Guinness Book of World Records*."

"I'll take your word for it." McNulty eyed the tree. "Does it appear to have been tampered with?"

Kitty studied the tree for a moment, then her jaw went slack. "Oh. My. Word."

"What is it?" McNulty asked.

"The tree was full of ripening fruit when I left on my trip. Now they're all gone!"

"I see," McNulty said. "Well isn't *that* interesting. Now, just who do you think would break into your greenhouse and take nothing except the fruit from an obscure tree nobody but you has ever heard of?"

"Could rats have eaten the fruit?" I called out from the doorframe, trying to be helpful.

"No." Kitty scanned the ground around the base of the tree. "At most, they would've nibbled one, died, and left the others."

"From what I hear, rats aren't good with bolt cutters, either," McNulty said sourly.

Kitty stared at the tree, then shook her head. "There were eleven fruits on it when I left. Now they're all gone."

"Eleven?" McNulty's eyes focused like lasers on Kitty. "That seems peculiarly precise. Did you have *plans* for these fruits, Ms. Corleone?"

"Uh ... not particularly. I just like to keep an accurate inventory."

"Why bother with an inventory unless you had plans?" McNulty asked. He shook his head. "I don't understand why you'd have such a deadly plant in your possession for no purpose whatsoever."

"For curiosity, I guess," Kitty said. "I love plants. Like I said. I'm a botanist. Or, I used to be."

"Humph." McNulty reached toward the tree.

"No!" Kitty cried out, swatting his hand away. "It's not just the fruit that's deadly. The sap is, too. Just touching the leaves or branches can inflame your skin. Even blister it."

"Is that so?" McNulty eyed Kitty carefully. "Well, then. Let me have a look at your hands."

"Whose hands?" I asked.

McNulty turned to face me. "All three of you."

My nose crinkled. "What for?"

"Don't play dumb, Diller." McNulty turned back to Kitty. "You said it yourself. You believe this plant was used to murder someone. If that's true, I need to know who handled it. Now show me your hands."

"But—" I started to object.

"Or should I come back with a warrant and charge you all with conspiracy to commit murder?"

I wilted. "No, sir."

Aunt Edna held up her hands like she was about to be arrested. McNulty gave them a cursory scan. "You're clean."

"See?" Kitty said. "We're not—"

"Not so fast." McNulty grabbed Kitty's right hand and held it up. "What have we here?"

I gulped. I already knew what he'd found. A blister on her index finger. The burn Kitty told us she'd gotten from her Bunsen burner.

Crap.

It wasn't looking good for Kitty. I hung my head for her. As I did, I caught a glimpse of my own hands. The skin between my right index finger and middle finger had turned red. And rising up from the inflamed area was the pale, circular, unmistakable form of ... a blister.

You've got to be kidding me.

Chapter Forty-Three

Something was desperately wrong with my life.

Instead of being recognized as a fancy VIP customer at fine dining establishments and posh day spas, I'd just been clocked as a repeat offender at the police station—by none other than Shirley Saurwein, ruthless busybody reporter for the *Beach Gazette*.

"Back again so soon?" she cackled, cracking gum between her bright-red lips. She looked me up and down as McNulty herded me across the lobby. "Oh, wait," she called out. "Don't tell me. Another fashion crime?"

As Saurwein's hideous laughter echoed off the industrial-green walls of the police station lobby, I knew what awaited me—and it wasn't a gourmet meal or an aromatherapy massage.

Not even close.

Soon, I'd be sitting in a small, stark room with no windows, feeling like a mongrel mutt at a kill shelter. Geez. At least this time I had litter mates. McNulty had hauled in everyone who had blisters on their fingers. That included Kitty, me, and, oddly, Jackie Cooperelli as well.

"Okay, ladies," McNulty said as we took positions around a metal table in a windowless room that might've once been a storage closet. "After seeing the Manchineel tree myself, I'm of a mind to believe it would take a trained botanist to even *identify* the plant, much less be aware of its deadly potential."

The cop's eyes narrowed in on Kitty. "And you just happen to be one. Isn't that correct Ms. Corleone?"

Kitty swallowed hard. "Yes."

McNulty's eyes narrowed even further on the petite woman in pink. "And you just happen to have all the symptoms of Manchineel poisoning on the tip of your tongue *and* your fingers. My, my. That seems like quite the coincidence."

"It's not like that," I said, coming to Kitty's defense. "We were just discussing different kinds of poisons over lunch."

McNulty's eyebrows rose a notch. His attention diverted to me. "And why would *poison* be a topic of lunchtime conversation?"

I grimaced. "Because we've been trying to figure out if someone tried to poison Sophia while she was at Shady Respite."

"Sophia?" McNulty said. "Does she have a last name?"

"Lorenzo," Kitty said.

McNulty eyed us with suspicion. "I'm investigating the deaths of Charles McDaniels, Ernest Jones, and Fred Sanderling. What's this Sophia Lorenzo woman got to do with it?"

"Uh …," Kitty fumbled. "Freddy was a friend of hers while she was at Shady Respite."

"That's right," I said, nodding perhaps a bit too eagerly.

"And her taste-tester, too," Jackie added, causing Kitty and me to wilt.

McNulty's left eyebrow arched into a triangle. "Taste-tester?"

"Yeah," Jackie said. "You see, Sophia's our Quee—"

"Quickly about to turn a hundred years old," Kitty blurted over Jackie. "On Tuesday. That's why we've been … uh … diligently trying to make sure she … *stays healthy*. We didn't want her to get food poisoning while she was in Shady Respite recovering from a fractured hip."

McNulty's eyes shifted between us. "I don't follow."

Kitty shot him a beaming smile. "It's kind of silly, you see. While Sophia was there, someone kept delivering sweets to her. She's pre-diabetic. So she gave the treats away to her friends there. She jokingly called them her taste-testers."

"Uh-huh," McNulty grunted. "And now the taste-tester named Freddy Sanderling is dead."

"And Charlie and Ernie, too," Jackie said, nodding cheerfully.

McNulty's eyes grew wide. "Are you saying *all three* men who died were Mrs. Lorenzo's taste-testers?"

I grimaced.

We are now.

Kitty cocked her head innocently. "Gee. I guess so, now that you mention it."

McNulty frowned. "Apparently *somebody* had to." He glared at each of us in turn. "But sugar intake alone doesn't usually kill someone."

"I know, right?" Jackie said. "That's why we think they were poisoned."

"Poisoned," McNulty repeated. "By the fruit of a Manchineel tree."

"Yes." Kitty's jawline tensed. "But there's no way to prove it in the case of Charlie and Ernie. They've both been cremated."

"Another convenient fact you strangely seem to know all about." McNulty crossed his arms and glared at Kitty. "I'm advising you that anything you say from here on out can be used against you."

Kitty blanched. "Are we under arrest?"

"No. Not yet." McNulty uncrossed his arms. "But what you've told me so far has done nothing to exonerate you and *everything* to incriminate you."

"We're just trying to be helpful," I said. "We want to catch who did this just like you do."

McNulty shot me a dubious look. "If that's true, then I need you all to be completely honest with me. Now, before anyone says another word, let me remind you that lying to a police officer is tantamount to perjury."

"Yes sir," the three of us said.

"Okay, then." McNulty turned to Kitty. "You said handling any part of the Manchineel causes skin irritation, correct?"

Kitty nodded. "Yes."

"Then explain to me how the three of you came to have blisters on your fingers."

"I must've gotten mine handling the poisoned lemon bars," Kitty explained. "There must've been a hole in my rubber gloves."

"So you admit to making the lemon bars?" McNulty asked.

Kitty's eyes grew wide. "No! I ..."

"I gave her the bars," I said. "I got them from Sophia's room at Shady Respite. Kitty was just testing them in her ...uh—"

"I was preparing samples to send away for testing," Kitty said, picking up where I'd trailed off. "That's when I got the hole in my glove."

"Right." McNulty turned to Jackie. "And you, Ms. Cooperelli?"

"I didn't use no gloves when I handled them," Jackie said.

Kitty gasped. "You handled them?"

Jackie smiled sheepishly. "I couldn't help myself. I reached into the bag and squeezed one before I gave them to you."

Kitty shook her head. "Why?"

Jackie shrugged. "I dunno. I'm Italian. I guess I just wanted to see if they were as moist as the ones my mama used to make."

McNulty blew out a breath and shook his head. "Enough already." He turned to me. "And you, Ms. Diller? How did *your* fingers come to be blistered?"

I grimaced and glanced at the small pustules forming on the red skin between my fingers. Had I gotten contaminated while prying open Freddy's jaws in the morgue? If so, how the heck was I going to explain *that*? Talk about incriminating myself!

"Uh ... I have no idea," I said.

"I see." McNulty scribbled on his notepad. I could tell by the gleam in his eye that whatever he wrote down was most definitely *not* in my favor.

He looked up from his notepad. "So let me get this straight. Your 'friend' Sophia Lorenzo was at Shady Respite recovering from a fractured hip. While she was there, three men designated as her 'taste testers' died, while she remained in good health."

Kitty nodded. "That's right."

"That doesn't make sense," McNulty said. "Why would you all take it upon yourselves to investigate the cause of three strangers' deaths?"

"To find out if somebody's trying to bump off Sophia," Jackie blurted. "And then figure out who the dirty bird is."

"That's why I was testing the lemon bars for poison," Kitty said, pressing her shoe down softly on my foot. "You know, with *one of those kits you can get at the drugstore.*"

"I see," McNulty said. "And?"

"The initial results were inconclusive. But now that I know what to look for, I can run a test specifically for Manchineel poisoning."

McNulty's eyes narrowed on Kitty. "And exactly how are you—"

"Uh, I'm sorry, but I really need to pee," Kitty said. "My bladder isn't what it used to be. If I don't go soon, it could get ugly in here."

McNulty grimaced. "Go ahead."

"Uh, mister officer?" Jackie said, raising her hand. "Me, too."

He blew out a breath. "Fine. Go."

I got up to join them.

"Not so fast," McNulty said. "I have a couple of questions for you."

I gulped and watched the two women disappear out the door. "What kind of questions?"

He shook his head as if in disbelief. "Like, who are these people? And how in the world did you get tangled up in a mess like this again?"

Because the Universe hates me?

"I was staying at my Aunt Edna's place while we sorted out the Tad Longmire case," I said. "Sophia and these two women are just little old ladies who live in my aunt's apartment complex."

"What's their relationship with Ms. Lorenzo?" McNulty asked.

"Friends. They all are. Just a bunch of unrelated women taking care of each other. You know, like the *Golden Girls*."

"I don't recall an episode where the *Golden Girls* poisoned people."

"Well, that's exactly my point. They didn't. I'm pretty sure of it. I honestly think it had to be somebody not in the Family."

"The *Family*?" McNulty's eyes locked like lasers on mine.

Crap!

"You know, the little family unit they cobbled together."

McNulty studied me. "I see. Why should I believe you, Diller? Your fingers are just as blistered as theirs."

"Why shouldn't you? I proved I was innocent of Tad's murder, didn't I?"

McNulty shrugged. "Yes, I suppose so. But—"

"So, can *I* go use the john now?"

"Yes. But hurry up."

• • • •

I SCURRIED TO THE LADIES room to confer with Kitty and Jackie on what our next move was. But when I burst through the door, nobody was there.

"Hello?" I called out. My voice echoed off the empty stalls.

Have I just been ditched and left holding a bag of poison beach apples?

I slunk back out to the lobby. It was empty, too, except for Shirley Saurwein. Through the glass exit door, I saw a flash of green go by. I ran over and flung the door open—just in time to see Jackie's Kia speeding off down the road.

My heart sank.

So much for Family loyalty.

"What's the matter, Diller?" Saurwein said. "You look like you just lost your best friend."

I scratched the itchy red blisters welling up on my hand.

Even worse. I just lost my only alibi.

Chapter Forty-Four

I slunk back to the ladies room and sat in a stall for as long as I could, waiting for the huge lump in my throat to go down. I'd just been hung out to dry by the Collard Green Cosa Nostra.

Bamboozled by a bunch of old ladies.

What an idiot I am!

Wait a minute. If they plan on throwing me under the bus, why not beat them to the punch?

After all, Kitty was a more likely suspect than me. I could tell McNulty about her secret lab. And how I'd seen her messing around in the courtyard early this morning. What had she really been doing there? She never let me into her greenhouse. She could've been in there taking those beach apples herself—to cover her tracks!

I stood up and reached for the stall handle, then had a change of heart.

If I turned her in, I'll be a rat just like Humpty Bogart.

I thought back to that day in the bakery, and recalled the disgust on the faces of Aunt Edna and Jackie when he'd come through the door. Was that what I wanted for my future?

I heard the main door to the bathroom open.

"Hey, Diller," McNulty called out. "You die in there or something?"

"Uh ... no. Just constipated."

"Well, hurry it up!"

"I will," I said. Then I flushed the rest of my self-esteem away and resigned myself to my fate.

• • • •

AFTER STALLING ANOTHER ten minutes in the bathroom, I gave up and poked my head back inside McNulty's interrogation room.

"It's about time," he said, glancing at his watch. "Where are the others?"

"Uh ... I'm afraid—"

The doorknob to the interrogation room jiggled. Kitty came bursting in.

I nearly gasped as my heart fluttered back to life.

"Sorry I'm late," Kitty said. "Jackie crapped her pants. I had to take her home so she could—"

"Spare us the details," McNulty said. "Is she here?"

"No. I took a taxi back. I don't drive."

"Right," McNulty said sourly. "You should be glad I didn't send some officers out to apprehend you."

"Your officers are the ones who should be glad," Kitty said. "If they'd seen Jackie's backside they'd have been scarred for life. Worst case of diarrhea I've ever seen. I gave her some—"

McNulty cringed. "Like I said, spare us the details. *Please.*"

"Of course," Kitty cooed. "Anyway, good news! When we got home, I found out the lab results on the lemon bars had arrived."

"Really." McNulty's face pinched with suspicion. "Show me the report."

"Sure thing. I got it right here." Kitty began digging around in her giant purse. "According to the lab, the test came back positive for Eserine."

"Eserine?" McNulty said. "I've never heard of it."

"Neither had I," Kitty said, still rifling through her huge purse. "I had to Google search it. Come to find out, there's only two naturally-occurring sources of Eserine. The Calabar bean, and the fruit of the Manchineel tree."

"Interesting," McNulty said.

"Sure is." Kitty looked up from her purse and shot me a surreptitious wink.

"What about this Calabar bean option?" McNulty asked.

"Unlikely," Kitty said. "It only grows in West Africa."

McNulty's hard face softened a notch. "And you believe Eserine is the poison used in the lemon bars."

"I *know* it," Kitty said. "Based on the test results. It's a done deal. The Manchineel is to blame."

"It's not the Manchineel that's to blame," McNulty said. "It's whoever used it to poison the victims with."

"Yes, sir," Kitty said. "That's what I meant."

I glanced at the fiery red blisters swelling up on my hand. They were really itching now. "Uh ... Kitty? We're not gonna die from touching it, are we?"

Kitty shook her head. "No. You need a pretty hefty *internal* dose for Manchineel poisoning for it to be deadly. We'll be fine with a little topical steroid cream. But elderly people like Freddy and Sophia most likely wouldn't survive a major ingestion."

McNulty cleared his throat. "Ms. Corleone, you seem to know an awful lot about the Manchineel."

"Nothing you can't find on an internet search."

"Fair enough," McNulty said. "You told us the symptoms of Manchineel poisoning are a sweet taste, followed by peppery, then by blistering of the throat."

"That's exactly right," Kitty said. "You're a great listener!"

"Uh-huh. So tell me, how did you know Freddy Sanderling's throat was blistered?"

"Uh ... lucky guess?" Kitty said, barely missing a beat. "It's a natural progression of the—"

"We went to the morgue at Shady Respite and examined his body," I said.

McNulty's shoulders straightened. "So I shouldn't be surprised to find your DNA on his body, then. That makes for quite a convenient excuse, now doesn't it?"

"Seriously?" My jaw tightened. "We're trying to be *helpful* here, and all you're doing is trying to trip us up, like we're guilty already. Well, how's *this* for convenient? How *convenient* is it that you should get an *anonymous* tip about us being murderers?"

"Well," McNulty said. "I can't—"

I crossed my arms. "I bet it was from an old lady, right?"

McNulty's eyes widened a notch. He sat up straight. "Like I said, it was anonym—"

"And I bet her name was Gloria."

McNulty's eyebrows rose an inch. "How could you possibly know that?"

"Gloria Martinelli is a patient at Shady Respite." I blew out a breath. "The woman is nuts. She saw me on that stupid TV show where I stabbed Tad Longmire." I shook my head. "She keeps calling me a murderer every time I go over there."

"So you admit you've been to Shady Respite numerous times," McNulty said.

The saddle on my high horse slipped. I grimaced. "Uh ... yes."

"We *all* have," Kitty said, patting me on the shoulder. "To visit Sophia."

I stuck my chin in the air. "That's right. Visiting the sick isn't a crime, is it?"

"No," McNulty said. "But only *one* of you has been suspected of murder *twice* in the last two weeks." He turned his laser glare toward me. "Since you arrived in town, Ms. Diller, people seem to be dropping like flies."

"What?" I shrunk back. "Why in the world would I want to kill some old guys at a nursing home?"

"And *I* might ask why you'd want to sneak into a nursing home morgue?" McNulty fired back. "To relive the thrill of killing your victims?"

"What? Gross!" Anger boiled up inside me. "Look. I wasn't even *in town* when the other two guys died."

"That's right!" Kitty said.

McNulty leaned forward. "So, Diller, your accomplices killed the first two men, providing you with an alibi. Then you returned the favor."

"Dream on!" I hissed. "That's insane!"

"She's telling the truth," Kitty said. "Doreen only went to the morgue because I asked her to accompany me."

McNulty's eagle-eyed glare shifted to Kitty. "If you had suspicions about Mr. Sanderling's death, why take the matter into your own hands? Why didn't you simply check with the attending physician?"

"I *did*," Kitty said. "His name is Dr. Mancini. When I asked him about how Mr. Sanderling died, the guy didn't seem concerned about foul play in the slightest. I might add that it was Dr. Mancini who ruled all three men's deaths to be from natural causes."

"People die of natural causes all the time," McNulty said. "Why didn't you take his word for it?"

"Maybe the first two I could chalk up to what you said, that people, you know, kick off from natural causes all the time." Kitty shook her head. "But when the third guy, Freddy died, I couldn't just sweep it under the rug."

McNulty frowned. "So you went and looked under the sheets instead."

Kitty nodded solemnly. "In a manner of speaking, yes. It may have been unorthodox, I'll give you that. But what we did proved that Freddy Sanderling was murdered. And, if you ask me, Dr. Mancini is either negligent or incompetent."

"Or complicit," McNulty said.

"Yes, or that, too."

McNulty rubbed his chin and stared at the table for a moment. When he glanced up at us again, the accusatory look in his eyes had faded a bit. "What did the coroner's report say? I assume you got your hands on a copy of that, too?"

"No," Kitty said. "Dr. Mancini didn't order an autopsy."

McNulty nearly blanched. "No?"

Kitty shook her head. "Look. Whether the doctor is in on the deaths or not, I don't exactly have the authority to demand an autopsy on Mr. Sanderling. But *you* do."

"Believe it or not, we're on the same side as you," I said to McNulty. "We want to know who killed Freddy and the other two men just as badly as you do."

"Okay. Fair enough," McNulty said. "But I'll need more facts before I upset Sanderling's family with the news he may have been murdered."

"An autopsy would give you those facts," Kitty said.

McNulty nodded. "Agreed."

"Then you better hurry," I said. "Because Dr. Mancini is having Freddy's body shipped to Neil Mansion today for cremation. Probably as we speak."

McNulty's eyebrow angled. "How do you know that?"

"He told us so himself," Kitty said. "A couple of hours ago. Right before we examined Freddy's body."

"Without his permission, I assume?" McNulty said.

"He would never have given it," Kitty said. "What choice did I have?"

"Wait here." McNulty jumped to his feet. "I need to make a phone call."

Chapter Forty-Five

"It's too late," McNulty said, returning to the interrogation room. "Sanderling's body is already being cremated."

"Talk about *convenient*," I quipped. "That Neil Mansion crew sure didn't waste any time."

"You think the funeral home might be in on it?" McNulty asked.

"I don't know." I frowned. "But it makes me wonder. Why would they be in such a hurry to get rid of the body?"

McNulty sighed. "It's summer. In Florida. Do the math."

I did. And it added up to *gross*!

"Do any of you own a pair of bolt cutters?" McNulty asked.

"No." Kitty shot me a smirk. "But Doreen told me she used a pair to clip a guy's toenails back in L.A."

I shook my head. "Why do you ask?"

McNulty formed a temple with his fingers. "Someone would've needed a pair to cut through the padlock on the greenhouse."

I blanched. "Are you really back to focusing on *us* again?"

McNulty closed his eyes for a moment. "Okay. Let's put a pin in that for a moment."

"Yeah, let's," I grumbled.

"You seem to have done a lot of homework on this case already," McNulty said. "What other facts or evidence have you ladies ... ahem ... *assembled*?"

"These." Kitty reached into her purse and pulled out a baggie with the tubes containing the long-stemmed cotton swabs. "I used these to take samples from Freddy's throat this morning."

McNulty took the baggie, then frowned at its contents. "We can't use them."

"Why not?" Kitty asked.

"Because the chain of evidence collection can't be confirmed," he said. "The samples could've come from anywhere. You could have altered them." He shook his head. "If you'd called the police instead of taking matters into your own hands—"

"We wouldn't have any samples at all," I said.

"Maybe," McNulty admitted. "What else have you got?"

I glanced at Kitty. "I know! Sophia's description of the guy who delivered the lemon bars to her room at Shady Respite."

"That's right," Kitty said. "Sophia told us the man wore a hoodie and spoke in a gravelly, English accent."

"Not great, but it's something to go on," McNulty said.

"Maybe, maybe not," I argued. "Anybody can fake an English accent." I straightened my shoulders, lowered my voice, and gave it a try. "Well blimey, fancy a pint at the pub?"

McNulty shook his head. "You know that's not helping your case, don't you?"

I cringed.

"Okay," McNulty said. "Let's say Freddy Sanderling was poisoned, possibly even accidently while serving as Sophia Lorenzo's taste-tester. What I want to know now is why someone would want to kill an old woman with a fractured hip in the first place?"

I gulped.

Uh ... because she's a mafia Queenpin?

Before I could think of an answer, Kitty stepped up to the plate.

"Have you ever met Sophia?" she asked. "As they say, to know her is to loathe her."

McNulty smiled cruelly. "Okay, then. We're finally getting somewhere."

"What do you mean?" Kitty asked.

"You just supplied me with your motive to poison her."

• • • •

AFTER DELIVERING HIS bombshell, McNulty left the interrogation room and locked the door behind him.

"Geez, Kitty," I said. "If loose lips sink ships, Jackie would be the lead singer on the Titanic. She practically told him about the Family and everything! Why would she do that?"

"What can I say? Jackie's brain is wired different from the rest of us."

"You mean that whole photographic memory thing?"

"Well, yes, partly. But there's more to it than that. Jackie is ... sort of incapable of abstract thought."

"What do you mean?"

"She can't bend reality to suit her own perceptions, like the rest of us. That's what gives Jackie her clear sight, I think." She let out a sigh. "It also means she can't lie. Depending on the situation, that can be her biggest strength *or* her biggest weakness."

I blew out a breath. "You aren't kidding."

Kitty shook her head. "You saw for yourself, you definitely don't want Jackie in an interrogation room, even if she's on your side. That's why I begged off and took her back home—that, and to get the test sample results."

"So you weren't just making up the Eserine results?"

"No. Why would you think so?"

"You never gave McNulty anything to substantiate the results."

Kitty smiled. "You noticed."

"Yes."

"*And* you kept your mouth shut." Kitty grinned and patted me on the back. "You know what, Doreen? You just might contain a little bit of the best of all of us."

"Really?" I glanced at the growing red patch on my hand. "I finally do something right, and now I'm going to die."

Kitty laughed. "What are you talking about?"

"My hand. I somehow got poisoned when I pried open Freddy's mouth."

"Let me see that." Kitty grabbed my hand. "You didn't happen to touch that poison ivy I showed you in the garden, did you?"

I grimaced. "Uh ... maybe."

"Uh-huh," Kitty grunted. "Thought so. You didn't touch anything *else* with that hand, I hope."

I shrugged. "No. Only my fork and glass at lunch."

"What about during the restroom break? You wipe with your left hand or right?"

"Uh ... right."

Oh no.

Either it was a case of perfect timing—or the power of suggestion took hold—but at that very second, my butt-crack began to itch.

I cringed. "What do I—"

The door flew open.

McNulty came in.

I couldn't help but notice he was carrying two pairs of handcuffs.

Chapter Forty-Six

I raced out into the lobby of the police station. It wasn't exactly a clean getaway. But like choosing the least-stained shirt in a pile of dirty clothes, it was the best I could do on short notice.

"Over here," Jackie called out.

She and Aunt Edna were loitering close to the exit door, as if they feared going into the station any further might seal their fate, too. I'd never been so glad to see two women's faces in my entire life.

"Coming!" I yelled.

"Hey!" a woman's voice rang out, interrupting my beeline toward my aunt and Jackie. I turned to see a too-tanned, too-blonde woman come rushing out of a hallway.

"Well, if it isn't the fugitive from justice," Shirley Saurwein said. "Did they let you go, or are you making a prison break?" She turned to Jackie and winked. "Oh, and thanks for the tip, doll. I'll see you all at the soiree on Tuesday."

I sneered at Shirley. "What are you talking about?"

Shirley's red lips twisted into an evil grin. "Didn't you know? I'll be covering Sophia Lorenzo's hundredth birthday party for the *Beach Gazette*." She looked me up and down. "Let me guess. You'll be wearing an orange jumpsuit?"

Crap!

"Come on," Aunt Edna said. "Let's get outta here."

I shoved open the door and followed them toward the parking lot. "Looks like Jackie's loose lips sank another ship," I grumbled.

My aunt eyed me funny. "What do you mean by that?"

"She told McNulty way too much."

"She's right," Jackie said, hanging her head. "Sorry."

"Hey, nobody's perfect." Aunt Edna stopped in her tracks and locked eyes with me. "But that don't mean they got no worth, Dorey. Don't you ever forget that."

I scoffed. "Tell that to my Ma."

"No. I'm telling it to *you*." Aunt Edna put her hands on my shoulders. "I don't know what Maureen taught you, or what you learned from all those schmucks in Hollywood. But around here, we don't slit each other's throats over some tiny mistakes."

I winced. "I didn't mean—"

Aunt Edna moved one hand to Jackie's shoulder. "Jackie here may be a blabbermouth, but I'll give her this—she's who you want to have around if you're in a crowd full of strangers."

My nose crinkled. "What do you mean?"

"Who needs Benny the pug?" Aunt Edna said, smiling at Jackie. "She's the *real* genius when it comes to sniffing out deadbeats. Ain't that right?"

Jackie shrugged, her usual perky smile beginning to curl her lips again. "Yeah, I guess so."

"Wait a minute," I said. "When you had Benny sniff me up and down after interrogating me, what was that? A sick joke?"

Jackie smirked. "Sort of. Hey, after we found out you was legit, I kinda felt like the situation called for some comic relief, you know? Anyway, I had Benny do it to make her feel useful. We all need to feel like we've got a purpose in life, right? Even mutts like Benny."

My heart pinged. "Sure."

"What about *your* lips, Dorey?" Aunt Edna said. "How'd you beat the rap when Kitty didn't? You didn't rat us out, did you?"

"No, ma'am. Kitty got me off. She explained the blisters on my hand were from poison ivy. She convinced McNulty to let me go."

"Just like that?" Aunt Edna eyed me funny. "That don't sound right."

"No," I said. "She also confessed that she was the most likely suspect and turned herself in. For desecrating a corpse."

"What?" Aunt Edna screeched.

"She took one for the team," I said. "So I could go free."

"So, I gotta know," Aunt Edna said. "You playing for our side, Dorey?"

I nodded. "Yes, ma'am."

"Good. Because up to now, I wasn't a hundred percent sure."

I grimaced.

Neither was I.

"All right then. Now, let's get to work." Aunt Edna turned and began marching toward the Kia, muttering and shaking her head. "Kitty's in the slammer and Sophia's about to turn a hundred tomorrow. I don't know which disaster to start plugging the holes in first."

"I do," I said. "Let's go back to Shady Respite."

"What for?" Jackie asked.

"To collect Sophia's things." I smiled coyly. "And to do a little bit of housekeeping of our own."

Chapter Forty-Seven

"Does McNutsack really think we're trying to kill our own Queenpin?" Aunt Edna asked as we pulled away from the front of the police station in the rusty green Kia.

"Pretty sure, and I can't blame him," I said, adjusting the driver's seat. "The blisters on our hands might as well have been blood stains."

Aunt Edna groaned. "Aye aye aye."

"But don't get too worried," I said. "I don't think things look all that bad for Kitty."

"How do you figure that?" Jackie asked.

I gripped the steering wheel tighter in an attempt to fight the urge to scratch myself in private places. Kitty had been right. In the bathroom, I'd used my right hand to wipe myself. And now it was coming back to haunt me in all the wrong places.

"Uh," I said, squirming in my seat. "It seemed to me like McNutsack ... Mc*Nulty* ... was starting to come around to our idea that Dr. Mancini from Shady Respite could be involved in the whole scheme, and is covering up Freddy's death along with the other guys."

Aunt Edna shook her head. "If that's the case, we gotta prove motive. Why would Mancini want to kill Sophia? It don't make sense to me."

"I don't know," I said. "The guy's got the bedside manner of a baboon. Maybe he's got a deal worked out with Neil Mansion funeral home."

"You mean like a 'kickbacks for stiffs' kind of scheme?" Jackie asked from the backseat.

"Why not?" I said. "Neil Neil told me the basic funeral package at his place costs over fifteen grand."

"Sheesh," Jackie said. "That's a lot a dough per capital head."

"You aren't kidding," Aunt Edna said. "I'm in the wrong line of work."

Jackie reached up from the backseat and patted her shoulder. "No you ain't, Edna. I hear it's a dying business."

I groaned. "Sophia said she thought Shady Respite had a conveyor belt running from the cafeteria to the morgue. What if she's right?"

"What?" Aunt Edna said. "No way. Sophia was just being sarcastic. This ain't no *Soylent Green* situation."

"I don't mean it *literally*," I said. "When Kitty and I were there this morning we didn't see an actual *conveyor belt*. But the elevator opened up right in front of both the cafeteria and the morgue, making it only steps to move a body back and forth to the two locations."

"Hold on a second," Jackie said. "If Neil Mansion *is* in on this poisoning scheme with Dr. Mancini, why would they bother with Sophia?"

"For the money," I said. "Fifteen grand a head. I thought I just explained that."

"You did," Aunt Edna said. "But you forgot one thing, Dorey. Sophia's funeral is already paid for."

"That's right," Jackie said. "There ain't no loot in it for them. When Sophia dies, it'll cost Neil Mansion out of their coffins. Right Edna?"

"*Coffers*, but yeah," Aunt Edna said. "But that don't rule out Dr. Mancini."

"It don't?" Jackie asked. "Why would he want to murder her then?"

"Not to reduce his workload," I said. "He'd just get new patients to replace them."

"True enough," Aunt Edna said. "But it still don't rule him out."

"Why not?"

Aunt Edna turned and locked eyes with me. "Because, Dorey. Maybe Mancini is one of those creeps who gets his jollies killing people. You know. The way some people like collecting poisonous plants. Or sniffing out deadbeats. Or pretending to be an actress."

Wait a minute ... ouch.

• • • •

"SHOULD I WAIT IN THE car, in case we need to make a quick getaway from Gloria and her deadly acorns?" Jackie quipped as we pulled up to Shady Respite convalescent center.

"Good one," Aunt Edna said. "But no. We go in strong. We go in together."

"Let's make this quick," I said, climbing out of car. "Afterward, I need to stop at a pharmacy. My fingers are itching like mad."

"Itchy fingers, eh?" Jackie smirked. "You got a desire to steal something, Dorey?"

"Huh?"

"Old wives' tale," Aunt Edna said. "Not this time, Jackie. I'm pretty sure it's just the poison ivy."

"If you say so," Jackie said.

"Here." Aunt Edna handed me a pink bottle. "It's calamine lotion. Try it."

I put some on my fingers. The relief was instant. "Thanks."

Aunt Edna reached over to take the bottle back. I resisted. "Uh ... mind if I hold onto it? In case the itch comes back?"

She shrugged. "Sure. Now, let's roll."

• • • •

THANKFULLY, THE RECEPTIONIST who'd caved to Kitty's extortion routine this morning wasn't the same one working the desk when we went back in. It was the harried Ms. Rodriguez. She seemed in a perpetual state of dishevelment.

"Excuse me," I said. "We're here to pick up the personal belongings of Sophia Lorenzo. She was ... um ... *discharged* yesterday?"

Jackie laughed. "That's one way to put it."

Rodriquez let out a huge sigh and dug through a plastic tub full of boxes and envelopes. "Hmm. I don't see anything here with that name."

"Look again," Aunt Edna said.

"I'm sorry," Rodriquez said. "But we've had a rash of things go missing lately."

Jackie glanced at my hand. "Who would want to steal a rash?"

"I understand," I said to the receptionist, and shot her my best smile. "Could you please tell us who was working the late shift on Saturday and Sunday?"

"Sorry," Rodriquez said and picked at a yellow stain on her scrubs. "We don't release employee records."

Aunt Edna huffed. "Well, that's a bust."

"No it ain't," Jackie said. "That glob of mustard's on a fat roll, not a boob."

"Excuse me?" Rodriguez said, glaring at us.

"Nothing." I herded the women away from the window. I'd considered putting up more of a fight with the receptionist, like Kitty would have. But, unfortunately, I had an even more pressing matter to attend to.

"Um...I need to use the ladies room," I said. "Wait here. I'll be right back."

Before they could reply, I sprinted down the hall. My lady parts were itching like mad. I slipped into the bathroom, yanked open a stall and slammed it behind me. The only thing on my mind at the moment was covering my private areas with the calamine lotion I'd stashed in my purse.

As I pulled down my pants and twisted off the bottle cap, the main door to the bathroom opened. A strange tapping sound traced along the floor. It grew nearer and nearer. Then it stopped right in front of my stall.

Perfect.

Quickly, I poured some lotion onto a wad of tissue, then assumed the position to wipe myself. Just before I reached my fanny, I froze. From under the stall door I spotted the pointed end of a purple umbrella.

Gloria! You've got to be kidding me!

Beside the umbrella tip were two sets of feet. One was clad in squeaky red loafers. The other one wore ugly, beige orthopedic shoes. I held my breath, afraid to move, even though it felt as if I were hosting a flea convention between my thighs.

Suddenly, one of the women spoke.

"Why don't you just do like the doctor said?"

"And look like a weak, old woman?" Gloria said. "No, way."

"You'd have gotten out of here sooner if you'd just done what you were told."

"Humph," Gloria grunted. "I did what he asked me to do, okay? It's not my fault if it didn't work."

"Well, I'll tell you this. He isn't happy one bit about the delay. I'm not sure how much longer I can keep—"

"Do you smell calamine lotion?" Gloria asked.

I froze mid-wipe. A millisecond later, my stall door flew open like it had been kicked by a mule.

"You!" Gloria yelled.

"Who?" the other lady asked. I couldn't see her face, and I prayed she couldn't see my fanny.

"It's *her*!" Gloria screeched at the other woman. "The one I told you about. The one who's trying to murder me!"

"It was a TV show!" I squealed, yanking up my drawers. I covered my head with my arm and dodged the swing of Gloria's umbrella.

"Come back here!" she yelled as I squeezed past her and scrambled out the bathroom door.

Still hitching up my jeans, I made a mad dash down the corridor. As I rounded the corner, I almost slammed into Jackie and Aunt Edna.

"What's going on?" Jackie asked.

"Hurry," I yelled. "Crazy Gloria is after me again!"

"Geez," Jackie said. "That woman needs a hobby, if you ask me."

• • • •

THE OLD KIA BOUNCED like a squeaky balloon house as the three of us scrambled inside and slammed the doors.

"Here, hold this," Aunt Edna said, shoving the brown bag into my lap. "I need a Tums."

"What's this?" I asked.

"Sophia's cherished possessions," she said sourly. "That ditzy receptionist found them after all."

As my aunt fished through her purse, I took a peek inside the bag. "A ratty bathrobe and worn-out slippers? I risked my life for *these*?"

"Hey," Jackie said. "When you reach a certain age, a soft robe and a comfy pair of shoes are worth more than all the teak in China. Am I right, Edna?"

Edna shrugged. "Jackie makes a good point. Now drive, Dorey. Before Gloria makes it rain again with those blasted acorns of hers."

Chapter Forty-Eight

We were halfway back to Palm Court Cottages when Jackie discovered a piece of paper in the pocket of Sophia's well-worn fuzzy bathrobe.

"What's this?" she asked, waving the paper at us from the backseat.

"Lemme see that." Aunt Edna grabbed the paper. "It's a list of people Sophia wanted to invite to her party."

I stopped the Kia at a red light and glanced over at the paper. "If that's the case, I see *I* didn't make the cut."

"Sophia made this before she knew about you," my aunt said. "You're definitely invited, kid."

"Thanks," I deadpanned. "Seems like a short list for such a big party."

"What else could it be?" Jackie asked. "It sure ain't no shopping list."

A thought hit me. "What about a list of *suspects*? You know, people she thought were trying to poison her?"

Aunt Edna's brow furrowed. She studied the list again. "Morty?" She shook her head. "We know it ain't him."

I glanced over at my aunt. "Just because you went out with him doesn't get him off the hook."

Aunt Edna glared at me. "It ain't him. Capeesh?"

I glanced down at the list. "Humpty Bogart is on here. Why would she invite him to her party if she doesn't like him?"

"This party ain't no popularity contest," Aunt Edna said. "It's about paying your respects. With gifts. Sophia likes gifts. And with most of the people she knows dead or dropping like flies, she's not in a position to be choosy."

I shrugged. "Fine. Who's Victor Ventura?"

Aunt Edna snorted. "Victor the Vulture. Clean-up man. You need to make a body disappear, he's your guy."

My upper lip snarled. "I'll keep that in mind."

"You do that," my aunt said.

"What about Dr. Mancini?" I pointed to the name on the list. "Why would she invite *him*?"

"Who has more money to buy her a nice gift than a doctor?" Jackie asked.

"Plus, she likes him," Aunt Edna said.

I frowned. "What about that last guy, Gordon?"

"Never heard of him," Aunt Edna said.

A horn honked. The light was green. I hit the gas.

As we traveled along, I thought about the names on the list. I kept coming back to Morty. What if he and Humpty really *did* have some kind of scheme going on together? Morty used to go out with Aunt Edna, so surely he'd have known about Kitty's greenhouse. And it would be super easy for him to bake the poison Manchineel apples into a dessert.

Easy as pie.

I glanced over at Aunt Edna. She was still staring at the list. Should I bring up Morty again? Why was she so touchy about him? I suspected it was because she was still in love with him. If that was the case, she'd just make more excuses for him.

"Look," I said. "If that *is* a list of people trying to kill Sophia, don't you think we should get some professional help sorting them out?"

"You mean like hire our own hitman?" Jackie asked.

"No," I said. "Hire our own cop. Officer Brady."

Jackie's eyebrow arched. "Like put him on our payroll?"

"No." I shook my head. "Get him on our side. Sergeant McNulty sure isn't."

"Dorey's right," Aunt Edna said. "Call Brady. Have him meet us at home in an hour. In the meantime, we got one more stop to make along the way."

"Where?" I asked.

"Morty's bakery," Aunt Edna said. "I need to check on the cake for the party. Plus, I got a hankering for a fresh cannolo."

Huh. I wonder what that means...

• • • •

"DELICIOUS, AS ALWAYS," Aunt Edna said, finishing off the cannolo. "I'll take a dozen to go."

"No can do," Morty said from behind the pastry counter. "I snuck that one out of an order just for you."

"What order?" I asked.

"For the Neil Mansion." Morty wiped the glass-topped bakery case with a dishtowel. "I do a lot of their catering. That cannolo was headed for the Sanderling service."

"Fred Sanderling?" I glanced around the display case. I saw cookies, brownies, cupcakes, éclairs, and croissants. But no lemon bars. Maybe Aunt Edna wasn't just covering for him when she'd said he didn't make them anymore.

"Yeah," Morty said. "You know him?"

I frowned. "No. Do *you*?"

"Not a clue," he said.

"When's his service taking place?" Aunt Edna asked.

Morty glanced at a clock on the wall. "In about an hour. Why?"

My heart thumped in my chest. "Come on, ladies. We better get going."

"Right." Aunt Edna gave me a quick nod, then turned to Morty. "You got everything on track for Sophia's party tomorrow?"

"Absolutely. You don't got to worry about a thing. I got everything taken care of."

"Humph," Aunt Edna grunted. "That's what they all say."
It was like she'd read my mind.

Chapter Forty-Nine

It wasn't hard to convince Aunt Edna and Jackie to take a detour to the Neil Mansion to attend Freddy's memorial service. We were eager to check out the crowd for potential suspects.

As for me, I had a secondary agenda as well. I wanted to see if Morty just happened to make a few lemon bars for the service.

Aunt Edna had told me he didn't make them anymore. Maybe he didn't—for Sophia. But that didn't mean he couldn't be baking up "special" batches for "special" occasions. And who knows? Maybe Sophia broke up the love affair between Aunt Edna and him, and now he wanted his revenge.

On another note, I still hadn't ruled out the folks at the Neil Mansion, either ...

"Aunt Edna, I noticed Neil Neil wasn't on Sophia's list."

"Why would she invite an undertaker to her birthday bash?" she asked.

"What if Jackie's right and that's a list of suspects?" I nodded toward the slip of paper still in my aunt's hand. "Sophia would never suspect the funeral home of being in on killing her, would she?"

"What would be their motive?" Aunt Edna asked. "It don't make no sense. Sophia's funeral is already paid for."

I frowned. "I don't know."

As I drove along, I wracked my brain for the answer. During my frenzied attempt to investigate my boss Tad's death a few weeks ago, I'd learned some valuable lessons from Sergeant McNulty. The biggest one was to look for the motivation behind the crime.

McNulty's words rang in my head.

"In my line of work, murder motives usually fall into three categories—sex, drugs or money."

Given the age of the suspects involved, sex and drugs seemed off the table. Unless the drug was Viagra. The mere thought made my stomach churn.

No. It has to be the third thing.

Money.

O.M.G.

"What if Sophia wasn't the main target?" I said.

Aunt Edna turned and stared at me. "What are you talking about?"

"What if Neil Neil and Dr. Mancini are poisoning random people after getting them to sign up for funeral services? I'm pretty sure Neil's husband has a cleft chin."

"You don't say," Aunt Edna said. "That could make sense, Dorey."

"I don't know much about the suspects on Sophia's list," I said. "But I *do* have an inkling about who has the most to gain from old people dying."

"At fifteen grand a pop, the answer's pretty obvious," Jackie said. "Even to me."

Chapter Fifty

When the three of us walked up to the front door of the eggplant-colored Victorian house, I wasn't surprised to see Neil Neil standing at the entrance ready to greet us. I *was* surprised, however, to see him handing out business cards.

"You two go on inside," I said to Jackie and Aunt Edna. "Check out who showed up, and if anyone looks suspicious. I want to question Neil Neil."

"You got it," Aunt Edna said. She nodded her respects to Neil Neil as she passed by, tugging a gawking Jackie along with her into the funeral home.

"Busy drumming up business?" I asked.

Neil Neil looked down his nose at me. "Excuse me, but aren't you the woman who wanted me to put an old lady on layaway?"

I winced. "That was a misunderstanding."

"Either way, you're too late."

I gulped. "Too late?"

"Yes. I'm sold out of Settler's Rests."

"Oh. So, will your husband be attending?"

Neil practically blanched. "What? No. Not that it's any of your business."

"You're right. It's not." I offered him an apologetic smile. "Look. I'm sorry, Neil. We got off on the wrong foot. It's just that I saw a picture of your husband. He has very striking features."

Including a cleft chin, I think ...

"Oh. Thank you."

"So, where did you two meet? Is he *British*, per chance?"

"No," Neil said sourly. "And if you must know, he's getting his teeth fixed."

"What? I didn't mean—"

A car horn tooted. I turned to see a white van pull up in the parking lot. A sign on the side read *Shady Respite Courtesy Van*.

"Look at that," I said. "Isn't it nice of the folks at the convalescent center to come and see Freddy off?"

"Right," Neil said curtly. "Those old vultures are just here to gobble up the free food and coffee." He looked me in the eye. "Why exactly are *you* here?"

I smiled inside, pleased with myself for having already come up with a line just in case he asked. "I wanted to see what your customers get when they pay for 'the works.'"

"This service certainly isn't the works," he said. "But we do what we can with every budget."

I nodded and smiled. "Good to know."

Neil glanced to his left and let out a big sigh. "Great. Here comes Mrs. Martinelli. That woman wouldn't miss a free meal if it were her own funeral."

I gulped. "Gloria Martinelli?"

"Who else?"

I turned and snuck a peek. Sure enough, the purple-umbrella crusader was making her way toward us, gnashing her teeth. Practicing for the cannoli, I figured.

"Uh, thanks, Neil," I said, then turned and scurried inside the funeral home.

• • • •

WHILE AUNT EDNA MINGLED with the crowd to eavesdrop on conversations, I slipped into the second row of pews right beside Jackie. Her job had been to get us seats as close to the front as possible. Once in position, she would serve as my wingman and dish the dirt on anyone she knew who attended the service.

"Where's the cleft-chin wonder?" she asked.

"Not here," I whispered.

Jackie shook her head. "It's Monday. Like I said, even a homicidal maniac needs a day of rest."

I glanced around. "See anybody you know?"

"Not yet." Jackie cocked her head and smiled. "Hey. What's that music they're playing?"

I listened, expecting it to be *Amazing Grace*. It wasn't. But it did sound vaguely familiar. As I strained my ears and my brain, it finally dawned on me. It was the Musak version of an old Motown hit.

A Curtis Mayfield tune called *Freddie's Dead*.

My jaw went slack. Either the music choice was one hell of a coincidence, or someone had a truly sick sense of humor.

I was about to whisper to Jackie when a man said, "Is this seat taken?"

I looked up to see the tall, slim, imposing visage of Sergeant McNulty. I nearly swallowed my tongue.

"What are *you* doing here?" I asked.

He sat down beside me. "I was about to ask you the same thing, Diller. I came here to check out the crowd. Killers sometimes like to attend their victims' funerals."

My nose crinkled. "Why?"

"Because they're sick bastards," McNulty said. "They want to see the pain they've caused. Some of them get their jollies from being so close to their victim again. Reliving the crime somehow, I would assume."

"Well, that's not why *we're* here," I said.

"I didn't say it was." McNulty eyed me even more suspiciously.

As I scrambled to think of something to say that wouldn't bury me even deeper in McNulty's eyes, Neil Neil approached the podium at the front and tapped on the microphone.

"Good afternoon, everyone," the gorgeous funeral director said. "The Sanderling family thanks all of you for coming. Fred Sanderling was a wonderful man. He will be sorely missed. We'd like to offer time for those who knew him best to come up and share a favorite memory of him."

"Oh, oh!" a woman's voice rang out. "Me first!"

A busty redhead who'd have fit right into Tad Longmire's lecherous playlist got up and wiggled to the podium.

I leaned over and whispered in Jackie's ear. "Who's that?"

"Victoria Polanski," Jackie said. "But Sophia calls her Slick."

"Why?"

Jackie smirked. "Because Victoria hates it."

The microphone crackled. "Slick" Victoria dabbed a hanky at her mascaraed eyes. "Freddy and I were very close," she said. "Nobody knew it, but we were secretly engaged."

"What?" I gasped. I leaned into Jackie. "What would she be doing with an old man like Freddy?"

"I heard a rumor at the nursing home that he was quite the lady killer," Jackie said. "Maybe the tide turned."

"Huh?"

"A lady killer got killed by a lady," Jackie said. "Classic gold-digger move."

"What do you mean?"

"Right out of the playbook," Jackie said. "Marry a rich old man, give him a bath, put him in a draft. Only this time, she went all Snow White on him."

"Excuse me, but that woman looks *nothing* like Snow White."

Jackie laughed. "That's for sure. But it looks like she knows her way around a poisoned beach apple, don't it?"

I stared at the woman still gushing tears at the podium. Slick looked like she knew her way around a stripper pole, too, if you asked me.

Huh. I wonder how much Freddy Sanderling had in his bank account...

Chapter Fifty-One

After the memorial service for Freddy was over, everyone lined up for coffee and desserts. Gloria Martinelli was first in line, so I stayed tucked behind Jackie and Aunt Edna. I kept a wary eye on the acorn assassin until she'd settled down at a table with her back turned toward us and began gnashing her mountain of food like a wood chipper at a sawmill.

"Did you see that piece of work?" Aunt Edna said, nodding toward "Slick" Victoria Polanski as she walked by us, her plate stacked with brownies. "I've seen better looking diamond rings in a bubblegum machine."

"So you think her jewelry's fake?" I asked.

My aunt huffed. "Dorey, it's as real as those boobs peeking out of her dress."

A tall, slim man with a head of frizzy, Bozo-like hair walked slowly along the line of people waiting for food. I noticed he was handing out something.

"Is that Neil Neil's husband?" Jackie asked.

"Not unless he's had some plastic surgery that went horribly awry," I said. "But he *does* have a cleft chin."

When the man got to us in line, he shot us a smile that was even faker than Slick's boobs.

"Ferrol Finkerman, attorney at law," he said. "Have a card. You never know when an injustice will occur."

"I think one just has," I said. "This is someone's funeral. Have some respect."

"Are you kin to Frederick Sanderling?" Finkerman asked.

"No."

"Beloved friend?"

"Err ... no."

"Then what are *you* doing here?"

My face reddened.

Finkerman smirked. "Uh-huh. That's what I thought."

Before I could think of a comeback, the ambulance chaser was already three guests down the line.

"Hold my place," Jackie said.

"Where are you going?" I asked.

"To introduce that jerk to Slick. Those two are made for each other."

I could hardly argue with that.

• • • •

OUR PLATES LADEN WITH pastries, the three of us headed for the table furthest away from Gloria Martinelli. As we sat down, Jackie picked up a cannolo. I recognized Morty's signature banana pudding inside.

"Don't eat that!" I whispered. "What if it's poisoned?"

"Gimme a break," Aunt Edna said. "We're too young to be targets for this old-folks scheme."

I studied the women for a moment. Jackie's pewter hair was in soft curls that hadn't been in style since Betty White played Rose on the *Golden Girls*. Come to think of it, Aunt Edna looked a lot like Bea Arthur.

Geez. Maybe reality and TV are the same thing ...

"Uh, right," I said. "But I think this could be more like a Russian-roulette situation."

"They got gambling going on?" Jackie asked.

"Gambling with people's lives," Aunt Edna said, and slapped the cannolo out of Jackie's hand.

"Well look who's here." I turned my attention to Dr. Mancini. "Why would he be attending Freddy's service?"

"To make sure Neil and his husband don't spend too much on the service?" Jackie asked.

It was as good a guess as any. And, unfortunately, that's all I had so far. Guesses.

I glanced around at all the silver hair and realized one head was missing. Sophia. She'd played us to get out of Shady Respite early. Maybe she's playing us again. I swallowed a knot in my throat.

Maybe that guy in the hoodie was hired by Sophia herself! Or Jackie and Aunt Edna. Geez! Maybe I'm being set up by the whole Family right this very second!

"What'cha thinking about, Dorey?" Aunt Edna asked.

I nearly gasped. "Oh. Uh ... nothing."

My aunt's left eyebrow was an inch higher than her right. "Don't look like nothing to me."

"Where's Jackie?" I asked, suddenly paranoid. She'd disappeared from her chair while I'd been lost in thought.

"Right here," she said, towering over me. "Take these and guard them with your life."

Jackie pressed a lumpy napkin into my hand. Was there a gun in there? A poison tree frog? At this rate, anything seemed possible.

"I wanna try a poppy seed muffin," Jackie said, and turned toward the buffet.

"What did we just say about—" I called after her. But it was too late. Jackie was already at the pastry table. I looked down at my hand as the napkin slowly unfolded.

Inside was a pair of dentures.

O. M. G.! Did she steal these from Freddy?

"Excuse me for a moment," I said to my aunt, then got up and made a beeline for Freddy's casket. I was about to slip the dentures inside when someone foiled my plan.

"What are you doing?" McNulty asked.

I quickly palmed the dentures. "Uh ... what do you mean?"

"I thought you'd be busy trying to get your friend Kitty off the hook."

"We are," I grumbled. "We're certainly not here for the free food."

"Right," McNulty said. "Well, take my advice. Don't try the poppy seed muffins."

I thought of Jackie and nearly choked. "Why? Are they poisoned, too?"

McNulty eyed me funny. "No. The little seeds get caught between your teeth."

"Oh." I smiled weakly. "Of course."

McNulty folded his arms across his chest. "I've got my eye on you, Diller. And your friends here, too."

"But we didn't do anything. I swear. And Kitty didn't either."

"You two desecrated this man's corpse," McNulty said, nodding toward Freddy as he lay in his coffin.

I winced. "Besides *that*, I mean."

"Listen to me, Diller. You need to step aside and let me conduct my own investigation into Sanderling's death. Can you do that?"

I looked down at his shoes. "Yes, sir."

"If I find you're meddling again, I can arrest you for tampering with an active investigation. Then you and Kitty can be cellmates."

I looked up at him. "But we've got the big party tomorrow!"

McNulty's eyes narrowed. "What party?"

Aww, crap!

"Uh ... my birthday party." It wasn't a lie, technically.

Suddenly, Jackie was beside me. "Our Dorey here turns forty tomorrow."

"I see," McNulty said. "Well, happy birthday. But one slip up Diller and you may find yourself celebrating it inside a jail cell."

Chapter Fifty-Two

"Great. Just great," I said as I drove the Kia out of the parking lot of the Neil Mansion. "Now McNulty suspects me even *more*. He told me one little slip-up and I'll be celebrating my big day in the big-house."

"Look on the bright side," Jackie said, and shot me a grin with her reinstalled dentures.

"Bright side?" I asked.

"At least you got out of there without being beaned over the head by Gloria Martinelli."

I sighed. "I guess. But do me a favor, Jackie. Don't ever hand me your dentures again."

"But I didn't want any poppy seeds to get caught in them."

"Put them in your purse next time."

She cocked her head. "I'm not carrying a purse."

"Geez. Put them in your pocket then."

"I don't have any—"

"You know what?" I said, eager to change the subject. "After what I saw at the service, I think Neil Neil and Dr. Mancini for sure have a thing going on."

"Mancini's gay, too?" Aunt Edna asked.

"No. But they're both in love with money."

Jackie laughed. "What man ain't?"

"Brady," Aunt Edna said.

"Brady!" I gasped. "I forgot about him!"

"*I* didn't." Aunt Edna patted my knee. "Don't worry, Dorey. While you were busy being Miss Detective, I called him. We got it all worked out for him to drop by our place later."

"Whew." I breathed a sigh of relief. "Look. Before we meet up with him, there's some stuff I want to know."

"Like what?" Jackie asked.

"Like what you two think of the other suspects. You know. The ones on Sophia's list."

"You mean Victor the Vulture?" Aunt Edna asked.

I nodded. "You said he deals with dead bodies. Could he be poisoning people to get more business?"

"Naw," Aunt Edna said. "He makes bodies *disappear*. Not show up to funerals."

"Edna's right," Jackie said. "Besides, from what I hear, Victor's got more business than he can handle."

My eyebrows shot up an inch. "Excuse me?"

"Never mind." Aunt Edna shot Jackie a dirty look in the rearview mirror. "It ain't Victor."

"Then who?" I asked. "What about that Humpty Dumpty guy?"

"Humphry Bogaratelli," Aunt Edna said.

"Why would he do it?" Jackie asked. "The creep's got plenty of money, thanks to his sticky fingers."

"Maybe his tastes have changed," Aunt Edna said. "Maybe he's developed a hankering for *power* to go along with his dough."

I nodded. "That's what I was thinking. Look, Aunt Edna. I know you have a thing for Morty. But you have to face reality. That day at the bakery—could Morty have been chipping in cash for Humpty to pay for a hit on Sophia?"

"No!" Aunt Edna groaned and reached for her purse. "I need another Tums."

I frowned, then glanced in the rearview mirror. Jackie was shaking her head at me, running a bony finger across her throat. I got the hint and backpedaled. "But what do I know? It's probably somebody else."

"My money's on that old gasbag Gloria Martinelli," Jackie said. "She sure has it out for *you*, Dorey."

I grimaced. "Don't remind me."

"And there's bad blood between her and Sophia," Jackie added.

"True," I said. "But the woman is no pro at hiding her feelings. If Gloria wanted to have a showdown with Sophia, she would've done it while they both were at Shady Respite."

"Who says they didn't?" Aunt Edna said, chewing her antacid tablet.

Jackie patted Aunt Edna's shoulder. "Not me."

I pursed my lips. "If that's true—"

"I think it's that red-headed tramp at the funeral," Aunt Edna said. She spat out her name. "Slick Vicky. What a piece of work. That bimbo is Freddy's fiancé? I don't buy it." She shook another Tums out of the bottle. "Let me tell you, Dorey. It ain't just *men* who love money."

"I know that."

Aunt Edna popped the Tums into her mouth. "Here's a theory for you, Miss Detective. What if that ditz ordered those poisoned lemon bars for Freddy, but told the delivery guy the wrong room number?"

I sat up straight in the driver's seat.

Huh. Right now, that's as good a theory as any.

• • • •

AS I UNFASTENED MY seatbelt in front of Palm Court Cottages, Aunt Edna grabbed my arm.

"Dorey. You familiar with that expression, 'A girl's gotta do what a girl's gotta do.'?"

I thought about the time handsy Arthur Dreacher had summoned me to his trailer in the back lot of the studio at two in the morning. I'd armed myself with a mouthful of pea soup, then spewed it all over myself when he opened the door. My fake *Exorcist* impression had earned me the whole night off, Dreacher-free.

"I'm familiar with the term," I said.

"Good." Aunt Edna hauled herself out of the passenger seat. "When Brady comes over tonight, he might need a little persuasion, if you catch my drift."

I climbed out of the Kia and shut the door. "Not exactly."

"You like Brady, don't you?" she asked.

"Uh … yeah, sure."

"We may need you to use your feminine wiles to help him see things our way."

"Wait a minute. Are you pimping me out?"

"It ain't pimping if you really like him. Besides, Brady's a good boy."

I frowned. "And you think I'm a bad girl?"

"No. Just use the assets Mother Nature gave you. Tease him a little. You don't gotta do nothing you don't want to do. Think of it as practice."

I blanched. "*Practice*?"

"Yeah. For your acting career. You got that big audition tomorrow, right?"

"Yes, but—"

Aunt Edna locked eyes with me. She looked tired and sad. "You care about Kitty, don't you?"

I cringed. "Sure."

"Well, she needs you. *We* need you."

I gulped. I've never been needed before. Tossed aside. Ignored. Taken advantage of. But never *needed*.

"Just be nice to Brady, that's all I'm saying," my aunt said. "Just flutter your Bambi eyelashes and find out what he knows. We only got tonight and tomorrow morning to figure this thing out. And while you're at it, see if maybe he'd be willing to help us get Kitty out of jail so she can come to the party."

My eyes grew wide. "You mean bust her out?"

"Yeah." Aunt Edna winked. "But on a *technicality*."

"Oh. Okay."

"Thanks, Dorey. But listen. Whatever you do, don't tell Brady about the Family. Capeesh?"

I nodded. "Capeesh."

Aunt Edna gave me a big bear hug, then hollered after Jackie, who was up the path a few steps ahead of us. "Jackie! Help our girl get dolled up a little! And you two come up with a cover story."

"I'm on it, Capo," Jackie said, turning back toward us.

"So it's all settled," Aunt Edna said. "Now, I'd better get a move on."

"Where are *you* going?" I asked.

"To make dinner. It's past five o'clock, already, for crying out loud!"

Chapter Fifty-Three

I guess it was my turn to take one for the CGCN team.
Kitty had confessed to the desecration of Freddy's corpse on the condition that I would go free. Aunt Edna had reluctantly faced the possibility that her old flame Morty could be involved in a plot with Humpty to kill Sophia. And Jackie? Well, I was convinced she was willing to do whatever it took to protect her Family.

Was I?

As I checked my look in the mirror, the lyrics to Bruce Springsteen's *Dancing in the Dark* ran through my mind.

I wanna change my clothes, my hair, my face.

Jackie's "makeover" for my date with Officer Brady was nothing less than stunning—but it the worst possible way. The sleeveless white shirt she'd insisted I wear bore enough sparkling rhinestones to cause an epileptic seizure. She'd also plumped my hair to epic volume with half a can of hairspray—and coated my eyelids with enough "smoky eye shadow" to start a forest fire.

I closed my eyes and took a deep breath.

Okay, Doreen. You can do this. Channel your inner Vicky Polanski.

I sighed.

Who am I kidding? Even Slick *didn't look* this *trampy.*

• • • •

"THANKS FOR PICKING me up," I said, leaning into the open driver's window of Brady's Ford F-150. "I didn't know where else to turn."

"Uh ... no problem," he said to my cleavage.

I glanced around, tugged the hem of my too-short skirt, and whispered, "Listen, if anyone asks, we're on a date, okay?"

Brady's eyebrow shot up. "Okay, but—"

"Hold that thought." I pressed a fake fingernail to his lips. "Let me get in first."

I hobbled in stilettos over to the other side of the truck. One of my spike heels caught in a crack between the bricks lining the street. I yanked it free, then tugged opened the passenger door.

"This was the only way I could get out of there without them suspecting me," I said, spoon-feeding Brady the cover story Jackie and I'd come up with.

"I see." Brady watched me climb into the cab of his truck with all the grace of a drunken she-goat.

"So," he said. "Do you usually sleep over on a first date?"

I blanched. "I beg your pardon?"

Brady smirked. "I'm a trained observer. I couldn't help but notice the luggage."

"Oh." My cheeks caught flame. I grabbed my old suitcase off the road—a prop Jackie had insisted I take along. God only knew why. At least she'd left it unpacked. I lugged the old brown case onto the floorboard beside my feet. "It's not what you think."

"No?" Brady smirked. "Too bad."

"What?"

He laughed. "So, Ms. Diller. What's going on?"

"Don't ask. Just drive."

• • • •

THE HOT COP TURNED left on Ninth Street and pulled up to what he said was one of his favorite haunts. The Dairy Hog.

The place was a complete dive.

Oozing the ambiance of an abandoned gas station, the Dairy Hog was the kind of hole-in-the-wall place where, during daylight hours, street urchins and bigwigs sat elbow-to-elbow and munched suspiciously red hotdogs at giant wooden picnic tables—tables selected because they were too heavy to steal. During nighttime hours, however, the Dairy Hog lost most of its charm.

I crinkled my nose. "What a dump."

"Not at all." Brady opened the driver's door and climbed out. "This is the perfect place."

"For what? A homicide?"

"Only if you order the fish sandwich," he quipped.

"Why in the world would you take me here?" I asked, trying to get out of the truck without being arrested for indecent exposure.

"Because here, no one will think twice about a cop talking to a prostitute."

"Prostitute?" I balked, wobbling on my heels as I followed him across the potholed asphalt.

"My bad." Brady stopped in front of the dive's walk-up order window. "That wasn't the look you were going for?"

"No!" I tugged at my skin-tight orange mini skirt. It was actually one of Jackie's old tube tops. "I was trying to look like I was going on a date with you." I stared at the spot where my stomach bulged the stretchy orange fabric. "Geez. I think I've put on a few pounds thanks to Aunt Edna's cooking."

Brady grinned. "I can see how that could happen." He turned to the guy in the order window. "Two dogs, Dairy style, and two chocolate milkshakes."

"You got it," the guy said.

Brady turned to me. "Hope that's okay with you. It's the most edible stuff on the menu. Unless you think the calories might make you pop a seam."

I punched him on the arm. "Ha ha."

We grabbed our food and found an empty spot at the end of one of the picnic tables.

"Sorry to dump all this on you, Brady. But if I didn't tell someone, I think my head would have exploded."

"Like your dress?"

I frowned. "One more crack like that and *you'll* be the one with your life in danger."

"Your life's in danger?" he asked, suddenly serious.

"Yes. No. I don't know!"

"From who? Your aunt and Jackie? Did they threaten you with a cane or something?"

I slumped in my chair. "It's ridiculous, I know. I ... I just can't decide whether to get out of here or stay."

"What's so bad about staying? From what you've told me, your life in L.A. was no pleasure cruise."

"No. But it seemed less ... I dunno ... dangerous."

Brady laughed. "Dangerous?"

I scowled. "You know what, trying to talk to you was a big mistake. Just take me back home."

I turned back toward the truck. Brady's hand softly gripped my upper arm.

"I'm sorry, Doreen. It's just hard to take you seriously in that get-up."

"I know. I ... I'm only doing this because I care about my family."

"I can tell." Brady let go of my arm. "Look, give me another shot, okay? I promise I'll take you seriously."

I looked up at him with Bambi eyes.

I didn't have to fake them.

I sniffed and said, "Okay."

Chapter Fifty-Four

"I can definitely see why you needed a reality check," Brady said after listening to me spill my guts about ... well ... *everything*. "Like I said before, the women in your family are in possession of some truly exceptional imaginations."

My family.

Brady's words caused a lump to form in my throat.

"Yes, they *are* my family," I said, my spine stiffening. "And I believe this isn't their imagination. Not all of it, anyway."

Brady slurped his chocolate shake through a straw and set it down on the wooden picnic table. "You really think Sophia's life is in danger?"

"Yes! That's what I've been trying to tell you." I wiped mustard from my chin with a cheap paper napkin. "Someone tried to poison her with a machine ... a mancini ... a mansion ... a *beach apple*."

"Beach apple?" Brady's eyebrow shot up. "Is that anything like a road apple?"

I shot Brady some side eye.

He laughed. "Be honest. You didn't drink another Long Island iced tea before you came here, did you?"

"No!" Frustration boiled inside me. "*Manchineel*. That's it."

"That's what?"

"The name of the poison Kitty said was in the lemon bars. We tried to explain it to Sergeant McNulty, but he put her in jail instead!"

"Oh." The humor left Brady's face. "I'm sorry. I didn't know it had gone this far."

"Well, it has." I frowned and stared at my half-eaten hotdog.

Brady reached across the table and took my hand in his. "Doreen, why would someone want to kill a harmless little old lady like Sophia?"

"So they can take over the Fa—"

I choked on my own words.

Crap! I can't tell Brady about the Family!

"uh ... her *money*," I blurted.

Brady's eyebrows rose a notch. "So Sophia's loaded?"

Well, she's loaded with something, that's for sure.

I nodded. "I know it sounds crazy, but I'm worried whoever is trying to kill her may try again at the Coliseum tomorrow night."

"In Rome?"

"No. On Fourth Avenue. That's where they're holding her birthday party."

"Oh. But why *then*?"

"To keep her from turning a hundred."

Brady's brow furrowed. "I'm not following you. Why would they care about that?"

I chewed my lip, trying to come up with a reason that didn't involve mafia hitmen. I shrugged. "How should I know?"

"Is it because of the Collard Green Cosa Nostra thing?" Brady asked.

I nearly fell off the picnic bench. "You know about that?"

He laughed. "I bought Jackie a beer once."

"Oh." Relief washed through me. "Look. It's a real thing. Mob men are lining up to do Sophia in!"

Brady's shoulders straightened. "Why?"

"Because Sophia says they're like hermit crabs. They all need bigger shells."

"Excuse me?"

I shook my head. "Forget it. You think I'm nuts, just like my aunt and Jackie, don't you?"

"No." He smiled softly. "Well, not completely. But I don't get the crab reference."

"Whoever knocks off Sophia gets to be the new head of the ... *you know*. But if she lives to be a hundred, she can name the new leader herself."

"Ah. And McNulty thinks Kitty wants to take over?"

I shook my head. "He doesn't know about the whole Sophia thing. He nailed Kitty on desecration of a corpse."

Brady choked on his milkshake. "What?"

"Look. That's not important right now. What I know for sure is that Kitty didn't want to kill Sophia. She doesn't want her job. Believe me, none of us do."

"Are you sure about that?"

My nose crinkled. "Being head of the Cosa Nostra and walking around with a price on your head? No thanks."

Brady smirked. "Don't be so dramatic, Doreen. I've seen trailer park kids that were more dangerous than the CGCN gang."

"Really?" I chewed my bottom lip. "Well, then, there's your answer, Brady. *We're not killers*. If any of us wanted to be the new head of the family, why would we be working so hard to keep Sophia alive?"

"In hopes she'll name one of you to the role?"

I frowned. "No. We take care of her because she's family. And we keep her alive because despite her being a cranky old cuss we ..."

"We what?" Brady asked.

I looked up at him. "We love her."

Brady locked his brown eyes with mine. "Sounds like you've integrated pretty well into the clan, Ms. Diller."

I blanched.

Geez. I guess I have.

"So, your love for Sophia is what's driving you to seek my help?" Brady asked.

"Yes, I guess so," I admitted. "But not just me. Aunt Edna and Jackie want your help, too. It was their idea." I looked down at the sparkles on my shirt. "So was this horrible outfit."

Brady blew out a breath. "Thank goodness. I was worried about that."

"Could you can it with the jokes, please? If someone kills Sophia, we're worried her replacement could be somebody horrible. Like Sammy the Psycho."

Brady blanched. "The cheese-curd guy? He's *real*?"

"My Family sure seems to think so." I grabbed Brady's hand. "I'm worried her birthday bash could turn into a bloodbath!"

Brady shook his head. "Look, Doreen. If you want my opinion, I don't think there's going to be a shootout at the Coliseum. But I agree, something could be up with the poisoning thing. Otherwise, why would McNulty have arrested Kitty?"

"Exactly my point! I didn't mean to dump all of this on you, but I couldn't go to McNulty, now could I?"

"No, I guess not."

"Can you help us?"

Brady pursed his lips. "I'll check into it."

"No! That's just it, Brady. There's *no time* left to check into it! The party's tomorrow!"

"Then how can I possibly help you?"

"Come with me to the party. As my date."

"What exactly do you see me doing for you at the party?"

"You know. Keeping an eye out for us." I shrugged. "You can kind of be Sophia's bodyguard. You can bring your gun, can't you?"

Brady stiffened. "I can't exactly go shooting suspects for you, Doreen. We need to gather proof of intent."

I frowned. "How are we supposed to do that?"

"By recording incriminating statements."

My eyebrows shot up. "You mean by wearing a wire? Like that stray dog Jackie saw?"

"No," Brady said. "This time, the wire would be real."

Chapter Fifty-Five

I couldn't remember walking from Brady's truck to Aunt Edna's apartment. Or how I ended up staring at pink globs floating around in the lava lamp atop the old, yellowing French Provincial bureau in the spare bedroom where I slept.

I only remembered it wasn't a walk of shame.

Officer Brady had kissed me goodnight. Or maybe I'd kissed him. Either way, neither of us had objected.

After that, my mind had gone blank.

And now, here I was, staring at the gooey pink shapes rising and falling inside a globe full of mysterious liquid. I don't know how long I'd been standing there, but slowly I became aware of my surroundings.

Down the hall, I could hear Aunt Edna softly snoring. I turned toward the bed. In the pink glow of the lamp, I saw my pajamas laid out neatly for me next to my pillow. On the bedside table, a plate of cookies and a glass of milk sat waiting for me. The last time someone had done that for me was ... never.

Suddenly, my heart felt way too big for my chest. I sniffed back a tear and picked up a cookie. Beside the plate was a handwritten note on a neatly folded piece of pink paper.

Dorey honey,

I was worried you didn't get enough to eat. I hope you had a nice evening with B, and that he was a gentleman.

Sleep well,

Aunt Edna

> P.S. I talked to Kitty. She said to tell you natives used the sap to poison their arrows.

"What the?" I muttered.

I set the note down and grabbed my toothbrush from the bureau. As I did, I caught a glimpse of myself in the mirror. I nearly screeched with terror.

I'd forgotten all about Jackie's makeover.

One brown eye and one pale-blue one stared back at me from dark, skeletal sockets, thanks to the brown eyeshadow Jackie's applied all the way to my eyebrows. My lacquered hair was the size of a frizz-ridden basketball.

Dear lord! I look like a zombie that just stuck its finger in a light socket!

As I stared at my hideous visage, a sudden thought melted my horrified expression into a dreamy smile.

And Brady had kissed me anyway.

· · · ·

AFTER PEELING OFF JACKIE'S sparkly top and tube-top mini skirt, I took a long, hot shower to remove every last trace of my stint as a low-rent femme fatale. I slipped on the pajamas so lovingly laid out for me and climbed into bed.

Suddenly, I realized I wasn't alone.

Something hard poked me in the elbow.

"Ack!" I yelped, then scrambled out of bed and flipped on the light.

Lying in the covers was Kitty's leather-bound poison journal. I picked up Aunt Edna's note and read it again.

> P.S. I talked to Kitty. She said to tell you natives used the sap to poison their arrows.

I sat down on the bed and picked up the journal. What was Kitty trying to tell me? We already knew the poison came from the Manchineel tree. Did she think someone was going to use a bow and arrow at the party? It seemed implausible. But then again, this *was* Florida.

I flipped through Kitty's hand-painted plant journal until I found the one I was looking for. The Manchineel.

I studied every entry Kitty had made next to the illustration of the sad-looking little tree-bush. Sure enough, the last note was about how the Carib Indians had poisoned their arrows with the toxic sap from the apple-like fruits, and used it to bring down small prey like birds, squirrels, and rabbits.

What had Kitty meant by this?

I thought about last night, when I'd been guarding Sophia at her cottage. Kitty had been messing around in the garden in the dark. She could've easily gone into her greenhouse and taken the fruits from the Manchineel tree. She could've staged the cut padlock to make it look like a robbery.

My eyes grew wide.

Is that why she never found the time to show me the greenhouse? Is she trying to throw me off her scent by giving me false clues as a pretense to helping?

Helping.

The word echoed in my head.

Wait a minute. Why wasn't anyone watching Sophia tonight? Had that whole guard-shift thing last night been a ploy to get me to stay inside Sophia's place so the three of them could hatch their poisonous scheme without my interference?

Am I being taken advantage of again? Duped like a fool by people pretending to love me?

A soft knock sounded on my door.

"Who is it?" I hissed.

The doorknob jiggled.

Then, before I could get up, a hand holding a shotgun forced its way inside.

Chapter Fifty-Six

"Get out!" I yelled, and hurled Kitty's poison journal at the intruder. It banged against the wall, missing its target.

"Geez," a familiar voice said. "You really need to work on your aim."

"Jackie!" I yelped, my eyes moving from the shotgun to her face. "Are you going to shoot me?"

"What? Heck, no, Dorey!" She leaned the shotgun on the wall. "I just came to check that you got home safe."

"Oh." I swallowed against the thumping in my throat. "Yeah. I'm okay. What are you doing walking around with the shotgun?"

"Guard duty. Tonight there was only me and Edna to take shifts watching Sophia. With you being ... you know ... *busy with Brady*, we figured you'd be exhausted. Edna went to bed early so she can work the midnight to six."

"Oh." I slumped back in my bed, ashamed I'd thought they might be plotting against me. *Again.*

Jackie's head cocked to one side. "What's wrong, kid?"

What isn't?

"I ... uh .... Nothing."

"You sure?"

"Why was Kitty's book in my bed?"

"Oh." Jackie laughed. "That was me. I thought it'd make good dead-time reading."

My nose crinkled. "You mean *bed*time reading?"

"Naw. Who can read when they're asleep?"

"I guess you're right." I felt the tension in my face slip away. Jackie's unique way of looking at the world was growing on me. "Jackie, can I ask you a question?"

"Sure, kid."

"Why do you keep unpacking my suitcase?"

She chuckled. "Why else? Because I want you to stay. That's why I had you take your suitcase along on your date with Brady. So you couldn't pack it without me knowing. I figured you wouldn't take off without your stuff."

I shook my head softly. "But why would you care if I stayed or not?"

Jackie's eyes grew wide. "Are you kidding? We love you, Dorey."

I bristled against the kindness Jackie was showing me. The vulnerability she displayed made me squirm with discomfort. Telling her I loved her back would be a sign of weakness, wouldn't it?

Damn, early programming dies hard.

"And we need you," Jackie said. "But more than that, *you* need *us*."

I frowned. "Why would *I* need *you all*?"

"Everybody needs somebody to watch their back." Jackie sat on the edge of the bed. "Take me, for instance. If it wasn't for Edna, I'd probably be living in the streets."

I gulped. In a way, I was in the same boat. "Me, too," I admitted.

Jackie studied me. "I thought you were a famous movie star back in L.A."

I laughed bitterly. "Hardly. If I don't get this job Kerri's offering me at Sunshine Studios tomorrow, I'll be so broke I'll have to cash in my plane ticket and get a new career in fast-food delivery."

Jackie winked. "Well, then, I hope you don't get it."

I frowned. "What?"

"Only so you'll stay, I mean." She reached over and patted my hand. "Otherwise, break an arm."

I smiled. "Thanks."

Jackie stood up. "Now get some shuteye kid. In the morning, you can tell us all about the plan you and Brady came up with to save Sophia."

I gulped. "Right."

Jackie turned to go, then glanced around the room. "Where's your suitcase? Did you use the goodies I packed inside?"

"What goodies?"

"You know." She waggled her eyebrows. "The naughty nighty and the packs of 'protection.'"

I grimaced. "No. I'm not that kind of girl."

"Playing hard to get, eh? I like your style, kid." Jackie grinned at me, then clicked off the light and disappeared like a shadow.

Suddenly, I was so wide awake I was certain the whites of my eyes were glowing in the dark.

I'd accidently left my suitcase in Brady's truck.

Holy crap! Please, Brady, please. Whatever you do, don't open that suitcase!

Chapter Fifty-Seven

I was at the Coliseum in Rome, wandering among the ancient stone columns and arches. Dressed in a cop's uniform, I was wearing a wire frying basket atop my head like a rectangular helmet.

A sudden movement at my feet made me look down. The ground was swarming with hermit crabs. Instinctively, I knew they were acting suspicious. I reached for my service weapon.

It was a wooden mallet.

I raised my mallet in the air like Thor's hammer and took off in pursuit of the orange crustaceans running amok like miniscule hoodlums.

I followed a gang of them through a stone arch and cornered them by the base of a broken column. As I prepared to play Whack-a-Mole with the culprits, I spied something that made me freeze in place.

Holding court on a throne-shaped boulder was the biggest hermit crab I'd ever seen. Atop its flat, triangular head was a tinfoil turban.

As I crab-walked cautiously toward it, the turban grew larger with every step I took. Suddenly, the aluminum headdress split open like a fully-cooked Jiffy Pop. Out of the crack, a claw emerged.

The claw gripped the slit in the foil and ripped away a chunk of...

"Dorey? You okay?"

My eyes flew open. Aunt Edna was standing over me.

"Wha?" I mumbled, and raised up in bed on one elbow.

My aunt's eyes were full of concern. "You were groaning. I thought maybe Brady fed you a bad meatball or something."

"Huh? Oh." I blinked the sleep from my eyes. "No. Just a weird dream."

Aunt Edna smiled tiredly. "Well, time to rise and shine. I'm making something special for breakfast."

"What?" I asked.

"Eggs benedict. With fresh crab meat."

• • • •

WHEN I GOT DRESSED and stumbled to the dining room, Aunt Edna was at the table setting out a gravy boat full of hollandaise sauce for the eggs benedict breakfast she was making.

"What's the occasion?" I asked, reaching for the coffee carafe.

She grinned. "Your birthday, Dorey. Or don't you celebrate it no more?"

"Oh." I shrugged. "Ma never made a big deal out of it."

Aunt Edna frowned. She looked exhausted. Then I remembered she'd been up since midnight, watching Sophia's cottage.

"Can I help you with something?" I asked. "You need me to go get Sophia?"

"Nah, Jackie's doing it. So, how'd it go with Brady last night?"

I grimaced. "Okay, I guess. I didn't have to ... *you know*."

Aunt Edna eyed me funny. "I *meant* did you two work out a plan for making sure Sophia's balloons don't get popped tonight?"

I felt my cheeks heat up. "Oh. Yes. He's going to the party with me. As my date."

Aunt Edna shot me an arched eyebrow. "*That's* your plan?"

"He'll also be carrying a concealed firearm."

"Uh-huh. Well, it sure would be good if we could tell him who to aim it at, wouldn't it."

I winced. "I know. All we know for sure is what kind of poison was used to kill Freddy. And if we don't figure out who took those beach apples from Kitty's greenhouse, she's in big trouble."

Aunt Edna let out a big sigh. "Tell me something I *don't* know."

"Look, Aunt Edna. I need to be honest with you. I saw Kitty wandering around in the garden the night before last. She could've taken the apples herself. Are you sure she didn't want to get rid of Sophia and be the new godmother of the CGCN?"

Aunt Edna's back stiffened. "Yes, I'm sure. I've known Kitty Corleone for over thirty years."

"Then why didn't she want to show me her greenhouse?"

"She *did* want to. She just ran out of time. McNutsack showed up before she could give you the tour."

I chewed my bottom lip. "Okay. But if you don't suspect her, why did you leave me that note about Kitty saying natives poisoned arrows with the sap?"

"Why else?" Aunt Edna said. "Because Kitty *asked* me to. I'd tell you to talk to her yourself, but she already used up her one phone call. And believe me, the police were listening to every word we said to each other."

I blew out a frustrated breath. "I'm just trying to follow every lead."

"I get that. But look, Dorey. Around here, we watch after each other. Whoever messed with those lemon bars, it ain't Kitty. Go point your poison arrows at somebody else."

"Believe me, I'd like to. But McNulty told us the Manchineel is so rare it would take a botanist like Kitty to even recognize it."

Aunt Edna rested a tired hand on my shoulder. "Dorey, I dunno what you had happen to you growing up with Maureen and being an actress in L.A. and all, but around here, we don't eat our own young. Drop it with Kitty. If I can't trust her, I can't trust nobody."

The tired, sad, earnest look on my aunt's face made me feel like a heel. "I'm sorry. I'm just trying to make sure nobody gets hurt."

"I know that, kid. But that ain't the way the world works. No matter what choice you make in this life, you hurt somebody doing it."

I grimaced. "So what are we supposed to do? *Nothing*?"

"No. You just live your life the best you can and try to do the least damage to the ones you love."

My eyes filled with tears. I hugged my aunt. "I meant to thank you for the cookies. And your note. And for caring about my birthday."

Aunt Edna patted me on the back. "You're welcome. Now, Miss Detective, you keep on snooping around. But stay out of *our* doghouse, okay?"

I nodded. "Okay. You know, I looked through Kitty's journal last night, but I couldn't find any other clues."

Aunt Edna locked eyes with me. "Maybe she wants you to look harder."

"At what? The plant itself? It's so homely, nobody would give it a second glance."

"Are you talking about me?" Jackie asked.

She came slowly into the dining room, Sophia on her arm. Jackie's outfit of the day was a lime-green top and orange-and-white striped pants. She looked like she'd just been mugged by a circus tent.

Aunt Edna frowned. "What's up with that outfit?"

"What?" Jackie balked. "It matches my cheerful personality. Plus we're celebrating somebody's big day today."

Aunt Edna winced and shook her head. "Dorey, you wouldn't happen to still have those big sunglasses of Jackie's, would you?"

Chapter Fifty-Eight

The crabmeat benedict was delicious. The conversation, however, turned out to be a little harder to swallow.

We were running out of time to figure out who the poisoner was, and to get Kitty out of jail. So I kind of threw caution to the wind and went for broke.

"Sophia, I mean Queenpin, why did you choose Freddy Sanderling for your taster?"

"If Kitty were here, she'd tell you why," Sophia said.

"Well, that's just it," I said. "She isn't here. That's why I need to know why you chose Freddy."

"Dorey's only trying to help," Aunt Edna said.

Sophia sighed. "I didn't choose Freddy. *Kitty* chose him. She said when it comes to determining a poison's effectiveness, size matters."

I crinkled my nose. "What do you mean?"

"Kitty said we needed to test the food on someone about my size. Someone with a similar digestive constitution."

"Oh. That makes sense. The poison might not have been lethal for someone bigger and stronger."

Sophia gave me the evil eye. "You saying I'm not strong?"

I shook my head. "Not at all. I meant you made a good point. When it comes to choosing poisoning victims, *size matters*."

"Also helps when picking a few other things," Jackie quipped.

"Poor Kitty," Aunt Edna said. "We gotta figure this out and get her out of the slammer. Otherwise, she's gonna miss your party, Queenpin."

Sophia frowned. I wasn't sure if it was because Kitty wouldn't be there, or she'd miss out on another gift.

"Okay," Sophia said, drawing her shawl around her shoulders. "Let's put our heads together on this. I'd like to hit the century mark without wearing a target on my back."

"Where do we start?" Jackie asked. "We got no solid proof of nothing."

"What about this blister on my lip?" Sophia said, pulling down her lower lip for our viewing pleasure. "Freddy tried to poison me with a kiss!"

Aunt Edna sighed. "It's probably just the acid from the tomatoes in the caprese salad."

Sophia scowled. "That old goat."

"Be glad it isn't poison ivy," I said, then squirmed in my seat.

Jackie elbowed me. "Hey. Did you know a goat can eat poison ivy with no problem?"

I frowned. "For real?"

"Yeah." Jackie laughed. "I guess that means Freddy wasn't an old goat after all."

"Freddy was just a stooge," Aunt Edna said. "Somebody used him to try and get to you, Queenpin."

"Maybe," I said. "But he could've been poisoned as part of a scheme to sell expensive funerals."

"That isn't it," Sophia said.

Aunt Edna turned to Sophia. "So, who do you think is behind it?"

She frowned beneath her silver turban. "I'd put my money on Gloria Martinelli."

"The acorn lady?" Jackie asked. "Why?"

"Jealousy," Sophia said. "She was always giving me the evil eye because the men liked me better. But then again, they always have."

"Kitty told me that poisoning was a covert business," I said. "Not to disagree with you, your Queenpin, but Gloria Martinelli doesn't strike me as the stealthy type. Her attacks on me were about as inconspicuous as a dumpster fire."

"You don't know her like I do," Sophia said. "Gloria is a hands-on kind of woman. She likes to do her own dirty work."

"Then why wasn't she on your list?" I asked.

Sophia scowled. "What list?"

"The one in your robe pocket," I said.

Sophia locked her cat eyes on me. "You been going through my things, Miss Busybody?"

"No," Aunt Edna said. "We found the list when we picked up your stuff from Shady Respite."

"What list?" Sophia repeated.

"You know," Aunt Edna said. "The one that had Morty, Ventura, Humpty Bogart, Dr. Mancini and Gordon on it."

Sophia's scowl softened. "Oh."

"Were those your list of suspects?" I asked.

"Why would you think that?" Sophia said.

"Are you saying they *weren't* suspects?" I asked.

Sophia's face puckered. "What is this? Some kind of interrogation?"

"No!" Aunt Edna kicked my shin under the table.

I knew I was asking too many questions, but Kitty's life was at stake here!

"Listen here," Aunt Edna said, glaring at me. "Like I told you before, Morty wouldn't hurt a fly."

"But I saw him at the bakery," I said. "When Morty handed Humpty a bag of cash."

"Geez, enough about that," Aunt Edna said. "That money was to help pay for renting out the Coliseum tonight, okay?"

"Oh." I grimaced. "But what about Humpty?"

"That jerk wasn't in town when Freddy got poisoned," my aunt said. "The dirtbag took a trip to the rat's mouth."

"Oh." I wanted to know what rat's mouth was a mob euphemism for, but as angry as Sophia was, I was afraid if I asked, I might end up there myself.

"What about Ventura?" Jackie asked. "Could he be trying to do you in, Sophia?"

"Poisoning ain't Victor's style," Aunt Edna said. "He deals with bodies that are already dead."

Sophia stared at me. "Victor doesn't need to drum up business. He's got all that he can handle."

"So I've heard," I said. "What about Dr.—"

"Don't you dare say a word about Dr. Mancini," Sophia growled at me. "The man's a legend in my eyes."

"Fine." I threw my hands up. "I'm only trying to help clear Kitty and keep you safe tonight."

"That's right," Jackie said. "Cut the newbie a little slack."

"What did you say?" Sophia growled.

"Your Queenpin," I said, "if these guys aren't people you suspect of trying to kill you, then who were they?"

Sophia shrugged and adjusted her shawl. "A girl can dream about getting married again, can't she?"

I nearly fell out of my chair. "You want to get married?"

"Hell, no," Sophia said. "I meant for Edna."

Aunt Edna gasped. "What?"

"It ain't over till it's over," Sophia said.

Aunt Edna's face softened. She shot Sophia a small smile. "Oh. So, who's Gordon?"

Sophia's lips formed a crooked grin. "A new fragrance I saw on TV. It's supposed to drive the men wild."

Jackie snorted.

Aunt Edna swore under her breath. "Mother of pearl! What am I gonna do with her?"

Sophia's grin disappeared. "Speaking of driving the men wild, who's going to press my outfit for tonight?"

"I'll do it," Jackie said. She stood and picked up her empty plate.

"Wait a minute," I said. "I still have questions."

"I bet you do," Sophia said sourly.

"Like what?" Jackie asked.

"Like who let the delivery guy in at Shady Respite? And what about Sammy the Psy ... err ... I mean, your son, Queenpin?"

"What about him?" Sophia grumbled.

I didn't want to upset the old godmother any more than I already had. The last thing I wanted was to give her a heart attack six hours before her shindig.

I winced out a smile. "Will he be coming to your party?" Suddenly, a sharp pain shot through my shin. Aunt Edna had struck again.

"You in charge of the headcount or something?" Sophia barked. "Jackie, take me back to my cottage."

"Yes, ma'am." Jackie helped Sophia to her feet.

As they left the room, I rubbed my shin and turned to Aunt Edna. "Is Sammy going to be at the party?"

She grimaced. "I don't know. But stop talking about him already. It's bad luck!"

I grabbed my aunt's arm. "But I need to know if Brady and I should be on the lookout for him tonight."

"Sammy don't exactly send me his agenda, Dorey. For all I know, he could be standing at the door as we speak."

Bam! Bam!

Loud knocking commenced on the front door.

"I'll get it," Jackie called out from the living room.

"No!" Aunt Edna hollered. "Jackie, don't answer that!"

Chapter Fifty-Nine

"Who is it?" Aunt Edna asked.

She, Jackie, and Sophia were huddled up behind me. I appeared I'd been assigned to take another one for the team.

"Is it Sammy?" Jackie whispered.

I grimaced, then cautiously took a peek through the peephole in the front door.

"It's Brady," I said, then sighed with relief along with the others.

"Thank goodness," Aunt Edna said. "Go ahead and let him in."

"Hi, Brady," I said as I opened the door. The handsome cop was standing there with a bunch of dark-red roses in one hand, my suitcase in the other.

Jackie laughed. "So, you moving in, Romeo?"

"What?" Brady looked at the flowers. "Oh. No. This is—"

"Red roses. How romantic," Aunt Edna said. "Those for Dorey?"

Brady grimaced. "Um. I found them lying on the doorstep. I'm afraid they aren't from me."

"Huh. Well, come on in." Aunt Edna took the roses from Brady and opened the small envelope stuck to them with a plastic pick. Her face turned pale.

"What's it say?" Jackie asked.

Aunt Edna's hand fell to her side. "Hope you liked the curds."

I gasped. "Sammy sent them?"

"Hold on," Sophia said. "We don't know that for certain. All we know is that whoever sent them knows about the cheese curds, too."

"Aww, geez!" Aunt Edna said. "Red roses mean death."

"No they don't," Jackie said. "They mean love."

"Po-*tay*-to, po-*tot*-o," Sophia grumbled.

Brady frowned. "What's that supposed to mean?"

"Nothing." Aunt Edna folded the note back up. "These flowers must be a birthday gift for Sophia. Brady, come have a cup of coffee. Dorey, don't you need to be getting ready for your big audition?"

"Oh, crap! Yes, I better get going."

"Will you be needing this?" Brady asked, holding up my suitcase.

I cringed. "I hope not." I snatched the ugly brown bag from his hand. "Uh ... you didn't look inside, did you?"

He shrugged. "I'm a trained detective."

My brow furrowed. "Is that a yes or a no?"

Brady smirked. "Let's just say I'm prepared to fulfill my duties, and apparently you are too."

Fan-freaking-tastic.

I spun on my heels and headed for my bedroom. I needed to drop off the case and brush my teeth.

I suddenly had a very bad taste in my mouth.

• • • •

"TAKE THE KIA," JACKIE said as I emerged from the bedroom dressed for my audition.

I wasn't sure what role to expect, so I kept my wardrobe simple. A pair of black slacks, a white shirt, and a pair of sensible sandals. I'd also lavished on a full set of makeup.

"Thanks." I glanced around the room.

"Brady's gone," Jackie said, then grinned. "I'll keep my fingers crossed."

"For my audition?"

"Nope. That the Kia starts."

"Thanks. I'll take it." I yanked open the front door.

"Good luck, Dorey!" Aunt Edna called out from the kitchen.

I turned and hollered, "Thank you!" I took a blind step out the door and suddenly found myself tumbling sideways onto the concrete porch.

"Ouch!" I yelped, rolling onto my knees.

"What happened?" Jackie asked.

I shot an angry glance back at the cottage. Piled up along the porch were five cardboard boxes. Whatever jerk had delivered them had put one right on the front door mat.

"I tripped on those fakakta boxes!" I hissed.

"What's going on?" Aunt Edna bellowed, bolting from the kitchen with the shotgun in her hand. Her eyes glued on me, she didn't see the boxes either. She tripped and fell on the ground beside me.

"Oh, no!" I scrambled over to her. "Are you okay?"

"Crap. I think I sprained my ankle," she grumbled. "Who sent the fakakta boxes?"

"That's what I want to know," I said.

Jackie leaned over a box. "Looks like they're from L.A."

"Geez." I shook my head. "I guess Sonya met Johnny Depp after all."

"Huh?" Aunt Edna grunted.

"Nothing." I turned back to her. "I'm *so* sorry. This is all my fault!"

"Horse hockey," my aunt said. "Now, get up and get going to your interview. I'll be fine. Jackie will take care of me."

"But—"

"I got this," Jackie said. "Go on. This is your big day, Dorey. We'll be okay."

I cringed. "Are you sure?"

"Yeah." Jackie squatted next to Aunt Edna. "I'll get her to her feet when she's ready."

I chewed my lip. "Well ... okay. But leave the stupid boxes where they are. I'll take care of them when I get back."

"Will do," Jackie said.

Aunt Edna winced out a smile. "Go get 'em, Dorey."

I took a step toward the street. Guilt washed over me.

Am I wrong to leave them here?

"Go!" Aunt Edna said.

"Okay, okay!" I turned and headed down the path, not at all sure I was making the right decision.

Universe, I need a sign.

If the Kia starts, I'll go to the audition. If it doesn't, I'll stay and help.

I turned the key in the ignition.

The Kia started right up.

Chapter Sixty

"What are *you* doing back?" Aunt Edna asked as I walked into her cottage. She was sprawled out in the hideous old brown recliner, a bag of frozen peas on her ankle.

"The Kia won't start," I lied.

"Cripes," Jackie said, walking into the room. "Lemme have a whack at that thing."

I shook my head. "No. I'm not going. I already left a voicemail for Kerri at the studio. It'll all work out."

Or it won't.

"You sure?" Jackie asked. "I can call a taxi for you. Or maybe Brady—"

"No," I insisted. "I don't think I could concentrate anyway. You know, with Kitty in jail and now Aunt Edna out of commission. You were right, Jackie. You guys need me."

And I need you.

My words, even though unspoken, caused a strange, warm feeling to envelop my heart. It was both exhilarating and a bit frightening. I smiled at the two women, and suddenly noticed how tough, yet vulnerable they were. Just like me.

Huh. Maybe it isn't Aunt Edna's food *I've become addicted to after all.*

Aunt Edna smiled through her pain. "But Dorey, missing your audition would mean you've already taken *two* for the team."

I thought it was three...

I shrugged. "Talking to Brady wasn't that bad. And I'm sure Kerri will understand. Besides, Family is a lot more important than some acting role. If we don't find out who's trying to kill Sophia, both she and Kitty are in big trouble." I spotted the roses sitting in a vase on the coffee table. "Any idea who sent those?"

Aunt Edna winced. "I didn't want to say nothing, but it looks like both the flowers and the cheese curds were probably from Sammy."

I nodded. "So he's definitely alive, like we suspected."

"Pretty sure." Aunt Edna adjusted the frozen peas on her swollen ankle.

Jackie chewed her bottom lip. "You think that means Sammy's coming to the party, or is he still in Idaho?"

Aunt Edna shook her head. "Who knows? Sophia sure isn't gonna spill the beans on where he is. He could be in New York, New Jersey, or the new deli down the street."

I blanched. "You think Sammy is *here*? In St. Petersburg?"

"He's Italian, and it's his mother's centennial birthday. Why would he miss it?" Aunt Edna asked.

"So he's here," I said.

Aunt Edna blew out a sigh. "I'd bet on it."

Chapter Sixty-One

I hauled the boxes containing my junk from L.A. into my room and checked my cellphone. I had less than four hours to figure out who was trying to kill the CGCN matriarch, and save my Family from her psycho son.

Awesome.

I searched through my purse for the little yellow book I'd come to depend on for guidance. It wasn't anywhere to be found. After rifling through my entire room, I padded back to the living room. Jackie was trading the soggy bag of peas on my aunt's ankle for a frosty bag of frozen collard greens.

"Have either of you seen my *Hollywood Survival Guide*?"

Jackie cocked her head. "What do you need that for?"

"For ideas on how to deal with this situation," I said. "What's going to happen if Sammy takes over as Kingpin?"

"God forbid!" Aunt Edna said, and crossed herself.

I crumpled into the brown recliner beside her. "I don't know what to do!"

My aunt reached out and laid a hand on my knee. "You're part of the Family now, Dorey. You don't gotta do everything on your own anymore."

I gulped back a knot in my throat. "So, you two have some ideas?"

Jackie shook her head. "Not a one."

• • • •

WITH NO ANSWERS FORTHCOMING from my aunt or Jackie, I went to the world's best source for accurate information. The internet.

As my fingers hovered over the keyboard on my laptop, I hit my first snag. What should I search for? How to deal with a psycho?

I typed that phrase in the browser and got 6,734,923 results.

You've got to be kidding me.

I glanced through the first dozen or so, but they didn't seem very helpful. Joining the witness protection program seemed implausible before six o'clock.

Now what?

I couldn't exactly call the police, file a restraining order, or tell Sophia to make her son stay home. I slapped my laptop closed. It tipped sideways and slid off kilter.

What the?

I picked up my computer and finally discover something useful—underneath was the little yellow book I'd been searching for.

Yes!

Like a madwoman, I thumbed through the *Hollywood Survival Guide*. Tip #366 seemed to fit the bill. *When life gives you lemons, make a grenade.*

I marched back into the living room and announced, "We're going to need weapons."

"For the party tonight?" Jackie asked.

"No," Aunt Edna said. "For our trip to the moon."

"You can't go," Jackie said. "You got a busted ankle!"

"It's only sprained. And yes, I'm going. I'll use Sophia's wheelchair. She don't really need it anyhow. It's just for show."

Jackie blew out a breath. "Really? I thought that—"

"Ladies," I said, clearing my throat. "We need to focus on how we can find and apprehend whoever might try to kill Sophia tonight, hopefully before they actually do it. Brady's going to have his gun. We need weapons, too."

"I got a new can of Raid," Jackie said. "Amazon just delivered it yesterday."

"A can of Raid?" I said. "Really?"

Jackie shrugged. "Everybody's got their weapon of choice, Doreen. I hear yours is cuticle scissors."

"Hilarious," I said. "What's the best weapon for taking down a bad guy?"

"Your brain," Jackie said. "If you use the old noodle, you never have to get into the soup in the first place."

"Well, it's a little late for that," Aunt Edna said. "The pot's already about to boil over."

I winced. "That's what I'm afraid of."

"Aww, don't worry so much," Jackie said. "It's your birthday."

"Yeah. Another lousy birthday," I grumbled. "Ma always thought they were bad luck."

"Not around here," Aunt Edna said. "Here, birthdays are always good luck."

My upper lip snarled. "I hope you're right. Because boy are we ever gonna need it."

Chapter Sixty-Two

It was D-Day at the lemonade stand—or, more accurately, the Coliseum on Fourth Avenue.

I wasn't packing lemon grenades, but I *was* packing—thanks to Jackie Cooperelli.

"I put the shotgun in your suitcase," Jackie said, pulling my ugly brown bag out of the back seat of the Kia. "Just *in case*. Get it?"

I frowned. "Why in the world would you—"

"Hello *Officer Brady*," Aunt Edna said loud enough for even Jackie to get the hint.

I turned around. Brady was right behind me, eyeing my suitcase. "You didn't tell me this was another actual *date*," he said. "You packing those thirty-eight caliber panties again?"

"No." The only heat I was packing was my flaming cheeks. "Am I the only one taking this seriously?"

"Sorry," Brady said. "What's with your eyes? They match tonight."

"I put a contact lens over the wonky one."

"Why?"

"So she can keep an eye out for Sammy!" Jackie quipped.

"Can it already," Aunt Edna said. "Jackie, help me into the wheelchair." She turned to me and Brady. "You two help Sophia inside, would you?"

"Of course." Brady leaned in and whispered, "Here we go."

"I sure hope you know what you're doing," I whispered back.

"You don't trust me?" he quipped.

"I have to. Besides you, I'm all alone in this mess and I don't have a clue what to do next."

"Looks like your family trusts you," he said, glancing over at them. "Maybe you should start trusting them back."

• • • •

"QUITE THE CROWD," I said to Sophia as she and Brady walked, arm in arm, toward the lights of the Coliseum.

I was a few steps behind them, talking to Aunt Edna as Jackie pushed her in Sophia's wheelchair. As we and the other geriatric partygoers formed a crowd in front of the entry doors, I got this weird vibe—as if I were an extra in *Night of the Living Dead II*.

"Geez, Louise!" Aunt Edna complained. "You'd think they'd have a special entrance for people in wheelchairs."

"They do," Jackie said, nodding toward a line to our left. "It starts way back over there."

"Are all these people, you know, *Family*?" I asked.

"No," Aunt Edna said. "Only about thirty are. The rest I invited from here and there. I didn't want Sophia to realize how small the Family has shrunk to."

"Here and there?" I asked.

"Ah-ha!" Jackie said. "*That's* why you had me post those flyers at all the senior centers!"

• • • •

FIFTEEN MINUTES LATER, we'd managed to swim across the gray sea of old humanity and make it to our reserved table by the stage. Glancing around, compared to the rest of the crowd, Brady and I looked like we'd just teleported here from a mothership sent from the future.

"Would you just look at all these BENGAY Bozos and Geritol gals?" Sophia complained as she settled into her seat.

"You wanted a big party," Jackie said. "I voted for a night with the Chippendales."

"Brady and I are going to walk around and keep a close eye on the crowd," I said.

"Uh-huh." Jackie winked. "I heard there's a kissing booth behind the exit doors."

Brady smirked. "I'll be scanning the crowd for weapons, while Doreen tries to glean information from people's conversations."

"Eavesdropping, eh?" Aunt Edna nodded approvingly. "A tried and true tactic." She looked at her table mates and sighed loudly. Sophia was picking lint off her black shawl. Jackie was counting the peppermints in a bowl at the center of the table. "Well, get going," she said. "You sure as heck aren't going to pick up anything useful at *this* table."

"Hold on," Sophia said. "You think somebody's gonna confess to you because you're young and hot?"

"No," I answered. "But if L.A.'s taught me anything, it's how to tell if somebody's full of it."

Sophia chuckled. "Good on you, kid. Hey, don't forget. The mafia is like a hot fudge sundae. Only room for one nut on top."

"That reminds me," I said. "Stay away from sweets, and keep an eye out for anything suspicious." I cupped my hands to my mouth and whispered, "Or psycho."

"Got it," Aunt Edna said.

"Thanks. And Aunt Edna? Please, stay here at the table with Sophia. If something goes down, we need to be able to find you two in a flash."

"What about me?" Jackie asked, dropping the mints back into the bowl.

"I want you to keep an eye on anyone or thing coming out of the kitchen," I said.

She shot me a thumbs up. "You got it."

Sophia frowned. "Excuse me, young miss. But who died and made *you* Capo?"

"*I* did," Aunt Edna said. "I mean, I didn't die. But I gave Dorey a, you know, *temporary* position. Only until I can walk again tomorrow."

"Humph," Sophia said. "Well, then, if anything happens to me tonight, I blame *you*, Doreen."

I blanched. "But how could it be my fault? I—"

"I didn't say it was your fault," Sophia said. "I only said I was going to blame you for it."

My nose crinkled. "What?"

Sophia let out a huge sigh. "Geez. I'm getting too old for this gig. I used to have wiseguys clipped. Now, look at me. I'm clipping coupons for Depends."

The Queenpin looked up at me and flicked a ghostly wrist. "What are you waiting for, already, Miss Hotshot? Go make your bones."

Chapter Sixty-Three

Brady and I took Jackie's advice and slipped out the exit doors. Soon, Brady had his hand under my silk blouse. But it wasn't a romantic rendezvous. He was clipping a recording device to my bra.

"There," he said. "That ought to do it."

It sure did. Just ask my lady parts.

"You ready?" he asked.

"What?" I gulped.

"To do this thing." He shot me a serious look. "If you hear anything even slightly suspicious, please don't do anything stupid. Come and get me first."

"Of course," I said, tucking my blouse back into my skirt.

"All right then. Let's go."

・・・・

AFTER WEAVING BACK and forth through the crowd and around the grounds of the Coliseum, Brady and I returned empty handed to the table reserved for the guest of honor. I never realized how hard it was to find something when you didn't know what you were looking for.

As we walked up, I heard Sophia and Aunt Edna groan in unison. From the sound of it, Jackie must've just laid another rotten egg of a joke. I was grateful I hadn't been around to hear it hatch.

"How elegant you all look," Brady said, pouring on the charm. Being the youngest, best-looking man in the room *and* dressed in a tuxedo, he didn't have to pour much for our cups to runneth over. "You three certainly are gracing the place."

"More like *dis*gracing it," Sophia said. "Look at the three of us. I'm old as dirt. Edna fell in the dirt. And Jackie's dumb as dirt."

She shook her head and scowled. "And nobody's even asked me to dance."

"You took the words right out of my mouth," Brady said. "May I have the next dance, please, Queen Sophia?"

The old lady's chin rose an inch. She shot Brady a smile. "The next waltz. I don't do any of those crazy Latin dances like the one on now."

"As you wish." Brady kissed her pale, liver-spotted hand. "It will be my pleasure."

Geez. Turn off the tap, Brady. Even I'm starting to swoon ...

"Ha!" Jackie laughed, killing the moment. "Look at that guy out there. He can really dance the flamingo."

"Flamenco," I said.

I glanced over at the dancefloor and spotted a familiar nest of red frizz that could only belong to Ferrol Finkerman, ambulance-chaser at law.

What could that funeral-hustling jerk be doing here?

Then I answered my own question.

Drumming up business.

My eyes narrowed in disgust, causing my contact lens to shift halfway off my pale-blue iris.

Not good.

"Uh ... I've got to go to the restroom," I said, cupping my hand over my eye.

"Itchy?" Jackie asked.

"What? No!" I said, mortified. "A little trouble with my contact lens, that's all."

"I'll go with you," Brady said.

I didn't argue. I might've taken a few for the team lately, but poor Brady had already taken at least ten tonight alone.

"I just heard from the clerk at the station," Brady said as we walked toward the restrooms. "He couldn't do anything to get Kitty released. He said McNulty wouldn't allow it."

"Why not?" I asked, frowning.

"I don't know. My buddy says there's a named suspect in the file, but it's not Kitty Corleone."

"Then who is it?"

"I can't say."

I cringed. "Does it start with Sammy and end in Psycho?"

Brady shook his head. "Like I said, I can't say."

My eyes flew open. "Is it *me*?"

"I can't say."

"*Why not?*"

"Because I don't know. He wouldn't tell me."

"Oh." I winced and wiped my eye.

"You know, you kind of look like you've got a lunar eclipse going on in your eye."

"Gee," I said sourly. "I bet you say that to *all* the girls."

Brady laughed.

I turned and headed for the ladies room door. "See you on the other side."

• • • •

AS I TRIED TO SHIFT my contact lens back to its proper position over my iris, the vanity lights above the bathroom mirror flickered. Startled, I lost my grip on the contact lens. It tumbled from my hand.

"Great," I grumbled, and searched around on the counter for it. I spied it in the sink. "Thank goodness!"

As I reached for it, the lights flickered again, and kept flickering like a black light at a disco party.

"Are you kidding me?" I said aloud.

But in a flash, the contact lens ended up being the least of my worries. As the lights flicked on and off, I spotted something in the niche between the two stalls.

It was a pair of mismatched eyes—and they were staring right at me.

Sammy the Psycho was here!

Chapter Sixty Four

I flew out of the ladies room and slammed right into somebody. Thank goodness it turned out to be Brady, or I'd be paying for somebody's hip surgery.

"Saw him!" I gasped.

"Who?" Brady asked.

I nearly collapsed. Brady grabbed my upper arms and held me steady.

"What is it?" he asked.

"Face! Man!" I gasped. "Sammy!"

"In the ladies room?"

"Yes!"

He let go of me and ran into the women's restroom, but came right back out a few seconds later.

"There's nobody in there, Doreen."

"What?" I ran back into the restroom, Brady right on my heels. He was right. It was empty.

I shook my head. "I know he was in here."

"Well, there's a small window above the tampon dispenser. But the guy would have to be Spiderman to get out that way."

"I saw him with my own two eyes!" I insisted. "Am I going nuts?"

"No," Jackie said. "Sammy's like the wind. He can disappear at will."

"Did you follow us over here?" I asked.

Jackie scoffed. "No. Last time I looked, this was a free-to-pee country. And when you're my age, you make sure and buy the express pass."

As I stood there, dumbfounded, Jackie looked us up and down and grinned. "Doing it in a public restroom, huh? Maybe I should add that to my bucket list."

Chapter Sixty-Five

Just when I thought the worst possible thing had already happened, Shirley Saurwein, reporter for the *Beach Gazette*, came flouncing through the entry door to the Coliseum.

Oh, crap.

"What's with the face?" Aunt Edna asked.

I nodded toward Shirley, who was wearing a skin-tight red dress that perfectly matched her pin-up-girl lipstick.

"Oh, geez," Aunt Edna said. "That woman has more issues than *Time* magazine."

"I only wish her fact-checking was as good as her wise-cracking," I said, as the snarky bleach-blonde made a beeline for our table.

"Well, if it isn't Miss Fancy Pants," Saurwein said, cracking her gum. She glanced at my crotch. "How's things down under? Still *itching* to make your big break?"

My eyebrows met my hairline. "How did you—?" I glanced across the table. "Jackie!"

"Sorry." Jackie cringed guiltily. "Hey, to change the subject, did you know iguanas taste like chicken? It says so on this flyer here." She waved a yellow slip of paper at us. "They eat them like crazy down in Central America."

"Where'd you get that?" I asked.

"From the lady with the big lizard. Here she comes now."

I turned to see Melanie the pet therapy lady come walking toward us in a red dress identical to Shirley's.

I shook my head. "Lemme guess. Big sale at Walmart?"

"Ha ha," Shirley said. "At least I don't wear animals or old lady sunglasses for accessories."

My contact lens down the drain, I'd had to resort to wearing Jackie's glaucoma glasses again. I pushed them higher up the bridge of my nose and took another look at Melanie. Her iguana, Iggy, was slung around her shoulders like a wrinkly, threadbare mink stole. My nose crinkled as she approached. Then I heard something squeak.

"What the—" I looked down and saw she was wearing expensive red loafers.

"I guess when you're nearly six feet tall, you don't need heels," Shirley said. "Lucky you."

"Thanks," Melanie said.

Wait a minute. I'd seen those shoes before. "Ha!" I sprang up from my chair and screeched at Melanie. "It was you!"

"What about me?" Melanie asked.

I heard a click. Saurwein had just pushed a button on her microrecorder. She hoisted her camera, her big eyes pools of liquid gossip.

"Yeah, what about her?" Saurwein said, egging me on.

Thrown off my game for a second, I stuttered. "I ... I heard you, Melanie. In the bathroom at Shady Respite."

"Ha! I'll alert the media," Saurwein snorted. "Oh, wait. I'm already here. Farts at eleven!"

"Shut up, Shirley!" I swallowed hard, hoping the knot in my throat would go fortify my backbone. "You ... you were plotting with Gloria Martinelli," I said to Melanie. "I heard you!"

"Plotting?" Melanie asked, crinkling her nose at me. "Plotting *what*?"

"Yeah, plotting what?" Saurwein echoed. "She run out of toilet paper or something?"

"No!" I grumbled. "I heard you tell Gloria that if she'd done what she was told, she'd have gotten out sooner. And that some big cheese wasn't happy about it. Are you two helping Dr. Mancini poison people?"

Melanie's eyebrows shot up. "Geez. And I thought *Gloria* was delusional."

Saurwein snickered and started clicking off shots with her camera.

I scowled. "If I'm delusional, then explain yourself!"

Melanie shrugged. "All right, I will. I was talking with Gloria because she was using her umbrella as a cane. If she'd have used her walker instead, like the doctor said, then she'd have gotten out sooner. He'd just told her so himself."

"Oh." I wilted, suddenly wishing I could be like that lizard on her shoulder and blend into the woodwork.

Melanie shook her head. "You got some kind of imagination, lady."

"It runs in our family," Jackie said proudly.

Shirley Saurwein hooted. "Ha! I can't wait to write up this one!"

I scowled. "What are you doing here anyway, Melanie?"

I invited her," Sophia said.

My jaw fell open. "*You?*"

"Yes, me." Sophia hitched up the sides of her shawl. "It's my party, isn't it? Besides, that lizard of hers has more personality than most of those old coots in that stupid nursing home."

"Thank you, Sophia," Melanie said, walking over to the Queenpin. "Just for that, I think Iggy wants to give you a kiss."

"Bring it." Sophia puckered up for a smack on Iggy's lizard lips.

"Gross!" I hissed.

Melanie spun on her loafer heels to face me. "What's your problem? Iggy and I are working hard to change the minds of reptile-haters like you."

I blew out a breath. "So I've heard."

"Here you go, Dorey," Jackie said. She smiled and reached across the table to hand me the yellow flyer. I didn't take it.

"Melanie, do you have any more of those petition forms on you?" Sophia asked.

The lizard lady shook her head. "No. Not today. This is *your* special day. That's why Iggy's wearing his special birthday hat. Say happy birthday, Iggy!"

Melanie held the iguana out for Sophia to pet. My nose crinkled.

"What's amatta you?" Sophia asked, stroking the iguana's head. "Everybody loves Iggy."

Jackie leaned over and asked Aunt Edna, "What'd she say that lizard's name was?"

"Iggy. You know, like Iggy Pop."

Jackie frowned. "Iggy popped somebody?"

Aunt Edna shook her head. "Tomorrow, for sure we get you a Miracle Ear."

Chapter Sixty-Six

I took off Jackie's glaucoma glasses and stared at my reflection in the bathroom mirror. I'd lost my contact down the sink, and just accused an animal rights activist of conspiring to kill people at an old folks' home.

I was batting a total goose egg.

"What an idiot I am!" I said to my reflection. "I mean, can I get any more incompetent?"

As if in reply, the bathroom lights flickered twice. As they did, I came face-to-face with my own utter stupidity.

Staring at me from between the bathroom stalls were those wonky eyes again. Only they didn't belong to Sammy. They were my own reflection in the stainless-steel tampon dispenser.

I looked around for a rock to crawl under.

Is it physically possible to flush yourself down the toilet?

• • • •

IT TOOK FIFTEEN MINUTES for my face to fade from fire-engine red back to a reasonably normal flesh tone. I slapped Jackie's glasses on and headed back to the party. At least I knew Sammy the Psycho wasn't running wild. Who needed *him* when I was around to fill the position?

As I emerged from the restroom, I spotted Melanie leaning over a table full of old men. It wasn't hard to spot her red dress in a room full of gray suits. Then I noticed the clipboard in her hand. An old man was signing something clipped to it. Then he handed her some cash.

What the?

I marched over to Melanie. "This isn't the time or place to be collecting for your stupid cause!"

"No?" Melanie said. "Better go tell Sophia that."

"I will!"

"Wait," she said, and turned the clipboard over for me to see. "It's a birthday card for Sophia. I'm collecting for her centennial gift."

Again I wished I could morph into the scenery like a chameleon. I cringed. "I'm sorry."

Then, mercifully, before I could dig myself deeper into the hole, someone yelled, "It's time for the cake!"

• • • •

"WHERE'S BRADY?" AUNT Edna asked.

"Good question," I said. "I haven't seen him since Saurwein got here."

Aunt Edna looked over my shoulder. "Ah. There he is."

I turned and walked over to meet Brady, who'd come through the front door. "Where have you been?"

"I saw you talking to those two women in red. I wanted to hear what you were saying, so I went out to my car and listened in on the recording."

My eyes nearly doubled. "You heard all of that?"

"Every word."

"When did you turn it off?" I asked, trying not to whimper.

"I haven't."

Something deep inside me curdled like sour milk. "I need a drink."

Brady smirked. "Where's a Long Island iced tea when you need one?"

At this point, I'd settle for a bottle of Ripple.

Chapter Sixty-Seven

"Here it comes," Jackie said, rising from her chair as Morty and Humpty rolled a huge birthday cake up to our table on a catering trolley.

The three-foot-tall confection was white and tiered, like a wedding cake. Silver swags of icing adorned the edges. Sugary purple plums and green icing leaves hung from the swags, and completely covered the top layer. In a word, it was gorgeous.

Flutes of bubbly were passed around the table. As I took my glass, I noticed the other randomly invited guests were beginning to circle us like vultures. I hoped it was because they smelled something sweet, and not dead.

"A toast," Morty said, raising his glass.

"Hold up a second," Saurwein said, bending over between Sophia and the cake. "I need to change my film."

"This is *my* day," Sophia said. "Get the hell out of the way, you two-bit gossip-monger."

Morty grinned. "To Sophia, the sweetest angel left on Earth."

"Here, here," we said.

I tipped my glass back and guzzled the booze down in one big gulp.

"You're not worried you'll be incapacitated?" Brady whispered in my ear.

"Nope," I said. "You can't incapacitate something that was never capacitated in the first place."

He laughed. "Don't be so hard on yourself. You screwed up with Melanie. So what? You were just looking out for your family. I admire that."

I looked up at him. "You do?"

"Sure. I ... um .... Oh, look. They're cutting the cake."

"Who wants to do the honors?" Morty asked, holding up a knife.

"Oh, I will!" Melanie called out.

"Come on over, then, beautiful lady," Morty said.

Aunt Edna grunted. "Huh. Morty always was a sucker for a floozy."

"Here, hold this," Melanie said.

Before I could react, she'd plopped her purse on the table in front of me and her five-pound lizard had taken up residence in my lap.

"What the?" I grumbled. But there was no time to object.

"To Sophia's centennial!" Morty said, then everyone applauded as he and Melanie sliced a piece of cake from the top layer like two giggling newlyweds.

Aunt Edna popped a Tums into her mouth and chew it savagely.

"Here you go, Sophia," Melanie cooed, handing her a slice of cake. "The plum piece belongs to you!"

Sophia smiled serenely. "You bet your bottom butt cheeks it does."

"Hold up a minute," Jackie said, springing to her feet. She sprinted over to the cake. "There's one more plum on there than there outta be."

"What are you talking about?" Morty said. "I put ten on there. One for each decade."

"I know," Jackie said. "But look. There's still ten on the top."

Morty shrugged. "What's your point?"

"There's ten on the top, and one on Sophia's plate," Jackie said. "Now, I'm no mathematician, but that adds up to eleven."

"She's right!" Aunt Edna turned to me. "Dorey, what color are those beach apple fruit things?"

"Yellowish-green."

Aunt Edna took the slice of cake from Sophia and rubbed her finger on the plum. Yellow peeked through the layer of sugar icing. I gasped.

"What's going on here?" Sophia asked. "Can't a person have a piece of cake in peace anymore?"

"Eat that and you'll be resting in peace," I said. "That's a Manchineel fruit. I'm certain of it."

Aunt Edna shook her head. "Morty, how could you?"

"But ... I didn't," he said.

I pointed a finger at the woman in red. "Melanie put it there!"

"Geez. Not this again!" Melanie said. "I gotta say, I'm beginning to feel a bit persecuted here, Doreen. You don't like iguanas. You don't like me. Maybe you don't like Sophia, either. You trying to take over the Family or something?"

"No!" I yelled.

But as I looked around, I realized that more than a few Family members were eyeing me suspiciously.

Chapter Sixty-Eight

"Look, I'll humor you, Doreen," Melanie said. "Would I feed a poison fruit to my darling Iggy?" She took the knife and cut the suspicious plum on Sophia's plate in half. Then she walked over to me and popped the piece into the iguana's open mouth.

Dear god. I've stepped in it again!

Sophia shot me a look. "Now, can I eat my cake, or you want to take that over *that*, too?"

Melanie shook her head. "Go on, Sophia. Enjoy your cake. This woman's nuttier than a squirrel."

Squirrel.

Suddenly, my mind began to swirl. Like a jigsaw puzzle swept up in a tornado, snippets from the past five days began twirling and colliding and interlocking in my mind.

Squirrels. Rabbits. Indians poisoned their arrows with beach apples to kill small prey.

Size matters when choosing a poisoning victim.

Iguanas are small prey. They taste like chicken. They eat them like crazy in Central America.

If iguanas are so tasty, why didn't the Indians shoot them with their Manchineel arrows?

"You okay, Dorey?" Jackie asked.

"Huh?" I glanced at Jackie's striped pants.

Stripes.

The stripes on Iggy's tail. Goats can eat poison ivy with no ill effects.

"That's it!" I yelled, springing to my feet.

I glanced around. Everyone was staring at me like maybe someone should fit me for a straightjacket.

"That's nice, Dorey," Aunt Edna said softly, patting my shoulder. "Now sit down and we'll get you a nice cup of—"

"There's only one animal immune to the Manchineel's poison," I blurted. "And it's the striped iguana!"

"Huh?" Jackie grunted. "Why would Iggy want to kill Sophia?"

In the split second while we were distracted by Jackie, Melanie dove for the other half of the plum on Sophia's plate. Fortunately, Brady was quicker on the draw.

"I don't think so," he said, grabbing Melanie's wrist. "That little plum is going in an evidence bag."

"That's crazy," Melanie said. "What do I have to gain from killing this old coot?"

"Old coot?" Sophia hissed. "After I gave you twenty bucks and signed your petition? On my own birthday, no less!"

I eyed Melanie. "I thought you didn't bring that petition."

I grabbed the clipboard sticking up out of her purse.

"I told you already," Melanie said. "It's a birthday card for Sophia."

"Right." I lifted up the card. Behind it was a petition on animal rights. "What's this, then?" I asked, and waved the clipboard in the air.

"It's not against the law to fight for animal rights," she said.

"No. But it proves you're a liar."

"That's not against the law either," she hissed. "Unless you're on the witness stand."

"Maybe not. But I'm pretty sure forgery is." I held up the clipboard for everyone to see.

A hole had been cut through the petition form where the signature line was. I flipped the page over. Beneath it was a power of attorney form. And the latest victim to sign Melanie's bogus form was none other than Doña Sophia Maria Lorenzo herself.

Chapter Sixty-Nine

The evidence against Melanie was strong enough to earn her a pair of silver bracelets and a free ride to Sergeant McNulty's guest house. After Brady told McNulty what had happened, he agreed to release Kitty immediately.

"Thank you so much, Brady," I said.

He smiled. "You know, you really amazed me tonight. But thanks to *you*, I've now got a mountain of paperwork to do." He winked at me. "Could you and Kitty catch a taxi home?"

"Oh, sure. No problem."

"Good." He looked up. "Oh, speak of the devil."

"You figured out my clue about the iguana!" Kitty said, rushing to give me a hug in the lobby of the police station.

"It took me a while. Why did you have to be all 'Indians and arrows' cryptic about it?"

Kitty pulled her pink purse up higher on her shoulder and glanced around. "I had to. The cops were listening. If I told them I thought an iguana kissed Sophia and gave her that blister on her lip, they'd have locked me in the looney bin."

"You know, there was a moment tonight when I thought I might be going there myself." As I hugged Kitty again, my brain suddenly slammed on the brakes. I locked eyes with Kitty. "Wait—that's what your clue was about?"

・・・・

ON THE RIDE HOME, I filled Kitty in on what she'd missed at Sophia's centennial party. "As it turned out, there were no hermit crabs with tommy guns. Just crabby old people with swollen gums."

Kitty laughed. "Wow. You make me sorry I missed it."

"You know, if you hadn't had the gumption to collect those samples from Freddy's throat, we might never have figured out the source of the poison, or Melanie's scheme to defraud the folks at Shady Respite."

Kitty shook her head. "Forging people's signatures on powers of attorney so she could bilk them out of their belongings. How low can you go?"

"I know, right?"

She shook her pink-haired head. "Melanie seemed so nice."

"You talked to her?"

"Yes. Before you showed up in our lives. I ran into her while I was stuck doing my tour of duty with Sophia at Shady Respite. Melanie said she was really into tropical plants, like me. She's even got a greenhouse in Boca Raton. She told me to drop by and see it some time. And I told her to do the same." Kitty's mouth fell open. "Oh, my word. I even gave her my address."

"Well, that explains what happened to your beach apples."

Kitty shook her head. "I guess you just never know, do you?"

"Nope."

"Oh, that reminds me. Who did Sophia name as heir to her throne?"

My mouth fell open. "You know, in all the commotion, I think everybody forgot about it. We were just glad to have foiled Melanie's plans and that Sophia was still alive."

Chapter Seventy

When we arrived back at Palm Court Cottages, the little glowing lights above the picnic table were on, but the table was bare. Kitty and I made our way along the path to Aunt Edna's door.

"Hey, Kitty! Hey, Dorey!" Jackie said as we entered the 1970s time warp that was Aunt Edna's living room. She shoved a cardboard box the size of a microwave at me.

"What's this?" I asked.

"One of those boxes you got today. I just happened to notice it was from Maureen." She grinned. "Looks like your ma sent you a birthday present!"

I took the box and frowned. "If she did, it'd be the first one."

"What?" Kitty gasped.

I shrugged. "Like I said, Ma thought birthdays were bad luck. I never even knew what a birthday was until I got invited to a party for the next-door neighbor's kid."

"Geez," Jackie said.

"Well, first time for everything!" Kitty said with way too much enthusiasm. "Go on! Open it up!"

"Hold on," Jackie said. "Let me get a knife to cut the tape. Or do you have your cuticle scissors handy?"

"Ha ha. Hurry up!"

Jackie disappeared, then returned a few seconds later with Aunt Edna trailing behind her.

I took the knife and sliced through the packing tape. Inside the box was a jumble of stuff, none of it wrapped.

"These are all my childhood things I left at Ma's," I said. "Why would she send me this?"

"I thought this might happen," Aunt Edna said.

"What would happen? Is Ma ditching me for good?"

Aunt Edna came and sat beside me on the couch. "It ain't like that. Not exactly."

I frowned. "Then exactly how is it?"

"Remember when I told you we were like a bunch of Prince Charles's, waiting for Sophia to die to take over the throne?"

I gasped. "Did Sophia *die*?"

"No. She just went home to get out of her girdle."

"Oh."

"The point is, your ma was like Wallace."

"What?"

"Maureen was a commoner. The kind of gal a prince shouldn't marry."

I shook my head. "What are you talking about?"

"Your ma got knocked up by somebody she shouldn't have been involved with. A big-wig we couldn't trust. That's why she moved so far away, and never kept in touch. To keep you a secret. To keep you safe."

"Safe from what?" I grumbled. "Love?"

"Don't say that." Aunt Edna patted my back. "Maureen is a regular woman, just like us. She ain't no superhero. She hid you from the Family because back then, if they'd found out, well, who knows what would've happened. She would've been a tramp, and you a bastard. She tried to make the most of it, but she resented having to give up her life for you. You can understand that, can't you?"

"Not really. But it does explain a lot."

"Maureen did you a favor, never telling you. So you could lead a normal life."

"Normal?" I scoffed. "That's rich. So who is this guy, or am I not supposed to know?"

"I ain't the one to say," Aunt Edna said.

"Who is?"

"Maureen."

I scowled. "I knew when you told me she went to Alaska that it was a lie. Ma hates the cold."

"You're right," Aunt Edna said. "She ain't in Alaska, Dorey."

"Then where is she?"

"No telling. Her phone's been disconnected. She's in the wind."

Chapter Seventy-One

"In the wind?" I asked. "What does that mean?"

Aunt Edna shook her head. "Only Maureen knows."

A knock sounded at the door. A woman's voice called out, "Let me in!"

Ma?

I sprinted to the door and flung it open. Sophia came hobbling in.

She looked around. "Where's the cake, already?"

"Right behind you," a man said.

Morty and Humpty Bogart came in, each carrying a torta alla panna heaped high with whipped cream.

"Finally," Sophia said. "A *real* Italian birthday cake."

"Sorry," Morty said. "I couldn't exactly make one of these to feed a hundred people."

A smile crooked Sophia' lips. "That's how many came?"

"A hundred and seventeen," Jackie said. "If I count you."

"Not bad." Sophia reached for the cake in Morty's hand. "So let's cut that thing, Morty. I'm starving."

"Not this one," Morty said. "Humpty's got yours. With bananas and blueberries, just like you like. This one's for Dorey."

My eyebrows ticked up a notch. "For *me?*"

"Yep," Morty beamed. "Underneath all this hand-beaten cream is a mound of the most delectable strawberries I could find."

"Strawberries," Sophia huffed. "I don't like things with little seeds. They get caught in your dentures."

"Me either," Jackie said, taking Sophia's arm. "Come on, let's all go celebrate in the courtyard, where there's room for everybody."

• • • •

"YOU DIDN'T THINK WE forgot about you, did you Dorey?" Aunt Edna asked as I sliced my first official birthday cake.

"I didn't dare get my hopes up," I said. "Ma never called today, did she?"

Aunt Edna shook her head.

"And my son never came to *my* party," Sophia said. "You don't see me all down in the dumps."

"He sent you flowers," I said.

"Humph," she grunted. "Did he? Nobody signed the card." She scooped up a forkful of her cake. "Red roses. Death or love. I got neither tonight."

"You got love," Aunt Edna said. "From *us*. So did you, Dorey."

"What's this I hear about love?" a man's voice called out from the shadows. Brady walked into view carrying two bouquets of yellow roses.

"For you," he said to Sophia, handing her a bunch and kissing her on the cheek. "And for you, Doreen." Brady kissed me on the cheek and whispered, "Happy birthday." His breath sent shivers down my spine.

"Yellow roses mean happiness, new beginnings, and friendship," Kitty said. "How wonderful!"

Wonderful? I noticed love wasn't in there anywhere. Still, this was my best birthday ever, and I was happy to have any or all of the other things the yellow roses meant.

"I guess it's time for gifts," Aunt Edna said.

"Yes!" Sophia said. "Where are they?"

"Um ... you got yours already, Doña Sophia," Kitty said. "We blew quite a bit on your party."

"And Dorey here saved your life," Aunt Edna said. "What more gift do you want?"

"Eh," Sophia grunted. "I'd love to have my old bladder back."

Everyone laughed, their smiles lit by the warm glow of the overhead lights. The moment felt like a delicious group hug.

"So, here we go," Aunt Edna said. "Presents for Dorey."

"What?" I said.

"Here's mine." Aunt Edna shot me a smile. "Room and board for six months, and linguini for life."

"Are you serious?" Tears welled in my eyes.

"You bet'cha."

"This is from me," Jackie said. She handed me an unwrapped cell phone.

"But this is *my* phone," I said.

"Read the text."

I glanced down at the display. There was a text from Kerri.

Tomorrow at 10:30. Last chance. I mean it this time. Oh, and happy birthday!

"How did she know it was my birthday?"

Jackie grinned. "A little birdie told her."

"Here, this is from me!" Kitty said, handing me a wrapped gift.

I tore into it. It was a beautiful, leather-bound journal.

"I thought you might want to write down your observations," Kitty said. "You may not be on the big screen yet, but you've got a great talent for seeing the big picture."

My heart swelled to near bursting. "Thank you all! And you, too, Morty. For the cake. It's delicious."

"You're welcome." Morty shot me a wink. "Strawberries are *my* favorite, too."

"Geez," Aunt Edna hissed.

"Sophia," Kitty said. "Sorry I missed your party. I heard you didn't name an heir to your throne."

"Hey, it's a woman's prerogative to change her mind," the Queenpin said. "And the day ain't over yet."

"Women." Humpty laughed. "I hope you don't think we're all after your pot of gold, Sophia."

"I ain't worried about you," Sophia said. "You'd be out of your depth in a paddling pool."

"Well, I don't want the job," Kitty said. "The only crown I wear came with a matching root canal. No thanks."

"Don't look at me," Aunt Edna said. "I'm up to my elbows in macaroni as it is."

Sophia's cat-green eyes surveyed us one by one, until her eyes fell on me.

"Dorey, it's good to see you coming up in the ranks. You're no soft, coddled egg."

"Uh ... thank you," I said.

"Hard boiled." Sophia nodded. "That's what this organization needs."

Aunt Edna nudged me with her elbow. "Remember when we gave you the flip-flops and told you that you've got big shoes to fill?"

I gulped. "Uh ... yes."

"What we need is fresh blood," Aunt Edna said. "Youth."

"You got that right," Sophia said. "Around here, forty years old is barely out of diapers."

My mouth went dry. "You want *me* to be the new Queenpin?"

Aunt Edna and Sophia burst out laughing. After a quick pause, Jackie, Morty and Humpty joined in.

"No," Aunt Edna said, wiping tears from her eyes. "We want you to take over as the Doña's personal assistant."

"What?" I gasped. "Why me?"

Aunt Edna put a hand on my shoulder. "After what you told us you had to do for those celebrities back in L.A., we figured you have the perfect skills for the job." She leaned in and whispered in my ear. "Besides, if I have to do it for one more day, I might lose it."

"Well, if Dorey isn't gonna be the new Queenpin, who is?" Jackie asked.

"Me," Sophia said. "Anybody got a problem with that?"

"Not me," Kitty said.

Everyone at the table shook their heads.

Sophia smiled and adjusted her silver turban. "So then, it's settled."

• • • •

AFTER THE GUYS LEFT and the dishes were washed, I said my goodnights and padded back to the spare bedroom where I'd been staying.

Where I *would* be staying.

As I changed into my pajamas and climbed into bed, there was a soft knock on the door.

"You decent in there?" Aunt Edna asked.

"Sure. Come on in."

She peeked her head inside. "It's nice to see somebody using that bed. You know, you never did say whether you were gonna take the job as Sophia's assistant."

"How could I turn it down, given your glowing recommendation?"

Aunt Edna laughed. "Sophia ain't that bad."

"Maybe not." I shook my head. "I didn't realize Sophia was such a comedian."

"You wouldn't unless she likes you."

"Sophia *likes* me?"

"We all do. Face it, Dorey. You're one of us."

I winced. "Because of the eye?"

"No. Because it's in your blood."

"Like Ma?" I said sourly.

Aunt Edna sat down on the edge of the bed. "Our Family is *our* people, Dorey. No matter how much we hate each other, we love each other more."

I looked down at my hands. "I guess."

Aunt Edna stood. "Now, don't stay up too late. You've got a busy day tomorrow."

I looked up. "As Sophia's assistant?"

"At your audition."

"Oh. Yeah."

Aunt Edna shot me a smile, then closed the door behind her. The warm glow I felt as she left had nothing to do with the pink lava lamp on the bureau.

I smiled softly, remembering Tip #53 in my *Hollywood Survival Guide*. *When you come to a fork in the road, pick it up and use it to eat cake.*

I didn't know if my future would turn out to be filled with angel's food or devil's food. But I'd just picked up my fork and eaten my own, bona fide birthday cake with it.

The first one ever.

And the way I figured it, taking care of Sophia couldn't be anywhere near as bad as clipping Arthur Dreacher's toenails.

Ma's starting her life over. So am I. I hope wherever she is, she's somewhere warm.

I didn't mean it *that* way.

I picked up the beautiful journal Kitty had given me, then cracked it open and wrote down my first observation.

Humpty Bogart has a cleft chin.

• • • •

THANKS FOR READING ***Almost a Clean Getaway***, book two in the Doreen Diller Humorous Mystery Trilogy.

Doreen's decided to stay in St. Pete and check out her job opportunities. Two are knocking. But which one will bowl her over? Find out the final, fun conclusion in *Almost a Dead Ringer*! Here's a handy link to check it out on Amazon:

https://www.amazon.com/dp/B0BMZCB4S9

Excerpt from Almost a Dead Ringer

Chapter One

The newspaper landed with a thump on the dining room table, right next to my bowl of Lucky Charms.

"Read it and weep," Aunt Edna said, shuffling past in her fuzzy slippers. She chuckled to herself as she took a seat across the table from me.

The paper was St. Pete's local tabloid, the *Beach Gazette*. My aunt had folded it to an article about Sophia's big party at the Coliseum downtown last night.

Twelve hours ago, the matriarch of the little-known southern branch of the mafia known as the Collard Green Cosa Nostra had turned 100 in style—if you considered narrowly escaping death to be stylish. And from what I'd learned so far about the gang of elderly mob ladies I was currently living with, I was pretty certain they *did*.

Sharing the same birthday as Sophia, I'd also turned a year older yesterday—only my odometer had clicked over to forty. I squinted at the newspaper. The only thing certain about my future was the need for bifocals ...

The article in the *Beach Gazette* was entitled, "*The Hundred Games*." The headline was spot-on, considering Sophia's age and the underhanded shenanigans that had gone down last night. But it irked the stew out of me that the article's annoying author, Shirley Saurwein, had been clever enough to think of it.

The sarcastic, loud-mouthed, bleach-blonde reporter was quickly becoming my least favorite acquaintance *ever*. And as a gal who'd tried for 15 years to make it to the big screen in L.A., the list of scumbags I knew was longer than a trip up the Nile in a leaky canoe.

I scanned the newspaper article. Saurwein had made no mention of my heroic deeds in saving Sophia's life during last night's soiree. Or how I'd uncovered a scheming crook trying to defraud seniors of their life savings. Instead, Saurwein had decided to focus on clichés about Florida's growing glut of "golden years" seniors with nothing but time on their hands and complaints in their mouths.

I had to hand it to her, though. The photo Saurwein had published to accompany her story drove home her point like a spear gun to the gut. She'd caught Sophia, our reining Godmother, glowering like an angry gargoyle at the two people cutting her centennial birthday cake.

The Queenpin's thin-lipped, Grinch-like scowl creased the lower half of her ancient, pasty face. Her catlike green eyes bulged with fury beneath the shiny silver turban she wore like a Jiffy Pop crown.

I pursed my lips. Sophia's tragic/comic visage reminded me of the absurd, bubble-headed aliens in *Mars Attacks*.

Well played, Saurwein. Well played.

I snickered, then caught myself. I glanced up at Aunt Edna.

"What's so funny?" she asked, peering at me over the rim of her coffee cup. A cultural relic from the 1970s, the only thing my aunt was missing were pink curlers in her hair.

"Nothing," I said, then set the paper down and picked up my spoon. "Well, at least it wasn't *me* caught in Saurwein's crosshairs this time. I think I might've made it through this whole 'turning forty thing' without any damage after all."

Aunt Edna raised a silvery eyebrow. "You sure about that?"

I frowned. "What do you mean?"

"Turn the paper over."

I did—and nearly choked to death on a mouthful of magically delicious cereal. Unfortunately, Saurwein's caustic article continued beyond the fold. The second part of it was punctuated by a photograph of me that was just as odd and unflattering as Sophia's.

I stared at the image of myself wearing Jackie Cooperelli's old-lady glaucoma sunglasses. I'd donned them to hide my spooky, pale-blue left eye from the public. But that wasn't what galled me about the photo.

During the party, I'd been stuck holding one of the guest's therapy animals—a grayish-green iguana the size of a wiener dog. Saurwein had captured the lizard and me both glowering into the camera like a pair of infuriated dimwits.

Even worse, my downturned mouth exactly mirrored the iguana's. The only difference was, *I* had lips. Well, at least more lips than that *lizard*, anyway.

Argh!

My grip tightened on the paper. I took a deep breath, then steeled myself as I read the caption Saurwein had written beneath the cringe-worthy photograph.

> *Younger hunger. Some seniors have forgotten how to age gracefully. Apparently, they're ready to do just about anything for attention—including, sadly, trying to look glamorous well beyond their expiration dates. Hitting a new low, accessories to attract attention now appear to include the exploitation of exotic pets.*

I gritted my teeth and hissed, "That woman is a menace to society!"

Aunt Edna smirked and shrugged her mannish shoulders. "Everybody's gotta have goals in life, Dorey."

My mouth fell open. As I waited for my brain to get with the program and spew forth a snarky retort, a different voice beat me to the punch.

"Morning, you two!" Jackie, Aunt Edna's ever cheerful sidekick, poked her pewter-haired head into the dining room. Wearing a flower-print shirt loud enough to bust an eardrum, she wagged her eyebrows playfully. "Brace yourselves, ladies. I've got the other birthday girl with me."

Jackie disappeared, then reappeared a moment later with Sophia on her arm. The rail-thin Godmother hobbled in, her silver turban slightly askew.

I snatched up the newspaper. "Did you see this?"

"Yes," Sophia said. She eased herself into a chair across the table from me. "Jackie. Coffee. Now."

"I'm on it," Jackie said. Springing into action like a soldier on a life-or-death mission, she scurried into the kitchen.

"What's so golden about the golden years?" Sophia muttered, picking lint from her black shawl. "My hair is silver and my butt's turned to lead."

My upper lip snarled. "At least *you* weren't upstaged by a freaking *iguana*."

Jackie returned with two mugs of coffee. She handed one to Sophia, then patted my shoulder. "Aww, Dorey. You got to learn to take things with a stain of salt."

"Jackie's right," Aunt Edna said, ignoring yet another classic Jackie malapropism. "Don't let sourpuss Saurwein get to you. She's just jealous. So, you ready to start your new job today?"

Jackie cocked her head at me and grinned. "Oh, yeah! You're taking care of Sophia from now on."

"*Her* taking care of *me*?" Sophia scoffed. "More like *I'll* be taking care of *her*." The ancient woman jutted her pointy chin toward me. Her thin lips curled slyly. "I'm going to make Doreen my pet project."

Aunt Edna leaned my way and whispered, "Better pray they're merciful at the kill shelter."

"So, young Doreen," Sophia said, eyeing me through her bejeweled bifocals. "Are you ready for lesson number one?"

"Um ... I can't right now," I said. "I have an audition this morning downtown. At Sunshine City Studios. If I miss it a third time, Kerri Middleton will have my head."

Sophia scowled. "And who says *I* won't if you go?"

"I do," Aunt Edna said. "Doreen made this lady Kerri a promise, Doña Sophia. And we CGCN women keep our promises."

Sophia sighed. "Fine. When will you return?"

I shrugged. "I don't know. It depends on whether they want me for the part or not."

Aunt Edna smiled and raised her coffee cup. "Well, here's to hoping those studio folks give our Dorey here an offer she can't refuse."

"This ought to help even the odds," Jackie said, handing me a baseball bat.

"What's this for?" I asked.

Jackie beamed. "So's you can break a leg, kid. What else?"

• • • •

READY FOR THE FINAL book in the trilogy? Grab your copy of ***Almost a Dead Ringer*** on Amazon now. It's going to be a blast!

https://www.amazon.com/dp/B0BMZCB4S9

About the Author

Why do I love underdogs?

Well, it takes one to know one. Like the main characters in my novels, I haven't led a life of wealth or luxury. In fact, as it stands now, I'm set to inherit a half-eaten jar of Cheez Whiz...if my siblings don't beat me to it.

During my illustrious career, I've been a roller-skating waitress, an actuarial assistant, an advertising copywriter, a real estate agent, a house flipper, an organic farmer, and a traveling vagabond/truth seeker. But no matter where I've gone or what I've done, I've always felt like a weirdo.

I've learned a heck of a lot in my life. But getting to know myself has been my greatest journey. Today, I know I'm smart. I'm direct. I'm jaded. I'm hopeful. I'm funny. I'm fierce. I'm a pushover. And I have a laugh that lures strangers over, wanting to join in the fun.

In other words, I'm a jumble of opposing talents and flaws and emotions. And it's all good.

I enjoy underdogs because we've got spunk. And hope. And secrets that drive us to be different from the rest.

So dare to be different. It's the only way to be!

All my best,

Margaret

Made in the USA
Coppell, TX
05 June 2025